THE LOVING DOMINANT

THE LOVING DOMINANT

John Warren Ph.D.
"MENTOR"

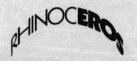

Second Rhinoceros Edition 1998

First Printing January 1998

ISBN 1-56333-600-6

Manufactured in the United States of America
Published by Masquerade Books, Inc.
801 Second Avenue
New York, N.Y. 10017

Acknowledgments

This book could not have been written without the assistance of many people, chief among them Libby Donahue, who provided the support and help so needed by an author as well as a deep and sophisticated understanding of a female submissive's needs and desires.

Another person whose contributions were vital for this book was M. M. of San Francisco, whose editing skills and tact made the book readable while preserving the author's ego.

Isobel Silkwood is gratefully acknowledged for her insight and support during many difficult passages.

Many thanks go to Mistress Margo, Lady J, Mistress Kay, and Goddess Sia for providing invaluable insight into the functioning of female dominant-male submissive relationships.

Others without whom this book might never have been written:

The posters on the D&S group on the Prodigy electronic bulletin board.

The members of Eulenspiegel, Nashville PEP, and Threshold.

Ceres of the BFB Bulletin Board for the illustrations of knots.

TABLE OF CONTENTS

INTRODUCTION

What is "domination and submission"? It is a form of erotic play that takes place when one voluntarily gives up some or all of one's power and freedom to another for the purpose of sensual excitement. For most practitioners, it is a kind of chocolate frosting on conventional sexuality—an enhancement and expansion rather than a substitute for genital sex.

To many who indulge in its pleasures, it is a cathartic sexual game based on fantasy, a sensual psychodrama. Moreover, the term describes both activities and relationships. Those who take part in D&S games at anything more than the most surface level usually discover that these activities intensify the emotional interconnections between themselves and their partners.

There are only two universals in the practice of D&S. First, there must be a transfer of power between or among the parties in the relationship; second, all activities must be consensual.

In the transfer, one person gives up a certain amount of power, and another person (or persons) accept it. The person who gives up power is the "submissive"; the one who accepts it is the "dominant." The amount of power given up by the submissive varies widely among couples and may also be different at different times for the same couple. At one end of the spectrum, the surrender can consist of one partner's simply agreeing to remain absolutely still and passive while the other reads a story or describes a fantasy. At the other end, it can be accepting a rigorous restraint while enduring—and enjoying—the application of intense and varied stimuli.

This transfer of power doesn't just have to be at the physical level of "You must do this" and "You can't do that." It can be on a much deeper spiritual level. Shortly after becoming my lover, Isobel showed me an ancient Hindu drawing of a couple making love; curved and straight lines led from various parts of one body, called *chakras*, to the comparable parts of the other's. She explained that they represented energy transfers the Hindus believed took place during sex. As I looked at the picture, I realized that during the scene I felt this energy transfer but hadn't considered visualizing it in such a way. In some kind of metaphysical way, she seemed to be sending me a force that I returned to her through my actions in the scene.

"Consensuality" means that not only has the submissive partner consented to the activities, but that the dominant also consents. The latter point is often overlooked, but is very important to understanding the true dynamics of the relationship that underlies the activities.

Consensuality also means that at all times during the activities, all parties continue to consent. Later in this introduction and in the body of the book, I will go into detail as to how this consent is maintained and confirmed.

Other terms that have been applied to these games are "B&D" (bondage and discipline) and "S&M" (sadism and masochism). The former is an accurate description of the activities of some members of the greater D&S community. However, there are many who revel in forms of D&S with neither a rope nor a whip to be seen. Although the term S&M is very popular with many D&S players, I feel that we would be better off cutting our ties with it. Many people disagree with me; some do so strongly.

My reasoning is that while masochists make up a significant part of the D&S community, far from all submissives are masochists and some masochists are far from submissive. Some masochists can be most emphatic about demanding and getting a proper 'dose' of pain during any given session.

However, what bothers me about the phrase S&M is the S. The Marquis de Sade, as anyone who has read his writings knows, favored unwilling victims for his cruel activities, which were concerned entirely with his own pleasure and not at all concerned with consent. To me, this is a true description of a sadist. Nothing could be farther from the spirit of the typical dominant, who engages in an erotic dance of power with the submissive. While some dominants choose to proclaim that they are sadists, I have noticed that even they will distance themselves from non-consensual practices.

Since there are true sadists in the world, I prefer to leave this term to them and describe us as dominants, a more neutral and less limited word. After all, people are confused enough by D&S play. We don't need to make the distinction more difficult.

Do not be fooled by my choice of the word "play" for what goes on in D&S. As any mother knows, play is inherently dangerous. Who among us survived through childhood without a cut or painful scrape? For this reason, I will never describe any D&S activity as "safe." I heard recently of a submissive who suffered a fatal heart attack while cleaning his mistress's toilet, an activity which would have normally been quite safe but was rendered fatal by the intense excitement he felt fulfilling his fantasy. A lady of my acquaintance suffered a dislocated shoulder while combining bondage with a truly mind-blowing orgasm.

However, some D&S undertakings are riskier than others. In this book, I will be taking care to differentiate the risky from the not-so-risky and to explain ways to minimize the risk inherent in any of them.

The truth about most D&S movies and books is that many things that are shown or talked about are extremely dangerous. True, many movies and a few books have a sort legalistic warning against trying to duplicate what is shown. However, such a generic warning is little help for someone trying to find out how to do it right.

I write from my own point of view, that of a male heterosexual dominant. However, I sought assistance from several of my sister dominants and have tried to provide the information that female dominants who work with men need. In addition, a number of male and female submissives have provided valuable and, sometimes, vital insights which I have included.

A good motto for any dominant: NO UNINTENTIONAL PAIN. I hope this book will help you and your partner find things that are exciting and creative and that you can do in an atmosphere of relative safety and complete consensuality. I've been playing D&S games for more than twenty years and seriously studying the art for almost a decade. This book is the distilled essence of that study and experience.

You will find the vertical pronoun "I" scattered throughout the book. Although an overweening ego may be in some way responsible, my primary intent is to emphasize that many of the comments in this book are my opinion and are fit subject for debate or refutation. I hope others will carry this orderly and ethical approach to the art of D&S to greater heights than I can manage.

The Loving Dominant is intended for a wide audience. My primary goal is to reach novice dominants or those who feel they are dominants and help them overcome the psychological barriers to undertaking such a politically incorrect activity. I also want to show them techniques they can use to bring pleasure to their submissives and themselves.

Experienced dominants may have largely overcome the discomfort of violating conventional sexual rules and will be familiar with many of the techniques I describe. However, the most experienced of us gets in an occasional rut. Most will find some new ideas here, and reading about what others do in the field may get the old excitement back and inspire them to new heights.

While I have written this book for dominants, I sincerely hope that submissives and those who feel they might enjoy being submissive read it. They can gain an insight into "how the other half lives," and it may give them the courage to act on their needs and desires.

Other individuals may have had the desire to experience D&S but, lacking the proper words, may have been unable to verbalize or visualize their yearnings.

In addition, I hope that some copies of this book fall into the hands of the general public. Too often their perceptions of D&S people are shaped by sensationalized media stories and pornography. The truth may not be as shocking, but I hope it will be interesting. To those readers, I am "defending my perversion." In fact, you many feel that some of the anti-D&S positions I try to refute are extreme, but I assure you they are not straw men set up by me to be knocked down. Every one of them represents a real point of view, often with a vociferous group behind it.

Although I have included a highly personal and opinionated glossary at the end of this book, I feel this is an appropriate place to go over some confusing terms. For example, throughout the book, I use the word "scene" to mean two different, related things. "The scene" is a umbrella term for all D&S activities and the people who take part in them. On the other hand, "a scene" is what takes place when a dominant and a submissive (or any combination of the two) get together and play. Thus, I might write "In the scene, it is considered unconscionable to ignore a safe word" and be referring to the umbrella term, or "When you are doing a scene, safety is of primary importance" and refer to a specific activity. People may also refer to "living the scene." This usually means that they attempt to maintain their D&S persona on a twenty-four-hour-a-day basis, but it can also mean simply that the person is serious about his or her participation in D&S and is putting down those are seen to be less "serious."

The most important word in the D&S vocabulary is "safe word." This is a word or phrase that serves as a signal from the submissive to the dominant that things have become unbearable. Common safe words are "red light" and "mercy." In general, we do not use words like "stop" or "no" because many submissives increase their enjoyment by playacting that they are not in a voluntary situation. Screaming and begging turns them on, the little darlings.

CHAPTER 1
All the Colors of Kinkiness

People often talk about D&S as if it were some sort of monolithic activity like accounting or poker. (My apologies to accountants or poker players. I know better, but the line was too good to pass up.) In fact, the umbrella of consensual transfer of power covers an astonishing variety of acts, attitudes, degrees of commitment and extremes of kinkiness. D&S or "The Scene" is like a very liberal Chinese restaurant. You can take as many, or as few, items as you want from Column A, B, and so on.

Each couple can decide what activities bring them the most pleasure. Some couples savor a highly intellectual D&S that can be so subtle that even someone observing their scenes would be unaware that anything "kinky" is going on. Others enjoy a level of "stimulation" sufficient to horrify many observers. Still others appreciate elaborate psychodrama that may or may not include stimulation. The only persons who can determine what is right for you and your partner are the two of you. There is no right or wrong way to do D&S.

Individual styles can also vary widely. Some dominants like to project a harsh, stern demeanor and keep the caring sensitivity carefully hidden. Others cherish the role of loving guide and protector. A scene can be as serious as a religious ritual or it can be a laughing, giggling frolic.

Submissives, too, project a broad range of images to the world. Some, particularly men, like to maintain a passive, stoic image that can be frustrating to a dominant looking for guidance. One female dominant complained in frustration, "How in the hell can I have any fun if I can't tell if he is?" Of course, other dominants value and encourage that sort of a show of unruffled endurance.

Some submissives say they can really let go only when they have intentionally adopted a role. In effect, they create an internal psychodrama in which they are captured secret agents, molested peasant maids, or blackmailed debutantes.

Ann, an Atlanta submissive, makes a point of distinguishing her "uppity submissive" from what people in the scene call a SAM (Smart-Assed Masochist). While the SAM tries to "top from the bottom," that is, to control all aspects of the scene, Ann's uppity submissive is more likely to signal her eagerness for stimulation by pinching the dominant's bottom in passing or looking up with innocent eyes and asking, "Is *that* as hard as you can hit?"

There have been numerous attempts to examine the

various approaches to D&S. One of the most successful of these was detailed by Diana Vera, writing in *The Lesbian S/M Safety Manual*. Based on her experience and observations she described nine levels of submission. These range from a kinky sensualism, where everything revolves around the submissive's needs, through play submission, where the submissive gives up control but the stimulation is erotic and pleasing to both, all the way to consensual slavery, where the slave exists solely for the dominant's pleasure. This short piece makes interesting reading for anyone who is interested in thinking about submission as well as actively submitting.

Another way of looking at conceptualizing the scene is shown by my own dear Libby. Instead of considering the severity of the activities or the portion of the day they take up, her approach examines the emotional intensity of the submission and the degree of trust put forward by the submissive. In her section, "A Submissive Looks at Submission," later in this book, she goes into detail about her three levels of submission: fantasy, clarity, and transparency.

Inspired by Libby's format, another submissive woman offered her three categories. Unlike Libby's, these are not in a hierarchical structure but, instead, are based on the needs of the submissive.

The first is "Stimulus Driven." Here, the submissive is taking part because he or she is seeking out a specific stimulus, like the "pain" of whipping or the "confinement" of bondage.

The second category is "Relationship Driven." In this, the main desire is for a relationship, often with a particular person. Individuals in this kind of relationship glory in the multichannel communication between the submissive and the dominant and enjoy the richness of the information flow.

The final category is "Fantasy Driven." In this, the submissive is seeking to make real a fantasy or fantasies. Sometimes this is accomplished by living through the fantasy; however, others find satisfaction in finding an individual who shares his or her fantasy, and no specific action need take place.

However you choose to play, welcome to a land of fantasy in the midst of reality. Here, perhaps more than in any other aspect of your life, you are free to choose your own route to ecstasy.

CHAPTER 2
Are You a Loving Dominant?

Well, are you? It may seem like an easy question to answer, but it can be more difficult than you realize. Sadly, in our society, domination, sadism, cruelty, and brutality have become confused and intertwined.

Crude, unrealistic fiction has made the situation worse. Publishers have found that to reach the broadest possible audience they must include themes that are repugnant to many. Because consensual, loving D&S in fiction is so rare, those who are interested in these themes must pick through thousands of pages, much like someone looking for jewels in a dung heap, to find sections they find provocative while other readers wallow in the nonconsensual brutality.

The following is a series of questions that you need answer only in your own soul. Be honest with yourself and look deeply into those answers to see if this scene is really for you.

Do you get as much pleasure or more from erotically exciting your partner as from your own enjoyment of the sexual act?

If this is true, you are likely to be a good dominant. The essence of domination is to take another's power and then use it for *mutual* pleasure. If you already seek to maximize your partner's gratification, you have a mind-set that will adapt well to D&S.

Do you want an easy relationship with you as the unquestioned boss?

Then, D&S is unlikely to be for you. A D&S relationship is more—not less—complex than one that is purely vanilla. This is because D&S relationships generally have all the components of a vanilla relationship *plus* those that are unique to D&S.

It is common to hear dominants talk about how hard they have to work. This is because in exchange for the power that is given us, we must find ways of using that power for the benefit and pleasure of both participants. At the same time, because of the trust given us, we must be very sure that nothing we do is harmful to anyone in the relationship. *This* kind of careful balancing act certainly isn't attractive to someone looking for an easy ride.

Have you been in an abusive relationship and would like to "turn the tables" on someone like the person who abused you?

This is another rough start. A significant number of people in D&S have been in abusive relationships, and some of them consciously use D&S psychodramas to help them work through the negative feelings that resulted from these experiences.

However, revenge is a poor motivation for such an intimate relationship and is likely to result in further damage to your self esteem.

Why do you want to control another person?

This is a sticky one. One of film star Vanessa del Rio's earliest fantasies was of having a group of tiny people in the palm of her hand. She loved to imagine that she had complete control of them; but, to me, the key was that she imagined that she would use this power to make them happy.

The desire to help, to enhance, or to make happy is common among dominants. This may be why so many of them are in the teaching and helping professions: medicine, social work, religion. Other-centered people make good dominants. Self-centered people often find that the strain of the responsibilities inherent in a D&S relationship is overwhelming.

In a consensual relationship, control applied purely to self-gratification is a self-limiting proposition. Submissives who do not get what they are looking for are unlikely to remain in a relationship for very long.

Do you have fantasies involving nonconsensual activities or harm to another?

This isn't as serious as you may believe. The trick is being able to keep the fantasies inside your head and separate from the scene you are playing with another person. Most of us have large, hairy monsters in the dark corners of our minds. What separates the civilized from the uncivilized is how tight a leash we keep on them.

Having the fantasies is all right; acting on them isn't.

Aside from being totally against the ethical principles of the scene, such 'play' can get you locked up with other people who believe in nonconsensual play—and may be bigger than you are.

CHAPTER 3
Dig All Those Crazy People

Why? Why do people do this? Why do people love this? Some of us are fascinated with the genesis of these feelings and enjoy searching for the root cause of our desires. Others, myself included, hold with Alexander Pope that "Like following life though creatures you dissect, you lose it in the moment you detect it."

Sometimes I suspect that too close an examination can actually destroy the feelings being studied, and I recognize that an understanding of causes is not necessary for enjoyment. I have only the vaguest idea of why chocolate ice cream tastes good, but that ignorance decreases neither my enjoyment nor my consumption.

I'll admit that my sexual tastes are more unusual than a love for chocolate ice cream. Still, no one made deep analyses of why some people like chocolate sauce on their pizza. People who love it pack the Hershey's syrup on trips to Pizza Hut, and the rest of us avert our eyes and shudder a bit—or maybe borrow a dollop and see how it tastes on the pepperoni. They are simply classified as "weird" or, if they are rich enough, "eccentric."

Psychologists, psychiatrists, social science theorists, theologians, and feminists haven't lined up to find answers for this chocolate "perversion," for people carrying handkerchiefs they never use in their coat pockets, or for voting Republican. These are simply "trite eccentricities" unworthy of study.

To make the question even more complex, the language of experience is not the same as the language of classification. Race-car drivers don't study physics—although they may pick up a good bit of it in passing. They drive. They experience. They don't think about the underlying mechanics, but about the feel of the car and the track.

People have studied poems since before Aristotle wrote *Poetics*. Their reactions still come down to "This poem speaks to me."

However, some enjoy sharpening their Aristotelian knives and having at "the search for why." If you tend toward this approach, I dedicate this search for causes to you.

Some give a simple answer to "Why?" "It is fun, enjoyable." "We like to do it." Unfortunately, this kind of simplicity isn't looked upon kindly by the members of the Ivory Tower Brigade who glory in philosophical head-knocking and counting dancing angels.

Unfortunately, too, all too many of these deep thinkers

have fixated largely on sadistic monsters and masochistic victims. Like Shakespeare's Horatio, they have failed to realize that there are more things in heaven and earth than are dreamt of in their philosophy. Neither loving domination nor sensual submission is part of the paradigms they develop—to admit that these exist might knock their carefully constructed houses of cards askew. To make matters worse, the competing theories are all different, and most of them are mutually exclusive.

I was strongly tempted to exclude much of the psychological theory on the grounds that it is inconsequential to the people most actively involved. Unfortunately, I have been repeatedly and forcefully reminded that anyone attempting to discuss D&S with a learned audience or with doctors is going to be presented with these spurious "explanations."

I suppose that it is better for you to encounter them here, amid interpretation and exegesis, than to have them flung into your face with an implication that they are, somehow, revealed truth. Just take a firm grip on your temper and read on.

Theories of Sadism and Masochism

In the labeling craze of the nineteenth century, when scientists still clung to the mystical concept that to label something was to control it, Dr. Richard von Krafft-Ebing came up with the terms "sadism" and "masochism" in his book *Psychopathia Sexualis*; this learned tome was a sort of Sears, Roebuck catalog of perversion, listing just about everything that two or more people could do together to get their individual or collective rocks off. Krafft-Ebing would have had a good laugh on modern thrill seekers perusing his volume; he put the boring stuff in English and the good parts in Latin.

As most people in the scene know, the term "sadism" came from the writings of the Marquis Donatien Alphonse François de Sade, and "masochism" from those of Leopold von Sacher-Masoch. Both de Sade's writings (including *Philosophy in the Bedroom, Justine, Juliet, 120 Days of Sodom*) and Sacher-Masoch's *Venus in Furs* are still hot-selling items today. A quick glance at any of de Sade's work will show you why many dominants are infuriated when they are accused of being sadists. Nonconsensuality was the order of the day for the marquis.

Sadly, Krafft-Ebing got it almost right with submission when he defined masochism as:

"A peculiar perversion of the psychical sexual life in which the person affected, in sexual feeling and thought, is controlled by the idea of being completely and unconditionally subject to the will of a person of the opposite sex; of being treated by this person as by a master…"

Aside from the near miss of failing to recognize that submission is independent of hetero- or homoerotic orientation and throwing in the term "perversion," he came fairly close to how many submissives would describe themselves. However, after that good start, he ruined it by adding three words—"humiliated and abused"—at the end. With just three words, he narrowed the definition to include only the small percentage of submissives who *do* enjoy humiliation, and convicted the master, a person who is doing what the submissive *wants done*, of being abusive.

Krafft-Ebing was even less kind to dominants, whom he implicitly lumps with sadists:

"Sadism is the experience of sexually pleasurable sensations

(including orgasm) produced by acts of cruelty, bodily punishment inflicted by one's own person or when witnessed in others, be they animals or human beings. It may consist of an innate desire to humiliate, hurt, wound or even destroy the others in order thereby to create sexual pleasure in one's self."

Unfortunately, aside from some amusing—or horrifying—examples, depending on your point of view, Krafft-Ebing is almost useless to anyone looking for insights. Sadism is simply seen as "a pathological intensification of the male sexual character," and females are seen as anxious, irritable, and weak. (I wonder how Mistress Mir, Goddess Sia, or any of the hundreds of thousands of dominant women feel about that!)

Freud, the father of modern psychology, took the ball and ran with it. Not one to do things by halves, he came up with three separate and sometimes contradictory theories. In *Three Essays on the Theory of Sexuality*, he claimed that sadism is a component part of the sexual instinct, an "instinct for mastery" that is inherently masculine, and masochism is "nothing but inverted sadism." Freud declared that sadism and masochism are interchangeable; masochism is only sadism that has turned inward upon the self.

According to this theory, sadists behave as they do because, during childhood, they were trapped in the anal stage of development, attempting to control the parent figure by releasing and withholding feces. (Does the term, "crock of shit" come to mind?)

In his later essay, *A Child Being Beaten*, Freud shifted the birth of sadomasochism to the child's first oedipal conflict and linked it with parental punishment and punishment fantasies. His thesis was that the child links forbidden sexual feelings with the fear of punishment. In effect, pain is the payment for pleasure.

With better footwork than a running back, Freud next feinted toward his first theory but then went wide and, in *The Economic Problem of Masochism*, hypothesized that masochism—not sadism—is the primary component and linked it with the death instinct. For one thing, masochism, in his eyes, was necessary so that women could endure childbirth.

Erich Fromm, a leading light of the Frankfurt School, a group of German intellectuals who desperately tried to explain the rise of Nazism, moved the discussion of sadism and masochism from the individual, where Freud had staked his claim, to society, or at least to the individual's reaction to society. In *The Fear of Freedom*, Fromm postulated that freedom itself was frightening in that it caused intolerable loneliness and that individuals adopt various strategies to escape from it. He maintained that sadomasochists use control as such an escape hatch.

For example, masochists were described as consciously complaining about being weak, inferior, and powerless, while at the same time seeking circumstances where these feelings were intensified. Fromm argued that the masochists, failing repeatedly at being strong and independent, became even more weak and passive to reduce the conflict between what they want and what they can accomplish, like someone who says, "If I can't play perfect baseball, I'll become the team clown and everyone will think I'm fucking up on purpose."

The sadists, on the other hand, were seen as recognizing their inferiority and powerlessness and seeking to control others to gain an ersatz strength in place of real strength. In effect, he saw us as failed admirals playing with toy boats in the bathtub.

French existentialist philosopher Jean-Paul Sartre drew on Freud's third field goal attempt in his classic, *Being and Nothingness*, in which he argued that both sadism and masochism were responses to a fear of mortality, of death. In French author Jean Genet's play, *The Balcony*, lawyers and other powerful individuals played out masochistic fantasies in a surreal house of domination. The theme implies that they are doing this to strike a psychic balance and atone for their sadistic behavior in the 'real world,' as if they were saying, "I hit him, now you hit me, and everyone will be even."

Swedish psychiatrist, Lars Ullerstam, supported Genet's hypothesis that masochism was an exculpatory behavior; however, he pointed out that the presence of powerful, rich men in such D&S brothels may also be because they, unlike their less-powerful counterparts, can afford to pay the fees involved. Thus, it may be that the overwhelming number of lawyers whom dominatrixes report seeing as clients are not expiating sins particular to this profession. They may simply be making an obscene amount of money and thus be able to afford the dominatrix's service.

In her book *Powers of Desire*, Jessica Benjamin alleged that both sadistic and masochistic behavior were fueled by a need for recognition. The masochist suffers to be recognized as worthwhile by the sadist, while the sadist subjugates another person to force recognition from him or her. Benjamin, on the other hand, gets her recognition by writing books.

During the conference that followed publication of the *Playboy Foundation Report* in the 1970s, researchers had a chance to differentiate sadism from dominance. Wardell B. Pomeroy, one of Kinsey's collaborators, described a segment of a filmed scene which depicted a waxing. He had noticed that the "sadist" was watching not just the place where the wax was falling, but also the expression on his partner's face. When this "sadist" detected that she was getting close to the edge, he raised the candle to reduce the intensity of the stimulation. Pomeroy commented, "It suddenly occurred to me that the masochist was almost literally controlling the sadist's hand."

Sadly, a less-imaginative colleague pooh-poohed the idea and insisted that "genuine" sadists are not interested in a willing partner. (I'm personally glad this myopic soul was not present at the discovery of penicillin. He probably would have thrown out the moldy bread.)

Working in what is known as the Object-Relations School of psychology, Margaret Mahler attempted to explain sadism and masochism by looking at a child's early relationship to—you guessed it—objects. Rather than placing the critical age in puberty as Freud did, she held that such desires begin before the age of four.

In sort of a Cliff's Notes explanation, I'll just say that object-relations theory says that children go through a series of phases in which they seek either greater independence or greater reassurance. Mahler argued that both masochism and sadism come from a failure to have these needs satisfied at the proper time. In effect, the person is trapped repeating the critical phase in hopes of "doing better this time."

For example, she believed that a sadist may have been unable to form a satisfactory relationship with his or her mother and is now trying to create a controlled relationship in which he or she can try to re-create that relationship. On the other hand, the masochist was able to form a satisfactory bond but was unable to break it at the appropriate time. Thus, he or she is seeking a relationship from which a clean break is possible.

In the *DSM IIIr (Diagnostic Statistical Manual, third edition, revised)* the American Psychological Association defines "sexual masochism" as:

"recurrent, intense, sexual urges, and sexually arousing fantasies, of at least six months' duration, involving the act (real, not simulated) of being humiliated, beaten, bound, or otherwise made to suffer."

It defines "sexual sadism" as:

"recurrent, intense, sexual urges, and sexually arousing fantasies, of at least six months' duration, involving the act (real, not simulated) in which psychological or physical suffering (including humiliation) of the victim is sexually exciting."

Interestingly, sexual fantasies alone aren't enough to trigger the diagnoses. According to the shrinks-in-charge, if you have fantasies about spanking a willing partner or imagine yourself in charge of a Nazi concentration camp, you can be perfectly healthy.

However, if you are disturbed by the fantasies or *if you act on them* (emphasis added), you are in need of treatment. It is an interesting Catch–22. A person can dream of going to a loving leather-clad woman; he can burn in his bed each night with unslaked desire for the hug of the rope and the kiss of the whip. However, one trip down to Mistress Harsh's House of Loving Leather makes him a candidate for the laughing academy.

Intent is immaterial. In the view of the authors, someone who pleases his or her lover with a bit of erotic spanking is lumped right along with a creep setting fire to kittens.

Even Madonna has a theory about why we like what we like. In an interview with *Newsweek* magazine, she suggests that her sexuality may stem from her Catholic upbringing:

> "When I was growing up, there were certain things people did for penance; I know people who slept on coat hangers or kneeled on uncooked rice on the floor…and as for me, I think somehow things got really mixed up. There was some ecstasy involved in that.
>
> "And the whole idea of crucifixion—a lot of that, the idea of being tied up. It is surrendering yourself to someone. I'm fascinated by it. I mean, there is a lot of pain-equals-pleasure in the Catholic Church, and that is also associated with bondage and S&M."

So be it, from the index cards of a nineteenth century cataloger to the musings of the Material Girl herself, this is a sample from the varied buffet table of psychological explanations of D&S—or, to be more precise, sadism and masochism. You are free to pick and choose as it pleases you.

Why Would Someone Want to Be Submissive?

I believe that many submissives are strong people who are taking a vacation from their responsibilities. By giving their considerable power to others, they benefit from the incredibly aphrodisiac nature of contrast. Shifting willingly from powerful to powerless gives their libidos extraordinary jolts.

This erotic nature of contrast may explain why, during the many years I spent in the Orient, I never encountered what I considered a truly submissive woman from those cultures. Most women in Oriental cultures are steeped in submission; it is not a choice, nor is it a change. Because of this, for me, the fire was missing from their submission. They got no more of a sensual charge from their submission than American women get from signaling a cab or buying a meal.

Many of the submissives I have talked to find that their attraction to the scene is based largely on this contrast between having power and control but releasing themselves to experience powerlessness at the hands of another whom they trust. Almost everyone knows the sheer joy of coming home after a hard day's work and slipping off the wingtips or high heels and putting on a well-worn pair of slippers. Many submissives simply carry it a step further and slip off the entire business-mandated Type A personality to submit to a trusted dominant.

There is a misunderstanding on the part of some wannabe doms and many in the vanilla public about the essence of submission. Part of the fault is our phrasing. We speak of "a submissive person"; that is not precisely correct. A better phrase would be "a person who is submissive to…"

This understandable error is created and compounded by playacting on electronic bulletin boards and misleading plots in pornographic novels.

In the real world, however, the nature of the submissive is often quite different from what is seen in these limited purviews of fiction and fantasy. This is particularly true in the case of submissive women. These ladies are not submissive to just any man who happens to want to play at being a dominant.

A woman who has elected to give her submissive side permission to play is, in my opinion, stronger and more courageous than those of her vanilla sisters who have that side and do not let it show. Such a woman is not likely to submit herself to anyone who just happens to be blessed with a Y chromosome.

Far from simply waiting for a dominant to appear, these women seek and select the person to whom they will submit. In turning over their power to this individual (or, much more rarely, these individuals), the submissive woman forms a bond that is often stronger than that of a conventional sexual dyad. Anyone intruding into this relationship should not be surprised to receive a cold shoulder from all parties.

By the same token, depending on the personal style of both the submissive and the dominant, the submissive woman in such an affiliation may be quite active and aggressive outside of the scene portion of the relationship.

Submissive men are both more complex and simpler than their female counterparts. Either because of the nature of the male/female dichotomy, because of early childhood conditioning, or because of the nature of our society, many male submissives are much less selective of whom they submit to. While a submissive female "on the prowl" is a rare sight in the D&S clubs, submissive males in search of a mistress make up the bulk of any given night's attendance.

Some submissives report that they have chosen their role because they found that the strength and control they have in their vanilla lives interferes with their sensual enjoyment. A number of years ago, I had a relationship with a brilliant and successful psychologist who had to be bound and helpless in order to reach orgasm.

Her explanation was consistent and cogent. Before discovering bondage, she found that, as she approached orgasm during intercourse, an anxiety would appear that would quite overwhelm her building passion. This anxiety did not appear during masturbation. Examining the anxiety in a cool and detached manner as if it were a symptom reported by a client, she concluded that she had been socialized to please and cater to her partner during sex. She concluded that her subconscious mind, recognizing that during climax she would be out of control, was sabotaging the orgasm.

Her solution was to make the desire-to-please irrelevant. Because when she was bound she could not do anything either to please or displease her partner, she found that bondage allowed her, in her own words, "to wallow in sensation." When she was tied, she was able to reach orgasm repeatedly.

An alternate explanation, offered by another member of the psychological community, suggested that the root cause was, instead, a deep-seated guilt about nonmarital sex. In effect, her subconscious was punishing her for engaging in 'sinful' behavior. In this scenario, the bondage "gave her permission" to enjoy sex because it wasn't her "fault." A submissive man allowed that guilt did play a significant factor in his love of bondage. As he put it, "It is difficult to get past the Calvinist idea that feeling good isn't enough; there must be some greater purpose, some tangible benefit for society." Being bound and helpless freed him from the need to search for that benefit.

Other submissives have said that they have found, in loving submission and certain pleasure/pain activities, a way of coming to terms with legacies of emotional pain. For example, it is not uncommon for a submissive to be drawn to re-creating scenes of abuse or rape with a loving partner acting the part of the aggressor. While, on the surface, this might be seen as counterproductive, those I have spoken to are unanimous in declaring that the psychodrama helped them "get control of the trauma."

The logic seems to be that the original act left the victim with a sense of powerlessness, but reenacting it in an environment of D&S, where he or she can set the parameters of the action and even halt the scene abruptly with a safe word, gives a feeling of empowerment.

I should note here that these submissive individuals, both male and female, themselves initiated the idea of using a scene psychodrama in this way. I would strongly caution any dominant not to coerce a submissive into such scenes with the thought of providing a sort of home-brew therapy. The dynamics of control seem to indicate that a suggestion of this sort must originate from the individual most directly affected.

Other submissives report that D&S helps them deal with emotional pain by allowing them to "go away," to escape into the intense sensuality and endorphin-engendered haze where memories and even rational thought become secondary.

Of course, this going-away isn't unique to D&S. I doubt that there are many of us who have not set down an engrossing book to discover we were cramped and aching from the position in which we had been sitting. The book literally took us away from our bodies.

A friend who is active in the arts observes that the first five minutes of a play or musical presentation may be accompanied by coughs and other noises from the audience. Soon these vanish as the performance lifts the audience from the mundane sensations of their bodies to a higher plane, where tickles in the throat and uncomfortable chairs cannot follow.

What is uncertain about these submissives' observations about their use of D&S to deal with their pain is whether they are describing a benefit or a cause. Did the emotional pain lead the person to choose a submissive role in D&S play? While this is possible, I could equally persuasively argue that the person was already submissive and was simply using the "facilities" of the D&S scene to deal with the existing pain.

Another "need" or "cause" cited by some submissives is that in their early lives they sealed away their emotions. In some cases, this was the result of abuse; in others, it was because the family had a norm of ignoring or concealing emotion. As one submissive woman put it:

> "By being submissive to my master and relinquishing all control to him, we are slowly tearing down the protective walls I built because of some things which happened in my childhood. For me, D&S is a way of confronting my fears and allowing myself to grow emotionally. What I find most appealing about D&S are the emotional and psychological aspects— although the physical is also fun. Would I still find it appealing if my childhood had been different? I don't know, but I doubt it."

Another woman commented that before she took part in D&S activities she had been very passive in vanilla relationships; however, after experiencing the intense communication necessary to make a D&S relationship work, she had found herself being more forthright in vanilla activities.

Is the increased ability to communicate simply a benefit of the scene, or did the blocking these women experienced cause their submissive feelings? Did the blocking and the feelings have the same original source? Obviously, there isn't any clear, single answer.

Why Would Someone Want to Be Dominant?

Some individuals take the converse of my relaxing-from-power explanation of submissive behavior to state that dominants, then, must be weak individuals who need to take the power from others to experience a contrast to their helplessness.

Aside from the knee-jerk reaction that this ain't so, the available evidence doesn't seem to fit. Before I took to writing full time, I was the vice president of a very old and successful market-research company. Many of my fellow dominants in and out of the major scene organizations hold stressful, high-pressure jobs and do very well.

If our motivation isn't the reverse of the submissive's motivation, what is it? I have come to the conclusion that the essence of what motivates *me* are two interlocking items. One factor is that I get a tremendous charge from my partner's pleasure. D&S is a wonderful way to "get someone off" more intensely than most vanilla people can imagine.

Many teachers and guides say that one of their major rewards is to see someone excited by a new idea or an unexpected vista. Having been a college professor, I know exactly what they mean, and I can see a definite kinship between that feeling and the feeling I get watching a woman in a paroxysm of pleasure. There is a feeling of accomplishment in knowing that I have helped someone climb higher and go farther than she could have gone alone.

Another factor in my attraction to the dominant role is that the D&S situation allows me to be in almost complete control. In today's modern world, this situation is becoming more and more difficult to attain. In fact, the more powerful one becomes, the more it seems that one is buffeted by collateral factors and outside forces.

For example, to a naïve observer, I may have seemed in complete control in my vanilla office. However, I had to depend on my employees doing their jobs correctly. I had to answer to the president and to the CEO. I had to depend on suppliers to be on the ball. Much of what I seemed to control was really "managed," a much less satisfactory situation. In D&S, I am in complete control, to fail or succeed as my talents and imagination permit. I control every factor, and I do not have to depend on anyone. Any *object* I depend on (whips, ropes, suspension gear) I can test and retest until I am certain it works. Being in that kind of control pleases me intensely.

This, of course, may not be the true cause of these feelings. No mirror is completely accurate, and ego is a subtle distorter of fact. I can only urge you to look into your own hearts and, most importantly, *enjoy*.

CHAPTER 4
Consent and Consensuality

Consent is more than just an ideal for D&S relationships; it is a touchstone, an axiom, a sacrament. Without full, knowing consent, they are in immediate danger of becoming brutal, exploitative affairs without beauty or elegance.

Consent can vary from the very specific ("You can do this, this and this, but not that") to a simple, knowing acceptance ("I trust that you will do nothing to harm me"). However, it must be constantly present and mutually respected within the relationship.

You Don't Have to Say Exactly What You Mean

For most players, the concept of "safe words" is central to consent in D&S. Using these phrases permits the submissive to withdraw consent to a particular activity or terminate the scene at any point without endangering the illusion that the dominant is in complete control.

An acceptable safe word can be "no" or "stop"; however, many submissives enjoy an illusion of nonconsensuality and relish being able to beg for mercy with unrestrained fervor. For these, the use of such blandishments is an inherent part of the trappings of the scene. For them, phrases that would not be used in the heat of the scene are the best safe words. Expressions like "red light" and "give me mercy, mistress" are common. One problem that can be encountered is that, by the time a safe word is needed, the submissive may be so caught up in the excitement of the scene that he or she has forgotten what the safe word was. I deal with that by having my submissives use their own names as safe words. Another approach is simply to say (yell, scream) "safe word."

Some D&S couples have adjuncts to safe words: "slow words" and "go words." A "slow word" is a signal to the dominant that, while the activity is not beyond the submissive's tolerance, the limit of tolerance is being approached. It is a signal not to cease all activities, but to ease off a bit and, perhaps, to take a different route. Those who use "red light" for a safe word, often use "yellow light" as a slow word.

A "go word" is simply a signal to the dominant that everything is all right and he or she can continue and increase the intensity of the stimulation. Again, some couples use phrases like "yes, please" and "more," but others, who wish to maintain the illusion of nonconsensuality, enjoy the irony of using "no" and "please stop." However, when this latter type of go word is used in a public or semipublic scene, it is advisable to inform at least some of those present that it will be used. Otherwise, an "inadvertent termination of the scene by outside influences" may result.

A second type of safe word is used by some people who use intense psychological stimuli as well as physical stimulation. This is a emotional safe word. While one word can be used to signal that either physical or psychological limits have been surpassed, some couples prefer to have separate safe words. This allows a submissive to signal, for example, that while the physical chastisement is still enjoyable, the humiliation has reached an unendurable point.

In some scene groups, there is a heated debate about the need for safe words. While the majority seems to concur that they are necessary, a vocal minority deems them contrary to the spirit of D&S. The most extreme members of this group put forth the concept of irrevocable consent. That is, once a submissive has given consent to a dominant, the dominant is free to do whatever he or she wishes. This outlook seems to be most common among the gay community. During a lecture at a D&S group, one gay dominant expressed this philosophy succinctly as "If he goes home with me, he's mine until I'm tired of him."

A female dominant reflected a more mutualistic viewpoint, but still rejected the concept of safe words, when she said, "If I can't tell when he [the submissive] isn't enjoying it anymore, I don't have the right to call myself a dominant."

A less radical outlook is that safe words are acceptable in the early stages of a relationship but, as the relationship matures, they become unnecessary and reflect a lack of confidence in the empathic abilities of the dominant.

Interestingly, this desire to drop safe words from a relationship's vocabulary is often voiced by the submissive, who declares that he or she wants to demonstrate absolute trust in the dominant.

It is important to recognize that a safe word benefits both parties. Many dominants value the use of safe words because it allows them to "work closer to the edge" than would otherwise be comfortable. Particularly at the beginning of a relationship, safe words offer "reality tests" that assure them that they are reading the submissive's responses correctly.

During her initial session, a novice submissive made such a fuss, pleading and begging, when she realized that I intended to shave her pubic region, that I was unsure whether she was 'going with the fantasy' or genuinely objecting. After she had cried, "You can't do this to me," I replied, "Of course I can—unless, that is, you use your safe word." She paused only a moment and then moaned, "I'll do anything you want; just don't do this to me." Reassured, I went on mixing the lather. Safe words work not only to make the submissive feel safe, they provide a margin of safety for the dominant.

Of course, as the relationship matures, a dominant will become more familiar with the submissive's reactions, and safe words become less important. However, they shouldn't ever be discarded. Fatigue, distraction, or changes in the submissive's physical or psychological functioning make them an important backup in all D&S relationships.

Protect Us From Our "Protectors"

Outside the D&S community, among some groups and individuals, there is a vocal contention that some people are not competent to give their consent. Like most generalizations, this one has a degree of truth. The law recognizes that some individuals are separated from reality to such an extent as to constitute a danger to themselves and/or to society at large. They are considered to be "non compos mentis," not of sound mind.

In the last few decades, exacting rules have been enacted to prevent people from being declared non compos mentis at the whim of someone in authority. However, in the past, people have been committed to mental hospitals for such minor idiosyncrasies as failing to bathe or for desiring daily sex from a spouse. In addition, certain groups, such as minors, are considered by law to lack competency: the ability to make trustworthy decisions.

Normally, it takes a pattern of irrational behavior to motivate a court to rule someone incompetent, and this ruling is deemed universally applicable. That is, a person who is found incompetent has *all* of his or her decisions removed and placed in the hands of another.

However, many of the previously mentioned groups would both narrow and broaden the definitions of competence and incompetence. For example, certain pseudo-feminist groups argue that today's society is so male dominated that a woman cannot truly consent to any form of heterosexual intercourse, whether it is vanilla or D&S. In effect, they argue that *any* act of heterosexual sex is rape, and the only consensual sexual activities a woman can engage in are with other women. By their definition, lesbian sex is based on equality.

Interestingly, although they would hold that a woman who desires heterosexual intercourse is not competent to make that decision because of the domination of society by males, they would not extend it to the point of denying her the right to make contracts, buy property, or go into business. They also fail to see that D&S relationships thrive between lesbians, as reflected in the rich and growing body of lesbian D&S fiction.

Others take a more moderate approach. Vanilla sex is considered acceptable as long as both partners mouth the right words about equality and acceptance. However, when someone—usually a woman—engages in D&S activities as a submissive, it is then taken as prima facie evidence that that person is incapable of giving consent, a classic Catch–22.

It is difficult to argue with these people. Their beliefs have often hardened to such an extent that they are unable to recognize loving, supportive couples even when they meet them in person.

Moreover, there *are* undoubtedly individuals and couples in the scene who desire or take part in activities which most people would find frightening or repulsive. *The Correct Sadist* (a highly overrated and not particularly informative book) describes a man whose cock had been mutilated until it resembled a peeled banana. Michele, a dear friend, told me of a man whose ankle had been pierced to such an extent that he could literally be hung from a meat hook.

However, while we might desire to avert our eyes from what, to us, are "disgusting" activities, taking the approach that the participants in these activities are somehow less sane than ourselves puts us on a slippery slope. If it is possible to reject a person's ability to give consent simply on the basis of a desire for mutilation, could it not be argued that a desire for whipping or bondage would be equally likely to indicate derangement?

Moving out of the emotionally laden sexual arena, how are we to treat those members of our society who bungee-jump, body-surf through pilings, or race motorcycles? A cherished friend spends her vacations hundreds of feet under the ground, crawling through openings a gopher would reject with disdain. Should I judge her mentally incompetent because of this proclivity?

When we argue that, because of a single desire, a person lacks the ability to give consent, we are headed for a safe, sane, boring society that will eventually stamp out every scintilla of excitement and adventure.

A Submissive Writes About Submission

This section has been written, at my request, by Libby, a lovely and sensual submissive woman. I'm providing it to give you a firsthand look at how one submissive sees her submission. Her words may not be true for all submissives, but she speaks for many.

I was quite squeamish as a kid, so when I told my childhood friends that I was going to study biology in college, they said, "You, I can't believe it, dealing with bugs, guts, and gross things. It used to make you sick to your stomach to see a piece of old spaghetti in the sink." Well, yes, but still, once I was exposed to the lure of science, I just couldn't keep from it. I'm sure I would get a similar or even stronger reaction if I were to share my interest in being a submissive woman. In my everyday life, I'm a strong, competent, and successful woman; yet, even before I was exposed to the submissive role, I was called to it by my earliest childhood fantasies. The attraction to it is even stronger than to my chosen professional life because I was called to it from a place deep within me. I'm not sure how the seeds of submission were planted within me but I am driven to nurture those seeds into full bloom by "following my bliss," as Joseph Campbell would say.

So, what is submission to me? To me, submission is a desire to be special or significant. My earliest fantasies, and they were when I was very young, always involved being somehow chosen and desired. I will borrow here from the image of the Goddess who is a composite of virgin, maiden, and crone, to describe how these forces, desires, and needs coalesce within me and reach expression as submission. The part of me that is virgin always wants tobe able to approach new things in an open-minded and curious way, without giving a thought to her own security. The part of me that is maiden seeks to explore passion and creativity. The chance to explore passion, sensuality, and sexuality, within the framework of safety that the virgin enjoys, takes my freedom onto the path of liberation. The crone is the wisdom part of me that is self-assured enough to look at my dark desires. If the virgin can be safe to enjoy the erotic pleasure that is awakened in the maiden, the crone may risk to surrender herself to the dark side of her soul.

Facing my uncensored soul, without turning away, looking aside, or getting preoccupied in divergent energy interferences, I see a desire to surrender completely to another who is that one special person with whom there is mutual love, affection, and emotional trust. Being able to do this makes me integrated, complete, and whole. Then, as the two of us become absorbed in each other, get increasingly unified, and become soul mates, there is always the polarity of the dominance and submission to keep the bond alive and vital.

Levels of Submission

Philosophically, I have been developing a way of looking at levels of submission. In this model, trust is an integral part. I have categorized three levels of submission: fantasy, clarity, and transparency. The fantasy level is where everyone starts out, and for many this is sufficient. The D&S fantasies are as varied and unique as the individuals who create them. Some are mild, like spanking or bondage, while others are what some consider edge play.

There really is no hierarchy of the fantasies, but some are obviously easier to realize than others. While they remain strictly a fantasy, no trust is involved. The fantasy level would also include mind play and some negotiated play or clearly defined and limited scenes during which trust can begin to develop.

In the next level, power transfer begins, and there is great opportunity for trust to develop. I call this level "clarity" because there is a clear understanding of what power is being transferred—this is often stipulated by contracts and is limited by the establishment of safe words. The submissive is watchful at first and careful to determine that the dominant is technically competent as well as being caring and comforting. The range of activities is again determined by the mutual fantasies involved.

Because of this, there is a great deal of diversity among the so-called "real players." As trust develops, so does the relationship. For some involved in D&S activities, it is sufficient to have these times set aside for scenes, but for others the trust-building helps to develop the relationship outside of the D&S activities. So there is a continuum within this level, with functional scenes at one end and real relationships at the other.

In the third level, called "transparency," the partners know each other well, and trust for personal safety is well established. Safe words are still operative, but they are not as necessary because the dominant has a sharper aware- ness of the submissive's limits. Paramount in this level is excellent communication and a willingness for each to trust the other with what is truly within their hearts and souls.

In this level, one begins to establish emotional trust, a kind of "Will you be there for me when I need you? I trust my body, safety, and pleasure to you; now, may I also trust you with my emotions, hopes and other desires?" It is here, with the passion-desires of the maiden having been met, that the fully realized woman incarnated as Goddess begins to hope and believe her relationship-desires, and her drive to be special or chosen can be met. Many D&Sers move into this level, but it takes ongoing work to maintain transparent trust.

The Experience of Submission

Well, what is it like to step across that threshold from fanta- sy into clarity? I had D&S or S&M or B&D fantasies ever since I can remember. As I came to realize these were sexu- al fantasies, I was a bit ill at ease thinking I was a maso- chist. None of the terms to describe what I felt seemed to capture what seemed to me to be very natural, exciting, and compelling.

I feared enacting my fantasies for several reasons: that I would not be safe doing so, that I would verify that I was a pervert, and that reality would not be as good as fantasy. I believed that somehow I would be able to negotiate safety nd be able to deal with the pervert label if I acted on this desire, but I was very reluctant to give up the exciting sexual energy that I derived from the fantasy.

After a while I knew that I would have to at least have to find out. It actually took more courage to get over being a D&S virgin than to lose my virginity in the first place. Behind the mask of a computer bulletin board, I felt safe enough to talk about it. I stalked my lover on this national family-oriented bulletin board after I found out that he had D&S interests and experience. I had long thought about answering D&S or B&D personal advertisements, but an image of a snickering and licentious sadist always prevented me.

This computer-bulletin-board stalking did allow me to find out things about him outside his D&S interest which made him seem like a reasonable risk to me. After stalking for a while, I wrote him by private electronic mail and said simply that I shared his interests. He wrote back, and a week later I was on my way to visit him in New York City.

It was on leap year day that we met. To me, this was symbolic of taking a leap into this new and wonderful world. In that twenty-four hours, we did several scenes, went to the Vault where, in spite of my reservations, I did my first public scene. In this first encounter, I felt that the innocence of the virgin and the wisdom of the crone were operative, but the passion of the maiden had not really been released.

Suffice it to say that, for me, not only was reality better than fantasy, it made fantasy pale in comparison. The world of D&S is replete with contrasts and polarity, but when I first entered this stage of clarity, I was quite surprised to feel an ambivalence when I reentered my vanilla routine.

When I awoke the first morning home, I felt ambivalent about proceeding any further despite a wonderful rest caused by having had my body sensually satisfied to the point of exhaustion. Yes, I wanted to run right back and do it all over again, but I kept asking myself if I wasn't dragging my body somewhere my mind was not yet prepared to go. I realized that, in giving D&S a try, I had been trusting myself and my perceptions about the situation. However, to go any further, I would have to trust Mentor, and this scared the living daylights out of me. I had tapped into my own passion, the lioness within me had roared, and she would not again be silent. The maiden was about to be liberated.

Losing control is a common fear in the trust-building stage of clarity. One submissive who was playing in the fantasy stage asked me how I could give my mind over to someone, and was it like a battle of wills to submit? My response was that, in the process of submission, my mind does drift off, and it can drift off quite a bit, but this happens in a most pleasant way.

Initially, fear can make it seem like a battle of wills, but as fear is replaced with trust, the battle becomes a dance. Often, when people dance together for the first time, they find themselves stepping on each other's feet. Eventually, as each becomes used to the other's style, they begin to move as one. If one listens to the music with the heart and responds with the will, it is truly a brand-new and exciting dance.

Physically, submission is hard to describe to one who does not have submissive tendencies burning within the soul. I had long ago accepted that I must be a masochist. This was not a very pleasant thought, but it was the only term I could find anywhere that described my taste for pain. I knew that I did not like being hurt; in fact, I am a wimp when it comes to what I call real pain, but I and many other submissives can only describe the joy of a whipping or a spanking as increased intensity. The language is truly impoverished in trying to describe the physical feeling.

Because there is clearly a sexual component and most people recognize the nebulous word "turn-on," perhaps I should just say that I am turned on by acting on my submissive urges and feeling the physical aspects of submission such as bondage, whipping, spanking, waxing, or needle piercing.

I have always been a spanking enthusiast; that still elicits the strongest sexual response in me. When I am spanked, my vaginal juices flow like a fountain, and sexual tension builds in my clitoris into a tidal wave force that longs to be relieved by an enormous orgasm. Whipping has the added smell and feel of leather, the caress and the sting of the leather providing contrast in sensation and in emotion.

Bondage was not initially a primary turn-on for me. I asked some of my submissive friends why bondage is such a turn-on, and typically the answer was that it made them feel secure or allowed them to be sexual. As I have grown to trust my dominant partner, I have become more willing to be rendered helpless before being disciplined. The symbolic consensual helplessness heightens the physical response and amplifies the pre-orgasmic sexual tension.

Waxing is something that I had never heard of before becoming involved in D&S, but I really love the sensation. First, there is much anticipation as I see the wax from the burning candle building up into a small hot puddle. The falling of the wax splashing on the skin is somewhat like a hot raindrop, but as it quickly cools, it feels like a point of massage oil. There does seem to be a direct line connected to the clitoris, making the sexual response even more intense.

These are just a few examples of how I experience submission physically. To those who still feel you have to ask, "Why do you enjoy pain?" the answer is, all the theoretical explaining aside, I have the strongest and best multiple orgasms this way.

Integrating Spirituality and Ritual

Looking at the stage of transparency takes me into the arena of deep trust and has, for many, a spiritual component. I am called to the reality of D&S from within what I understand to be my soul. All of my religious upbringing and the development of faith that took place in adult life leads me to accept this truth.

I do not know why I am thus called, only that I am. I can no more deny this call than the biblical prophets could deny their call. I have seen this in others as well, others who risk more in the way of heart and home than I do by answering the impulse within.

The word "soul" represents an individual's ideas, feelings, hopes, fears, and desires. Everything that shapes us, surrounds us, or in any way influences us rests within this soul. When one senses the stirring within one's soul, it is nearly impossible not to heed these signals, whatever they may be. For me, the most satisfactory image of soul comes from the ancient Greeks, who viewed the different aspects of the soul with different deities. Psyche, the spirit, was married to Eros, the body. To me, this is why the call is so strong, it is a call to be whole, to be integrated and happy within.

It often comes up that there is a strong similarity between religious experience and D&S experience, and I have been asked, "Do the submissive's feelings in a D&S relationship compare to other control/surrender situations?" For me, it is more than a similarity, D&S is part of my spiritual journey. Myself, I would call it a faith experience rather than religious. Anyone who experiences the joy of newfound faith is often willing to give up control to God. In mature faith, however, one finds that God speaks to one's heart through the community and through the aching and longings within the heart.

To listen to the spirit that calls beyond what you are takes courage. You know it is a right move spiritually when you feel a peace within about your decision and when your move is affirmed by the community. Often, in new faith and in new D&S experience, people think that they are giving themselves totally. In both cases, preconceptions and "the way it ought to be" mentality are cast aside in order to make room for new fulfillment. But in neither case do people abandon what they are at the core of their existence. Instead, they often find that they become more true to themselves.

Ritual within the D&S scene may seem like a very strange concept, but please do not discount it. Patriarchal religions have long attempted to separate the holy from the body—especially from the sexual aspects of the body. Yet, if there is one way the Almighty could be sure that we would "go forth and multiply," it is by this marvelous gift of sexual drive.

I associate the act of submission with ritual. Many of the toys we use in D&S play are phallic symbols: knives, sticks, the energy of fire, candles, and needles. The vaginal symbols are more subtle: bowls, water or other liquids that flow, such as melted wax, roses and their scents, circular or undulating movement, and repetition. During a scene, beyond the enjoyment of the participants, there is a symbolic reality expressing that sexuality is part of who and what we are.

My Catholic background makes me think of a D&S scene as similar to a liturgy where the actions or props are symbolic of a spiritual truth. For me, the spiritual truth in D&S is that we are greater together than alone. The polarity of our D&S roles symbolizes the uniqueness of the individual. We approach the divine by the ecstasy of the scene being acted out.

I often play out in my mind a scene where I symbolically make my gift of submission. It starts with two of us walking to the center of the "scene," or ritual space. My outer clothing is vanilla, and I have on a priestlike stole (symbol of authority and power) that is rainbow colored. This shows that we start out as equals. Pachelbel's *Canon* begins softly and slowly grows louder. As the music becomes manifest, I kneel down, bow, and then take off the stole and place it on my lover (the power transfer made manifest).

He motions me to take off my vanilla outer clothing, and I do (a symbol of a willingness to become vulnerable). He puts the cuffs on me (a symbol that I trust being helpless before him). Here I would feel the fire. It might be real fire on skin or skin reddened and warmed by the whip (symbolic of passion). Pachelbel ends and Webber's

"Music of the Night" begins. This music by itself is symbolic of spiritual journey as it talks of letting "fantasies unwind" and letting the "darker side give in." At this point, there is a waxing (the double symbols of fire and light). The fire of the candle is symbolic of the fire in the soul, and the image of light coming into darkness is replete with symbolism.

As the music builds, the lyrics ring out: "You alone can make my soul take flight; help me make the music of the night." We embrace and caress. This, to me, is symbolic of reaching heights in a journey that one could not reach alone or if one did not risk. As the music dies down and we move apart, he takes off the stole and holds it out in front of him, draped over his hands. He bows. I return the bow and, while my head is still bent submissively, he replaces the stole around me (a symbol of power returned). We again embrace and kiss as equals.

While this D&S ritual is in many ways reminiscent of the liturgical dance, it fits my own fantasies of being exposed and becoming known deeply and intimately by another, so it is still a personal expression. When I think of a private scene, it seems like private prayer and as such is open to a multitude of diverse expression.

Submission as Personal Growth

Being a submissive woman has taken me on a journey that has challenged my preconceived ideas and has forced me into clarification of my values. The life force or spirit within me has been strengthened, and I have been and continue to be guided by the spirit of Goddess/God in every step of the journey. I have gone beyond pain and pleasure and into a world of self-discovery, personal fulfillment, and community outreach. I have discovered a side of me that is curious about my previously repressed bisexual nature and a receptivity to open relationships.

At times, I have felt like Abraham in the Old Testament, when he was asked to give back to God the son who was to be the instrument of God's promise. How could I give up the values of my youth or the hard-won advances of the feminists who have gone before me? Listening to that small voice within, I have been abundantly blessed, as Abraham was, when I trusted the spirit within rather than conventional wisdom. At other times, I've felt as if I were an unwilling prophet like Noah or Paul. It has seemed that I have been as compelled to be a prophet of a new sensuality as they were to spread the word of God. My early faith development and refinement, even though it was in a very patriarchal religion, has taught me to live the questions. Being submissive may have put chains on my body, but it has removed my soul from bondage.

CHAPTER 5
A Feast of Joy... A Dish of Pain

One of the things that makes discussing D&S so difficult is the word "pain." Submissives don't necessarily seek "pain"—even though many enjoy many forms of "pain" as part of the play. What many of us do would seem to be painful, but most dictionary definitions of pain include phrases like "leading to evasive actions" or "which are avoided." Yet, these stimuli, far from being avoided, are sought. Therefore, they cannot be pain. Or can they?

This paradox reminds me of a story about a politician who, being asked if he opposed liquor, said, "Are you referring to the Demon Rum that destroys lives, reduces families to ruin, and is the shame of our cities; or are you referring to the delicious elixir that rejuvenates the tired, gives peace to the troubled, and contributes so much in taxes to our national treasury?"

The problem seems to lie in a failure of the English language; obviously, there seem to be at least two—and perhaps more—kinds of pain. I've never known a submissive who got off on a stomach ache from a bad hot dog. However, many people enjoy the very similar pain resulting from an enema. A swat from a closing spring-loaded door is annoying; one from a leather-clad lover is exciting.

Nor is it simply situational. More than once I have had to pause during a session to untangle a strap which was pinching my submissive or to ease her leg cramps. Why did these pains "bring her down" when she was receiving substantially greater pain from the whipping, strapping, or waxing?

The answer could be that the pains are different. Popular myth has it that Eskimos have dozens of different words for snow. We have only one word for pain (and only one for love, which is another interesting shortcoming for English. But not one I want to address—not here, at least.)

As far as I know, psychologists have not examined this terminological shortfall (perhaps scientists involved in D&S prefer to remain in the closet); however, there has been considerable research into stress, which affects the body much like pain. The stress researchers found that there are two kinds of stress: eustress (good stress) and distress (bad stress). Interestingly, the distinction between these two stresses is completely within the soul of the individual. Where one person might see a roller-coaster ride as the high point of her day; to another, it might be a glimpse into hell.

Even the same stress can be distress (let me out of here)

for an individual at one time and eustress (having a ball) at another. We all know individuals who glory in the push and tug of office politics; however, occasionally even these "political animals" get fed up and need to get away when the eustress of political infighting becomes distress.

People in D&S recognize instinctively that there are positive pains and negative pains. Our discussions are laden with indirect references to them. We may talk about something with "gets me off" or "sends me somewhere else" while another activity/toy/person "turns me off" or "brings me down."

Often, at the beginning of a session, we are dealing with a relatively narrow cone of positive pain. Most submissives prefer to begin with some relatively light, sensual, familiar stimulation. As the level of endorphins builds and the submissive "gets into his or her space," the cone of positive pain widens, and the dominant has a broader range of stimulation to choose from.

This is where experience and sensitivity come in. By riding just short of the edge, where positive pain becomes negative, the dominant can take the submissive to heights of pleasure he or she never expected to be able to reach. However, crossing over that edge, moving outside the cone of positive pain, can distract the submissive and shatter the mooe of the scene.

This is what creates the intensity of communication between the submissive and the dominant. The body language, tone, and timbre of cries—even odor—provide clues that allow an experienced dominant to bring the submissive right up to the edge without crossing it.

To make matters even more complex, this "edge" does not lie at a particular point on the submissive's pleasure map, nor is the passage to it analogous to reaching a conventional wall or barrier. The position of the edge varies from day to day and is responsive to the pace and timing of the stimulation and to the tool employed. In fact, in the non-euclidian space of domination and submission, it is also possible to go beyond the edge without passing it.

For example, a particular submissive may be in sheer heaven with hours of firm, measured spanking but may reach the edge rather quickly with a few swats of the cane. Conversely, the cane may produce a marked negative reaction *(red light!)* when used early in the session, but be welcomed as a scene ender which drives that particular submissive right into paroxysm of pleasure *(yes, my God, yes)* when preceded by extensive stimulation with other toys.

Another thing that differentiates the kinds of pain is a sense of control and trust. Recently, doctors have been fitting patients with small pumps with which the patients can dose themselves with pain medication. To many people's surprise, the patients used less medication than they would have been given in a typical nurse-supplied situation. It wasn't that doctors and nurses had been overdosing patients; the patients who could control their own pain could tolerate more of it. They were in control of the situation.

This may explain why a twisted strap or cramp can be painful and a whip pleasant. The strap and the cramp are unexpected and uncontrolled. There is no assurance that no harm will be done. The whip, on the other hand, is controlled by someone who is seen as trustworthy, one who would not inflict lasting or gratuitous harm. The submissive recognizes either overtly or covertly that he or she has the overriding say in the scene.

Because the previously mentioned cramp wasn't "part of the script" between me and my submissive, it was therefore frightening—and painful. It was an alien intrusion into this dance of trust and submission. Since I did not control it, my submissive did not even have the indirect control over the stimulation to which she had become accustomed. This created a sense of negative pain, and she used her safe word to bring the situation under control once again.

This sense of control over the outer parameters of the scene may also explain why experienced submissives playing with unfamiliar dominants are unable to tolerate the same degree of stimulation they would enjoy with familiar partners.

It is the development of this trust that is the test of a true dominant. It is fragile, broken easily, and can rarely be mended seamlessly. However, it is a treasure beyond price, the key that opens fantasy to reality.

CHAPTER 6
Stalking the Wild Submissive

The single most common question in D&S is "How do I find a submissive?" (I'm also asked "How do I find a dominant?" but that is another book.) Occasionally, it is spoken with a an air of angry frustration as if there should be a branch of Subs Are Us on every corner. More often, the tone is one of frustration and disappointment.

I won't sugarcoat the truth. It is difficult and frustrating for both sides in this eternal dance. If you are seeking a male submissive, remember that you are asking him to admit to desires contrary to every precept he was brought up to hold. If you are seeking a female submissive, keep in mind that by admitting her desires, she could be seen to be rejecting gains that women have slowly and painfully made over the last 20, 50, 100 years.

Is it any wonder the streets are not filled with people wearing buttons reading "I'm Submissive; Take Me"?

There are basically two routes to your goal. One is to attract an individual who has already made up his or her mind that submission is the desired path. The other is to help a potentially submissive person liberate his or her feelings. Neither is easy.

Let's look at the first path. On the surface, it looks smooth. We have a group of submissives looking for dominants and a group of dominants looking for submissives. Put them together and all will be well—and, in an ideal world, this would be true. Unfortunately, within each group, there is a smaller group of people who are not what they seem. Each group includes mindfuckers, blackmailers, and outright confidence tricksters. Removing them from the mix sometimes seems like an overwhelming task.

To make things harder, submissives are looking for someone strong in spirit and confident, someone to whom they can entrust their safety. A seemingly frenzied search does not present these qualities to the onlooker.

Perhaps the best approach for a dominant to take is presented, somewhat tongue in cheek, in this short parable written on Prodigy by a Midwestern dominant.

Somewhere in the stormy North Atlantic, aboard the U.S.S. *Dominance*:

"Captain...our sonar shows subs lurking in the area."

"Easy, Mr. Libido. We'll let them come to us."

"Begging your pardon, captain, but shouldn't we be seeking them out?"

"Mr. Libido, you obviously don't know how the

U.S.S. *Dominance* retains its control over the high seas. "

A klaxon horn goes off, and an urgent voice blares from the loudspeaker. "Sub sighted off the starboard bow!"

"All hands, this is Mr. Libido! Man your battle stations! Full speed ahead!"

"Mr. Libido! You will rescind those orders and never dare to overstep your authority on my ship again!"

"Captain, the U.S.S. *Dominance* is a dominant ship!"

"Exactly, Mr. Libido. And, as a dominant ship under my command she will stay her course while the sub approaches. Stand down from battle stations. Steady as she goes."

"Captain, as executive officer on this ship, I must protest your extraordinarily passive behavior in the presence of a sub."

"Mr. Libido, protest if you will. But the sub will be handled my way, or it will not be handled at all."

"Sir, do you mean we will capture it by projecting a calm, secure image on the rough seas?"

"Mr. Libido, continue to learn. One day you will be a captain of a dominant ship yourself."

Rose, a New York submissive, phrased it this way:

"I like a guy who respects himself; he is more likely to respect me and my gift to him. He is more likely to take care of himself and, by extension, of me. I like a guy who understands that trust of this depth can evolve only if we take our time.

"Some guys always overdrive their headlights, no matter how rotten the driving conditions. That doesn't mean that I don't like to travel fast—only that there is a time and place for that, and the beginning is figuring out where all the buttons are and what they do.

"Finally, since this is all about domination and submission, shaping behaviors and pleasing each other, I like a guy who understands at least the rudiments of shaping behavior. Some people are natural-born dominants, masters, or trainers, but that doesn't mean the skills can't be learned. And there are lots of rules about shaping behavior that apply, no matter whom you're shaping."

Contact Media

There are various media for avowed dominants and submissives to seek each other out: newspapers, magazines, electronic bulletin boards, clubs, and associations.

Whatever the medium, the method is to give trust, for a dominant must earn the trust of a submissive by being trusting, while keeping alert for those who are flying false colors. True submissives look for this trust in an attempt to separate us from the sadists and those who would do them harm. Unfortunately, there are those among them who would use this trust to hurt us.

Because of this danger, it is a good idea not to reveal too much about yourself during initial contacts. Naturally, this is directly at odds with the need to give trust. It is a delicate balance, not susceptible to easy solution.

My method is to rent a post office box to receive replies to my advertisements or responses to replies I have sent out. Others prefer to rent boxes from private companies. These have a significant advantage. It is often possible to obtain a street address for a P.O. box from the post office; private companies recognize that discretion is part of the service they sell and are often much more careful about giving out information.

I usually include my telephone number in initial transfers; however, I have specified that the telephone company neither print my address in the directory nor give it out to those who request it. This way, I can tell the potential submissive to call me so that she can maintain her privacy while checking me out. A dominant friend uses another way to avoid annoyances while giving out his telephone number. He subscribes to a voice-mail system and gives out that number. He says it is relatively inexpensive and saves a lot of hassle.

Mindfuckers, Confidence Tricksters, and Blackmailers

If you spend any significant amount of time in the scene, you will encounter mindfuckers. Some of these have no malevolent intent, but are simply confused by what they want. Others are just intentionally cruel. The most common encounter of this type begins with the exchange of a series of passionate notes or phone calls, in which she or he seems to be everything you ever wanted and more. You get hotter and hotter—and suddenly the contact is broken off. A crueler scenario has you traveling hundreds and perhaps thousands of miles, to have no one waiting for you when you arrive.

There is really no perfect defense from these people. The old saw "If it seems too good to be real, it is" applies. So does getting as much information about the submissive as possible before committing to any major inconvenience or making any significant commitment. However, many genuine submissives are reluctant to give out much information to a relative stranger. (Don't forget that there are nuts masquerading as dominants, too.) Therefore, you must strike a balance between what you perceive as a risk and what you have as a need.

The same rule applies to the confidence tricksters. However, they generally reveal themselves in their single-minded search for money. The scenario goes like this: she (male dominants are most often the victims here) seems to be your dream submissive. There is an exchange of letters and, perhaps, phone calls. She informs you that she wishes to fly to your arms and dungeon, but she doesn't have the price of a plane ticket. Would you...

This is not to say that there are no submissives who are short on traveling money; however, such a request should send up warning flags. Other clues are typed rather than written letters and an inability or unwillingness to phone you. Again, some submissives find it easier to type person-al letters than to write them, and a small percentage does truly lack the freedom to send and receive calls. However, caution is called for.

Fortunately, most tricksters who sink to this kind of work are woefully lacking in skill and intelligence. If they were smarter, wouldn't they have been running a savings and loan company? I have received "personal" letters that were photocopied. Unsigned computer-generated letters. "Personal" photographs that had been copied from bondage magazines. I don't really object to their trying to trick me; I just wish they had a higher opinion of my intelligence.

Blackmailers are more difficult to deal with. Fortunately, the numbing of the American mind has made this a vanish-ing breed, except when political figures and socialites are the targets. If you don't fit into either category, you proba-bly have little to fear.

Writing an Advertisement

Placing an advertisement can be tricky. You don't want to write a biography. That gets expensive because most magazines and newspapers charge by the word. It can also convey a sense of desperation that does not reflect the calm and controlled demeanor that attracts a submissive.

On the other hand, advertisements like "Are you submissive? Write me" are unlikely to attract a high-quality group of submissives but are likely to be the natural feeding ground of the unsavory groups I mentioned. Keep in mind that this is the first step of a seduction. Outright commands ("Drop to your knees and write") can attract a certain group of fantasy players, but to attract people who seek a long-term submission and concomitant relationship, a more informative advertisement is needed.

The best approach is to think seriously about what kind of submissive you want and what he or she would want to read. Be as realistic as possible; at this stage fantasy is counterproductive.

Your advertisement should include information about yourself if you want to provide it, but lying is almost always a serious mistake. Some lies will be discovered almost immediately. One wannabe dominant who described himself as "tall and imposing" was quite successful at meeting submissives, but the meetings rarely went beyond that. He couldn't understand why. A glance in the mirror might have helped. He was 5'6" and weighed less than 120 pounds. You can imagine the suspicions submissives might have felt about any other information he had given them.

Other lies may take a while to come out. Marital status,

amount of experience, group membership, and such are difficult to lie about consistently. Every person is different, but the intensity of trust necessary for a D&S relationship rarely survives such falsehoods.

Honesty *is* the best policy.

In general, the approach in seeking male submissives can be a bit more "abrupt" than that in seeking females. Speaking even more plainly, what will scare the bejesus out of a novice female may be just right to attract a novice male. Of course, the perfect strategy is a matter of hot debate among those who use this approach. I have noticed that those of my female dominant friends who run the worship-at-my-feet-while-I-whip-your-ass type of advertisement do tend to get more responses than their more sedate colleagues. However, they also tend to attract a greater percentage of mindfuckers and no-shows. All in all, it seems to even out in regard to the number of male submissives who actually appear.

When writing my advertisements, I act on the assumption that submissive women are *not* looking for someone who will declare dominance. Almost all men will loudly claim that they are dominant; most are wrong. In any case, the simple declaration of dominance is not enough to motivate most submissive women. They are not looking for declarations of brutality or strength. Almost anyone can swing a whip or a paddle. Nature has made most men stronger, at least in their torsos and shoulders, than most women.

What they are seeking is some evidence that the person behind the advertisement is trustworthy and sensitive to their needs. Writing an advertisement that reflects these qualities is much harder than simply announcing dominance. Rather than providing a set of catch phrases or sample advertisements that anyone could copy, I suggest that you male dominants look deep inside yourselves.

If, once this reality is brought to your attention, you still cannot convey the requisite sensitivity in words, you may not be ready to hang a riding crop from the left side of your belt.

When you get a response to your advertisement, don't be surprised if a submissive—particularly a female submissive—is forthright in demanding more information about you. After all, the submissive is the one who must feel secure in giving up freedom. There may be a few maniacal ax-wielding submissives around, but I haven't heard of them. The Ted Bundys of the world have made submissives understandably nervous.

The most extreme example of demanding information I ever encountered was M, a thirty-year-old female submissive, who was a top-level executive in a nationwide store chain. She began with a standardized thirty-minute interview probing into details of the potential master's experience and background. As she put it, "I look at it as if I were hiring a vice president. After all, I am going to have to put my safety into his hands. I want to know if he can handle it."

She went through more than fifty candidates before settling on one. They are quite happy together.

Bulletin-board Systems

Electronic bulletin board systems (BBSs) can be used simply as modern versions of the classified advertisements. However, anyone doing this takes a chance at missing out on the medium's potential.

Electronic bulletin-board systems are specially programmed computers attached to telephone lines. To use them, you need a computer and a device called a modem, which allows the computer to communicate over the telephone lines. Then you just instruct your computer to call the BBS (bulletin-board system), and you can read other people's messages and leave your own messages on the BBS.

The simplest of the BBSs are quite similar to conventional bulletin boards. Users can post messages, requests for information, or advertisements which other users can read and respond to. Most, also, have an electronic-mail system for the exchange of private messages.

More complex systems have several phone lines so that several users can be using the system at the same time and even communicate in "real time" by typing messages that others 'on-line' can read instantly.

These systems range from small home computers run by hobbyists (some of whom are in the scene) to large mainframe complexes like CompuServe and Prodigy, which are only a local phone call from most of the people in the country. Most charge a monthly or yearly membership fee to cover expenses; others charge an hourly fee.

One attraction of BBSs is the speed with which a message can be posted. A magazine may take up to six months to run your advertisement, a newspaper, two days to a week, while an advertisement in a BBS can appear almost instantly. But the greatest attraction is anonymity. On most BBSs, you are identified only by a "handle." Some, like Prodigy, require real names. This requirement is not a major problem for those with a little imagination and creativity.

The handle serves to identify you to the BBS's computer and acts as a mailing "address" for electronic mail. There is generally no way for other users to obtain your real name, address, or telephone number if you do not wish it.

For example, you might see a message from a submissive who sounds promising. You could either reply to that message in the public board or send a private message (E-mail). He or she could use either mode to reply. "Conversations" of this type can go on for considerable lengths of time with neither party knowing anything more about the other than what that person wishes to tell.

The major qualitative difference between BBSs and conventional printed publications is that they allow users to "strut their stuff" in public as well as simply posting advertisements. This is possible because there is rarely an extra charge for posting messages.

I make it a point to post helpful hints regularly on the BBSs where I have accounts. I also respond to requests for information. The posts can be as simple as a list of D&S books I have found enjoyable or as technical as scene design and execution. In fact, many of the sections of this book first appeared as messages on a computer screen.

These notes allow cautious submissives to evaluate me as a dominant without even revealing their presence. They can get an idea of my level of skill and how closely my philosophy of D&S matches what they are looking for.

By the time *they* contact *me*, the "hook" is set firmly. All that is necessary is for me to decide the extent of involvement I will permit. In many cases, it is limited to guidance and advice; in others, the involvement can become much more intense. However, the computer has permitted each of us to exercise control in an area that was appropriate.

Initial Meetings

With all initial meetings, scene or vanilla, I let the other person choose a public site. This reduces her insecurities while permitting us to meet and look each other over with a minimum of pressure. Remember, a D&S relationship is still a relationship and should be approached like any other. The intensity that can develop and the extreme trust required make it "more" than most unions, not "different."

I strongly recommend that you not meet with the intention of having an intense scene immediately. The first meeting is a time to exchange a lot of information, and it is difficult to keep someone's attention when she or he is worrying or looking forward to what will be happening in the next few minutes.

The initial discussions should be quite detailed, but they can also be a mini-scene in their own right. The conversation can be played as a job interview with a young person attempting to get a well-paying job with a dominating, powerful person of the opposite sex, a medical examination, a Catholic-type confession before a priest or mother superior, a respondent to a Kinsey-type sex survey. Some sample questions are in Appendix G, which contains a questionnaire that Sir Spencer uses when interviewing new submissives.

You need to go over the submissive's medical history.

Important facts are:

Old injuries, particularly broken bones and tendons (For example, a person whose Achilles tendon has been reattached surgically is not a good candidate for many kinds of inverted suspension)

Diabetes (A diabetic can faint unexpectedly and is much more prone to long-lasting bruises)

Contact lenses (These can dislodge during blindfolding. In any case, the dominant should have a supply of artificial tears in case something gets in the submissive's eye)

Asthma (Gags are definitely a no-no, and you should keep the medication handy)

High blood-pressure or heart problems (obvious)

Allergies (For example, some people have severe skin reactions to alcohol; this would eliminate both fire-on-skin and basic sterilization techniques)

Glaucoma (This does not go well with inverted suspension)

Orgasmic syncope (People with this condition faint during orgasm; it is frightening, but not dangerous)

Skin sensitivity (Some people have skin that is exceptionally sensitive to cutting and bruising)

Tendency to muscle cramps or old sprains or strains (For example, a person with a history of charley horse shouldn't be forced to stand on tiptoe or be put in extreme positions)

Back problems (This would call for care in requiring high heels and the elimination of any hog-tie or arched-back positions)

Tendency to bladder infections (Women with this problem have to be very careful about cleanliness in the area of the urethra)

Hemorrhoids (This obviously would put a limit on playing with the ass)

Any psychological problems (A person with claustrophobia is *not* going to react well to hooding or mummification)

You should also ask the submissive about what are his or her turn-ons and turn-offs as well as what is seen as frightening. However, something that a submissive admits to being scared of is not automatically banished from your repertoire; actually, it may turn out to be a major turn-on for that submissive. After all, the sensation of fear is one of the major driving forces of the scene. Helping a submissive ride that crest of fear is one of the strongest highs for a dominant.

If you wish, you can ask about the submissive's pain tolerance, but except with highly experienced submissives, I have found such responses to be unreliable. One woman who described herself as a "big sissy" gloried in fifteen to twenty strokes of the cane, something well beyond the tolerance of most submissives. A muscular man who told a female dominant, "I can take anything a woman can dish out," was screaming his safeword before she ran out of her first Baggie of clothespins.

This initial conversation is a good place to assign a safe word or words or to allow the submissive to choose them. For a detailed discussion of the types and levels of safe words, check the chapter on consent. Here, I will only say again that it is absolutely necessary to have at least one safe word so the submissive can stop the scene before it gets too intense. Using a safe word is not an insult to your abilities; it is simply a recognition that Murphy's Law exists in D&S as well as everywhere else. Things can go wrong.

At this point, you should also discuss any limits on activities, including sexual. It does not have to be detailed. It can be as simple as "I will not have sex with you, and you may not come without my permission" or "I feel free to use you sexually in any way that strikes my fancy as long as I use safe sex techniques," or, if you wish, you can go deeply into precisely what can and cannot be done.

While you are gathering this information, you should keep in mind that this is an opportunity for the submissive to look over an unfamiliar dominant: you. For the submissive's peace of mind, you should be careful to maintain a dignified and professional demeanor.

You can either ask about the submissive's fantasies or try a more sensual, voluptuous approach I enjoy. Its basic idea is taken from Sigmund Freud. He recognized that people can be extremely sensitive to body language and other subliminal clues when they are talking about highly personal matters. Freud suggested that the doctor sit out of sight of the patient during the session to minimize the cues that might make it difficult for the patient to be open. My method modifies Freud's technique for my own erotic purposes.

If your submissive is comfortable with being nude, have him or her undress and sit in a comfortable chair. If not, have him or her change into loose, comfortable garments before sitting down. Comfort is important; you don't want any distractions. Stand behind the submissive or put your chair behind theirs. The important thing is to be outside he line of sight. Reach around the chair and gently run your hands over her breasts and neck or his chest and balls. Do not play hard enough to give more than a slight turn on. The imagination—not your hands—should be the primary stimulant.

An alternative is to have him or her put on a blindfold and lie on a bed. You can, if you wish, use light bondage techniques from the other chapters. Since there should not be any struggling, there is little need to worry about binding or nerve damage. The ropes, scarves, or whatever should be tied loosely and used primarily for psychological effect. The idea is to stimulate fantasy, not do a full-fledged scene.

If possible, put on some soft, relaxing music. Everything should be designed to promote relaxation and flights of fancy without giving any clues as to what "appropriate" responses should be.

In a low, gentle voice say something like "Just relax, my darling. Close your eyes. Feel sexy. Be aware of being turned on. Let your imagination run wild. Don't try to guide it or keep from thinking about anything, no matter how erotic. Nothing you say now is real. It is all fantasy. Just let me ride through your subconscious with you. There are no rules, no taboos. Tell me what you are thinking, dreaming about."

For the first ten minutes to half-hour, you will usually get conventional sex fantasies. As these begin to wane, there may be a bit of resistance. After all, you are getting into a very, very, personal space. Don't be insistent, but just continue as you have been. "You are so exciting, my dear; tell me more. Let's continue to explore. You are turning me on so much. Share your fire with me."

Never, under any circumstances, show the slightest sign of shock or disapproval. Even a gasp or an "oh, my!" can destroy the entire atmosphere. Listen and learn.

Whatever technique you use, you need to explore the submissive's fantasies. While you are not bound to follow any script, this information will allow you to create scenes that can excite and please both of you.

Public and Private Clubs

To many people who have not experienced them, public clubs sound like nirvana. Hundreds of leather-clad dominants and submissives mixing in an erotically charged atmosphere. *Your* perfect submissive waiting on bended knees for you to grasp the collar and drag him or her off to your lair. In real life, they *are* fun and exciting. However, as is so often the case, the reality is not quite the same as fantasy.

What Are the Clubs Like?

There are two types of clubs: scene and nonscene. At a scene club, you can actually whip, spank, or otherwise play with your submissive. Nonscene clubs are places where you can show off your gear, talk to potential partners, and relax with others in the scene, but no actual discipline can take place—at least overtly.

Perhaps the three most famous scene clubs in the United States are The Vault, Hellfire, and Paddles. Not surprisingly, they are in New York City.

Club Etiquette

Both scene and nonscene clubs can be very exciting places. However, there are some problems that prevent their being the answers to a dominant's dream.

Both attract throngs of tourists. Either because of a deep-seated fear or through simple bad manners, some of the tourists may behave rudely and inappropriately. For example, you will never hear anyone in the scene shouting "Hit her again, harder" during someone's scene. Some clubs, like Fetish Factor, a former scene club in New York City, try to minimize the tourist trade by imposing a strict dress code. To enter Fetish Factor, you must be dressed in leather, latex, or other fetish gear, or you must be a transvestite or transsexual in drag. Alligator-T-shirt-wearing frat rats usually don't get past the door.

Strict dress codes are the rule in most of the London clubs with which I'm familiar. Many of them use the premises of what are more conventional clubs when kinkiness is not in session. For example, The Pussycat Club in Hendon spelled out its stand clearly in advertisements: "Strict dress code. Leather, Rubber, Bondage, PVC and TV. No Denim, No Fur, No Cameras. No Swingers." Severin's Kiss in Soho took a similar stand.

In most scene clubs and nonscene clubs, leather and black clothing is standard wear, but conventional street clothing is acceptable. However, you will probably want to dress up a bit to fit in and distinguish yourself from the tourists and to get into the "flow" of the scene. After all, as one psychologist, who was talking to a scene member, exclaimed delightedly, "You get to have Halloween every weekend."

This doesn't mean you have to go out and buy a full leather rig. For men, black pants and a black shirt do the job. Women have a wider range of options—from riding clothes to, well…one dominant often shows up in a Victorian schoolmistress's outfit, complete with cameo at her throat.

Even the part of the crowd that is made up of scene members, like the scene itself, is disproportionately male. The vast majority consists of male submissives—much to the pleasure of the female dominants. Female dominants and male dominants are present in almost equal numbers.

However, unescorted female submissives seem almost nonexistent.

This is not to say that male dominants should avoid these clubs. They provide a useful place to meet others in the scene and to make (or ruin) one's reputation. Word of mouth is highly respected in the scene, and if the escorted submissive women come to like and trust you, you can be certain that their unattached sisters will soon learn about it.

Naturally, male dominants should treat escorted women with the greatest respect and courtesy. There are few greater sins than being dominating or rude to another dominant's submissive. If you fail to obey this unwritten rule, the nicest thing that will happen is that you will get the cold shoulder. Make sure to include the lady's dominant in any conversation; doing otherwise is extremely rude.

Another reason that unattached male dominants choose to visit these clubs is that a significant number of the "female dominants" are actually submissives dressing in dominant fashions so they can visit the club without being inundated by the attentions from wannabe doms.

Female dominants have an easier time; however, clubs present problems for them, too. Far too many apparently submissive men are actually SAMs (Smart Ass Masochists) who are intent on using them—or any other woman—as a prop in their fantasies. Far from being submissive, these men can be very uncooperative with anyone who does not look or behave in a manner fitting precisely into their fantasy.

I was with Ace, an attractive female dominant, at Paddles one night when a man approached her and said, "Mistress, may I worship your boots?"

With appropriate courtesy, Ace gave him permission. But then, after a few minutes, the man said, "Mistress, may I take off your boots and worship your feet?"

It had been a long evening, and Ace was tired. In a gentle voice, she told him that she had been standing all evening and felt that her feet were swollen. If she took off her boots, she would be unable to get them on again. However, she said, he could continue to worship the boots.

He simply dropped the leg he was holding, looked at Ace, and said, "That's no fun." Then he turned and walked away. While this man was far from being representative of all male submissives, unfortunately his kind is common in the club scene.

Female dominants *will* have a considerably easier time than males in finding someone to play with at public clubs. However, those who are seeking more than a simple bit of play may be just as disappointed at first as their male counterparts. The solution is to use the same strategy employed by male dominants in search of a submissive. Mingle; get to know the regulars, both male and female, dominant and submissive; plug into the grapevine, and eventually you are likely to have good luck.

Scene Organizations

Another way of meeting submissives already in the scene is through organizations, like Eulenspiegel, People Exchanging Power, Threshold, and Black Rose.

Unlike the public clubs, most of these are nonprofit organizations run by and for the members. The vast majority hold public meetings, but also have some members-only activities. Most are quite inexpensive to join and, even if you live too far away to attend meetings, their newsletters and other publications can be a valuable source of information and guidance.

For me, the most valuable reason for belonging is the joy of being with people who share my needs and desires. There is a feeling of family that can be infinitely comforting to someone whose desires are looked upon by the rest of the world with distaste and, sometimes, hostility.

If there is such an organization near enough for you to visit, by all means, do so. For the first meeting, sit, listen, and observe. Get a feel for the dynamics.

As a dominant, you may feel compelled to make your presence known immediately. Don't. Dominant means strong and secure. If you come across as pushy and insensitive, this reputation will stay with you for a long time.

I recall the close of an Eulenspiegel meeting. As was customary, everyone was putting away chairs. One man, whom I had not seen before, motioned to a woman whose collar and cuffs clearly indicated her status. He told her imperiously to put away his chair. When she looked at him in amazement, he informed her that he was dominant. She turned around and walked away. This exchange had not gone unnoticed by others, and this particular "dominant" soon stopped coming to meetings.

Talking to people is perfectly OK, but you should be careful not to angle your attention only at submissives of the opposite sex. Not only is this rude, but it gives an impression of a single-minded pursuit that is most undominant.

There are no hard and fast rules on how to act, but erring on the side of caution is probably a good idea.

I do not know of a single organization that pays much attention to clothing at their meetings. After all, many people will be coming directly from work, and few corporate organizations include black leather in their dress codes. On the other hand, some members come in full scene gear. What you wear is entirely up to you. However, a bit of black and a bit of leather will probably send the message that you are not entirely ignorant of the ways of the scene.

If, as is common, there is a point where those in attendance identify themselves according to their orientation and interests, take advantage of it to make yourself known in the most favorable terms possible. Just remember, as with advertisements, lying is inadvisable. Most lies will be found out eventually and may do irreparable damage to your reputation.

With organizations as well as at clubs, it is a mistake for a male dominant to expect to make contact with a female submissive immediately. It usually takes some time to build up a reputation to the point that your approaches will be welcomed. A female dominant may face the opposite problem: because of the abundance of male submissives, she may be faced with the pleasant difficulty of having to pick and choose.

Searching Outside the Scene

For one reason or another, a dominant may be unwilling or unable to avail herself or himself of advertisements, clubs, or associations. Still, it is good to remember that the vast majority of the submissives have not yet declared themselves or have not even realized the full range of their desires and, therefore, cannot be reached through the conventional routes.

Although there is some overlap between the techniques for identifying and seducing submissive men and women, there are enough differences to justify taking each group separately.

Identifying a potentially submissive woman is a situation fraught with peril. Not only is a direct question inappropriate, but many women have repressed their submissive tendencies because of embarrassment or because they have been taught that such feelings are evil or a betrayal of their fellow women.

I look for intelligent, strong, self-assured women. Frightened little mice do not have the courage to accept and act on their needs. Also, a woman who feels inferior can be manipulated into a submissive role against her will. This is ethically indefensible. With them, I tend to use a technique that I cause "plausible deniability," a method that allows me to back off with no loss of face in the event of rejection.

During the dating process, I put her in situations where she is lightly restrained. For example, I hold her hands behind her back during a kiss or kiss her while she is still entangled in clothing she has been removing. If she panics or withdraws, I apologize and "admit" to having been overcome with enthusiasm. If she reacts with passion, I try a bit harder. The trick is to keep it light and playful.

During sex, I watch for her to do things like grabbing sheets with wide-spread arms; this is a position often adopted by people who are fantasizing that they are being restrained. I also try holding her hands above her head or "accidentally" tangling them in the sheets when I am on top or holding them against her thighs or behind her back when she is on top.

Conversational probing can be as subtle as the physical testing. Literature is a good icebreaker. If she has read books by A. N. Roquelaure or *The Story of O*, it gives me a chance to discuss the situation in a suitably abstract, non-threatening atmosphere. If she brings up de Sade's writings, it gives me an opportunity to compare his writings with reality: "Yes, I've read some of his stuff, but what I hear about people who do bondage and stuff like that is that they are nothing like characters in his books. They seem really to care about consent and sensuality instead of just pain for pain's sake."

It is amazing what people will discuss in the abstract that would be extremely threatening to discuss on a personal level. I use such abstract discussions to get a feeling on "where a woman is" on this subject. Even a violent reaction to any kind of D&S literature is not necessarily a negative sign. Many women, as I have noted above, are fighting a great deal of social pressure to defeat what they have been taught to believe are bad feelings. I pay more attention to gut-level feelings, perhaps based on subliminal body language, which come out of the discussion. Of course, the danger here is that my desires may interfere with my judgment. The partial solution is a lot of introspection on my part.

If the discussion turns from abstract to specific, I do not deny my impulses, but avoid all terms like "domination," "submission," "sadism," "masochism," "bondage," or "discipline." These are emotionally laden terms that are defined slightly differently by every individual. Nor do I speak in terms of *my* needs and desires. Instead, I tell her what I enjoy doing for my partner, while stressing sensuality and respect. As in the initial stages of all D&S relationships, I try to earn the degree of trust that will allow her to submit to me.

Despite the teachings of certain psychological schools, my experience is that not all women are submissive, and only a relatively small percentage of them can act on submissive tendencies. However, through these approaches, I have been able to make some wonderful friendships and build a number of lasting relationships.

These techniques can also be used by dominant women to find a submissive man who has not yet declared—or perhaps even realized—his submissive nature. For example, the sensual bondage scenes in *Basic Instinct* are a sure conversation starter. One female dominant reports that the film, which includes the murder of a man while he is in bondage, seems to exercise an aphrodisiac fascination for some men.

Also, because of fashion, women are able to send more overt signals than men about their orientation. A man, wearing a kinky leather outfit with a whip earring, will probably be taken as gay by many women. A woman in similar regalia will certainly rate a second look from most men, even those who haven't explored their submissive desires.

The greater latitude for accessories is also a factor. Outside of the punk-rock scene, handcuffs aren't a common accessory for men. However, a woman can casually dismiss one hanging from her belt with "The chrome sets off my black dress."

The differences in body language between men and women can also work for the dominant woman on the prowl. While a man would be unwise to assume anything about a woman who dropped her eyes in the face of an appraising stare, a woman who gets that reaction from a man would be wise to press her advantage.

A word of warning: Novice dominant women often

restrict their search to men who are overtly submissive and/or effeminate. Experienced women report that they find their most satisfactory "conquests" among aggressive, masculine men. It is unwise to dismiss any specific "type" from consideration. Submissives are everywhere. They just need to be found.

CHAPTER 7
Winning Over the Vanilla Lover or Spouse

A common situation in marriages or long-term relationships is that one member discovers or finally admits to a D&S orientation and then is faced with the problem of convincing the other to join in these activities. If you are in that situation and hoping to convince your partner to submit to you, you may have a difficult task.

As I have written previously, even when submissive feelings are strong, admitting to them is a traumatic experience. For someone who does not have these feelings, being asked to act the submissive role is intimidating and humiliating. If, on the other hand, you have discovered deep submissive drives within yourself, there is a short section addressed to your specific needs at the end of this chapter.

When you suggest the possibility of trying D&S games, never use the terms S&M or B&D. Even the less-familiar D&S should stay in the closet for a while. Perhaps your major problem is that most people think they know what these things are all about; the mere fact that they are dead wrong doesn't alter the situation.

Sit down and think. What turns you on? Everything? Come on. Scat? Golden showers? Blood sports? Let's cut it down to the bone. What is it that you want? If you don't know what you want, you can't get it.

As a dominant, you should practice putting yourself "in the submissive's head." Do this for a moment. Put yourself in the place of a vanilla person whose spouse has admitted a liking for *sadism*. Do images of Ted Bundy or the Blond Bitch of Buchenwald leap to mind? They should. If you stir up these fears, the only people who will benefit are divorce lawyers. What you need to put in your lover's head is the image of your true desires. You also need to stir the emotions your lover may have repressed. There are several ways to do this, and they are not mutually exclusive. They can be combined as you see fit. After all, you are strongly attached to his or her person; who could know him or her better than you?

One approach is the direct one. If bondage is your turn-on, bring a scarf or the belt from a bathrobe to bed. Don't charge right in; mix a lot of horseplay with play bondage. Normally, a scarf is terrible for serious bondage, but we are talking light play right now. Share the fun; let him or her have a go at tying you up.

Stimulation is trickier on a direct approach. You must be certain it is recognized both consciously and unconsciously as sexual and not punitive. Spanking is probably the best "entry level" stimulation. It is familiar and doesn't involve instruments that might evoke a negative response. ("Where in hell did you get *that?*")

One approach I have used when dating overtly vanilla women is to exclaim during sex, "You bad girl! You scratched me with your fingernail." (No woman, even the most dedicated nailbiter, will feel entirely comfortable claiming innocence.) "You should be punished for that." Then I pull her onto my lap and give her a few swats with one hand while keeping her well excited with the other. Spanking can also combined with an intercourse position. Just put him or her on top and swing away.

When converting a vanilla lover, as when seeking out a submissive lover, talking about books and movies is a good way to lead the conversation to your own desires. Before I got into a relationship with a romance author, I had always dismissed romance novels as chaste escapism. They may be escapism, but they are *not* chaste. A husband who discovers dominant tendencies and has a wife who reads authors like Rosemary Rogers, Linda Barlow, Jayne Krentz, and Sandra Brown is halfway to heaven. Read a few of her romance books. Then let her "catch" you doing it. Suggest that some of the scenes in them are "interesting." It is wonderful duel that both of you can win.

Otherwise, bring home a few books to leave where she can find them. As I noted before, books by Anne Rice writing as A. N. Roquelaure and as Anne Rampling are a nice start to introducing someone to D&S fantasies. The original *Joy of Sex* has a nice section on bondage; unfortunately, later printings have watered it down. Madonna, the lady who made sleaze nice, has several books where she sings the praises of D&S.

Vanilla video tapes abound with D&S scenes. Bring some home for an evening of watching. A casual comment while watching *Bull Durham*, like "Wow, doesn't Susan Sarandon look like she is having fun," or "I bet he enjoys that" can begin an illuminating conversation. Avoid X-rated D&S tapes, they are so intense they can be threatening. Remember: you want to keep it fun and nonthreatening. Some vanilla films that have good bondage scenes are *Bull Durham*, *The Collector*, and *The Nightcomers*. Spanking fans have particularly recommended John Wayne's *McClintock*.

Generally, the only reason most television talk shows have D&S subjects is to attack them. Don't watch them live with your spouse; first, tape them and consider how effective each would be as a recruiting tool. Casually slip the good ones into your evening viewing.

Always keep it light and move slowly and patiently. There is a possibly apocryphal story in the scene about a man who greeted his wife while dressed completely in leather, wearing a leather mask and carrying a bullwhip. While she stood there in shock, he proclaimed, "You are now my slave. I am your master. Your only thought is to please me."

She recovered from her shock, place-kicked his balls up to about his neck, and went back to cooking dinner.

As I said, slowly and carefully.

On Creating a Dominant Spouse

A submissive approaching a vanilla spouse for domination faces a somewhat less complex—but more confusing—situation.

Right now, some of you are probably thinking, "This is a book for dominants. Why is this here?" The answer is simple.

Submissives may buy this book to give their vanilla lovers. Why cheat them of an opportunity for happiness? Besides, including them is a way for me to boost my royalties.

First, I'll speak to the novice submissive. Before you approach your significant other, you need to narrow things down to specifics in your own mind. It isn't enough to admit to a desire to be dominated. What one person calls domination can be either lukewarm tapioca or unthinking brutality to another.

Look into your own fantasies and decide on where you really want to start. The two of you will be beginning a journey of exploration. Having a firm starting point will make things easier later on. You need to decide what are your absolute turn-offs.

One danger in broaching this subject is that you may initially agree to do some things that you really don't feel comfortable with or which absolutely turn you off. If you backtrack later, this can be confusing to your partner, who may take it as a rejection or betrayal. You are probably both quite insecure right now. Consistency is the best course for the beginner. However, there is nothing wrong with admitting that some things both attract and frighten you and telling your partner that you might like to try these later. It is also OK to find that you really don't like something. That is what safe words are for.

Now give this section to your lover and ask him or her to read it.

You're probably a bit confused at this point. Someone you thought you knew pretty well has admitted to a passion you may not even have suspected. But, think about it: you have been given a profound compliment. A lot of trust has gone into making this disclosure.

First, let me explain that what your lover is talking about is not really that abnormal. I have written this book to help you. I'd like you to look the whole thing over later, but right now, you're going to need a little guidance as to what your lover meant. Fiction and the media have probably given you a very distorted idea of what it means to be a dominant or a submissive. First, and most important, it means sharing love and trust. You already have that, or your lover wouldn't have put this book into your hands.

Your life isn't going be turned upside down. You won't have to don leather garments or carry a bullwhip. (You can if you want to, lthough.) Your lover won't be showing up at the PTA wearing nothing but chains and handcuffs. All that is going to happen is that the two of you will embark on a sensual dance, will begin playing an erotic game that thousands enjoy every day.

You aren't going to be called on to be brutal or insensitive. On the contrary, you will discover that playing the dominant role will multiply your present sensitivity to your partner many times over. At the same time, it will allow you to experience sensual pleasures that you may not have dreamed of.

Your lover will not become weak or passive. Think about the strength and courage it has taken for him or her to admit to having these feelings. That strength and courage isn't going to disappear. In fact, by joining with him or her in this game, you will be adding to that strength and nurturing a level of confidence you haven't seen before.

For the moment, the best thing is for the two of you to talk it over. To a large extent, D&S is *communication*. Your lover has fantasies he or she wants you to enter. You need to hear these fantasies for you to make up your mind.

In the previous chapter, "Stalking the Wild Submissive," you can find some techniques for exploring fantasies near the end of the section titled "Initial Meetings." You may want to use these somewhat erotic techniques, or just to sit down with your lover and talk. The only important things to do are to recognize how stressful this is for both of you and not to make any judgments while the two of you are talking.

Afterward, take what you have learned and, using your imagination, turn it into something that the two of you can act out. It need not be anywhere near as complex as the fantasies you have heard. You aren't De Niro, and you don't need a cast of thousands. Look at the basics. Is there bondage? Stimulation with a whip or other instrument? Fantasy characters? Humiliation? You don't need to try them all at once. Break out one or two major ingredients and create something you can do. The rest of this book is just chock-full of ideas.

Some individuals instinctively have the ability to create an amazing alchemy and turn what most people would call pain into pleasure. Others can learn to do this. Still, others, as much as they may desire to do it, cannot make the change. For example, if the fantasy includes whipping or spanking, start slowly, give five or ten relatively gentle strokes of the whip, and then pause for reassurance; include a lot of feedback, including "go" words as well as safe words.

One novice couple came to me with a fantasy in which she was captured by a pirate and whipped on her breasts. We developed a scenario in which he demanded that she perform fellatio. By staying in her role as a well-brought-up young lady, she, of course, refused. He then whipped her breasts, stopping every few strokes to renew his demand. By refusing haughtily, she signaled him that all was well and that she was enjoying what was going on. When the intensity of the sensation approached her limits, she "submitted" to his demands.

With men, the fantasy often revolves around humiliation. This is a delicate road to tread for both of you. Some people cannot engage in humiliation without feeling considerable discomfort, even when they recognize that it is based in fantasy and play. It can result in a negative image of the person being humiliated, in a negative self-image on the part of the humiliator, or the other way around.

Remember, too, that D&S is based on *consensuality*. This goes in both directions. If you are not happy—or at least at peace—with what you are being asked to do, sit down and discuss your feelings. It is just as wrong for someone to make you, as a dominant, do something you do not wish to do, as it would be for you to force an unwilling submissive to do something.

However, if everything works, you will be amazed at the new dimensions that are opened up for both of you. D&S doesn't replace vanilla sex; it simply adds new vistas of which most people are not even aware.

CHAPTER 8
Making a Scene Sing

Defining "scene" is about as easy as defining a love affair. Some people like scenes that are very casual; others prefer formality and a specific set of signals to determine the beginning and the end of a scene which is played in a specific time and place. The majority do both as the spirit strikes them.

However, for the purposes of this section, I'm going to explore the possibilities of a formal, prearranged, relatively lengthy scene. It is the most complex kind, so you can feel free to pick and choose from my suggestions when planning your activities. Feel free to add your own "twists" and "kinks."

Whether a scene is to be with an unfamiliar submissive

or an old and treasured one, it begins for the dominant long before the submissive arrives—with thought. I generally run a scene much like a jazz dance; I know where I am and where I want to go, but the spirit of the moment, my sense of the rightness, the influence of my partner, all come together in a complex set of dynamics that changes minute by minute—even second by second.

On a higher plane, there *is* a strong link between the spontaneity, intensity, and passion inherent in the creation of any work of art and that involved in a scene. William Wordsworth defined poetry as "the spontaneous overflow of powerful feelings." He might well have been referring to the joyful exaltation of the whip and the rope. However, even a poet must prepare the pen, the artist the brush.

Preparation

Is the equipment you plan to use available and in good working order? The actual maintenance can be left to a submissive or submissives; for some, it is sheer bliss to be allowed to maintain the instruments of their joy. One mistress sets her submissives to chewing the tails of her whips to make them soft and supple.

Still, *you* are the one responsible for the scene and the safety of everyone in it. You must check the equipment personally.

If the scene will last more than an hour or so, make sure that an adequate supply of food and drink will be available. Both you and the submissive are going to be expending incredible amounts of energy. Hunger and thirst can be a distraction from the exciting sensations you want to feel. At a very minimum, I lay in a supply of some small, easy-to-swallow treats. Hershey's Kisses are a favorite. They are perfect for popping into a submissive's mouth when he or she least expects it. The candy provides a quick burst of energy, and the sweet sensuality of it is a marvelous contrast to the dynamic sensuality of what you are doing.

There is some small risk in doing this because of the level of excitement the submissive is feeling, but I'm sure you know the Heimlich maneuver. If not, read the poster that seems to violate the decor of every restaurant in the country.

Some people plan their scenes with the precision of a German railroad timetable. I've seem some that went: 8:00 to 8:20 spanking, five-minute rest, 8:25 to 8:50 whipping with deerskin cat, and so on. If this is your turn-on, so be it. Personally, I feel this kind of scheduling takes much of the spontaneity out of the scene.

This kind of Teutonic scheduling is often desired by male submissives and seems to have two sources. With an inexperienced submissive, it is most often an attempt to work out a fantasy which he has had for a number of years. This should be strongly discouraged. Such a person generally has very unrealistic expectations regarding his personal limits and endurance. Also, it is an attempt to seize control of the scene from you. Either situation is a potential disaster.

Less often, such a program may be presented by an experienced submissive who is attempting to re-create a previous experience. While this is much less likely to fail, you should still discourage such attempts. First, you are not the other dominant. It is unlikely that you could re-create what actually happened; and worse, it is almost impossible for you to be able to re-create what his mind now "remembers" of the experience after he has had time to embellish it in fantasy.

Second, and more importantly, repeating such scenes offers no potential for a submissive to grow. Part of the dominant's role is to expand the submissive's awareness and experience. We cannot do that by simply repeating the past.

However, even without a detailed design, you should have some plans for transitions between various activities. For example, in an initial scene with a new submissive, I set aside some time between each increasingly intense activity to talk about her reactions to what was done and how she is feeling.

With more familiar submissives, I still try to alternate intense stimulation with gentler activities. For example, although I may use touches of the vibrator during a whipping, I will set aside a few minutes of vibrator play after the whipping is complete and before, perhaps, I go on to waxing. Having such hiatuses gives both of you a rest. The contrast also gives a greater intensity to each individual feeling.

Limits and Surprises

If you are unfamiliar with the submissive, spend a bit of time thinking about his or her limits. Of course, no dominant would ever ignore a safe word, but one of the more enjoyable games is finding ways to slide around a submissive's limits. Frontal assault is rarely effective in these cases, but a flank attack can occasionally succeed.

For example, my submissive, Gale, was very sensitive about her anus. If I so much as looked at it too long, she was ready to call an end to the session. However, I suspected that the sensitivity that she felt could be converted to sensuality with the right input. Before her arrival, I put a bouncing-ball vibrator in a condom, lubricated the condom thoroughly, and put the whole thing in a plastic bag so it wouldn't dry out. The condom served two purposes. This type of vibrator is attached to its battery pack by a single fragile wire. If that wire broke, there would be no way to extract the vibrator without the condom. Second, it kept the vibrator clean.

Gale loved over-the-knee spanking. I began lightly along the top of her buttocks and slowly worked my way back, toward the "sweet spot" where the buttocks join the legs, while increasing the severity of the stimulation. As the spanking was reaching a peak, I gave the area near her anus a few extra hard smacks with my left hand and continued to spank the lower slopes with my right. Then, with my left hand, I extracted the vibrator from the bag and slid it carefully into her anus.

She was so distracted by the spanking that she felt nothing. Then, I paused to let her get her breath back. After a few seconds, I turned the vibrator speed control to half-speed. I could feel her puzzlement. Then she shouted, "What did you do to my ass?" Before I could respond, the orgasms hit her. Later, when she could talk again, she admitted that she had always been afraid of letting anyone touch her anus precisely because it was so sensitive.

Music and Scent

For many people, music is an important part of the scene. It seems to touch the primitive areas of the brain while bypassing the consciousness. Of course, the music must fit with the scene you have planned. For example, during an Inquisition role-play, I play Gregorian chants. The religious overtones and the monophonic nature of the music fit right in.

Most often, I simply fit the music to my mood. Because I often want to mix both fast and slow passages, I may use Pachelbel's *Canon*, the theme from *Chariots of Fire*, *The Firebird*, by Igor Stravinsky, *Close Encounters Suite*, by John Williams, or *Rhapsody in Blue*, by George Gershwin.

For music that builds toward a peak, there is nothing better than "Music of the Night" from Webber's *Phantom of the Opera*; however, it is a bit short. For a slower, longer buildup, I use albums by Mike Oldfield, like his older *Hergest Ridge* and recently released *Tubular Bells II*, or Ravel's *Bolero*. Other pieces of this type are Simpson's *Ninth Symphony* or the symphonies of Arvo Part.

Isao Tomita, who works with the Moog synthesizer, has an album, *The Planet*, that supplies a variety of music ranges. His "Mars" piece, in particular, is full of thunder; others are joyous; while others are soft, delicate.

For a change of pace, I use the minimalist composers like John Adams and Steve Reich. This music is so deliberately repetitive in style as to be annoying to many people in many situations. Under the right circumstances, it is exquisitely hypnotic.

Some other music is written by Jean-Luc Ponty, Philip Glass (*Satyagraha* and *Music in Twelve Parts*) and Carl Orff (*Carmina Burana* and *Veni Creator Spiritus*). For some wild musical effects, try Ives's *Symphony No. 4*, anything by Edgar Varèse, or some techno like "O Fortuna" by Apotheosis.

For truly exotic music, Bridge Records has some very interesting recordings by David Lewiston. Two of these are *Kecak: A Balinese Music Drama* and *Tibetan Buddhism: Shartse College of Ganden Monastery*.

Don't neglect odor. Incense, like music, creates a mood

by bypassing the conscious. Depending on the scene, I use light florals or a heavy musk. The trick is that the odors should tickle the nose, not anesthetize it. You want to accent, not overpower.

You can use incense to provide the odor, or a bit of perfume. One effect that I find quite powerful is to take some of the natural lubrication from my submissive's pussy and just touch it to her upper lip.

Beginning the Scene

While the kind of detailed discussion I outlined in the beginning of this section may need to take place only once, prior to the first scene—before every scene at least in the early stages of a D&S relationship—a few minutes of review are valuable safeguards. During this review, you should go over the safe word or words. If there is going to be role playing, you should inform the submissive about his or her role and the role you will be playing. This does not have to be in detail. It is enough to say something like "You are a young noblewoman brought before the Inquisition and I will be your confessor."

Some people use a symbol to begin the scene. For example, I often have a submissive lock her neck chain in place and give me the key. She is mine until I unlock the chain and give her back the key. A dear friend on the West Coast uses a blindfold. Others simply begin. Generally, it is just a matter of taste. However, in role playing, there should be a distinct beginning and end for the scene to minimize role confusion.

Clothing is another matter of personal choice, as is its removal. I usually demand that the submissive strip herself as a reminder of her status in the scene. Background music can transform this simple act into a seductive dance. Segments of the scene can be marked by a progressive disrobing, or the submissive can be disrobe completely at the outset.

Depending on your desires, you may or may not undress. If you do, do so in such a way as to add to the scene. Men should *never* take their pants off before their shirts. A glance at the covers of romance novels clearly shows the female fascination with males naked to the waist. However, the reverse, with a shirttail flapping about bare legs, is a spectacle that no amount of inborn dignity can survive. Female dominants may wish to put their submissives into precisely this undignified situation, but male dominants should avoid it.

The Scene Itself

The combinations and permutations of activities in a scene are almost infinite, and I am not about to lay down a "right" schedule of activities. However, for maximum effect, both psychological and physical stimulation should begin relatively gently and then increase steadily. For example, most submissives are not ready for caning at the beginning of a session, but they may welcome that kind of intense stimulation toward the end. Do not forget that the physical activities—bondage, whipping, spanking—are merely the keys that unlock the journey of the mind.

Just which act is "more intense" than another is a suitable subject for discussion with specific submissives. For example, some see waxing as extremely intense, while others find it a gentle stimulation. The perception of the submissive should be the final guide. However, a progression of increasing intensity for most people might be spanking, whipping, waxing, caning, pricking, cutting. This is only a general guide to intensity and, most assuredly, does not mean that every activity must be present in every scene, or even in the repertoire of every dominant. Some very respected and experienced dominants limit their activities to spanking and whipping. The most valuable characteristic of a good dominant is common sense.

Like humiliation, psychological stimulation should also proceed along a continuum. As your submissive becomes more involved emotionally, demands that might trigger a revolt just after the scene's onset will be welcomed with enthusiasm.

With experience, your subconscious will learn to read the subliminal cues that a submissive sends out. Without really knowing why you are doing it, you will feel that it is time to increase or decrease the stimulation or begin another phase or ease up and rest a bit. Much like two dancers "working" each other's bodies, the two of you will become caught up in a communication with a range so much wider than that provided by voice or sight alone.

A scene is not simply an extremely erotic activity; in a very real sense, it is a work of performance art.

Ending the Scene

The scene can end in a number of ways. You complete the scenario, or end it for another reason. The submissive uses his or her safe word, or the scene can be ended because of outside influences.

The ideal way for the scene to end, of course, is for it to run to its natural conclusion. However, you should terminate it if you are getting tired or sense that the submissive has passed his or her endurance limits. If you are tired, you aren't going to enjoy yourself as much. Even more importantly, you will become sloppy and careless. A scene is no place for a tired dominant.

A perfect way to end a scene is shown in the video, *Geisha Slave*. In it, Sarana says to her slave, Mariko, "When I remove your collar and call you 'lover,' the scene will be over." She follows her words with action, and then the two make passionate love. Many D&S films are filled with harmful misinformation. This one is a pleasant exception.

As part of your preparation, you should have provided a place for both of you to rest after the scene. In my scenes, a bit of gentle cuddling is mandatory, both to reassure the submissive and to give me a chance to get my mind out of the scene. One—or both—of you may want to sleep at this point. Remember: a scene *should* be intense, but it can also be shattering to a submissive, particularly one who is new to the world of D&S. If he or she seems to be shaken or have doubts, be supportive. Submissives often need to be reassured about their inherent worth.

Talking It Over Afterward

There is some disagreement about *when* a debriefing should take place, but most people in the scene seem to feel that having one is a good idea. An obvious time is right after the scene ends, while cuddling. Memories are freshest at this time. However, many people in D&S feel that waiting up to a day is a good idea because it gives both of you time to develop a psychic distance from the scene itself.

With experienced couples, it can be as little as "Was it okay, dear?" or "How did it go?" With couples just getting to know each other, the questioning should be deeper and more detailed. You cannot "read" a near stranger with anything like complete accuracy; however, as you combine what you have observed during scenes with what you learn during the post-scene talks, you can begin to approach the ideal one-soul two-body amalgam. Each person brings a different set of needs and a different set of sensitivities to the scene. A very concrete example would be that Libby loves the paddle more than any other toy, while Isobel prefers a whip and finds a paddle's impact too diffuse for maximum pleasure.

Of course, you don't want to beat the experience to death with analysis; it was a D&S scene, not a presidential speech.

The essence of a good dominant is strength and control, and during these post-scene talks, you must turn those characteristics inward. This is not a time for flowery compliments. These are serious questions. To treat them as perfunctory time-wasters is to miss a chance to expand and grow for both of you. You must press and probe to find ways to improve both your skills and empathic abilities.

The submissive will always be reluctant to say anything that could be taken as criticism. However, by eliciting negative comments and by welcoming them in an open and adult manner, you can do much to build both the submissive's self-worth and his or her opinion of you. Besides, wouldn't you rather hear it now and have a chance to discuss any problems, than hear how bad the scene went from Judy, who heard it from Karl, who was told by Lisa, who had talked to your submissive?

Now we'll look at a few specialized types of scenes.

Guided Fantasy

A guided fantasy is a wonderful way of exploring scenes that are too dangerous or too complex for realization in the real world. It works by establishing a fantasy in the submissive's mind and then guiding it to an explosive conclusion. However, this technique is not for everyone; it takes quick wits, careful preparation, and a flexible imagination.

We have all experienced guided fantasies as children, when we read stories of wonderful worlds and great adventures. We would sit back and let our imaginations fill in the spaces between the words. Now that we are adult dominants, it's time to start telling *our* kind of tales.

It's that simple: telling a fantasy to the submissive. The descriptions alone are powerful sensual devices that can bring hours of gratification. However, guided fantasy goes a step farther and makes the submissive an active participant in his or her own erotic tale.

To make the guided fantasy work, you must cut off or control as much sensory input as possible. A blindfold is indispensable. I prefer the fur-lined ones because they completely block out all light. I have also used headphones with a low hum to cut off all background noises when I am not talking, although this isn't necessary if the scene takes place in a relatively quiet room.

Most of the time during the fantasy, the submissive should be bound in a comfortable position. Any discomfort that is not part of the fantasy can be distracting. You may want to use snap fastenings so that he or she can be moved about if the plot requires it.

Begin your story in a low, sensual voice. Set the scene and then ask your submissive to describe people and things in it. Keep track of these descriptions and weave them into the story. For example, if he or she describes a dark-haired man with a leather vest, refer to the character in those terms and work in references to his stroking his dark hair or adjusting his leather vest.

By doing this, you are reinforcing the submissive's fantasy by making your story match what is going on in the imagination. The two build on each other in the sensory vacuum you've created.

Sound effects can be very valuable. The crack of a whip or the sound of a knife sliding out of a scabbard reinforce the illusion until it becomes almost indistinguishable from reality.

Don't forget the submissive's sense of touch. If you have a vest, remind her of the description of one of the characters by saying, "As the dark-haired man takes off his clothing, he drops his vest on you" and follow your words with the action. To feel the whip at the same time as imagining a whipping is unimaginably intense. One mistress regularly puts her submissives through a degrading male-on-male rape fantasy during which she employs three dildos simultaneously.

Odor, one of the most subtle senses, has an intense impact directly on the most primitive portions of the brain. It is a good idea to keep a few small vials of scent and other liquids about. For example, in a cycle-gang rape fantasy, I use the odors of oil, gasoline, and rubber to emphasize aspects of the fantasy.

In another fantasy, my submissive surprised me by mentioning that she visualized the floor of the dungeon covered with rose petals. (Isn't imagination a wonderful thing?) I was nonplussed for a moment because I lacked a rose scent. Then, I remembered a package of assorted incense I had purchased that day. In less than a minute, the room was redolent with the scent of roses.

Because of the relatively relaxed pace and the comfortable position the submissive is in, guided fantasies can go on for a long time. I did one that lasted for more than six hours, and there is nothing that prevents one from going on for days.

The six-hour scene is a good example of the heights of fantasy that can be reached. The submissive, Marty, had a deep interest in the darker side of the supernatural. She had confided to me that she fantasized that she was the reincarnation of a witch who had been burned at the stake.

The fantasy began with her tied horizontally in a modified crucifix position with her legs spread. I explained that she was going to be inducted into a witches' coven. In the background, the stereo was playing a long tape of religious chants. We developed the scene with my outlining the entrance of the witches and her filling in details which I used in my descriptions.

The induction was frankly sexual; during it she had to satisfy each witch orally. To simulate the witches' vaginal areas, I used my own hand flavored with Marty's own secretions. The touch of her tongue on my hand was erotic in the extreme because I could almost see what she was imagining. All the time, candles above her breasts and cupped hands contributed a bit of stimulation as they melted.

Then the witches summoned Satan to take his newest bride. A pistol shot and a bit of burning sulfur provided the background. For Satan's voice, I used a deep, rough tone and spoke with my lips close to her ear. When Satan entered her, Marty let out an incredible scream. Ancient books always spoke of the devil's cock being cold. This one certainly was. I had left the dildo in the refrigerator overnight.

After a bit more erotic play, I changed the pace. I told her that soldiers had broken in, and the entire coven was arrested. I stood her up and tied her hands and arms to her body with a number of coils of rough rope. Another part of the room, where I had broken open a bale of hay, became the rough cell into which she was thrown.

Naturally, the jailers had to take full advantage of her helpless position. She was repeatedly "raped," a part of the fantasy that both of us enjoyed immensely.

After allowing her to recover, still bound, from the "rapes," I continued the story with her being taken before the Inquisition, where she was tortured to make her confess. I had not told her the details of the scenario beforehand but I had told her that her safe word for this scene was "I am a witch."

The traditional tortures for a witch were flogging, scalding water, and being searched for the mark of Satan. The flogging was simple, and I simulated the scalding water by putting her hands repeatedly in very cold water and then shifting them to a container of very hot—but not scalding—water. The contrast made the hot water seem hotter.

The theory behind the witch's mark is that each witch has a place where she has been kissed by Satin. The place is numb. The investigators keep putting needles into the unfortunate's body until they find a point where pricking her does not make her scream. I imagine that most suspects confessed while the "search" was still going on. The investigators may not have used sterile needles or sterilized the area before beginning. However, when fantasy collides with safety, fantasy must give way.

Eventually, Marty "confessed."

I told her that she was going to be burned at the stake and guided her roughly across the floor. Lacking a proper stake, I tied her hands to a hook above her head, then turned on a quartz heater directly in front of her. After a few minutes, when her skin was getting a bit red from the heat, I came up behind her, holding a taper of smoldering sulfur, and whispered in Satan's deep, rough voice, "I've come again for you, my bride" and drove home the rechilled dildo in her pussy.

The resultant orgasms left her incoherent for more than half an hour.

In guided fantasy, anything is possible. You can travel the length and breadth of the universe and do things that, in real life, would leave the submissive a broken, twisted shell. Since much of the action is only in the imagination, the only limits are those of your imagination.

Interrogation Scenes

One of the classic ways that vanilla film makers slip a D&S touch into their products is an interrogation scene in which usually the innocent hero or heroine is helpless in the clutches of the evildoers. Therefore, it is not surprising that a common psychodrama in the scene is an interrogation.

There are several common themes in an interrogation scene. We have already covered one: a witch being forced to confess. Another is the military interrogation. The theme here is that the submissive is innocent—a brave solder or rebel maid—and you, the Nazi, Vietcong, English (you may have an IRA submissive) officer, are doing the questioning. In this kind of scene, there is often a threat of extreme force, even death, made explicitly.

An interesting facet of this stage setting is the use of symbols that normally would be offensive—in particular, Nazi regalia. Because of this, there is considerable debate within the scene about the appropriateness of this kind of play. My personal feeling is that there is an ironic justice in the use of these symbols in the service of a sexual fetish. Imagine the ire of a Himmler or a Hitler upon discovering that a "bunch of happy perverts" were playing with their revered emblems. Rather than honoring them, we are reducing them to a kind of kinky toy.

Of course, for some, these symbols are just too powerful to consider using. Because of this, no responsible dominant would ever spring such a scene on an unsuspecting submissive without probing his or her sensitivities in this area beforehand. Also, if you choose to do and talk about such scenes, be prepared for criticism from some members of the community.

The police interrogation is another form of the standard interrogation scene. Here the submissive may adopt the role of the bad guy or innocent victim of circumstances. You are or can be a good cop or a corrupt cop. Force and threats of force are more moderate here than in the military scenario, although the actual activities may be very similar.

Like the fantasy rapes covered in the next section, the interrogation requires the dominant to take on a role that may be quite different from his or her personality. For this reason, I recommend a clear starting and stopping point for such scenes. One of my favorite couples goes a step farther. Near the end of the scene, he blindfolds her, explaining that he is going out to get some nefarious device. Then, shifting roles, he reappears as her rescuer, lifting her and carrying her out of the dungeon to safety.

You don't have to do anything this complex—although it can be fun. A simple prearranged phrase ("You are free") or an action (removing the Nazi officer's cap) can signal the transition from scene to "reality."

In this kind of scene, the polarity between dominant and submissive is more marked than in most D&S play. You are the bad guy or gal. All cooperative endeavor is carefully concealed under a camouflage of brutality or coldness. Despite the underlying mutual consent, the mood of this kind of scene is clearly adversarial.

Scene setting is particularly important during this kind of psychodrama. You *want* the submissive to be caught up in the excitement of it all, and this means providing enough visual, auditory, and even olfactory clues so that he or she can achieve what the English poet Coleridge termed "the willing suspension of disbelief."

I like to make the transition between not-scene and scene with the submissive blindfolded. The blindfold is put in place outside of the place where the interrogation is going to take place and then removed after she has been bound in place.

Usually I begin with chair bondage. Not only is this position familiar through hundreds of late-night movies ("You vill speak, fraulein, or you vill suffer."), but it also puts the submissive's head at a lower level than mine, an important aspect of psychological dominance.

While for most scenes you want your dungeon/black room/scene room a bit warmer than ordinary room temperature, an interrogation scene calls for a bit of a chill in the air. We want the submissive to shiver a bit. While I rarely use chains for bondage, during an interrogation scene the cold metal just seems so appropriate. Often, I prepare it ahead of time by leaving it in the refrigerator for a few hours to give it the proper "dungeon chill."

It will be a special treat for your submissive if you can find somewhere other than your regular scene room to perform the interrogation. For example, all along the East Coast, there are abandoned World War II fortifications. Several times, I took a favorite submissive out to Dutch Island in Narragansett Bay, where I had "decorated" an isolated pillbox. It made a perfect place for a "Nazi interrogation" scene. These trips were suspended when an inquisitive soul discovered my hideaway and precipitated a search for what local police believed to be an underground group of American fascists.

However, even in your own house or apartment, you can create the appropriate atmosphere. A bright light shining in the submissive's eyes creates both the appropriate harsh ambience and distracts from any incongruous items in the background that cannot be removed or altered. I would recommend that you light the rest of the dungeon with red lights. Psychologists say that red lighting intensifies hostility and tension. This may not be appropriate for all scenes, but for an interrogation scene, it is perfect.

The old saying is "Clothes make the man (or in this case, perhaps, the woman)." Just a few bits of costume can make the scene come alive. A Nazi armband, a black leather trenchcoat, a Chinese Communist cap—all add to the verisimilitude of the experience. Posters, wall hangings, even a field telephone on the table, can add to the reality.

I have a collection of Nazi marching songs—they were rotten people, but they had great marching songs—to play in the background of my scenes, but any almost any appropriately military music will do.

In this kind of scene more than almost any other, you need to keep your submissive off balance and confused, just like a real prisoner. One trick I use is to tie her to an office chair and occasionally spin it around. This effect can be made even more powerful if some of the lights are strobe lights. Even when a person is standing still, these lights can be exceptionally disorienting; when a person is spinning out of control, the effect is mind-blowing.

Another approach is to tip a conventional chair backward with the submissive firmly tied in it. I have been told that the suspense and anxiety are overwhelming.

Of course, prisoners are threatened. I have a dramatic knife (no edges or point) I got from a theatrical-supply store. It is useless for cutting clothing or anything else, but it looks terrifying. If you are using a real gun as an intimidation tool, check again to see there are no bullets in it. (Obvious, but you want to be completely secure.) *Do not* count on the safety. Unload it and *confirm* that it is unloaded.

The section on guided fantasy covers some of the stimulants available in a witch interrogation scene. I have also used branding irons for intimidation. No branding actually took place, but the woman involved had a great deal of difficulty tearing her eyes off the branding iron slowly heating over a charcoal heater. (*Safety note:* Do not use a charcoal heater in a room where the air circulation is less than excellent. Carbon monoxide poisoning is insidious.)

Electrical devices are often used in interrogation scenes.

Remember that field telephone I mentioned before. It can have more uses than just as a visual prop. Be sure to read the "Electricity" section of the "Fun and Games" chapter for appropriate hints.

As I noted before, you can end the scene by having the "victim" rescued or simply by giving a prearranged signal. However, in any case, I strongly recommend that you spend a bit of time cuddling and reestablishing the intimacy that this sort of scene pushes into the background.

Fantasy Rape

Anyone who has read *Forbidden Flowers* or any of the other books about women's fantasies knows that *rape as a fantasy* ranks high on many women's lists.

Hold up, ladies. Don't skip by this section because you have a male submissive. Being raped by their dominant is one of the fondest dreams of many a male sub. Don't let the female pronouns throw you. If your submissive knew you were leafing through this section, he'd be so hard he could fuck a rock.

Unfortunately, because of the way many men were brought up, actually doing the first rape fantasy can be incredibly difficult. Consensual whipping seems positively easy compared to the playacting a dominant must do in a consensual rape. As in the interrogation scene, you are acting out a role that is much different from your true self-image. This can be disconcerting and, if you discover that you are enjoying it (very likely), deeply troubling.

A large portion of this discomfort, I believe, is fear—fear of ourselves. Any man who has come to terms with his dominant tendencies has learned what monsters roam around in the basement of the mind. We have found ways to take them out and parade them for our submissives, even to make them do tricks. But we want them in control, and rape is the biggest and hairiest of these monsters. However, we *are* descended from men who raped. In the history of humanity, consensual sex is a relatively new invention. There is always a bit of nervousness that, once we let this shambling horror out of its cage, we will never get it back in again.

Take heart from knowing that the very existence of this fear indicates that re-caging the monster will not be as difficult as you expect. The fear grows from a basic rule of civilized behavior that is part of the bedrock within you. The people I fear are those who are willing and anxious to try this the moment it is suggested. They are the ones who should spend a bit more time on the maintenance of their psychic locks.

Besides, this is a *fantasy*. The best analogy I can give is to ask if you've ever had a fantasy about flying. Of course you have. With some people, it is Superman-like flight; with others it is more like a bird hanging on the wind. Well, why haven't you walked to the edge of a building and stepped off?

Because it is a fantasy! You had no difficulty telling the difference between a fantasy of flight and the reality of a broken and twisted body on the street. Give your submissive the same credit. She recognizes the difference and can enjoy the fantasy while having no desire to participate in the "same" events in the reality.

Once both of you are comfortable with this kind of playacting, you can do it on an impromptu basis. In a way, this is easier than the interrogation scene, which I strongly recommend should have a specific beginning and end.

For example, I know one man who "kidnaps" and

"rapes" his wife about once a month on her way home from work. She never knows when this will happen, but she looks forward eagerly to each incident.

However, for the first time, a bit of discussion and planning is in order. Sit down, in or out of scene, whatever makes both of you more comfortable. Talk about rape fantasies. How they work, what she thinks would be exciting. As with all scenes, you are not limited by her desires, but they provide a good jumping-off place and excellent guidance for what orientation the scene should take.

Explore a bit of history. Has she been raped or molested? Ask; don't assume you know. This is not something that comes up in casual conversation, or even in the intense dialogue that precedes an initial scene. The fact that she is interested in playacting a rape does not mean that she has never experienced one in real life. As I noted in a previous chapter, *some* women look forward to the chance to desensitize a raw psychic scar by reenacting it in a situation of support and love.

Emphasize that she should not hesitate to use her safe word if things proceed further physically or emotionally than she is able to go. Urge her to stop the scene if she experiences even moderate emotional distress. While physical discomfort builds slowly and relatively evenly, emotional distress tends to appear in a rush. Waiting until it becomes overwhelming can be dangerous to her emotional well-being.

One rather exciting variation on the rape theme is to have the submissive go through her closet and choose some clothing that is too worn or doesn't really fit anymore. Insist that she wear nothing that is not dispensable. After all, a rape can be a relatively messy business.

Have her put it on and then tie her hands behind her back and slowly cut and rip everything off.

The position I prefer to place the submissive in is with her hands up by her neck. It is described in detail in the "Bondage" section of the "Fun and Games" chapter. It opens the body almost completely to the knife and does not have to be changed if you want to place her on her back later.

I use the word "knife" in a metaphorical sense. Using a knife next to a woman who may be struggling goes strongly against common sense. What I will often do is show my submissive the knife, and then, walking behind her, discard it and use my EMT scissors for the actual cutting. Make no mistake; you will need to cut. Modern fabrics are tough and, even if you can tear them, grunting and swearing when you get to the seams won't create the image you are after of unstoppable male power.

Amusingly, the hardest part of this scenario is often convincing her to wear old underwear. Women either want to keep them until they fall apart, or they are ashamed of letting you see them with anything but perfection. In either case, you will get the request "Can't we just take off the underwear?" Don't give in. One of the hottest parts is the final unveiling. The panties have to be cut off. You can cut them off with only two strokes: waistband and crotch. Or you can slowly and sensually cut holes in them until they resemble erotic Swiss cheese.

One alternative is for you to buy her a set of inexpensive underwear specifically for the scene. I gave one to a young lady with a card that said: "A woman's underwear is intended to make a man want to tear it off. That is just what I am going to do with these." *Indecent haste* is a good way to describe her reaction to this message.

If she has a bra with a front closure, you can put the knife between her breasts and then snap the bra closure open with your fingers. That allows the illusion that it has been cut without damaging the bra.

Naturally, neither tying nor cutting is necessary. You are probably bigger and stronger than she is. Just make sure she does not get too caught up in the playacting. There is more than one male soprano who underestimated the power of a fighting woman.

If you are planning on a "struggle," make sure that you will be doing it in a safe area. Struggles can be very uncontrolled, and doing them in places having furniture with sharp corners, extension cords on the floor, or movable throw-rugs is asking for an accident. Take care, also, to handle her carefully. Caught up in the spirit of the scuffle, she may forget the availability of her safe word. Bruises are all right, but a broken arm or a wrenched joint will spoil the fun for both of you, to say the least.

Of course, as in the interrogation scene, you can threaten her with a gun or knife. Naturally, you should take the same precautions using a weapon in this kind of scene as you would in the interrogation scene.

Language in a rape scene can also be difficult for some dominants who have a deep block against using crude language. However, again, remember that you are playing the part of a crude, rough character, a rapist. It is he—not you—who is telling her to "spread your legs, bitch, and let me see your pussy." For some submissives, the shift from your normal tone and language can be a terrific turn-on.

Gentlemen, at ease. I'm going to direct the rest of this section to the ladies who have been so patient.

The rape of a male submissive can be done in two

ways: forced genital or oral intercourse, or anal rape with a dildo. The first is merely seizing control of the situation. It usually consists of pushing the man on his back and using him for your pleasure. You can also combine this with various discipline techniques which may strike your fancy. I know one female dominant who likes to ride a tongue while waxing the owner's cock. I personally feel that it must distract from his precision, but the lady does not complain.

A dominant lady of my acquaintance, Lady Pam, has a lovely lavender dildo harness which is designed to accept two dildos: one extending from her pubis, the other entering her cunt. So while she performs the psychologically pleasing act of fucking another, she is also treated to a real fucking for herself.

Dildos can also be held in the hand, but then they somehow seem less complete. The best positions for penetration of a submissive by a dildo are the same as those described in the section on enemas. While the male submissive should generally be forced to suck the object of his defilement before to being penetrated, you should use large quantities of lubricant for the actual penetration. Saliva is really not effective enough.

For an added bit of excitement, a bit of forced cross-dressing fits well with the general theme of the entertainment. Cross-dressing is covered in more detail in the "Humiliation" section of the "Fun and Games" chapter.

CHAPTER 9
Opening the Toybox

Toys add so much fun to the scene. Not only do they have a physical effect; their psychological impact is impossible to overestimate. Toys like whips, ropes, and suspension cuffs are covered in their appropriate section of the "Fun and Games" chapter. Here, we are going to look at more "free style" toys.

Blindfolds and Hoods

The best kinds of blindfolds completely block out the submissive's vision without putting *any* pressure on the eyeballs. While the sleeping-aid-type blindfold is useful, it usually doesn't fit tightly enough to keep the submissive from peeking out next to his or her nose.

My favorite is a set with separate eye patches on a leather headband. Each eye patch is lined with rabbit fur. When these are on, nothing can be seen. Instructions on how to make these are in the chapter on leatherwork.

Because contact lenses can fall out under a blindfold, you should have the submissive remove the lenses before putting on the blindfold. Of course, with some submissives, removing the contact lenses *is* the equivalent of putting on a blindfold.

Another approach to blindfolding is hooding. This can be as simple as a bag over the submissive's head or as complex as a custom leather arrangement with removable eye pads, ear pads and a gag. However, because a hood conceals more of the submissive's face than a blindfold and hides familiar facial clues that show distress, you must carefully monitor his or her condition.

Hoods can also trigger claustrophobia and restrict breathing.

A trick for covert public scenes: Get the eye pads sold in drugstores. Put them over the submissive's eyes with flesh-colored bandages, then cover the lot with a pair of large, dark sunglasses. The feeling of helplessness can be overwhelming for the submissive, but bystanders see only a kind person assisting a blind one.

Clips and Clamps

Nipple clips are almost a cliché in bondage films and photography, and clips and clamps are popular tools. These can be used on almost any portion of the body, but breasts, labia, cocks, and balls are natural and obvious targets. You should always remember that taking these off is more painful for the submissive than was the initial application.

Test every clip on the skin between your thumb and forefinger. If it is too painful for you, have second thoughts about using it on a submissive. Although it would be unusual to do any kind of permanent damage with a clip, one should not be left on longer than fifteen minutes because it does cut off blood circulation to the skin underneath. The triangular paper clips available at stationery stores should be treated with considerable respect.

Complex-looking adjustable clips are available at leather stores. However, many dominants swear by simple wooden clothespins. Not only are they cheap and easy to obtain, but you can vary their severity in several ways. The simplest way is to buy several brands. Different companies have varying degrees of "zing" in their pins. Test them on yourself, and color-code each pin with a drop of model-airplane paint. I use red for the strongest down to blue for the weakest.

You can also weaken individual pins by putting elastic bands around the part where your finger grips the pin. This is particularly useful when the pins are going to be used on sensitive sections of the body.

Some people even disassemble the clothespins and readjust the spring tension. This is done by heating the spring with a blowtorch, altering its alignment with a pair of pliers while it is still red-hot, and then quenching it in a container of oil.

Before using clothespins on submissives, cut or sand off the tips so the pins end in a flat surface. This will allow them to get a firmer grip on the skin and prevent unintentional pain.

Initially, you should place a substantial fold of skin between the tips. The larger the amount of skin which is gripped, the weaker the stimulation felt by the submissive. As you become familiar with both the strength of the pins and the tolerance of the submissive, you learn just how large the fold should be to produce a given amount of stimulation. Avoid putting the clip where pieces of bone or cartilage would be caught inside. These bruise more easily than soft tissue.

Alligator clips are not generally used in stimulation because their serrated teeth can easily break the skin. However, you can cover the teeth by taking a piece of shrink-wrap tubing, putting it over the jaw of the clip, and then heating the tubing. It may take several layers of tubing before you have a thick-enough covering on the teeth.

Mouse and rat traps are fun to play with. They look infinitely more painful than they are because the spring's clamping action is distributed along a relatively wide striking wire. However, before you use them, I recommend that you take off the release arm and the trigger. Not only are these unaesthetic, but the gripper for the cheese can tear the submissive's skin.

To use them to maximum effect, hold the trap about a foot in front of the submissive's shocked eyes and let the striking wire *snap* onto the wood. Then, take it and insert the breast or cock and *lower* the striking wire onto the skin.

The degree of stimulation from a clip can be increased by several orders of magnitude by attaching weights to it. To hang things from clothespins, run a cord through the spring coil. Alligator clips come with a handy screw that is convenient for attaching cords or small chains. Some versions of adjustable clips in leather stores are designed to clamp harder when weights are suspended from them. Always add weight slowly.

Another approach is to pull on the string or—an even more erotic approach—put the string in your submissive's mouth and have him or her pull on it for you. This can also be done when you have two clips attached by a string or chain, a common technique when clamping nipples.

A variation on these dangling weights can be obtained by attaching the weights by heavy elastics or light springs. Any movement will set the weights bobbling, and it will take a while even when the submissive is standing stock-still for the weights to stop bobbing.

If a clamp causes a minor cut, treat it with antiseptic; however, torn skin requires a doctor's care to prevent permanent disfigurement.

Collars

The ultimate symbol of submission is the collar. It can be as simple as a dog collar or as complex as the kind of collar worn by O in *The Story of O*, that was made of many layers of thin leather and had an attached ring. Rings provide convenient attachment points for leashes or wrist cuffs.

The most common error in buying a collar is choosing one that is too wide. Unless it is only for short-term wear, one inch is the best width. Anything wider will have a tendency to abrade the neck over a period of hours.

Neither collars nor other around-the-neck devices should be used to attach a standing submissive to anything solid. Think what might happen if he or she stumbled or fell. If a person is attached in this manner, use cotton thread. This will provide the feeling of capture, but in the event of an accident, it will break without causing further harm.

Another common error is to attach the collar too tightly. If you cannot slip two—count 'em, two—fingers under the collar, it is too tight.

Contracts of Submission

While a contract isn't exactly what we generally call a toy, drawing up, signing, and living under a contract of submission can be an exciting experience. While contracts are obviously not enforceable in court, they do have a very practical function: they clearly spell out the various rights and responsibilities of each member in the relationship and require both individuals to think about them.

Clauses usually include:

The duration of the contract

Restrictions on where and with whom the submissive (or either) can play

Limitations on the forms of bondage and discipline used

Sexual activities permitted

Types of behavior required for, conduct of, and/or work to be done by the submissive

Safe words

How the contract may be terminated or modified

Most sample contracts like those in *The Leatherman's Handbook II* and *The Lesbian S&M Safety Manual* strike me as a bit too one-sided. They certainly spell out what the submissive owes to the dominant; however, the dominant's duties are considerably more vague. Part of this, I suspect, is because these are *sample* contracts and, as such, contain more than a bit of fantasy. To give you some fair and realistic models, I am reprinting, in the appendices, two actual contracts between couples who are actively in the D&S scene. I think you will see the degree of give-and-take that was necessary to work out these agreements.

Gags

I don't use gags much. They cut down on the complex verbal interaction between the submissive and the dominant—I like screaming and begging. They can also be risky.

However, in a semi-public environment (like an apartment with thin walls or motel rooms), gags can avoid "premature termination of the scene through external influence" (someone calling the cops). Some submissives also enjoy gags. The mild ache from the stretched jaw muscles is a reminder of their status. The ball gives them something to bite down on while you are stimulating them; and, for those who enjoy humiliation, the uncontrollable drooling provides the dominant endless opportunities for comment.

Before you use a gag, establish a safe *signal* that will work when the gag is in place. Like a safe word, it should be something that would not take place as part of a scene. This eliminates random grunting, but using a rhythm is acceptable. Don't get too complex. It may be easy for your submissive to hum "The Stars and Stripes Forever" when the only thing you are doing is watching. It is entirely a different matter to do it when you are playing Connect the Dots on his or her skin with a needle.

Simple physical signals are effective, too. Some submissives use opening and closing both hands to signal unacceptable discomfort when gagged. Others use slow and purposeful eye blinks.

Before playing with any submissive, you should ask about breathing problems, asthma, and allergies. If you are going to use a gag, ask again and listen carefully. A blocked-up nose can *kill* someone who has a gag in his or her mouth.

There is a multitude of commercially available gags, and an even greater variety that you can improvise. At one point during a session in an expensive hotel, the phone rang. It was the front desk. I just grabbed my companion's panties and put them in her mouth. She later told me that the mere casualness of this action made it extremely arousing.

Most important, the gag must be comfortable. If it isn't, that is a signal that it doesn't fit and can cause harm. Have the submissive inflate an inflatable gag. Dominants invariably overestimate how big it has to be. I have seen some face masks that cover both the face and the nose. I neither like them nor trust them. If either the nose or the mouth is blocked, the other should be completely free.

Ball gags that do not go completely into the mouth are particularly good if a person has a bit of trouble breathing. If the ball is attached with a single elastic, in an emergency it can be easily pushed out of the mouth by the submissive's tongue.

A submissive friend lists three benefits that go with gags. It is fun to bite down on during intense stimulation, it gives the submissive a feeling of being controlled and, finally, it causes drooling which, in turn, gives the dominant an opportunity for a bit of verbal humiliation if both enjoy this type of activity.

Dildos

For whatever reason you are using a dildo, it is always a good idea to cover it with a condom before use. At the very least, it makes cleanup quick and easy and assures that you and/or your submissive will have a sterile surface in contact with all that sensitive flesh. If you will be doing a scene where the dildo will be moving back and forth between people (yourself and the submissive or between two submissives) or will be used in both the anus and vagina, one or more condoms are mandatory.

If I am planning a complex scene, I may put four or five condoms on a single dildo. As soon as I am ready to shift from one area to another, I just take off the top condom, and the next is already on. (This is a neat trick I borrowed from my motorcycle-racing days, when I would wear five or six face shields, one under the other. When one got muddy, I'd just pull it off.) This has the added advantage that, if one condom tears, the others are intact.

In my opinion, the best dildos are made of silicone rubber. They have a more lifelike texture, are exceptionally smooth, and retain body heat (or cold—see the section on guided fantasies in the "Making the Scene Sing" chapter) best. However they are expensive. Thirty to forty dollars is not an unusual price for a life-size silicone-rubber dildo.

Latex dildos are less aesthetic, but are also less expensive. Dildos made of harder material must be used with care, but are often useful in the scene to make a psychological point. One mistress has a custom-machined eight-inch stainless-steel dildo with brass balls. It is enough to drain the color from the cheeks (both sets) of the hardiest submissive.

Obviously, when using any dildos in the anus, copious

lubrication and care are the order of the day. You must always keep a good grip on the dildo and allow no more than two-thirds of it to enter the anus if there is nothing at the base to prevent it from going all the way in. For safe anal play, buttplugs are more sensible, or you should use a dildo with a flange or set of "balls" at the base.

Some dildos are made with a clitoral stimulator at the base. While some find this fun, I think that it limits the range of movement of the dildo if you want to use the stimulator at the same time. A well-lubricated thumb is infinitely more versatile.

Avoid dildos which have machinery to make them move and rotate. I have heard of cases where the moving wire has worn a hole through the dildo and done serious harm. At least with clear or translucent dildoes, you can see the mechanism and check to make sure this isn't happening.

Squirting dildos which simulate ejaculation should be cleaned very carefully. The artificial urethra provides an ideal environment for bacterial growth. However, squirting a bit of bleach-water mixture or alcohol through it should be enough to clean it out.

Male Chastity Belt

Male chastity belts are popular items in leather stores. Some are made of leather, some of metal. I have seen a few that were made of clear plastic. (I suppose so the dominant could judge the effectiveness of the device.)

However, evidently these toys pre-date the current interest in D&S. In doing research for this book, I encountered the McCormick Male Chastity Belt, patent number 587,994, patented in 1896—yes, 1896. According to the application, the purpose was to protect a man from himself; however, it seems ideal for any lady seeking to make sure her submissive remains pure and sweet when he is not under her supervision.

The "appliance" had a plate "having an aperture through which the proper member is passed." The plate was attached to the body by a belt and had a series of what the inventor termed "pricking points." (Could this be the source of the slang word for the member in question?) "When, from any cause, expansion in the organ begins, it will come in contact with the pricking points." This, in turn, was considered enough to turn the wearer's mind to purer thoughts.

Although the inventor wrote that he intended this device to be worn voluntarily, he did note that arrangements could be made to permanently attach it to certain "irresponsible wearers."

While I have never encountered Mr. McCormick's gadget in any store, a similar device can be made using leather through which the prongs of snaps have been forced. Normally, these prongs are bent over to hold the snaps in place; however, if they are left extended, they can provided a "pointed reminder" for the wearer. Another product is a nonskid rug mat designed to protect carpets from rolling chairs. The bottom of these is covered with sharp plastic prongs. A small piece snipped off and placed in a jockstrap provides most interesting sensations.

Sport Sheets

This is an interesting little product that uses a Velcro loop sheet to provide points of attachment for a set of Velcro-hook wrist and ankle cuffs. Because the sheet fits tightly over a conventional mattress, you can convert any bed into a versatile bondage surface. It takes a bit of practice to attach the cuffs so that a strong person cannot break the attachment to the sheets, but it can be done. An added bonus is that the sheets are comfortable enough to sleep on.

Spreader Bars

These are simple wooden or metal bars with loops at the ends or at points along their length which attach to wrist and ankle cuffs. When properly in place, they prevent the submissive from bringing together the limbs to which they are attached. Some of the commercially produced models are adjustable, but many dominants simply make their own from lengths of one-inch dowel.

While there is rarely a problem using a spreader bar between wrist cuffs, care should be taken not to use one that is too long between either ankle or knee cuffs. If a submissive is forced to spread his or her legs too widely, they could be injured. This is particularly likely if weight is placed on the hip region while the legs are spread. As the appropriate angle varies among individuals, you should demand feedback from the submissive the first few times you use a leg spreader.

For an interesting effect, a second bar can be attached at right angles to a leg spreader. This bar can hold either a vibrator or a dildo, which the submissive can move in his or her anus or vagina by straightening or bending the knees.

However, because submissives have been known to desire too much of a good thing when they become excited, I recommend attaching the two bars together with a rubber band rather than cord or tape. This way, if the submissive tries to agitate the device too violently or tries to drive it home too firmly, the elastic will stretch and moderate the action or will break entirely—hopefully, before injury is done.

Vampire Gloves

Vampire gloves are a delightful addition to any dominant's toy bag. These are leather gloves with the palms and fingers lined with tiny sharp points. The points are short enough so that they won't break any but the most sensitive skin, but their effect is electric. The degree of pressure and the area being touched control the amount of stimulation. For example, one of my submissives gives me heavenly backrubs while wearing them, but turns pale if I so much as look at her nipples when I have them on. They are particularly useful in places where a whip or a riding crop might cause unwelcome attention.

Vibrators

Just hearing the hum of a vibrator is enough to bring joy to most submissives' hearts. I like to use a vibrator for (1) teasing and contrast during the scene, (2) pushing the submissive over the pleasure-pain-pleasure edge, and (3) for cooling down after the scene ends.

There are basically two ways to produce vibrations. The first type to appear was the coil-driven vibrator. These usually have the vibrating head at right angles to the body. They usually have only two speeds: low (60 beats per second) and high (30 beats per second). (That isn't a misprint. The body interprets the slower speed as faster than the faster speed, and the manufacturers went with perception rather than reality.)

Motor-driven vibrators use a rotating, off-center weight. This allows them a broad range of vibrating speeds. There are two types of these. Wand vibrators look like an old-fashioned hand-held microphone, and Swedish vibrators which strap on the back of the hand and turn the entire hand into a living vibrator. Most wand vibrators are exceptionally large, but this spreads out the vibrations and makes it a more effective massage tool. I tend to like the heft of a large vibrator.

Swedish vibrators are sensual and versatile tools. Their drawbacks are that the softness of the hand mutes the impact of the vibration a bit, the constant vibration can make *your* hand go numb fairly quickly, and the straps that hold the vibrator on your hand can catch pubic and body hair.

Vibrators are also classified by their power source. In most cases, I shun vibrators powered by replaceable batteries. They are generally shaped like dildos but give you the worst of two possible worlds, as they are ineffective dildos and underpowered vibrators. The only setting where I find them useful is in "wet" scenes: baths, showers, and hot tubs. Because they are battery-powered, there is no chance of a dangerous shock, and their size lets me waterproof them by slipping them in a condom and knotting the end.

If you want to transfer vibration into the vagina or anus, instead of using a plastic vibrator, insert a dildo or buttplug and then hold an AC-powered vibrator against it.

One class of battery-powered vibrators I do like are vibrating buttplugs and the Jonie's Butterfly type of clitoral stimulators. Because these can be worn under the clothing, they allow you to take your submissive for a walk or to a restaurant while stimulating him or her covertly. The speed control/battery box can be draped over the waistband, and you can play discreetly with the controls throughout the public session. If you use an egg in the anus, you should put it in an unrolled condom first. This will allow you to withdraw it safely if the cord breaks.

There have been rumors about a dominant who mated a Jonie's Butterfly to a pager so he could sensually torment his submissive from a distance simply by making a phone call. If it isn't true, it should be. The technique could give a whole new meaning to "reach out and touch someone."

A type of battery-powered vibrator I have discontinued using had a vibrating head at the end of a six-inch probe connecting it to the speed control–battery box. While it did allow me to place concentrated vibration on specific parts of the inside of the vagina (Raiders of the Lost G-Spot), it came apart during one play session. There are too many ways to play without using dangerous toys.

AC-powered vibrators are more powerful and have a greater range than those powered by replaceable batteries. Their only major drawback is the need for an electrical outlet. However, when you are playing in an unfamiliar area, that can be a major inconvenience. For example, in one club, the Vault, both major play areas are in the center of the rooms. Using a vibrator usually means running an extension cord through the shifting, milling crowd; this is hardly a satisfactory state of affairs.

Rechargeable vibrators are generally built along the same lines as a wand vibrator, and their batteries are good for about fifteen to forty minutes of stimulation. This may not seem like a lot, but you should remember that AC-powered vibrators overheat. Most manufacturers recommend sessions of no longer than thirty minutes without a cool-down period. Therefore, you may not get significantly longer sessions with AC- than with replaceable-battery-powered vibrators.

Like dildos, many vibrators can be covered with condoms for safety and ease of cleaning. You will be surprised how much you can stretch those suckers, and it is unnecessary to cover the body of the vibrator. For example, only the "foot" of a coil vibrator actually touches the skin, and this is relatively easy to cover. However, a few of the wand vibrators are just too big. Use a rubber glove to cover their heads.

Once, what I had expected to be a single-submissive scene became a two-submissive scene, and I didn't have any condoms or gloves; however, I had two riding crops. Rather than stop using what I find is a very effective tool, I mentally designated one crop for each submissive and, holding the shaft of the crop against the head of the vibrator, used the tip of the crop to touch the submissive. Since each crop only touched one submissive, there was no chance of cross infection. An added bonus was that the submissives found the intense, localized stimulation of the vibrating crop so arousing that I made the technique a standard part of my repertoire.

Finding Toys in the Vanilla World

One thing that consistently amuses me is the recurrent drives by single-minded do-gooders to, as one of them puts it, "close down the places where people buy devices of pain and agony." I won't quibble about the "pain and agony" part, but what is so amusing is that there is more kinky stuff in the average Kmart than in any leather store.

This last section isn't about specific toys or how they are used; I want it to be more of a consciousness-raising exercise. Let's take a walk through our local discount store and see how many things we can do kinky things with. I'm not going to try for a complete list; I'm just trying to give you some inspiration for your future shopping trips.

You've already read about the wonderful things that can be done with clips and clothespins. The "Secret Dungeon" chapter has other cute ideas, but let's start our stroll and see what we can find.

Garden Shop

Not even inside the door yet, and there is this lovely display of canes. I suppose they expect us to use them to train tomato vines. Any other ideas about what to train?

Kitchenware

We may have discovered the mother lode, with wooden and plastic spoons, mixers and spatulas—what wonderful spanking devices. Look at this cheese board with the convenient handgrip. Wouldn't it make a nice splat on some rear end? Hanging on this wall, we have clips and clamps galore. Here's an egg opener. It looks like a pair of scissors with a loop on one end. Notice how the loop is just big enough for a cock.

Toys

What interesting stuff. They call it Slime™, and it really looks sickening. Might it have potential for a humiliation scene? This Nerf™ paddle may not do any harm, but it certainly stings. Look at these jacks. Wouldn't it be interesting to see how someone would walk while she was holding them between her legs? My goodness, a treasure trove of little girls' play makeup. Wouldn't this be handy for a reluctant TV? It has an added bonus: it comes off easily.

I think I'll take a pass on these toy handcuffs. The plastic has hard edges; they could hurt someone who struggles.

Hardware

What a wonderful place with all the hooks, pulleys, ropes, and clamps. Anyone who can't imagine uses for Vice Grips™ should be sent back to D&S 101. The trick is to close the handle before putting it on and use the little screw to adjust the tension. Here are five locks that open with the same key. That is a handy safety precaution.

Automotive

These ratcheting tie-downs are designed for pickup trucks, but would be handy for *firmly* attaching a submissive to a frame. Here is a key ring with a nice feature. It has two rings attached by a mechanism that needs to be pushed together to separate them. Wouldn't it make a handy emergency release for light bondage?

Sporting Goods

Sir Spencer was once going to a birthday party for some scene people. He knew the crowd would include a sprinkling of vanilla people who knew nothing of the birthday girl's "interests." His lovely and brilliant wife recommended that he buy a game that featured a pair of charming Lucite paddles. As she pointed out, the vanilla guests would take the gift at face value. The scene people would realize that the real value of the gift was somewhat lower than the face and on the other side.

Here we have some weightlifter's kidney belts. The same kind of belt, to protect a submissive's kidneys during a whipping, cost five times as much in a leather shop. Wow, are these sinkers heavy! I bet they would be a lot heavier hanging from nipple clamps.

Hobby Supplies

These are such nice beading needles; cleaned and sterilized, they are marvelous for temporary piercings. And look at the wonderful materials for making cuffs and bondage toys.

Jewelry

Nylon replacement watchstraps with Velcro fasteners can be backed up with a felt pad (to keep them from cutting into the skin) from the hobby department to make a fine cuff. One warning: jewelry for pierced ears shouldn't be used in body piercings. It can cut and cause damage.

Pet Supplies

This aisle is just full of leashes, collars, humiliating squeaky toys that you can run a cord through and make into a great gag. Giant corkscrews that screw into the ground might be intended to hold Fido's chain, but when used in pairs or fours, they are wonderful for spread-eagled outdoor bondage. Nylon leashes can be tied to bed legs and then clipped to cuffs.

Miscellaneous

A mysterious scissor-shaped wooden clamp is, in the vanilla world, a glove stretcher. We have other uses for it. Here are some EMT scissors. A baby's pacifier makes a nice symbolic gag.

Finished here? Let's drop by a tack shop.

This place is packed solid with riding crops and whips, as well as all kinds of leather straps and such. Even better, they are less than half the price you'd pay in a leather shop. What *could* an imaginative person do with a bridle? Stirrups are useful for supported suspension. One gentleman at the Vault modified a standard saddle and delights in giving ladies rides about the place.

Look around. If you keep a kinky thought in your head, the world becomes a kinky place. You may never look at a cucumber the same way.

CHAPTER 10
Fun and Games

Spanking

It is so classic. The stern schoolmistress, strict nun, or angry father orders the miscreant to bend over, and the pleasure begins. Hey! Wait! Isn't that "punishment"?

Well, to each his or her own. To some people, being in one role or the other of this little scenario would be but one step away from heaven. Spanking is perhaps the most common D&S activity. Drop by your vanilla video store's classics collection, and you can spend hours watching mainstream stars warming each other's celebrity fannies.

Spanking has also served as the entry point to D&S by more than one couple. Spanking seems so much fun, so wholesome, so American. Besides, could anything that John Wayne did be so awful? In a very practical sense, spanking is probably one of the safest of the D&S activities. The buttocks, while abundantly supplied with nerve endings, are well padded, and the physics of the event guarantee that the hand partakes of much of what it gives.

Only when straps, paddles, and "strapples, a short strap with the characteristics of a paddle," make their appearance is it necessary to consider a modicum of safety, and that is only to avoid the portion of the upper buttocks where the bone is close to the skin. There are nerve junctions in that area which do not take kindly to being pounded. However, the rest of that delightful protrusion is fair game. The area between the top of the leg and the point where the arse begins to turn in again should be a particular target; as one masochistic lady put it, "It is the 'sweet spot,' with a direct line to the pussy." Comments from two submissive gentlemen indicate that the same effect is present in their anatomy...with a slightly different destination.

Bondage

Bondage—who can look at the bound and helpless submissive and not feel a stirring of excitement and pride? In a very substantial way, this is the scene made real. While not all submissives long for rope, leather, and chain, all long for the spiritual essence of these things: confinement, restriction, being controlled and held.

A man in a French maid's costume kneeling quietly at his mistress's feet can be more tightly restrained than one in a cocoon of rope and leather. Freedom through constraint is the quintessential nature of D&S.

Sadly, however, few things are done more poorly than bondage. Like Olympic-level gymnastics, to do it well is to make it look easy. Bondage is far more than simply grabbing a length of old clothesline, wrapping it around your partner, and tying a granny knot at the end.

Before we go any further, remember that bondage—unlike diamonds—is not forever. You should always have the means to release your submissive quickly and efficiently. No one should ever do any bondage without a set of EMT scissors (also called paramedic scissors). They have extremely sharp, serrated blades that can cut rope or even heavy leather. The bottom blade has a spoon-shaped end so that the scissors can be used next to a struggling person's skin without doing any damage. Of course, the scissors won't cut heavy chain. If you are doing chain bondage, keep a bolt cutter handy.

What Should Not Be Used for Bondage

Let's look at the actual tools for bondage. First, what should *not* be used? If a submissive is going to lie quietly, without any movement, almost any long, flexible material including (ouch!) barbed wire could be used. However, short of posing for a cover shot for *Hogtied Quarterly*, submissives do not lie there quietly. Many enjoy struggling, for the confirmation of constraint it gives them. Others are "stimulated" to movement by the dominant's activities.

Therefore, it is best to assume a certain degree of struggle. This eliminates many of the favorites of the bondage artist. Handcuffs, for example, are notorious for causing abrasions and can even cause nerve damage and broken bones. While this quality may be considered a plus by policemen seeking a docile prisoner, it is definitely *not* a plus in the scene.

At the very least, if you are going to use them for anything more than an attractive ornament on your belt, buy good-quality handcuffs. These are available to the general public in many states through police-supply stores. Avoid the cheap handcuffs sold in novelty and leather shops. The differences are twofold. First, the machining on the professional handcuffs is much better, and there is less likelihood of burrs or rough edges which can tear the skin.

The second reason is even more important. Professional handcuffs have a lock that prevents them from continuing to tighten after they have been applied. This lock is either missing or ineffective in the cheaper models. *Never* use a pair of handcuffs without this lock, even for the lightest play.

Regardless of the quality of the handcuffs, they should never be used for suspension or even for holding the hands above the head for a substantial period.

Police have begun to use long plastic strips with self-locking tabs as disposable handcuffs or "plasticuffs." Because they were developed by electronics companies for bundling cables, these are available through stores like Radio Shack. While they should not be used when the submissive may struggle, they are nice props for psychological scenes. Once the tab has been inserted through the lock, the plasticuffs are sealed permanently and must be cut off.

Hose clamps are another bondage item that should not be used in connection with any potential struggle. They are long strips of metal with a screw-locking mechanism designed to tighten over hoses until they are sealed to a nipple. They come in sizes big enough to hold a pair of legs. However, they have several important drawbacks. They are metal and can do damage if they are overtightened or if the submissive struggles. They are slow to take off because the tab must be unscrewed slowly. Because paramedic scissors may not be able to cut them, if you are going to use these, you should have a pair of bolt cutters handy in case something goes wrong.

Articles of clothing, like scarves and pantyhose, figure commonly in bondage fantasy; however, in the real scene, they should be used with care. Both can clump until they are very narrow and can cut deeply into the skin. Hold a silk scarf; it feels soft. However, if you pull it tightly between your hands, it forms sharply defined folds. Imagine those folds cutting into your submissive's wrists, and you can see what I am warning about.

Knots in scarves and pantyhose are also notorious for jamming. Eventually, you are going to untie your submissive. It is definitely anti-erotic to break fingernails while struggling unsuccessfully with a bulky knot. *You* are the dominant; *you* are supposed to be in control. Being bettered by a inanimate hunk of silk is not the image you are trying to project. Even more importantly, it interrupts the flow of the scene and destroys the mood for both of you.

Plastic clothesline rope is a definite no-no. Not only can its wire core cut deeply into the submissive's flesh, but it has an uncanny ability to jam almost any knot put in it.

Leather laces are definitely another no-no for immobilization. First, they are so narrow as to be almost certain to cut into the skin and stop circulation. Second, leather shrinks when it gets wet. Even if you're not into water sports and don't plan to dunk your submissive into a bathtub, he or she is going to sweat. Just a bit of sweat is enough to turn a tight—but safe—tie into a tourniquet. Worse, this same contraction will turn a relatively safe knot into a solid mass of dense leather.

Thin cord or line can be used for a decorative binding to produce interesting patterns on the submissive's body or for controlled compression of body parts, like the breasts or penis, but it should never be used for immobilization. For example, these should never be used for securing the wrists to each other or to a solid object. Keep thin cord for decoration or for secondary tying where a lot of strain will not be brought against the binding.

What Can Be Used for Bondage

What to use, then? The best bondage tools are well-made leather restraints. Although they are expensive and may be daunting to the novice, they are actually the safest way to render a submissive helpless. Their width and the nature of the material make it harder—although not impossible—to do something wrong, like cutting off the blood supply.

Of course, leather binders do cut into the dominant's creative flexibility. Wrist cuffs go on wrists. They won't go around waists or upper legs. When using them, at least part of the choreography is already laid out.

Rope is cheaper and inherently more versatile. Sisal or manila rope is rough and stiff. Some submissives like the harsh touch of these materials, and some dominants enjoy manila's ability to hold knots without jamming. Both, however, must be handled carefully because they can cause severe rope burns. Polyethylene rope—the yellow stuff that floats—is stiff and hard to handle as is mountain-climbing rope, which consists of a core of nylon lines inside a jacket of woven nylon.

Before the ghost of my father, a Merchant Marine officer, descends to crack me alongside the head and yell, "You're talking about *line*, son!" I'll admit that what seafarers call rope is more suitable for fastening the *QE2* to a dock than a submissive to a table. However, rope is what most people call it. Sorry, dad.

Perhaps the best all-around material for bondage is plaited cotton rope. Cotton rope used to be used primarily to hold sash weights in windows and for clotheslines. With the passing of sash weights and the use of weatherproof nylon for clothesline, cotton rope largely disappeared. The modern version has a plastic stiffener inside which renders it inappropriate for use in bondage. However, some pure cotton rope is still available, and those who have been able to obtain it swear by the material and guard their supply with care. A number of these lucky individuals report buying theirs at a magicians' supply store.

If you are lucky enough to find some without the plastic stiffener, wash it first to get rid of the starch that manufacturers use to make it look pretty in the store. Follow the directions in "Scrubbing Up" in the appendixes for washing unless you want to spend the next few hours untangling a Gordian knot.

The best generally available material, in my opinion, is nylon rope. It is smooth and flexible and takes knots well without jamming. I prefer 5/16- and 3/8-inch rope for immobilization bindings, while 1/4-inch and the so-called "parachute cord" are best for decorative bindings. Ropes of 1/2-inch diameter or larger are relatively difficult to work with, but can be worked into the scene as psychological props.

Nylon rope usually comes in two surfaces: three-strand-twisted and plaited. Plaited rope slides more evenly over skin, while the three-strand can leave "interesting" patterns when it is removed and lends itself to splices. Three-strand-twisted should be cut by wrapping it with electrician's tape and cutting through the tape. This also provides a nice temporary whipping.

The ends of both kinds should be sealed with a flame so that they will not unravel. When you are melting the ends, keep away from the smoke: it is *not* healthy to breathe it. Work outdoors or in a well-ventilated room. The melted ends are also *very* hot. Use a stick or pencil end to tamp them down. Don't even consider using your finger. If you are cutting a lot of nylon rope, you might consider getting an attachment that goes on a soldering gun and turns it into an electrically heated knife.

For a really kinky look, dye the rope black or red. Cotton rope dyes easily with any commercial dye. However, nylon rope requires something stronger. I use a dye manufactured in Germany called Deka L. It is available in 1/3-ounce packages from Earthguild. (The address is in the appendix.) A 10-gram package is enough to easily dye 50 feet or so of 5/16-inch nylon rope.

Another interesting bondage medium is mountain-climbing webbing. Available in a number of colors, this nylon webbing is fairly thick and comes in widths from 1" to 3" inches. Because it is so broad, there is less chance of cutting off circulation, but it can be tied as easily as rope and does not jam. You can cut and seal it in the same way as nylon rope.

The most common mistakes beginners make with rope are first, to buy too little of it and, second, to cut it into lengths that are too short. The shortest useful length is generally 5 to 6 feet. Anything shorter tempts the dominant to tie the submissive incompletely and too tightly.

You should have several lengths available. My kit usually contains five 5-foot lengths, five 10-foot lengths, and a 20-footer. If I am planning a webbing (see further along in this chapter), I bring two 50-foot lengths. Of course, specific plans may call for a different mix, but this combination is good for, say, a visit to a scene club like Hellfire or to a private party.

It is a good idea to code your ropes according to their lengths so you can quickly and easily select the proper one for the job. I use plastic tapes on each end of the rope. As a mnemonic aid, they are coded by the spectrum. Blue (blue has the shortest wavelength of the visible colors) is for the 6-foot length, yellow is for the 10s, green is for the 20s, and red for the 50s.

Colored tapes are also useful for establishing ownership at the ends of group scenes. All of my ropes have a black piece of tape at one end in addition to the color code.

Of course, rope isn't the only material to use for bond-age. Fiberglass-reinforced packing tape is impossible to break. I like to run a few turns of gauze bandage over the area before putting the tape in place so that the adhesive does not bond to the submissive's skin. Although that isn't necessary, if you are going to use the tape against the submissive's skin, experiment by putting a small piece on his or her skin in an earlier session and checking later for any redness or other signs of an allergic reaction. In later scenes, keep checking because a single exposure may not be enough to trigger a reaction. Also, pulling out fine hairs as the tape is being removed may not be what your submissive would call positive pain.

I've seen photographs of submissives bound in 12- or 14-gauge heavy-duty electrical extension cords. It looked attractive, and the thick plastic coating would provide more than adequate protection against cutting into the skin.

Velcro provides impressive opportunities for creative bondage. One couple I know has glued strips of hook-and-loop Velcro together to make a versatile tool. To "tie" it, all she does is gives the strip a half-turn and press it against the opposite side. I have seen Velcro replacement wrist-watch bands that look as though they would be quite effective as cuffs if they were attached to wide pads so that they wouldn't cut into the skin.

Hook Velcro will also stick to nylon rope, although the bonding is not as strong as against the proper loop material. Velcro does have the tremendous advantage in that the dominant can free the submissive quickly and easily from most bonds using this material. Sport Sheets, mentioned in the preceding chapter, use Velcro in an interesting fashion to turn any bed into a bondage device.

Knots: Knot So Mysterious

There is nothing mysterious about knots, and a dominant need not become an apprentice to a pipe-smoking old tar to learn how to join two ropes together or how to fasten a submissive down securely. However, a thorough knowledge of a few knots should be part of your repertoire.

Square or Reef Knot—This is one of the most common knots. It works best with two ends of the same rope or with ropes of the same size and material. It is simply two overhand knots, one in each direction. Millions of ex–Boy Scouts tie it every day, muttering under their breaths, "Right over left; left over right."

Slipped Reef or Safety Knot—This is a modification of the square knot, in which one end has been doubled back like a half-bow under the other rope. In an emergency, the dominant can give a good yank on the doubled-back end, and the knot will just come apart.

Two Half-hitches—Because this knot can tighten, you should never use it directly on a submissive's body. However, it is an effective knot to attach a rope to a ring or other inanimate object. Run the rope completely around the object and then back along the rope. Loop it around the rope with the end coming out under itself. Go down the rope a bit and then repeat this.

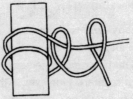

Bowline—The bowline lets you make a loop in a way that is less likely to slip than two half-hitches. However, especially with nylon rope, you have to be careful to tighten the knot after you tie it. The classic description of a bowline is "The rabbit (the end of the rope) comes out of the hole (the loop you have made), goes around the tree (the part of the rope above the loop), and then goes back in the hole." It sounds cutesy, but it is an effective memory aid.

Fisherman's Bend—This knot allows you to use rope as a less-effective substitute for bondage cuffs. First, wrap three or four loops of rope loosely around the submissive's wrist or ankle leaving at least two feet of free end. Then wrap the end around the rope, loop it through the loose loops, and then tie it off with a two half hitches. This makes the loops less likely to tighten independently and cut off circulation.

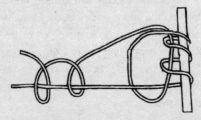

Sheet Bend—This knot is used to connect two ropes of different size or to connect a rope to an eye. Make a loop in the larger rope. Then run the smaller rope through the loop, around both portions of the loop, and then under itself.

That's it. There are many other useful knots, but these are the basics. If you want to learn about bottle knots, Spanish bowlines, or rolling hitches, read any book on knots.

When tying and untying a submissive, you should always be aware of the rope ends. More than once, I have seen enthusiastic novices inadvertently smacking the subject of their attentions with the end of the rope while attempting to tie or untie a complex knot. When being pulled through a loop, a rope can move at substantial speed. As the end of the rope approaches the loop, it can easily be slingshotted to one side or the other. Under such conditions, 3/8-inch rope with a fused end can have a substantial impact.

Trying to work too fast can also lead to rope burns. While such burns are less common with the recommended cotton and nylon ropes, they can happen. Work slowly and carefully. When you must drag a rope across the submissive's body, put your hand under the rope so you are aware of the potential for burning and are partially shielding the submissive from it. If your submissive is rope burned, clean the area with warm water and a mild soap. Then sterilize the affected skin with alcohol or Betadine.

A precise, careful dominant is a lot more impressive and gives far more pleasure than one who works fast but seems to be on the edge of losing control or, worse, actually injures the submissive because of ill-advised speed.

Bondage Positions

Of course, the tying is only part of a gestalt, the whole of which goes together to excite both of you. While a wonderful feeling of helplessness can be created by simply tying a submissive's hands behind his or her back, there are positions that amplify that feeling.

They can be as simple as adding an additional tie at the elbows to bring the arms closer together. This is particularly exciting with a woman because the position forces her breasts into greater prominence. However, there are two dangers with this position. The elbows should never be forced. While some people can bring their elbows together behind them, doing that with others can result in permanent shoulder injury. Also, a person should never be placed so that his or her body is resting on tied wrists for more than a very short time.

Another position that puts the submissive in a very erotic helpless position is with the hands up behind the neck. First, run a length of rope (climbing webbing is even better) behind the neck, bring it around in front of both shoulders and then back across the upper part of the back. With a female submissive, moderate tension on this rope will also make her bring her breasts into greater prominence. Then, with another length of rope, tie the hands together in *front*, with about a foot of rope between them. Leave another foot of each end of the rope loose. Bring the hands up and over the neck and tie them to the rope across the back and neck.

This position leaves the submissive completely helpless, exposes the entire body, back and front, and can be used either standing or lying down. This is the position I use when I am doing a knife stripping as described in the "Fantasy Rape" section of the "Making a Scene Sing" chapter.

A very versatile position is to have the submissive sit on the floor, knees bent and leaning forward slightly. Tie the wrists to the ankles and the elbows to the knees. A spreader bar can be attached between the ankles but, in most cases, only the most flexible submissive will be able to bring the legs together in this position. Because the genitals are in forced exposure in this position, one of my submissives coined the generic phrase "naked-making."

Another position that many submissives find naked-making is to be placed horizontally on the ground or on a bed with their legs vertical and spread widely. I used to have ringbolts in my ceiling beam for just such a situation (among others). A spreader bar attached to a single line also works, but I have found that the feeling of helplessness is greater when each ankle is attached to a separate point. You may want him or her to wear boots (and nothing else) during this, both for erotic contrast and to protect the tendons. If the tendons are protected, the legs can be left up and spread for quite a long time.

The Fold is a very secure position. Tie your submissive's hands behind his or her back. The forearms should be horizontal, and each wrist should be tied to the opposite elbow. This folds the arms behind the back. Next, have him or her sit cross-legged—what the yoga people call the "lotus position," and tie each ankle to the opposite calf. Take a 10-foot rope, fold it in half, loop the middle under the already-bound forearms, and tie it off. This will result in your having two 4-foot-long (or so) lengths of rope tied to the submissive's forearms. Bring one length over the shoulders on either side of the neck. Lean the submissive forward until there is a bit of stretch, but no discomfort, then tie each length of rope to a calf or to the ropes connecting the wrists and the calves. He or she can be left in that position to "mediate upon sins" or tipped backward, an action that exposes the genitals for casual play. Because the arms are bound in the small of the back, there is less pressure on them than in the conventional wrist-wrist tie.

Hog tying is a classic position but should be used with care. It can put a lot of strain on the back and knees. Position the submissive on his or her stomach. Tie the hands behind the back, wrists together, with enough rope so that you have a 3-foot tail on either end after you have finished. Tie the elbows together with a number of coils of rope. Take care not to put pressure on the shoulders doing this. As I wrote before, some people cannot touch their elbows without severe injury; you want the submissive secure, not injured.

Tie the ankles together, and fold them up against the thighs. Run the rope tails from the wrists and tie them around the ankle rope. This positioning of the final knot makes it much harder for a SAM to reach it.

Hog-tied submissives should not be placed on their backs, nor should any portion of the tie go around the throat. This is a popular photographic subject, but is much, much too dangerous for real play.

There is no hard-and-fast rule for how long a person can be left in bondage. Some positions are extremely stressful and should be used only for a few minutes. Others are so comfortable that sleeping in them is possible. Submissives' tolerances also vary. *It should go without saying that you should carefully watch anyone in bondage, and he or she should never be left alone.*

Aside from asking them how they are, you should check that their extremities do not become cold and that they can wiggle their fingers and toes on command. Blue skin is a good indication that circulation has been cut off, as is a complete loss of sensation.

This does not mean that a bit of circulation restriction can't be part of the bondage scene. Some submissives love the helpless feeling a numb limb gives them and glory in the pins-and-needles effect of returning circulation. However, this sort of scene must be monitored even more closely than conventional bondage.

For submissives who enjoy these feelings, I prefer to let gravity rather than ropes restrict the circulation. Anyone who has his or her hands held above the head can attest to how fast they go numb. After around half an hour, most people begin to lose sensation in their elevated hands. Releasing them produces the sought-after tingling.

Decorative Bondage

Many women enjoy having their breasts singled out for special bondage attention. Some report that the reduction of the circulation by the bondage increases the sensitivity; others just like the way it looks.

There are several ways to do this.

An approach that is often the choice of bondage photographers is to encase each breast in a coil of rope. A thin rope, like parachute cord (1/4 inch), is easier to use for this than the thicker rope we have been using for immobilizing ties.

Have her lean forward, then begin with an anchoring loop over one shoulder and down under the arm. The rope then passes under the breast, up between the breasts, and down the outside. Each successive coil should go outside the previous one. The rope should be tight enough to that it gets a good grip on the skin but shouldn't be so tight that it will cut off circulation.

Repeat this for the other breast. Finally, tie the ends of each rope behind her neck for a very effective rope bra. As this will reduce blood circulation, it should not be left on for too long. In any case, many women report that the breasts lose the extra sensitivity created by the rope bondage after about ten minutes.

Some breasts are simply too small and firm to offer the rope a good grip. As this can be a very hurtful point for some women, your failure to achieve a solid decorative bondage with rope can have more impact than you realize. You can avoid this by doing a full chest binding.

One way to do this is to wrap several layers of plastic wrap around the chest. When the chest has been wrapped, take a pair of EMT or bandage scissors (do not use anything with a sharp point) and cut holes through which the breasts or just the nipples can protrude.

You can also use coils of rope around the upper chest to provide a similar experience, except that you can't simply cut holes in the coils. While you are wrapping, leave room between strands for the nipples to protrude.

Naturally, since both of these techniques have the

potential to interfere with chest expansion—and therefore breathing—you must monitor the submissive very carefully while the bondage is in place and be ready to cut it off if she becomes disoriented or dizzy. Also, when a woman is menstruating or is about to begin her period, her breasts may be extrasensitive, and what would be pleasant at another time becomes very painful.

For the female dominant, men's cocks can provide hours of delightful fun. In the scene, this is often known as cock-and-ball torture or CBT, and bondage is an important part of this specialty.

Since this is a binding rather than an immobilization, you can use parachute cord or other relatively narrow twine. One scenario that parallels the previously described breast binding is to anchor the cord around the base of the genitals and then circle the scrotum with successive coils. The balls are forced farther and farther into the scrotum. The same approach can be used on the cock. However, its more uniform shape provides a surface for more artistic endeavors. At least one mistress preforms macramé with a thick yarn over her submissive's cock and balls until they resemble a teapot in its cozy.

Of course, eventually the cock will lose its erection and escape the bondage, providing an excuse for the mistress to punish her slave for this infraction.

Another approach is, after making the loop around the base of the genitals, to bring the cord around and between the balls, separating them and pulling them upward. This process is repeated until the a series of Xs are in place.

If your submissive has a tight little sack that makes getting a good grip difficult (fear often makes the balls retract), let them rest in a pan of moderately hot water. The reproductive system's temperature-control scheme will lower them right into your waiting hands.

Some leather shops and bondage magazine advertisements have clever little toys for binding, restricting, and clamping cocks and balls. The best of these lace rather than snap, to provide a snug fit regardless of the size of the endowment.

As with any bondage that has the potential to interfere with circulation, you should undo or reposition cock-and-ball bondage every ten to fifteen minutes.

Whole-body Bondage and Mummification

A subspecialization of bondage is whole-body bondage. The goal is to extend the experience of binding over much of the body surface.

Japanese bondage is one technique that combines the whole-body experience with an aesthetic exercise. Because it is essentially a binding, you can use almost any smooth, flexible material including twine, parachute cord, or yarn. I tend to prefer my favorite—3/8-inch rope—but will admit that sufficient rope to do a proper Japanese bondage can be rather bulky.

Because this is a lengthy tie, you *must* have a pair of sharp bandage or EMT scissors handy. In an emergency, this type of bondage *cannot* be untied quickly and must be cut. Also, because it is usually done with the submissive standing up, you should make sure that at no time does the little rascal lock his or her knees. That makes it easier to stand still, but it also makes it likely that he or she will faint on you.

One easy approach to Japanese bondage requires a minimum of 50 feet of rope or cord. Double up the rope.

About a foot from the bend which marks the center, hold the ends together and tie a simple overhand knot (half a square knot). Put one end of the rope over each of the submissive's shoulders. The knot should rest (not press) against the back of the submissive's neck.

Tie another overhand knot just below the rib cage and above the navel. The third knot goes about 8 inches below the clitoris or the cock. The fourth knot goes 3 to 4 inches below that.

Pass both ends of the rope through the submissive's legs and bring them up along the submissive's back and tie another knot about halfway up the back. Pass the rope through the loop made by the first knot (just behind his or her neck). Draw all the rope through this loop but don't pull it tight. It will get tight soon enough.

Pass each end of the rope around one side of the submissive's body. You can "trap" the arms at this time or pass the ends under the arms and secure the arms later. Both ends of the rope go through the loop between the first (behind the neck) and the second (below the rib cage) knot and then each end goes *back* around the submissive on the same side that it came forward. Thus the rope that came around the submissive's left side would go through the loop and then back around the left side toward the back. Do not tie the rope at this point. The whole point is that the rope is free to slide over itself.

Pull the rope moderately tight. The third knot should move above until it is just forward of the arse. Above the knot in the middle of the back, pass both ends of the rope through the two ropes and then bring the two ends back around again on the same side. This time they go through below the second knot and then go back around the submissive's body. This will bring the third knot on a woman right over her clitoris or on a man just under his cock. The other knot should be pressing on the arse.

By now, you see the pattern: an interlocking series of diamonds progressively tightening the entire pattern of ropes. At this point, you have plenty of rope remaining, and from this basic design, you can extemporize, looping and tying, until the submissive is a lovely piece of macramé.

Because there is not enough constriction to impede blood flow, a submissive can remain in Japanese bondage for an extended period and can, with some designs, actually don street clothes and venture out in public while remaining in this exotic bondage. When the entire pattern is completed, any strain should be distributed evenly across the entire body so the submissive can be lifted off his or her feet by attaching a hoisting rope to the web.

If the submissive's hands are tied to the web, this should be treated as an immobilization tie, and appropriate precautions taken. For example, it is acceptable to web the entire arm to the body web with twine or narrow cord because the pressure will be distributed across several loops. However, if you are doing a wrist tie with a single strand, you should use a wider rope and knot the rope with a fisherman's bend or use cuffs to protect the wrist from damage.

View

View

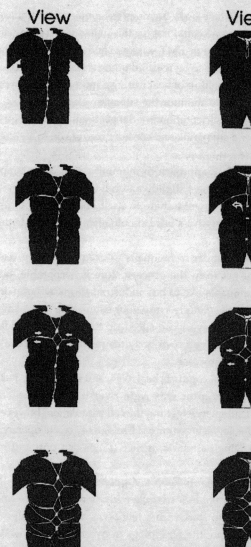

Another whole-body bondage technique is mummification. Again, you should not try this unless you have a pair of sharp bandage or EMT scissors handy in the event the submissive needs to be released quickly. Because there can be a gradual buildup of heat during a mummification, you regularly should monitor the submissive's alertness. Any faintness or disorientation is a danger sign. You must give him or her a cool drink and consider moving on to another activity.

The simplest approach to mummification is to dampen an ordinary sheet slightly and roll the submissive in it. The moist sheet will adhere to itself and to the submissive. The submissive's head should always be outside the roll.

Another, similar technique is to use plastic wrap. The kind you get from the grocery store is acceptable, but many dominants like to buy industrial shrink wrap in 36- to 40-inch rolls. Simply wrap your submissive like a large leftover. A hair dryer can speed up the shrinking action, but the submissive's own body temperature will activate the process in any case.

This material conducts heat, cold, and impact very well. So you can whip or wax right over it, with the well-wrapped submissive getting the full stimulation; however, you may enjoy using your EMT scissors to create openings through which all sorts of nice things can pop and be played with.

Many dominants keep a supply of regular or elastic bandages available for whole-body bondage. The usual procedure is to start with a few turns around the upper body and apply the wrappings in overlapping turns. As each bandage is put in place, it is secured with butterfly clips (usually supplied with elastic bandages) or with adhesive tape. A figure-eight pattern is used over the nipples to leave them exposed, as you don't want to cut elastic bandages, and if regular bandages are cut, they tend to unravel at the most inopportune times.

There is some debate about whether it is better to wrap the arms at the same time as the body, either crossed over the chest in Egyptian style or along the sides, or to bind them separately. Those who prefer the same-time wrapping argue that it is more aesthetic to have a single package. The arms-separate school holds that keeping them separate allows more options in the continuing bondage process.

The most important thing to remember with whole-body bondage is that it usually cannot be undone quickly. You must have some means by which you can cut the submissive free if something untoward happens.

Self-bondage

I'm setting aside the last part of this chapter for submissives, in particular those who are thinking of self-bondage.

First, and foremost, this is *dangerous.* If you have read the sections on bondage carefully, you will notice that I emphasize the importance of being able to free a submissive on a moment's notice. In self-bondage, this is generally difficult, if not impossible.

The best thing is to find a dominant and have him or her tie you up. OK, I accept that it isn't all that easy, but please consider doing this.

The next best thing is to do only partial immobilization. Many submissives secure only their feet and one hand. The main incentive for this is that the hand is used for masturbation, but it is also available for getting out of bondage in the event of a fire, break-in, or other emergency. Others secure only their hands and, in an emergency, could escape from their homes or apartments.

However, I recognize that, for some people, nothing but complete immobilization will do. In most cases, they use a locking device with a system to withhold the key for a certain interval. Many of these systems are extremely dangerous. One, which has appeared in more than one bondage film, is a burning candle that cuts a cord, dropping the key within reach. Unless you enjoy being helpless in a burning building, I do not recommend this approach.

Another, less-dangerous approach uses keys suspended from a string which runs through a pulley and down to the minute hand on a CrayLab timer. When the hand approaches the zero position, the cord slips off, and the keys drop from where they have been hoisted.

A common technique is to freeze the keys into a block of ice. The keys are unavailable until the ice melts. The size of the block determines the length of the bondage, and submissives have used gallon milk containers as molds for their "bondage cubes."

It is possible to arrange a weak equivalent of the safe word in self-bondage. Put an extra set of keys into a valued vase on a high table. The logic is that in a real emergency, you won't hesitate to knock over the table, smashing the vase and making the keys available. If you lack a Ming antique, put the spare keys in a regular jar in the middle of the living-room rug—then fill it with vegetable oil. Again, knocking this over isn't something you will do casually, but it will provide you with a set of keys when you need them.

However, remember that you won't be able to get your extra keys with anything like the speed with which an attentive partner can free you. Self-bondage is only a choice if a trustworthy partner is not available and you feel you *must* be in bondage. It is *not* something that should be tried casually.

Whipping

A whip is almost the icon of the scene. Hanging from a dominant's belt or flying through the air to land with a resounding *crack* on a submissive's back, the whip, to many people, *is* the scene.

Selecting a Whip

Contrary to popular impressions, it is the multi-tailed cat rather than the bullwhip that is the whip of choice for most dominants. Although the bullwhip is spectacular and makes an impressive *crack* in the air when used properly, even a short one requires an inordinate amount of room and is very difficult to employ so that the expectant submissive (and occasionally the novice dominant) is not reduced to bloody shreds. After all, the loud, snapping sound characteristic of the bullwhip is caused when the tips travel *faster than sound*. It is very difficult to caress anyone with a hypersonic piece of material.

Bullwhips are used in the scene, but their role is generally restricted to that of a noisemaker and intimidation device. Using one on a submissive is either the mark of a highly skilled whipper or a complete fool, and the distinction is rarely in doubt for long.

On the other hand, the cat is a tremendously versatile

tool. It can deliver as stimulating a whipping as most sub-missives can tolerate, or it can be as soft and gentle as a baby's touch.

The most common material for cats is steerhide. It is relatively inexpensive and easily available. However, it can be a bit rigid and inflexible, especially if it has not been prepared well. I and many other dominants I know prefer deerskin or moosehide. These are softer and more flexible than steerhide and have a very pleasing feel.

Suede is an interesting material. It has a lovely texture and is very soft, but anyone using it should be aware that it has a tendency to abrade rather than cut. Only a few strokes with a suede whip will redden skin. Too much may draw blood despite a complete lack of visible cuts. Whips of this material are a good adjunct to a dominant's kit, but I don't think they should be used as a primary whip for extended whipping.

Another popular material that can be deceptively harsh is horsehair. Horsehair "flicks" are sold in both tack and leather shops. Used lightly, they are an unmatched erotic tease, while with forceful blows they can be quite stimulat-ing. However, this is another material you should watch with care because its surface is so rough that abrasion will take place during an intense whipping. This effect can be reduced somewhat by using soaking the hair in a solution made from a capful of hair conditioner to a gallon of water and allowing it to air-dry. For those desiring a fashion statement, commercial hair dye can be used to make the flick match your own hair color or the color of your outfit.

Midnight, a Boston dominant who is an artist with the horsehair flick, says, "I use it as a warm up; it tends to red-den the bottom a little faster for me. It also leaves very,

very small welts (you cannot see them) so that the stings seem to last much longer. I also use it to caress."

Cats with beads or knots at the end of the tail should be avoided early on. Later, you may want one or two for special effects or as scene enders when you want a burst of high-intensity stimulation. However, they have to be watched carefully, and you can't use them for too long. To me, that cuts into the fun.

In my opinion, the best whip for a novice is a cat with five to ten broad, moderately heavy tails between 12 and 18 inches long. It is a fallacy that thinner tails are less injurious. Actually, they cut and abrade the skin very easily. One of the most feared whips in my collection is a simple ring with four leather shoelaces attached to it with hitches at their midpoints, making an eight-tailed whip.

On the other hand, a weighty, wide strip will make a satisfying splat when it hits and sting a bit but won't cut the skin. Lighter whips also have the disadvantage of making the dominant work harder.

Although they are not technically whips, canes belong more logically in this section than in the spanking section. These canes aren't the sturdy supports elderly people use to get to the corner store but are, instead, the light, whippy pieces of birch, rattan, and bamboo so beloved by the English schoolmaster. In recent years, fiberglass and even graphite canes have made their appearance for those more interested in durability than tradition.

Canes call for considerable care in their use and should not be used unless you are very familiar with both the specific cane and the submissive's limits. More than one budding affair almost came a cropper over a too-enthusiastic application of a cane too early in a relationship. The feel-

ing from a cane is *much more intense* than that from a paddle—or even, most whips—and a cane stroke, especially
where it passes over an existing welt, can draw blood.

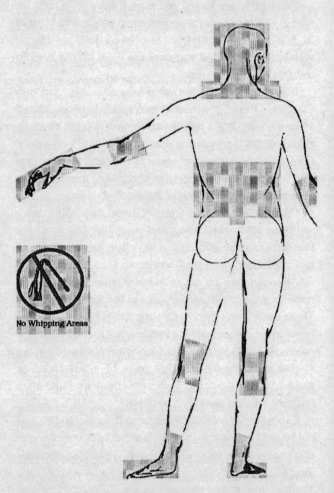

No Whipping Areas

Using a Whip

There are several standard techniques for using a whip. The standard stroke comes largely from the muscles in the back and arm. The motion is much like that a child would use spreading on paint with a paintbrush. Because several of the body's major muscles are involved, it can be quite a powerful stroke. It is generally delivered diagonally but can be delivered at anything from 0 to 90 degrees from the vertical.

The slingshot stroke is more precise. The handle of the whip is held away from the body in one hand and the ends of the tails are held close to the face in the other. The handle is moved farther away until a degree of tension is built up in the tails. When the tension feel right, the tails are released and the handle is moved toward the submissive with a snap and, just before the tails strike, the handle is jerked back. With a little practice, a whipper can become quite accurate with this motion. However, the impact is deceptive. It is considerably harder than it seems, so careful monitoring is advisable.

While the slingshot stroke is best for accuracy, the spin provides the most continuous stimulation. The whip is held by the end of its handle or by its handle lanyard, if it has one, and is spun like a biblical sling. If this is used on the breasts, you should place your hand under the submissive's chin and lift her head up and back. This not only moves the vulnerable face out of primary danger, but if the strokes are hitting too high, you will feel them on your hand before any damage is done.

It should be obvious, but I think I should point out that the whipping area should be well lighted. To have the kind of control you need, you have to be able to see what you are doing. If you want darkness for dramatic effect, use a spotlight to illuminate the submissive and leave the rest of the room dark.

The secret to a satisfactory and safe whipping is to hit only fleshy, muscled meat. You don't want to hit skin that is pulled tightly over a bone, nor do you want to hit any place where internal organs are close to the surface. The primary safe zones are from *below* the shoulders to *above* the lower middle of the back (not including the spine), *below* the upper curve of the buttock to *above* the knees.

These are places where a moderate whipping is unlikely to do any permanent damage. The biceps and the back muscle of the lower legs are also acceptable targets. Extreme danger zones are the kidneys, spine, joints, hands, and feet. When whipping the upper back, avoid letting the whip hit inside the armpit. There is a nerve junction there that is quite vulnerable. Naturally, these danger areas also apply when something other than a whip—like a strap or cane—is being used. In these areas, you have to be very careful that the ends of a whip don't "wrap" around the body and hit there.

Other portions of the body, including cocks, balls, breasts and pussies can be whipped. (You were wondering when I was coming to those.) However, even more intense monitoring of the submissive's reactions must be maintained when you are stimulating these areas. For best results, a whip with 3- to 6-inch tails should be used for these areas. The shorter tail gives better control and allows you to concentrate the stimulation on the intended area, rather than having it spread about.

As a personal idiosyncrasy, I tend to prefer to stimulate

the genitals with a short strap or a riding crop. However, that is something that is completely personal. There is nothing wrong with a carefully and lovingly applied whip.

Whipping should always begin slowly so that you can increase the intensity as the excitement builds. Even submissives who insist "I'm not into whipping" can get quite turned on by a gentle introduction followed by a slow escalation. Here is where the soft, heavy whips come into their own.

For example, one technique would be first to require the submissive to kiss the whip you are going to use. Then, tie his or her hands to an overhead hook, stand behind the submissive, and just drape the whip over his or her shoulder, then slowly pull it back. The sensation of the soft leather mixed with the knowledge of what is coming next is almost impossible to stand. Next, very leisurely, whip the back lightly with a standard diagonal stroke and, walking slowly around the vertical body, whip the sides and front. Don't work at it—just flick the tails onto the skin. If you are hitting hard enough to tear a sheet of newsprint, you are hitting too hard. At this stage, don't worry about safe zones because you can't do any damage in any case. Obviously, the submissive's head and face are never legitimate targets, but the entire rest of the body is fair game.

Now, step up both the timing and the intensity of the strokes. One per second would be about right. Now you are at a point where the place where you are whipping is becoming important. For the rest of the session, do not allow your whip to strike in any of the danger zones.

Watch the marks left by the whip. Do only the amount of "damage" you are comfortable with. As you judge it appropriate, increase both the tempo and the force of the strokes, stopping every once in a while to stroke the submissive with the whip, your hand, or a piece of fur. Genital stimulation short of orgasm is appropriate here. However, the recess should not be longer than a minute, or you might lose the plateau that you have built.

Cane should be used full force only on the thickly muscled buttocks and thighs. However, they can be used *lightly* on the chest and upper back. In any case, you should remember that the cane is flexible and, for best results, you should *use* the flex instead of fighting it, as some novices do.

All caning should be done with the end of the cane placed beyond the submissive. Allowing the tip to hit skin is both bad form and likely to cause cuts and deep bruises.

Genital Shaving

While shaving—of and by itself—isn't limited to D&S, it often figures into scenes, and shaven genitalia have a special attraction to some people. Dominants often view them as symbols of possession, and submissives remark on how the "special, intimate" nakedness reminds them of their status.

As with so many other activities, success is often more a matter of preparation and follow-through than the actual execution. Many people who have tried genital shaving have been put off by the appearance of ugly red spots and itching and burning after the initial shave. While even intense stimulation during the scene can be an erotic turn-on, stimulation that appears hours later and continues for days is just annoying.

However, this unfortunate side effect of shaving can be

minimized by a few simple procedures. Trim the hair as short as possible with scissors or a clipper. The less tangle the razor has to deal with, the more smoothly it will cut. Steam the remaining hair with a towel soaked in hot water. This will both soften the hair and partially clean the skin.

Use shaving cream or shaving gel and a *slightly used* razor. This is very tender skin, and I have found that a razor which has been used once before is less likely to scrape than a brand-new one. An electric razor—especially one of those battery-driven units that is designed for use on a wet surface—can also be used.

Once the hair has been removed, wash the area with a mild soap and apply an antiseptic lotion. Although it has an unattractive color, Betadine is an excellent choice for this. The red marks are often caused by minor infections in nicks in the skin. By killing the bacteria on the skin's surface, you are reducing the chances of such an infection.

For this reason, the area should be cleaned regularly with a mild antiseptic. Four or five times a day during the first three days would not be excessive.

Regardless of the appearance of red marks, you should plan on shaving the submissive daily for at least four days, or he or she should be instructed to shave each day during that period. Eventually, the red marks should disappear.

Naturally, the shaving can be made part of the ritual of a scene. Bind the submissive for maximum exposure, and work slowly and carefully. An alternative approach is to have him or her kneel before you and do the shaving without assistance.

A straight razor makes an interesting prop, but requires a high degree of skill to use. Novice barbers train by scraping shaving cream off inflated balloons. Once you are capable of doing this without bursting the balloon, you should practice on your own body before exposing your submissive to your nascent skills. Also keep in mind that, regardless of your skills, if the submissive is incapable of remaining absolutely still, the razor can inflict serious injuries from the slightest twitch.

A safer and easier approach might be to sharpen the straight razor conspicuously while the submissive watches, and then blindfold him or her. Then put aside the straight razor and use a conventional safety razor for the actual shaving.

Suspension

Suspension is a touchstone of bondage films and fiction. Unfortunately, this has given many the perception that it is both indispensable to enjoyable bondage and is safe. *Both are wrong!*

Many people enjoy years of intense bondage activity without anyone's feet leaving the ground. There is nothing that makes suspension the sine qua non of bondage. On the contrary, suspension is an activity fraught with hazards—one that needs to be approached, if at all, with care, thought, and preparation.

Some of the physical conditions that would make suspension unwise are the submissive's having had his or her shoulders dislocated previously, diabetes, or any other condition that would restrict the flow of blood to the extremities. Suspension usually causes a shortness of breath because the rib cage is compressed by the body's weight, so think twice about suspending someone who has difficulty in breathing.

If you are intent on going ahead with suspension, I recommend having at least one additional person to assist you. While a two-person suspension scene is possible, a third person provides the extra margin of safety needed in the event of an emergency.

Where to Suspend

Your preeminent need is locating a suspension place. Ask any mountain climber; finding a place to support a person's weight safely is harder than you might realize.

After they succeed in pulling down the shower-curtain rod, the towel racks, and a closet hook or two, the next thing most people think of is sinking a screw eye through their ceiling and into a support. This has three basic problems.

First, if the supports are there—a significant number of modern buildings have surprisingly little support holding up the ceiling—how are you going to find them?

Knocking on the ceiling or using a stud detector (go ahead and pun) usually gives you a good-enough idea of a support's location to hang a picture, but consider what would happen if your screw eye did not hit the center of the support. As weight was applied, the screw would work its way sideways and, splitting the wood, it would come out unexpectedly through the side of the support. You must be able to *see* the support you are using.

Second, the supports between a ceiling and a floor are designed to accept pressure *from above*. There is no guarantee that they can stand a very concentrated pull on their underside, especially after you have weakened them with a hole that is an appreciable fraction of their total width.

Third, a vertical screw eye is one of the worst things you can use for suspension. *Never use anything that can unscrew.* What makes this specific situation so much worse is that if you use a screw eye vertically, weight on the eye makes it easier—not harder—for the screw to come out.

The safest support is something strong enough to support *three times the weight you intend to put on it* when that weight is bouncing up and down with enthusiasm. The safest way to attach something to that support is to use a length of chain looped up and over it and then bolted or snapped together.

That piece of information usually leads people to the cellar, where there are lots of pipes running along the ceiling. It is very easy to throw a length of chain over a pipe...and isn't a steel pipe strong enough to support almost anything?

True. However, not having energetic perverts in mind, most plumbers don't attach the pipe to the ceiling with clamps strong enough to support much more than the weight of the pipe. So, therefore, while steel pipes can be fashioned into an outstanding bondage-and-suspension frame, putting unexpected strains on the pipes that are in your house for other purposes isn't advisable.

Also, the pipe is likely to break if you pull it loose from its supports. If it is a water pipe, you will get very wet. If it is a sewer line, you will get very sorry. If it is a gas pipe, you will get very...

However, while you are in your basement, look at the floor supports. These are usually 2x6 or 2x12 boards on edge. These are relatively safe to use. Take an eyebolt (an eyebolt is like a screw eye, except that instead of ending in a point the grooved part has a nut on it), drill a hole through the support about two-thirds of the way up, put the bolt through and tighten it in place using washers to prevent either the eye or the nut from sinking into the wood. The part of the eye that is open, although bent back against the shaft, should be at the top, in the unlikely eventuality that it works its way open under stress. Some dominants use hooks instead of eyes. I avoid anything that can release the rope or chain unexpectedly. It may be easier to lift a rope or chain out of a hook than to pull one through an eye, but I see it as a safety factor, not an inconvenience.

Consider the load you are going to be putting on the bolt and get one more than large enough to handle it.

Because you are able to put things into this support horizontally, as opposed to one hidden behind a ceiling where the only approach is straight up, screw eyes can be used here. Vertical weight on a horizontal screw tends to hold it in place, rather than allowing it to work out. Again, drill the pilot hole about two-thirds of the way up, and make sure that the screw eye is big enough for the load.

This technique can also be used with exposed ceiling beams and with room supports in the attic. Some exposed beams in cathedral ceilings are some distance down from the ceiling itself, making it possible to run a rope or chain over and around them, eliminating the need for a eyebolt.

Suspension Gear

Suspension can be done with either rope, chain, or a combination of both.

The chain should have welded links. The light-duty chain with unwelded links or plastic decorative chain intended for supporting plants and lamps is completely unsuitable. Twisted-link chain is capable of supporting the strains on it, but it lacks aesthetics and is uncomfortable to work with—or even to brush against when it is under strain. If you are using locks and snap links, you should make sure that the individual links in the chain are large enough to accept them.

Snap links and locks can also be used when chain is attached to eyebolts either by directly linking the chain to the eyebolt or by having the end of the chain pulled through and then attached to itself with the snap link. Permanent connections between two chains or between the end of a chain and part of itself can be made with split links rather than the "S"-shaped pieces of chain material sold in some stores. These "S" links can open under pressure.

When using snap links as temporary connectors, you should note that it is difficult or impossible to open them under strain. At some point in your chain arrangement, you should have one or more panic snaps. These are snaps that are designed to open safely despite strain on the chains they are holding. Panic snaps allow you to release the submissive quickly and safely if something goes wrong. Obviously, panic snaps should never be located where suspended SAMs can get their hands on them.

Although it has never happened to me, I have heard about panic snaps breaking under stress. Because of this possibility, I recommend that you have a separate safety chain that bypasses the panic snap. Because this safety chain is not under stress while the panic snap is intact, you can use an ordinary snap link to attach it to the chain above the panic snap.

In an emergency, first disconnect the safety chain's snap

line. Then release the submissive, using the panic snap. However, if the panic snap breaks during the scene, the safety chain will take up the strain and prevent what could be a serious fall.

Locks can act as a kind of inferior panic snap; most can be opened under pressure. However, chains can get caught in the clasp's notch at the worst possible times. Only the best-quality locks should be used; inexpensive locks may open under strain. For a psychological effect, inexpensive locks can be used to fasten chains that already have snap or panic locks taking up the strain.

Keys should be clearly marked and kept on a hook near the suspension or on your person at all times, and spare keys should be kept in the first-aid kit.

The kind of care that is involved in tying knots for bondage is all the more important in suspension. This is not the place to have a poorly tied knot come undone or tighten unexpectedly.

Neither chain nor rope should be used against bare skin during suspension. I prefer heavily padded suspension cuffs designed for just that purpose. They have an extended brace so that submissives can grip the cuff itself and ease the pressure on their wrists. If you use conventional cuffs, make certain that the inside of the submissive's wrists, where the veins are, are toward the *outside*. This way the weight is borne by the outside of the wrists, and the danger of cutting off circulation is reduced. In any case, you must monitor circulation regularly and terminate suspension at any time you notice symptoms or your submissive reports numbness or chill in the supporting extremities.

Once you have everything—and everyone—rigged,

you still must suspend them. After all, that *is* what it is called: suspension. Even with rope through a simple pulley, it is difficult to lift a full-grown human; trying to pull links of chain through an eyebolt with more than 100 pounds of flesh on the other end is something that would challenge Conan.

With chain, the best approach is for the submissive to step off a box or other movable object, as in an old-time hanging. However, in this case, the drop—the distance between where the person is standing on the box and where she or he will be while hanging—should be not more than 4 inches. This short distance makes it possible to get back on the box after being exhausted by the session.

Most dominants, however, prefer to hoist their submissives into position. Auto-supply stores sell chain falls that are ideal for this purpose, and hoists are available from boating and hardware stores. The safest kind is a screw hoist, which uses a crank attached to a screw drive to turn the drum. Unfortunately, it lacks the wonderfully erotic click-click-click of the cam hoist. Surprisingly, the safety of the screw hoist is a disadvantage in an emergency. Because the cam hoist uses a cam riding on a notched wheel to prevent the cable from unwinding, it is possible to lower someone quickly by moving the crank to remove tension from the cam, lifting the cam off the notched wheel, and then letting the drum rotate freely as someone else supports the suspended person. Because of its design, a screw hoist cannot allow the drum to run free.

Do not expect to run the rope all the way to the hoist, which should be attached firmly to a wall or other immovable object. Rope—especially nylon rope—has an amazing ability to stretch. A 15-foot length of nylon rope can be expected to stretch to 25 to 30 feet under strain. Not only does that mean a lot of cranking before anyone leaves the ground, it also makes the suspended individual bounce in an annoying manner that is more comedic than erotic.

Use wire-cored plastic or wire cable to run most of the way from the hoist to the lifting rope or chain. The cable will not stretch, and the submissive will stay about where you want him or her. Where the cable has to change direction to convert the downward pull of the winch to a lift, you should use a pulley, both to cut down on the friction and because cable is more vulnerable to abrasion and more likely to abrade what it rubs against than rope.

When lowering and releasing a suspended submissive, you will welcome an extra set of hands. The submissive is likely to be confused and disoriented, both by the suspension and by the activities that went with them. Expect a sort of collapse, and be ready to support him or her when the strain is removed.

Inverted Suspension

Cuffs for inverted suspension are also available, but, if care is taken to protect the Achilles tendon, tight-fitting boots can also be used. The ideal devices, however, are the 1970s fad—gravity boots—which can occasionally be found at yard sales and flea markets. A more recent sport, bungee jumping, also provides suitable equipment for inverted suspension. The feeling of partial inverted suspension can also be obtained by using tables intended for meditation or relaxation therapy, to which someone can be strapped while the entire tabletop tilts.

Some submissives report that the feeling of being suspended in an inverted position mimics, in a somewhat safer way, erotic asphyxia, an extremely dangerous activity, but one that a number of people find stimulating. Unfortunately, this position also tends to cause sinus blockage. Because of this, the dominant should monitor the submissive's condition during inverted suspension even more carefully than during conventional suspension.

You should not suspend anyone in an inverted position who is extremely nearsighted, has glaucoma, high blood pressure, heart conditions, diabetes or other circulatory problems in the extremities.

Great care should be taken while raising and lowering the submissive. A moment's carelessness can result in a fall directly on the skull and back of the neck. A compression fracture can mean a lifetime as a quadriplegic.

A common-sense safety precaution is leaving the submissive's hands and arms free during hoisting, and releasing them prior to lowering. I also like to have a third party present to steady and support the submissive's body while I tend to the winching.

Supported Suspension

Supported suspension eliminates many of the problems inherent in conventional, by-the-wrist suspension while providing the off-the-ground, out-of-control feeling valued by submissives. In supported suspension, the primary stress is either distributed at several points or is placed so that it mimics the normal stresses of standing or sitting.

Obviously, regardless of how the submissive is suspended, there is no reduction in weight, so you shouldn't scrimp on the risers (supporting ropes or chains) or on how you attach them to the supports. None of the hardware requirements I have specified earlier are in any way relaxed.

The simplest and most popular form of supported suspension is the swing. This can be as simple as a child's swing, with the submissive's arms tied above the head along each of the risers. This way, the submissive's entire weight is resting on the horizontal board, and there is no pressure on the wrist ties.

More complex swings or bondage swings allow the submissive to lie back and have both his or her feet and hands firmly attached to the four supporting lines. These swings are often sheets of leather or canvas, or meshes made from broad nylon strapping. The support is more broadly spread and, because of this, these swings are more comfortable than the simple board.

Of course, with both of these swings, there is limited access to the parts of the body, the ass or the back, that is doing the supporting. However, a creative dominant can lower the conventional swing until it is just above floor height and have the submissive stand on the seat. Extra ropes can hold the ankles and wrists against the rope. In fact, the entire length of the arms and legs as well as the waist can be attached to the swing's risers. This leaves both the front and the back of the body available for stimulation.

A homemade swing with an extra-wide seat is useful here. In this way, the seat substitutes for a spreader bar and keeps the legs well apart. As with any spreader, you can include a place for a dildo or vibrator support.

A more complex solution to the problem of supported suspension utilizes a harness. These range from a simple climbing harness like those used by rock climbers to something similar to a parachute harness. In fact, enthusiasts often haunt flea markets and surplus stores and snap up surplus parachutes. The shroud fabric is useful for many applications. The chute cord can be used for decorative bondage where there is no tension on nerves or blood vessels, and the harness itself is a joy forever.

However, for those who are unable to obtain the conventional parachute harness or who find it unaesthetic, a leather harness can be acquired from a number of leather craft shops around the country—at a considerable cost.

To create one style of climbing harness, you need about 10 feet of nylon webbing of the sort sold in mountainsports shops and mentioned previously in this chapter, and a device called a carabinier from the same source. A carabinier is a kind of D-ring with a spring-loaded gate that snaps shut whenever you put something into the ring.

I prefer the 2-inch-wide nylon straps. The 3-inch-wide straps provide better support but are harder to tie. This fabric feels soft but there is a chance that it can abrade the submissive's skin. Dominants should be aware of this and monitor closely. Some dominants prefer to put lamb's wool or other padding under stress points.

Put the middle of the strap across the submissive's back and tie it over the navel with an overhand knot (first tie). The two free ends go between the legs. Each free end should cross one of the buttocks diagonally and then go under the horizontal strap at the point where the outside pants seam would be if you were nice enough to allow your submissive to wear pants. Bring both ends forward and knot them over the navel with a square knot (second tie). Now, take a carabinier and put both the first and second tie inside it.

That completes the climbing harness. The carabinier provides a point of attachment for your hoisting rope or chain. You may wish to tie the submissive's wrists to the hoisting rope or have him or her hold on while you lift. There is a certain tendency for people to hang upside down in this harness so, naturally, a behind-the-back wrist tie is a very dangerous idea unless you somehow secure the upper torso to the rope so this does not take place.

Suspension is a lot more difficult to do well and safely than most people realize. Many of the desired effects can be obtained by other, safer approaches, such as standing bondage or tight spread-eagled bondage. However, if you and your submissive feel that suspension is what you desire, do it carefully and sensibly.

Waxing

Candles. They cast such a lovely glow across the bedroom or dungeon. Their gentle light hides and reveals. Their flickering flames draw the eye like little magnets. In the scene, candles can also perform another function: waxing. At first, it may sound horrifying. Dripping hot candle wax on bare skin will certainly sound horrifying to a novice submissive.

However, properly applied candle wax can be no more stimulating than a brisk spanking and considerably less so than whipping. The secrets are choosing the right candles and letting the wax cool by letting it fall a distance before it hits the skin.

Most novices attempting their first waxing are likely to go out and buy expensive candles. After all, this is a special occasion; it calls for special candles. Unfortunately, these are precisely the wrong candles to use. Expensive candles are, almost always, made from beeswax. This is because it is easier to mold into exotic shapes and burns for a long time.

Unfortunately, the reason a beeswax candle lasts for a long time is that it has a melting point considerably higher than the cheaper paraffin. The stimulation caused by melted beeswax striking the skin is very likely to exceed a submissive's ability to transmute it into pleasure. This, in turn, can lead to a truncated session and general unhappiness all around.

The best candles to begin with are the cheapest: the ugly white votive candles sold for chafing dishes and such, or standard Jewish Sabbath candles. I recommend that you test the temperature of any candle before using it on a submissive by letting it drip from various heights onto the skin on the underside of your forearm. Unless you know the various intensities, you will be unable to judge precisely how far away to hold the candles.

In my first waxing session with a submissive, I prefer to have her tied down firmly. This is because the stimulation provided by the hot wax can inspire considerable thrashing around. However, once she is familiar with it, I can generally forgo bonds unless they are needed for psychological reasons.

Generally, I begin dripping the wax at a height of three feet, slowly working downward as I feel her going into that transcendental state. The final height depends on where I want her and what I am planning for the rest of the session. I also keep a bowl of ice cubes handy. They come in handy for chilling down a bit of wax that was too hot, and they *are* handy for some erotic techniques I'll describe later.

Dripping can be done in several ways. You can hold the

candle horizontally and rotate it with your fingers so that the top is melted evenly and the drips are fairly regular. To speed up the dripping, you can lower the lit end so the flame is flowing over the wax. To get better control of the timing of the drips, you can tip the candle, drop a bit of wax, and then return it to an upright position until you want to drop a bit more wax.

Splashing is more shocking. You allow a pool of wax to build up in the candle and then dash it on the submissive's body. Because of the unexpectedness of the action and because the larger quantity of wax holds heat better, this is much more stimulating. Another way to splash is to use a brandy warmer, one of those little gadgets that holds a brandy glass above a small alcohol lamp. (Personally, I cannot imagine a better way to ruin the bouquet of a fine brandy by overheating, but it does lend itself to waxing.)

Simply take some wax; the flakes you remove from your submissive at the end of a session are fine. (Recycling can be fun.) Put the wax in a brandy glass and let it sit over the flame until the wax is melted. You can then slowly dribble the melted wax or dash the contents all at once. *Warning:* test the temperature of the wax with a finger before using it; the alcohol flame can raise the temperature of the wax considerably above the melting point. Also, a pool of wax will not cool anywhere nearly as fast as single drops. If it does not run off as a thin sheet, spread it around with your fingers or use an ice cube (more on that soon) to cool it down.

If one candle is good, aren't more better? I wonder how many antique candelabra are sold for purposes that the dealer couldn't even guess at. This is particularly effective with different-colored candles (more soon on colored candles) in each cup. Some dominants like to spin the candelabrum so the wax literally flies off the candles. Of course, this makes a major-league mess and often results in the dominant getting as completely waxed as the submissive. But it *is* spectacular.

With a little common sense, the entire body is an appropriate target. Obviously, open sores, eyes, and vulnerable places like that are off limits, but more than one man has watched in pleasurable horror as his mistress has converted his cock to a surreal wax sculpture.

Colored candles burn hotter and contain dyes that can irritate a submissive's skin. For this reason, I do not use them during an initiation to waxing. Normally, I'll add a few drips of each color in my "paintbox" to the next session. Later, I carefully examine where each of the drops landed. All by itself, this examination can be fun. If there is any redness or irritation, the color which caused it is off limits in future sessions.

Colored candles also allow the artist in the dominant to come forth. It is possible to produce very attractive designs using your submissive as a canvas. One of M's greatest pleasures was to parade around the Hellfire club or Fetish Factor clad primarily in different colors of wax.

Avoid dripless candles. They contain chemicals that are very likely to irritate skin.

D&S is a study in contrasts. This is nowhere more appropriate than in a waxing scene. There is no reason why you have to limit yourself to hot wax. Drop by the kitchen for a refreshing drink and pick up a glassful of ice cubes while you are there.

There is a host of ways to combine fire and ice. The simplest is to alternate touches: nipple, cold; neck, hot; stomach, cold; armpit, hot. Particularly if the submissive is blindfolded, it is amusing to vary the kinds of stimulation randomly. It keeps the submissive guessing.

Another approach is to use both on the same spot. For example, a section of skin is chilled for a few seconds with the ice cube and then receives a splash of hot wax. After a while, your submissive may be surprised to discover that he or she can no longer distinguish between hot and cold.

Most waxing is done with the submissive horizontal. That affords the maximum of available targets and the easiest application. However, sometimes this may not be possible or aesthetic. A vertical body calls for some variations in technique.

First, and obvious, is to use or create horizontal surfaces on which to drip the wax. Some are natural—breasts and cocks come immediately to mind—but don't forget feet and shoulders. If a man has allowed himself to become so out of shape as to develop a potbelly, this an obvious time to make him regret his lack of exercise. The head can be bent forward or back to put the neck in an appropriate position for waxing, and legs and arms can be brought out to the horizontal.

One danger should be noted here. Keep a close eye on what is above your candle flame. I was present when a careless mistress badly burned a submissive's stomach while she was waxing his cock. True, his protruding stomach was most unattractive, but the injury was unintentional—an indefensible error for a dominant.

Vertical bodies are also appropriate for the splashing technique noted earlier. However, you must exercise care that the forward, toward-the-submissive motion is as smooth as possible. Jerking when you begin your "toss" is likely to splash wax on you or waste it on the floor. The jerk should come as the candle stops its forward motion so that the liquid wax is projected toward the submissive with skill and accuracy.

There is a wealth of ways to remove wax. One is simply to allow the submissive to wear the wax. M, the first submissive with whom I tried the brandy-glass trick, greatly enjoyed being paraded around wearing little but cooled wax. Of course, this option in a less-public place may mean that flakes of wax will be turning up in the most unlikely places for the next millennium.

Of course, the submissive can be set to removing his or her wax, but I feel this is declining an opportunity for me to get in a bit of additional provocative stimulation. It can, however, be visually amusing, especially when the submissive is forced to remove significant amounts of body hair along with the wax.

While this advice is superfluous when the submissive is removing the wax, the wax should be allowed to cool completely before the dominant begins to remove it. This makes removal easier.

You can, of course, pick the wax off with your fingers. This method is particularly alluring when done by a female dominant with long, attractive fingernails. Other dominants attempt to whip the flakes of wax off the submissive's skin. My preference is for a large, sharp knife. (For personal protection, I generally eschew large knives. After all, vital organs are rarely more than two inches away from an opponent's skin. However, the scene puts image above practicality.) Watching a submissive's widened eyes following the shiny steel sliding over her breast and caressing her nipple while the flakes of wax are removed can be a most delightful experience.

There are two pre-waxing exercises that can make the wax removal much easier. The more erotic of the two is shaving. Most people have fine hairs over most of the body, not to mention the not-so-fine collection at several of the most logical targets for waxing. When these hairs are trapped by the cooling wax, it becomes quite difficult and time consuming to remove the result. (See the section on shaving in the "Fun and Games" chapter.)

Another approach that makes wax removal a snap is using plastic wrap. Both ordinary kitchen plastic wrap and the industrial-strength product conduct heat and cold quite efficiently and provide a surface to which the wax will not cling. Prior to waxing, you can elect to mummify (see comments on mummification in the "Bondage" section in the "Fun and Games" chapter.), or you can simply put the plastic firmly over the sections to be waxed.

In most cases, the plastic wrap goes on quite tightly and sticks very well. Unfortunately, this is not true in the case of the genitalia. Both cocks and balls and pussies are so irregular—and often so hairy—that the plastic wrap cannot find a smooth surface on which to stick.

This problem can be remedied by taping both ends of the plastic. Some people use masking tape. I have found the clear plastic tape sold in hardware and stationary stores for sealing boxes is better. Because it comes in 3-inch-wide rolls, there is plenty of adhesive surface to distribute between the plastic wrap and the skin. It also bonds quite effectively to skin.

Have the submissive lie on his or her back; attach one

end of the plastic wrap to the stomach; have the submissive roll over; pull the plastic *tight* and attach the other end to the back. Not only will the heat or cold be transmitted directly to the submissive's skin through the tightly drawn plastic wrap, the sight of the "shrink-wrapped meat" is an appropriate topic for light banter.

Wax removal consists simply of removing the plastic wrap. The wax comes right off with it.

Fire on Skin

A more spectacular—and a bit more dangerous—activity akin to waxing is putting fire itself directly onto the submissive's body. The trick to use a mixture of ethyl alcohol and water, rather than pure alcohol. You can obtain ethyl alcohol at chemical supply stores or by buying Everclear at a liquor store. Rubbing (isopropyl) alcohol will also work but not as well.

Put about an inch of water in a glass; add a bit of alcohol. After you add the alcohol, dip a stick into the mixture and then touch the wet stick with a flame. If the mixture burns, you have the right concentration. If it does not, add a bit more alcohol. The secret is to have a minimum of alcohol and a maximum of water so the water can form a protective film of steam between the fire and the skin.

Next, take an applicator (I use a Q-tip for testing) and rub a bit of the alcohol-water mixture on your arm. After all, we use submissives for play, but we test techniques on ourselves. Dip the Q-tip again and light it; then touch it to the wet spot on your arm. If the mixture is right, you will get a patch of blue flame that will burn for a moment and then go out. It should feel hot, but not especially painful. I'll talk more about that "interesting" smell later.

During a scene, I use a riding crop with a relatively narrow slapper as an applicator. I wet the slapper and place a bit of mixture on the submissive and then use the wet slapper as a torch to ignite it. If the fire burns for more than a second or two, I put it out with my own hand. Letting it burn for too long can lead to a first-degree burn.

This technique works best in a relatively darkened room so the pale flames stand out. Although the intensity of the stimulation from the burning mixture is slightly less than would be experienced from a close-in waxing, the psychological effect the submissive feels watching his or her own skin flickering with a bluish flame is quite intense.

When I set up for this scene, I try to avoid areas with strong drafts from fans or air conditioners. These either blow out the flame prematurely or cause it to burn in unexpected directions.

Obviously, you shouldn't put the mixture anywhere where you wouldn't put alcohol (e.g., mucous membranes, on the face). Also, as with candles, you should also be careful that the flame does not burn anywhere where there is something above it. For example, do not allow it to run under a breast where the flame will be burning upward against the skin. The vapor barrier works only when it is *below* the active flame.

As I have noted before, if you get careless about making up the mixture or using the technique, you can cause a first-degree burn. This is where a bowl of ice cubes like those used in waxing scenes comes in handy. First aid for minor burns is covered in the first-aid section.

One effect of the flaming-skin technique is that it will burn off body hair because hairs stick up into the active flame area. Because I have a sensitive nose, I avoid areas where much hair will be cremated, but I know some, especially female dominants, who use this odor as an effective intimidation tool—and, of course, this technique can be used to remove body hair before a waxing session.

Humiliation

Nowhere is the difference between the psychologies of male and female submissives so markedly different as on the subject of humiliation. While any generalization is suspect, and I am scarcely an expert on *all* submissives, the gender differences I have observed are much too consistent to ignore.

The majority of male submissives seem to crave some degree of humiliation as part of their servitude. Sometimes this craving is for extremely intense humiliation. The vast majority of female submissives—even those who seek out intense physical stimulation—seem turned off by humiliation. This, of course, does not mean that all women reject humiliation as part of a scene. I have met a few whose cravings are fully as intense as those of any man. However, this is an activity which a male dominant should approach with caution.

A quite handsome English gentleman came to the Eulenspiegel Society meeting one night. He was middle-aged, with a ramrod-straight posture and a neatly trimmed thin mustache. It was quite clear that he was making a most positive impression on the ladies, especially the unattached submissive ladies.

However, later, during a general discussion among members and visitors about their needs and desires, he said that what he enjoyed most was humiliating a woman. While condemnation and criticism of another's orientation is unthinkable in that environment and no one moved an inch after he had said it, I got the definite impression that a vast gulf had opened up between him and the women who, until he made that comment, had been hanging on his every word. Later, one submissive woman commented, "Damn, up to then, he was turning me on."

Male submissives often have a very different outlook. At another meeting, a submissive man recounted, before a rapt and admiring audience of other male submissives, how his girlfriend had lured him into the woods with the promise of sex, made him strip, rolled him in mud, urinated on him, and left him naked and bound.

Part of the answer to this difference may be that one essence of D&S is contrast. Consider that the only women I have ever found deeply attracted to this role were strong, intelligent, and forceful. Many say it is precisely the surrender of control that is so seductive.

Taking it from this point of view, you can see why humiliation is not attractive to most women. It offers little contrast between many women's daily lives and the scene. They are served a full daily diet of humiliation by our society. They hardly need to seek more.

Men, on the other hand, are largely shielded from humiliation and, when they experience it, are permitted by society to strike back, often in a physical manner. To experience humiliation in a controlled environment is a novel and exotic experience.

Another explanation for the love of many male submissives for humiliation was put forward by Michele, a lovely and intellectually dynamic female submissive. Her suggestion was that, because men are dominant and controlling, they are unable to tell whether a women desires them for their power or for themselves. If a woman strips them of their power, their dignity, and self-respect, and still cares for them, they are reassured of their essential worth.

A submissive man explained his love for humiliation by citing the Woody Allenism that sex feels dirty only if you are doing it right. "I guess that I feel a bit of shame at my submissive tendencies. Humiliation plays on this, magnifying it and making it more intense, more 'forbidden' and, therefore, more desirable."

To further confuse the issue, humiliation is quite different from embarrassment. Quite a large number of submissives of both sexes are turned on by embarrassment. To me, the primary difference between humiliation and embarrassment is how the activity causes the submissive to feel about himself or herself. Humiliation degrades, causes the person to feel that he or she is less valued and treasured, while embarrassment can bring out a greater sense of self-worth.

Here is an illustration quite separate from the scene itself. Imagine that you are at a formal dinner and the speaker says several complimentary things about you, then asks you to come up and say a few words. You might be embarrassed by the activity, but it would make you feel that you were valued. Then, as you walk to the rostrum, the speaker steps forward and pulls your pants down, and the audience laughs. *That* is humiliation. There is no gain or advancement there.

Recently, there was a Best Submissive contest at Manray, a local D&S club. I entered Libby, one of my submissives, in it. She was embarrassed as I led her to the stage, but was also turned on that I thought enough of her to enter her. She was also flattered by the attention of the audience. However, when one uncouth type called out during the whipping, "Hit her harder," I spun and snapped my whip within inches of his face. He shut up. His cry humiliated her, and I would not stand for it.

In short, embarrassment is what happens when you force submissives to do what they would like to do anyway if society and their own inhibitions would let them. Humiliation originates outside and is imposed from outside.

As with many psychological aspects of the scene, humiliation can hurt more than any whip. Also, the "level of discomfort" seems to build at an exponential rather than an arithmetic rate. For this reason, I strongly suggest to my submissive that, as soon as the humiliation seems to be building to an intolerable point, she should use her safe word. Macho shit on the part of the submissive can do more lasting damage in this kind of scene than in any other.

Another factor to consider is that humiliation often occurs in a public place. I am of mixed feelings about these scenes. They seem to be a terrific turn-on for those who enjoy them, and in a place like the Hellfire club, where everyone knows what is going on, there is no problem. However, an axiom of the scene is consent—consent by everyone in the scene. A woman walking her five-year-old in a public park did *not* give her consent to be confronted by a half-naked man being led on a chain.

I'm not ruling out the public places. However, I ask that you think carefully before forcing members of the public to be part of your scene. Spencer's M greatly enjoys public bondage. I have taken her for walks in Central Park with her hands tied behind her back. But the ropes were hidden by an artfully draped coat. Another time, her master, Spencer, displayed her at The Renaissance Faire in chain bondage. However, both of them were in period costume, and she was presented as a witch on the way to the stake. In each case, the public was used—not abused.

There are many techniques for humiliation. Because this activity is an almost exclusively male penchant, I will use the masculine pronoun from here on in.

Forced cross-dressing is a potent tool. The incongruity of a male form in female clothing is often enough. However, when the clothes in question are especially frilly or feminine, the effect is quite marked. Perhaps the height of this approach is to force him to wear a negligee or outlandishly erotic garments. The inherent instability of a man in high heels and a French maid's costume is a subtle but effective means of bondage.

Baby clothing is wonderfully humiliating attire. Several manufacturers have lines of oversized diapers and other items intended for the middle-aged "baby." Forbidding the use of toilets because the "baby" is too young for them and requiring him to use diapers augments the indignity.

Men have filled the English vocabulary with insulting terms for women. It is completely appropriate to use these terms on the "horny slut" who grovels at your feet. However, don't neglect the animal kingdom in your search for the appropriate term.

As cleaning has largely been the work of women, putting him to work, especially in appropriate clothing, can be an effective humiliation. There is no need to make his work easy. Toothbrushes do a better—if slower—job than scrub brushes, and mildew is best removed with a Q-tip and toothpick.

A dominant friend has a toilet brush that has been reshaped to be held in the clenched teeth. As she puts it, "This brush puts him close to his work." She also rewarded a submissive who had been cleaning her bathroom for several hours with a beating. She explained that he had missed something. When he returned to his labors, he discovered that she had shit in the middle of the floor.

Food can be a source for humiliation. Obviously, baby bottles and formula can be used, and as formula often causes diarrhea in adults, this will lead to more productive use of the diaper. However, the consumption of almost any foodstuff without use of the hands can be humiliating, especially if a firm grasp on the hair is used to "assist" the process.

I had one of those rare female submissives who desired humiliation. Her specific scene was "treat-me-like-a-dog." To this end, I had her name placed on a dog dish. She thought it was just a bit of scene setting until I emptied a can of a popular brand of dog food into it and commanded her to eat. Later, she admitted that she had come within a hair's breadth of her breaking point.

While real dog food is perfectly safe to eat occasionally, as some elderly people on a fixed income have discovered, I had cleaned out the can without her knowledge and replaced the contents with beef stew. She remained unaware of the substitution throughout the scene.

We all remember the scene in *Robinson Crusoe* where Friday, in submitting to his master, puts Crusoe's foot on his head. There is something powerfully evocative about the foot. Foot play can be an important part of a humiliation session. Simply having the submissive remove your shoes and get down on all fours so you can use him as a hassock is a good way to begin. While you are comfortably reclined, you can consider other activities.

Look down at your feet. Are they perfect? If not, it is his fault, and he should rectify the situation. Set him to work washing your feet (you may specify tongue or a soft cloth—or both), then clipping, smoothing, and painting your nails. Foot massage feels heavenly, and any slacking or carelessness should be punished.

A perfect position for all this is to have him lie on his back with his feet and legs under your chair. His cock and balls should be directly under the front edge of the chair. With him in this position, you can knead his cock with one foot while extending the other for his loving attention.

Food can be combined with feet for further humiliation. A bit of food on the foot is offered to the submissive, and he is required to lick it off. For more intense humiliation, grind your feet into the food before offering it to him. If you leave dirty footprints on the floor, so much the better. He can clean them, too.

Too often, submissives from whom we demand oral services become overly enamored of what they see as a power to give pleasure. This attitude should be carefully guarded against. Prior to her initial submission, the editor of a well-respected magazine expressed a certain interest in humiliation, and also said she had a justified pride in her skill at fellatio. Early in the scene that followed, I reclined in a chair and directed her to demonstrate her vaunted oral skills.

Her expression of nonchalant confidence vanished when, after she had made only a few tentative licks, I put my foot on her shoulder and pushed her backward to the floor. "You are careless and clumsy," I shouted. "You don't deserve my cock. Here, practice on this." And I extended my foot. After a few minutes, I let her, chastened and contrite, return to her original task. Later she admitted that it was one of her most exciting experiences, precisely because it was so unexpected.

Before the appearance of AIDS and an increased sensitivity to the threat of disease, humiliation scenes occasionally included the forced consumption of urine or feces from the mistress. Obviously, this is no longer acceptable behavior. If you and your submissive have a strong desire for this sort of scene, collect *his* urine and feces for the "meal."

Medical authorities give mixed opinions about the use of urine and feces on the body. The majority seems to hold that this practice constitutes no serious danger if done on unbroken skin and well away from mucous membranes. Others consider the potential risk as still too great to be acceptable.

Enemas

Enemas are occasionally used as a sensual/discipline/stimulation device in D&S. My observation is that they seem to be used most frequently by gays and by female-dominant couples. However, they are far from unknown in male-dominant games.

The theory is quite simple. A quantity of water or water-based substance is placed in the lower bowels through the rectum. It is held for a period of time and then released. The practice admits quite a bit more variation.

For one thing, there is a strong psychological element in giving and receiving an enema. First—and most obvious—is the humiliating position and the sense of being invaded in a most intimate area. Moreover, many find it exciting that you are taking away their control of one of the most forbidden bodily functions. People—especially men—can adapt to urinating in public; but almost everyone retreats into privacy where defecation is involved.

The enema also brings into play an intense contrast: the submissive will want mightily to defecate but can do so only with your permission. You are commanding something that lies close to the innermost being of the submissive.

The mechanics are easily mastered. For example, while water is often used, medical authorities suggest adding two teaspoons of salt per quart to minimize negative effects from the enema. A small amount of castile soap or Liquid Ivory creates a cramping effect that some D&S practitioners seek. Castile soap is available in gourmet and camping stores.

Although some enema players have been known to use dilute alcohol, this *is not* a good idea. The lining of the intestine is more permeable to alcohol than the stomach, and it is impossible to judge a safe dilution. Alcohol poisoning can be *lethal*. In any case, even a slightly drunk submissive cannot properly judge tolerances and limits and therefore cannot judge when to use the safe word.

Hot (not scalding) and cold water can be used to produce different effects. Again, as with all D&S techniques, this is something the dominant should try on himself or herself before using on a submissive.

For safety reasons, no more than two quarts of liquid should be used in any single "cleansing" operation, and the bag containing the solution should not be more than

24 inches (some authorities recommend no more than 18 inches) above the anus to keep the pressure from becoming too great.

Although enema bags come with their own nozzles, gay and D&S suppliers have come up with a multitude of specialized types, including some that are actually modified dildos and buttplugs. One popular commercial type of nozzle is the Bardex, which has a balloon tip. This tip can be expanded after it has been inserted in the anus to prevent the tube's being expelled.

Always use an enema bag or syringe. I have seen arrangements where tubes were connected directly to faucets. However, unless there are complex control systems (like those used in photo-processing labs), you will be unable to control the pressure and temperature reliably this way.

While wearing gloves, lubricate the rectum with K-Y or other water-based lubricant, let a bit of fluid run out of the nozzle to make sure that there is no air in the tube and then insert the nozzle no more than 3 to 4 inches into the anal canal. Be careful. The lining of the intestines is much more delicate than skin, and a tear or puncture is very dangerous.

Insertion can be made with the submissive in a "bend-over-and-grab-your-ankles" position, kneeling with his or her head on the floor, or lying on his or her side. Insertion while the submissive is in a seated position is possible, but I believe there is too great a chance of ripping the intestinal wall in this position.

After the submissive has been "filled," you can remove the nozzle—if you are using a Bardex, deflate it first—and replace it with a buttplug, available in most sexual-supply stores. Do not use a dildo unless it has some guard to prevent it from completely entering the anus. If there is nothing to keep dildos from going in all the way, they can be "lost" in the rectum.

After an enema session, the submissive may complain about diarrhea or gas. This can be dealt with through a diet of yogurt (sorry, the frozen kind does not work) or through packets of intestinal bacteria that can be purchased from a drugstore.

If cramping continues more than one hour after the session ends, or if there is a bloody discharge, go to an emergency room.

The effects of an enema can last for several hours, and you should be prepared for "accidents," especially when a submissive has an orgasm. If such an accident happens over a sheet of plastic, it can give you an excuse for a delightfully scathing and humiliating lecture; however, should you be unprepared, it can be a messy and inconvenient end to an up-to-then enjoyable scene.

Fisting

While neither anal nor vaginal fisting is a D&S activity per se, both are commonly used by members of the scene as part of their play. Naturally, the first rule is play safely. The human body is a remarkably resilient device, but the linings of the anus and the vagina are much more delicate than the skin. A jagged fingernail can create havoc.

Prior to the AIDS epidemic, in the lesbian community—even more than the red handkerchief in her left pants pocket—the mark of a fister was a right or left hand with short, carefully filed nails. Now, of course, any responsible fister dons latex gloves before beginning, so the length of the nails is of less importance.

The best gloves are individually packaged surgical gloves. They not only fit better, but they are a bit longer than the laboratory gloves which come in large packages. If you are going to do anal fisting, which often involves deeper penetration than vaginal, you might like to use a "calving glove," which has a longer sleeve. These are available from farm-supply stores. Anal scenes should also be preceded by one or two enemas to clean the area.

There are two requirements for a fisting: lubrication and patience. *There is no such thing as too much lubrication.* I tend to favor ForePlay, Probe, or Elbow Grease, but any thick sexual lubricant is satisfactory. K-Y tends to be a bit too thin and dries too quickly for my taste, but others use it.

Crisco, an icon of the fist-fucking scene, is rapidly fading from popularity because it is a very effective culture medium for bacteria. Those who still use it are careful to avoid contaminating their supply jar. Before the scene, a quantity of Crisco is placed in a smaller container—or containers, if there is to be more than one submissive. If there is any left after the scene, it is discarded.

The secret of a good fisting is to seduce the body into doing something it doesn't expect that it can do. Fiction may show the dominant smashing a dripping fist into someone's arse or cunt; but, in real life, it is a much more gradual process.

A single finger at a time, you touch and tantalize. Only when the body is comfortable with the intrusion do you add another finger. The process is not a simple progression. For best results, it is more a series of advances followed by slight withdrawals. Both verbal and tactile communication should continue throughout the process with the intent of soothing the submissive's very real fears and building the sexual tension.

The crux comes with the insertion of the thumb and the advance of the knuckles through the quivering ring of tightly stretched muscle. The alignment of the hand should be up and down rather than horizontal at this point, and generally entry can be made with a gentle rocking motion rather than a direct push.

Once you feel the muscle closing around your wrist, pause for a moment and reassure the submissive that everything is all right. Then begin a gentle series of motions with your encased fist. One of my favorites is to open and close my fingers slowly and gently.

The hand's strongest muscles are flexors in the palmar fascia which are responsible for closing the fingers. The extensor muscles on the back of the hand are relatively weak. However, I have found that they can be strengthened somewhat by enclosing the thumb and fingers with a heavy elastic and exercising by repeatedly opening the hand against pressure.

You can also use a push-pull motion or rotate your wrist. The important thing is to do everything slowly and carefully. You want to stretch and stimulate, not tear.

At this time, if you are fisting a vagina, you can also slide a lubricated gloved or cotted finger (a finger cot is a condom for a finger) into her ass. It is best if you plan this ahead of time. Putting on a latex glove with the other hand trapped in a vagina is an exercise in creativity—and frustration.

Don't get over-enthusiastic; a little goes a long way. One or two fingers is plenty. Once your other hand has touched the ass, do not use it to touch anywhere near the vagina.

When the session is over, removal should be gradual, so as not to shock the system or, in the case of anal fisting, "prolapsing the rectum," in effect turning the submissive inside out.

The opinions on a slight amount of blood from an anal fisting vary. Some individuals feel that it can be ignored; others insist that any blood at all is cause for major concern. My gut feeling (yes, I meant to say that) is that fecal material (shit) and blood just don't mix. Peritonitis is a lousy way to die. There is no disagreement about a significant amount of blood. Go to an emergency room *immediately*.

The vagina is a bit safer environment, so a smear or two of blood is probably nothing to be concerned about. However, again, a significant amount of blood is a sign that something very serious is going on. Go to an emergency room.

Cutting and Pricking

Contrary to what most vanilla people think, ordinary cuttings and temporary piercings (prickings) are not extremely painful. The primary impact of the scene is in the submissive's head. Having metal penetrate our skin touches something deep in our primal instincts. Of course, some of the more "creative" approaches also can cause intense stimulation that could easily pass the pleasure/pain threshold.

Cutting and pricking should be done only after the most careful consideration of the risks and ramifications. The skin is the body's first line of defense against disease. While this has always been true, AIDS and hepatitis have made it literally a matter of life and death. In fact, anyone who is planning to do this activity should seriously think about getting vaccinated for hepatitis B.

While pricking almost never leaves a scar, cutting may, depending on a person's physical makeup. This is particularly true of those with an African genetic heritage. People from that part of the world seem to have a marked tendency to develop keloid tissue over cuttings. Therefore, the possibility of a permanent marking from even a small cutting cannot be ignored.

Never penetrate the skin casually. While the preparations for a relatively safe cutting or pricking may interrupt the flow of a scene, aesthetic considerations have to give way to safety. Cleanliness is a primary consideration. Both the area to be played with and the tools you are going to use must be absolutely clean. Despite sterilization procedures, you should *never* use the same tools on different people.

The submissive must be absolutely immobile. For any initial play of this type, regardless of a submissive's certainty of her ability to remain still or our mutual experience with other forms of stimulation, I insist on using stringent bondage techniques. A futon frame is perfect for this because its slats provide a multitude of tie-down points.

Later, as I become more familiar with the submissive's ability to handle this specific stimulation, I may forgo the bondage. However, I always remain acutely aware that a single unexpected, involuntary movement on the part of the submissive could have serious repercussions.

Always wear latex gloves. Not only are you broaching your submissive's skin, you will also be exposed to his or her blood. In today's world, anyone's blood has to be considered a bio-hazardous material. A tiny hangnail or scratch on your hand might expose you to an unacceptable risk. However, keep in mind that gloves *do not provide a protection against needles or blades*. Anything that can penetrate skin can go right through latex. A moment's carelessness with a needle or a blade can still be fatal.

The best gloves are surgical gloves that come packaged in separate sterile containers. Ordinary lab gloves will do, although they do not provide the tactile sensitivity of surgeon's gloves. Remember that lab gloves are not sterile. Wash your hands with Betadine after putting the gloves on.

Be generous with the antiseptic when sterilizing the part of the submissive's body with which you will be playing. Some dominants use Betadine for sterilizing the skin. It is cheap, and the submissive shivers so delightfully both at its chill and at what it promises for the future. Betadine does a better job than rubbing alcohol, but has a distinctly unappetizing color. However, you can first sterilize with Betadine and, then, after a minute or so, clean it off with alcohol and have a fairly sterile area.

Whatever you use, spread it around with your gloved hands. This is both sensual and helps makes sure that any airborne bacteria that have landed on the gloves will have a short and unhappy life.

In my opinion, the best toy for a cutting is a surgical scalpel. It is easy to handle because it is designed for exactly what we are setting out to do. Also, it is much sharper than art or (shudder) utility knives. Sharpness is very important. A sharp blade is less likely to result in an unintentional scar. Also, you want to be able to work as smoothly as possible. One-piece scalpels are intended to be discarded after each use. Others are made so that the blade can be replaced with a new, sterile one. In any case, you should never use the same edge on different individuals. Straight razors with disposable blades are also used by some dominants. These can be obtained from beauty-shop-supply stores.

I met a West Coast dominant who carried a tiny knife in a locket between her breasts. Seeing her extract the knife from the hidden scabbard was a distinct turn-on, but I think I'll still stick with my scalpels.

I like to use acupuncture needles in my pricking scenes. They are very thin and easy to use. The address of Eastern Currents, an acupuncture mail-order supply house is in the appendix. For more intense stimulation, I use beading needles from a craft store. Other dominants use medical suturing needles or those designed for carotid angiography or arterial catheterization. In locations where they can be legally obtained, hypodermic tips are popular. The popular sizes of hypodermic tips range from 25 (quite small) to 10 (Oh, my, you're going to stick *that* in me?). Sail needles are also popular because of their curved shape.

Except for those packaged for medical use, the needles must be sterilized. The ideal sterilization tool is an autoclave, a device that disinfects with live steam. However, if you don't work in a hospital or a laboratory, you can use a pressure cooker. Keep the pressure up for at least 40 minutes.

Ideally, needles should be thrown way after each scene. In no case, regardless of sterilization, should a needle that has been used on one submissive be used on another.

Naturally, neither cutting nor pricking should be done in any area where joints, nerves, or blood vessels are close to the surface. Safer—but not absolutely safe—places are the upper arms and legs and buttocks.

When cutting, hold the blade perpendicular to the surface of the body. Begin with a light pressure and increase it only to the point that the blade breaks the skin. You are doing a shallow, erotic cut, not dissecting a frog in biology class. Take your time. Allow the first cut to clot before you begin the second.

When you are finished, lightly swab the entire surface again with a Betadine-soaked pad. Some people, to make the cutting *permanently visible*, put a bit of autoclaved ink on the skin before wiping it. The ink is then trapped under the skin when it heals and makes a tattoolike mark. Remember, this is permanent. It will not go away, and surgical removal is troublesome and not always effective.

In the pre-AIDS/hepatitis era, it wasn't unusual for a dominant to taste the blood from a cutting. I greatly enjoyed doing this; in that day, it was a powerfully symbolic bit of eroticism. Today, doing such a thing is a form of feebleminded Russian roulette.

Unlike a cutting blade's vertical position, needles should be put into the skin at a very sharp angle. The intent is not to penetrate deeply (there is little sensation below the skin), but to produce the desired stimulation. Grip the needle firmly close to the tip to minimize any wiggle and insert it smoothly. I use a hemostat to get a good grip. If you want to insert it farther, slide your grip farther back and push again. You can even have the tip come back out through the skin. When the needle is removed, it is important to disinfect the area again.

Some people create further excitement by making several prickings and connecting them with sterilized thread. I have observed very erotic scenes in which several submissives were connected with threads running between their temporary piercings. However, several medical authorities have warned that sterilizing thread can be extremely tricky.

Permanent Piercings

A friend summed up the difference between nonpierced people and pierced people succinctly: "Pierced people don't wonder what it would be like *not* to have a piercing."

While some people do permanent piercing as part of a scene, I prefer to leave that to professionals because the puncture will remain open for a significant length of time and because there are considerations regarding placement and such that require experienced judgment.

You'll find that most piercing professionals are very obliging—if not active—members of the scene, and they will usually go out of their way to accommodate any ritual you want to include with the piercing.

Almost any area of the body can be pierced, but I'll list the most common types of piercing. For both men and women, aside from the ear, the nipple is probably the most common kind of piercing. Aside from aesthetic considerations, nipple piercings often make the nipple more sensitive.

In India, nostril piercing is as common as ear piercing and is becoming more common here. The most customary type of piercing is through the outside of a nostril, but a ring or bar in the skin at the end of the septum (the piece of cartilage separating the nostrils) is being seen more and more.

The human mouth is not very clean; therefore, tongue and lip piercings require special care when they are healing; however, they *are* show stoppers. Also, members of the oral sex cognoscenti have been known to rave about the effect of a tongue piercing.

Less common piercings are in the eyebrow, on the bridge of the nose, and in the navel. The latter is another piercing that requires special attention when healing. Clothing rubbing against sore skin may be exciting for a few minutes, but even the most dedicated masochist can get very tired of it over a few weeks!

There is something about a cock that has drawn the eye of piercers for centuries. The *Kama Sutra*, India's equivalent to *The Joy of Sex*, mentions the *apadravya*, a vertical piercing of the glans (head) of the cock. The *ampallang* is similar but horizontal. The apadravya can also be made behind the glans in the shaft. According to legend, the women of Borneo refused to have sex with men lacking one of these piercings. (This gives a whole new meaning to "Justify My Love.") The *dydoe* is a piercing through the ridge of the glans. Dydoe piercings are often done in pairs.

Foreskin piercings were developed in ancient Rome as a means of enforcing chastity. According to some authorities, they retain that function today.

The frenum is a piercing through the skin of the cock just behind the glans and often includes a cockring. The Prince Albert is a piercing that goes through the urethra and exits behind the glans. Legend has it that Prince Albert, Queen Victoria's consort, had it done so he could strap his cock tightly against his leg so as not to spoil the fit of his tight trousers. (And we think we are slaves to fashion!)

A piercing through the outer skin of the scrotum is called a *hafada* and originated in the Near East, where the piercing went considerably deeper and was part of a rite of passage. Finally, the *guiche* is a piercing in the flap of skin that connects the anus and the scrotum. Because of its proximity to the anus, there is a significant danger of infection while this particular piercing is healing.

Although a woman's genitals are less "outstanding" than a man's, they afford a number of interesting sites for piercings. The hood of the clitoris is often pierced; however, authorities and aficionados have mixed opinions about piercing the clitoris itself. One group holds that it is unwise to puncture something with such a concentration of nerve endings; others argue that this is exactly the reason to do it. In any case, all agree that piercings in this area increase the sensitivity of the clitoris. However, some women have had the piercings removed, reporting that it *is* possible to have too much of a good thing.

Although both the inner and outer labia can be pierced, most people prefer piercing the inner. Paired piercings on both lips provide an opportunity to put a lock or seal across the opening as both a symbolic and practical chastity belt.

A piercing that goes from the end of the vagina toward the anus (much like a guiche) is called a *fourchette*. This piercing has the same inherent dangers as a guiche.

Earring jewelry should never by used in a body piercing. The wires that hold earrings can tear the skin if the jewelry catches on clothing or, as has happened, part of your lover. Body jewelry is expensive, because it is handmade in small quantities. However, one piece per piercing is quite sufficient. Body jewelry isn't changed regularly like earrings; you don't need different sets for the office, for dates, for formal affairs.

Generally, jewelry is made from gold, niobium, or stainless steel. Other metals can be used after the piercing has healed *completely*. However, some people have allergic reactions even to niobium and stainless steel.

There are several types of common jewelry used with body piercings. The most common is the bead ring, a simple ring that is straightened, inserted in the piercing, and then bent back into a circle. The break in the ring is held closed with a bead. Occasionally, the bead is not attached to the ring, but simply held there by tension in the ring. This is called a captive-bead ring.

A barbell is a bar with a screw-off bead at each end. Sometimes the barbell is bent into a partial ring. Another variation substitutes a fine wire for the screw-off beads.

If you choose to have a permanent piercing, remember to follow the piercer's instructions about after-piercing care carefully. This may mean a period of sexual abstinence. However, everything nice has its price. Infections are not fun.

As noted, simply wearing body jewelry can add to sensation. However, body jewelry on a submissive has other uses. As with clips and clamps, they provide handy attachment points for weights of various sizes. You can also run strings through them and attach them to each other. By tightening the thread, you create all sorts of interesting stimulation. As with temporary piercings, two submissives can be attached to each other by strings through their body jewelry.

A word of caution, though: Be very careful of how much pressure you put on a piece of body jewelry. They are threaded through the piercing by a relatively thin wire which can cut the skin. Light, even, pulls, with a lot of checking, are the order of the day. *Never jerk* at pierced jewelry, and never bind a person by the jewelry when you might expect him or her to jerk. (For example, do not bind a person in this way and then spank or whip.)

A minor drawback to piercings: they can get conduct an uncomfortable amount of heat from saunas and hot tubs to the inside of the body.

Finally, two common questions people who are thinking of getting piercings ask:

What happens if I have an car accident and get taken to the hospital?

Relax. Even if you are in East Podunk, Idaho, emergency room people have seen *lots* weirder things than piercings. (Ask one about people who have sex with gerbils.) A friend's stomachache became full-fledged appendicitis. When she woke up in the hospital after the operation, one of the first things she saw was a bottle on her nightstand, neatly labeled "body jewelry," with all her rings and barbells inside.

Won't the jewelry set off metal detectors at airports?

It depends on how much you are wearing. However, given the current state of paranoia, the security people have been cranking up the detectors until they would probably detect the iron in a leaf of spinach. You have two alternatives. First, take off the jewelry for the trip. Second, behave as one of my friends did on her way to *Living in Leather*. After the alarm went off, a guard used a hand-held detector to localize the "suspicious metal" to the area of her breasts. When he said, puzzled, "Do you have any metal in there?" She smiled, pulled up her blouse, and showed him. His jaw—and about a dozen others—hit the floor. As she walked away, the waggle in her hips indicated that she had enjoyed the entire process.

Electricity

In my first fiction book many years ago, I wrote a scene wherein a young woman was tortured by a mad scientist. While she was bound spread-eagled to a frame, he connected wires to her body and gave her electrical shocks until she confessed. Whenever I meet anyone who has read that piece of trash, the conversation shifts around to that particular segment and I'm complimented on how "hot" the scene was.

Electricity has a certain fascination for those in D&S. Although few have used this specific mode of stimulation, it seems to play an important part in many fantasies. Perhaps this is just as well. *Electricity is dangerous.*

First, the don'ts.

Don't use line voltage. Many movies and books have the villain stripping off the insulation from a lamp cord and using it as an impromptu torture device. This may happen in real life, but it isn't anything that D&S people want to play around with. One hundred twenty volts will kill.

Don't use anything that uses converted line voltage. In short, if you plug it into the wall, don't use it on a person. I know of a couple who enjoyed playing Foreign Legionnaire and Algerian Maiden with an old electric train transformer. They don't use that toy anymore. A transformer works by using insulation to isolate the input current from the output current. Insulation tends to crack when it gets old. Sometimes workers at the assembly plants aren't paying as much attention as they should. In any case, at any given moment, a transformer designed to put out 12 volts DC can easily and unexpectedly start putting out 120 volts AC.

Don't use anything above the waist. The heart is up there. The beating of this rather essential organ is controlled by minute electrical impulses. If you start pumping your own electrical signals into a person's chest, the heart might stop. This is *not* a good thing.

That's the bad news. Now for the good news. There are lots of things out there that can give a pleasurable "zap" without resulting in a call to the paramedics. One mistress uses a single nine-volt battery to deliver tiny but noticeable shocks to the tips of her submissives' cocks. She uses no amplifier or wiring. She just puts the battery onto the dampened skin.

Fortunately for those who enjoy more technological gadgets, back in the early part of this century, quacks were fascinated by electricity. There was a multitude of devices manufactured so that the quacks could give people a tingle of electricity and a lot of lies.

A good friend of mine, Goddess Sia, has such a device. It is called an Electreat and looks a bit like a flashlight, takes two flashlight batteries, and can deliver quite a jolt when the sliding control is all the way up. What it was claimed to accomplish no one seems to know, but her submissives are quite outspoken in their enjoyment of the stimulation it provides.

Another gadget I've seen actually wraps the balls in a metal mesh before delivering some substantial shocks. Again, I don't know what it was supposed to cure, but I'm sure that I'd be yelling, "I'm cured! I'm cured!" shortly after it was turned on.

Up until the 1960s, one company manufactured a passive-exercise machine (Jane Fonda step aside) called the Relaxacisor. It worked (or rather didn't work) by stimulating the muscles with tiny electrical impulses. Here the erotic charge is not from conventional electrical shock, but from the disconcerting feeling of having one's muscles performing without having willed it. Some couples have reported combining the Relaxacisor with conventional vaginal or anal sex with considerable success.

One battery-operated device is still manufactured. It is called the Titalator and is sold by the Sandmutopian Supply Company. Their address is in the appendix. It has several dials that allow a user to set intensity, frequency and pulse rate. As with any DC unit, it should not be used above the waist. (The "tit" in Titalator is said to have derived from "titillation" rather than from any portion of the body.

Another "quack" device, the Violet Wand, is enthusiastically sought after by those folks who enjoy electrical play. Fortunately, it is still being manufactured. It can often be located in barber-supply stores, where its overt purpose is to give "stimulating scalp massages." (Let's not tell them, shall we?)

The Violet Wand is an exception to the rule given above. Because it uses exceptionally high-frequency electricity-which doesn't enter the body cavity and should present no danger to the heart, you can use it everywhere on the body except the eyes. The machine consists of a power unit and a cord to which attachments can be connected. Most of the attachments are glass which glow bluish violet and give it its name. When these attachments are brought near anything, a spark will jump from the attachment to the object. The effect is like that from walking across a nylon rug with rubber shoes during dry weather and touching a doorknob.

One interesting effect is for the dominant to grab the attachment when the unit is turned on. If it is gripped directly, there will be no spark and no pain; but then, by reaching out toward the submissive, he or she can "fire" sparks from a fingertip. Since there is a bit of a sting when the spark leaves as well as when it arrives, I like to control it with a small piece of wire held between two fingers.

A favorite electrical interrogation device around the world is the old hand-crank telephone. Turning the crank sends a substantial charge down the line. Interrogators in Cambodia would remark that they guessed "they would have to call information" when they were about to use this technique. Pepperpot generators in old-fashioned telephones can be used in the same way.

There are two ways of reducing the stimulation level produced by these devices. The first is simply to turn the crank slowly. The faster the crank is turned, the more electricity is produced. The second is to remove several of the U-shaped magnets.

Another "popular" shock device is a cattle prod. In general, these produce too much of a shock for most submissives. However, the shock can be reduced by removing one or more of the batteries and replacing them with dowels wrapped in aluminum foil.

The so-called "stun guns" powered by nine-volt batteries have no place in D&S play. The electrical impact they produce is well beyond the threshold I consider safe. Although I have never used one except as a psychological prop, I know of one submissive who was traumatized when her dominant used one on her. Although she had a substantial ability to transmute pain into pleasure, she spent several hours in a state of semi-shock after a single application.

Obviously, electrical play is one area where a dominant is required to test any stimulation on himself or herself prior to using it on a submissive.

Catheterization

Catheters have been used by human beings for centuries. Some ancient Chinese carvings even indicate that they may have been first used as sexual toys. Ah, the infinite ingenuity of humanity in getting its collective rocks off sometimes awes me.

However, this particular trick seems to have suffered a well-deserved decline until recently when some D&S practitioners, principally gay, made it part of their repertoire.

Simply put, catheterization, as it applies to D&S play, is to insert a specially made soft-rubber tube into a man's cock or a woman's urethra—actually, I'm talking about the same thing, but people unfamiliar with urethras have got a pretty good idea of what a cock is—and letting urine escape and/or filling the bladder with another fluid.

If your reaction is "That doesn't turn me on," I'm overjoyed. Make no mistake about it; catheterization is dangerous. If it were less known, I would gladly have left any mention of it from this book. However, given that I was relatively sure you would hear mentions of it, with reluctance I will try to tear away the confusion surrounding the technique.

There are two principal dangers. The urethral tube into the bladder isn't designed to handle anything except a warm liquid under slight pressure. If you doubt this, think about the agony from passing a kidney stone. *That* can be an educational experience.

In a woman's body the urethral tube may bend a bit on

its way to the bladder; however, in a man's body, the route might be described as a prostate roller-coaster ride. Combine the tube's fragile nature with its less-than-straight course and you have a situation fraught with peril. While stories abound of people shoving swizzle sticks, pipe cleaners, and even pencils up the urethra, most of these are just that, stories. The rest had their end in an emergency room.

The second danger is infection. While many people consider urine "dirty," it is almost sterile. It is the rest of the world that is dirty. The major trick in using a catheter is to keep the rest of the world's dirt out of the urinary tract. Failing to do this can lead to a world of hurt.

First, if you are bound and determined to do this, try to find someone to instruct you. A book is a poor place to learn what is essentially a motor-skills task.

Second, let me give you some serious warnings. Use only medical-urethral-catheterization kits. An amateur may be able to make rubber and plastic hoses look like what comes in the kits, but they are rarely as soft or as smoothly cut, and they are *not* sterile.

Do not use naso-gastric catheters that are sometimes available in leather stores. A rose may be a rose be a rose, but a catheter is not necessarily a catheter. There are several reasons for avoiding them, but the best is simply that they aren't as flexible as urinary catheters. Remember that roller-coaster ride?

While doctors use solid rods called "sounds" to work in the urethra, in untrained hands they can be extremely dangerous. If you must play in this area, I recommend passing up anything except the basic urinary-catheter kits.

Finally, if your submissive has a history of bladder

infections, of venereal diseases like gonorrhea, which affect the urethra, or of kidney stones, catheterization is not for the two of you.

You will need the following equipment: sterile gloves, Betadine solution, sterile water, catheter kit with a 5-cc syringe, paper tape, and a small sterile packet of K-Y jelly. Some of these items will come in the catheter kit; some you will have to find on your own. Check whether your submissive has any allergic reaction from the paper tape by having him or her wear it next to the skin for a few hours.

First, you must open the catheter kit without touching the equipment inside with your hands. Open the package of K-Y jelly and drop a large dab onto a one of the gauze squares in the kit. Do not let the outside of the K-Y package touch anything in the kit.

Next, put sterile gloves on and take the folded sterile paper towel from the kit and place it on a convenient surface so that there is enough room to put the catheter on it. With a female submissive, it is best to have her legs spread widely and work between them. With a male, work from one side with the toweling next to the hip.

Next, sterilize the area. This means, with a man, grab his cock. Remember that the hand you do this with is now *not sterile* and shouldn't touch anything that is sterile throughout the rest of the procedure. Wipe the entire length of the cock, paying particular attention to the tip, with gauze soaked in Betadine. Spread the lips of the urethra and wipe inside. Do not force the gauze into the opening, just clean the area. Then repeat the whole process with another gauze soaked in sterile water.

With a woman, it means spreading her labia with one hand, which is now *not sterile*, and keeping it open. With

234 / John Warren

the Betadine-soaked gauze, first wipe one side of the clitoris and urethra; then wipe the other side; then wipe the center. Repeat this procedure with another gauze soaked in sterile water.

The remainder applies to working with both sexes. With your sterile hand, take the catheter and hold it about one inch from the opening of the urethra. Make sure you have found the opening of the urethra. You *do* want to go into the right hole. With your nonsterile hand holding the outside of the K-Y packet, generously lubricate the tip of the catheter. Use lots of KY; it's cheap.

Now, *gently*, begin to insert the tip into the urethra. Your submissive will feel a slight stinging feeling at this point. That is normal. Continue to insert it until you see drops of urine coming out the end; that indicates the catheter is in the bladder. Take the 5-cc syringe and place it in the special tubing for the balloon on the end of the catheter and inject 5 cc of sterile water. This will inflate a tiny bulb on the end to hold it in place.

You can remove the tube by deflating the bulb and sliding it out.

Generally, people use catheters to drain bladders for golden-shower-type activities. However, some use the catheter to put fluid into the bladder. Obviously, this fluid must not interfere with the bladder's normal function and must be completely sterile.

The best material, I am advised, is an isotonic solution such as Normal Saline, which can be purchased at a drug store. Do not open the bottle until you are ready to use it; the contents must remain sterile. I once heard about a less-than-attentive dominant who put ordinary ice cubes into the solution to chill it. Obviously, it never occurred to her that the ice cubes were not made with sterile water. If you want a cold solution, chill the whole unopened bottle in the refrigerator.

To transfer the solution into the bladder, you will need to get a Tomey syringe. It looks like a huge hypodermic, but the opening at the top is wide enough to fit snugly on the end of the catheter.

Gray's Anatomy reports that a healthy bladder should be able to hold a pint of fluid and that women have slightly larger bladders than men. However, I wouldn't want to push things past a cup or so.

First, allow the existing store of urine to drain out; attach the Tomey syringe to the catheter and slowly, *very slowly,* inject the solution. If there is cramping, stop and wait until it subsides. If it does not, you have reached the limit.

A word of warning: While an occasional inflation may not be dangerous, if it is done often, the submissive may develop a flaccid bladder, which could require medical intervention. As with all else, moderation is the watchword here.

Branding

Ask most people who have seen or read *The Story of O* for a list of the hottest scenes, and most of their lists will include the branding scene at Anne-Marie's. The slow buildup, the glowing coals, the white-hot iron, and the agonizing scream all combine for an overwhelmingly erotic effect

However, in real-world D&S, branding is an exotic subspecialty rarely practiced outside a relatively small group. It is both dangerous and *permanent*. While it is difficult and expensive to remove a tattoo, it is almost impossible to remove a brand. Much of the material in this section comes from Raelyn Gallina of Oakland, California, who is an expert at branding and piercing.

When most people think of branding irons, they visualize those heavy, cast-iron monsters used by cowboys on nonconsenting cattle. Human brands are more delicate. They are made of sheet metal—favorite sources are coffee cans and heating-duct material—and are something like cookie cutters. The "iron" doesn't have to be very thick because the brand spreads over a period of months and will eventually be four or five times the thickness of the metal.

If a burn goes completely around a piece of skin, the entire surface will turn to scar tissue because the encircling burn cauterizes all the capillaries feeding that section of skin. Therefore, the branding irons should be made without closed loops. For example, the Q and O should have openings at either the top or the bottom, and the vertical part of the B and P should be separated from the curved part by a strip of healthy skin.

While your submissive may desire to wear your initials as a gesture of subservience, it is incumbent upon you to overcome the admittedly intoxicating feeling of power and to refuse. There is no guarantee that this relationship will last forever. Because submissives give us their power, it is our duty to look out for them and protect them from their own folly. A geometric or symbolic symbol may be more appropriate in the long run.

Brands should never be placed on any part of the body where major blood vessels, bones, or nerve clusters approach the skin, nor should they be where the skin is being constantly bent or where clothing is going to rub against the brand. Remember, this is a *burn*; it is going to take several weeks to heal. A moment of pain is exciting; three weeks of it can become tedious.

Curved areas should be avoided for aesthetic rather than physiological reasons. For example, it is difficult to apply a brand properly on an upper arm. While highly experienced branders can "roll" the brand so that it is a consistent depth throughout, even they occasionally find that, after they have branded curved skin, the middle has gone too deep while the edges have barely touched the skin.

The first stage in making a brand is to draw the design on a piece of graph paper exactly as you want it on the submissive's body. Don't forget that the branded lines will spread. A delicate precise design with a lot of narrowly spaced lines will most likely end up as an ugly lump of scar tissue.

The branding iron is made from that design; because of the necessary breaks to avoid enclosing an area of skin, it is not unusual for a single brand to be made from a number of small irons.

There is no need for a complex branding iron with an attached handle. The most common approach is to use pair of a locking pliers as a detachable handle. Hemostats are not recommended because their tiny grasping areas preclude a good grip on the hot metal and because they tend to conduct heat too well. The idea is to brand the submissive's body, not the dominant's fingers.

Once the set of irons is finished, branders will practice in exactly the place where they are planning to do the actual branding with exactly the same equipment. A professional should be adaptable, but the middle of a branding scene is no place to have to be dealing with surprises. They may use wet leather, potatoes, or a notepad of paper. The notepad has the advantage of allowing them to check precisely how deep the brand has penetrated.

Because branders are not dealing with a thousand pounds of steak tartare on the hoof, they only need to go in about 1/16th inch to make a very permanent scar. Holding the iron against the skin for one second is often enough.

Before having the brand done, you draw the design and transfer it to the submissive's skin.

First, trace the design you made on the graph paper onto a piece of tracing paper.

Second, turn the tracing paper over and put it on a blank piece of white paper so you can see your original tracing clearly.

Third, retrace the design (now it is reversed) on the back of the tracing paper with a transfer pencil like a NOBLOT Ink Pencil.

If the area to be branded is hair covered, shave it or have it shaved. Then have your submissive stand so that the skin will be "hanging" properly. A person wears his or her skin differently when sitting, standing, and lying down because of the pull of gravity and the tension on various muscles. Put a coat of Mennen Stick Deodorant on the area to be branded and place the tracing paper on the coated skin with the negative side down, and press along each line with your finger.

Most branders recommend having a few assistants present at the scene itself. The submissive should be held down as well as tied. Not only are people more adaptable in restraining a struggling figure, but the touch of humanity has a soothing effect that no leather cuff can match. The brander may also have someone heating up the next part of the set of irons while he or she is making a part of the brand.

The submissive should be secured horizontally. Each component part of the set of irons will be heated red hot just before it is used. The person doing the heating should aim the propane torch so that the metal heats from the gripper outward to the branding edge.

Healing will be a lengthy process. Each brander has his or her favorite technique to make the burn heal safely. You should make sure that your submissive follows it to the letter.

Fortunately, a branding iron is almost guaranteed to be completely sterile. However, the wound can become infected later. If cloudy pus comes from the wound, redness or black marks appear, or the skin becomes hot, a doctor should be contacted immediately.

To reiterate, a branding is a serious, serious piece of business and should be done only by trained, experienced people. However, I offer the following as an example of how you might be able to satisfy the need in a safe and sensible way.

A number of years ago, a submissive begged me for a branding. At that time, I had never even seen a real branding, and I was certain that I had neither the skills nor the interest to make such an experience work.

Consensuality *is* a two-way street, and I firmly refused. However, she was lovely and quite persuasive. I was beginning to appreciate the feelings of Adam when he entered the first not-guilty-by-reason-of-insanity plea: "Lord, the woman tempted me."

I never agreed to do the branding, but one day after she had been firmly tied to the bondage table, I brought out a small hibachi. On it was a branding iron with my initial "W." I had borrowed the branding iron from a set used for branding steaks as rare, medium, and well done.

As the iron heated, I played with her a bit with various toys, but whatever I did, her eyes rarely strayed far from the red-hot iron. Occasionally I took it from the fire and held it close to her thigh while I pretended to evaluate whether the temperature was suitable.

She could not take her widened eyes off the steel block and the colors that chased themselves along its surface in response to the heat-roiled air. Time after time, as the tiny hairs on her skin writhed in the radiated heat, I pronounced, "Not yet, let's let it get a bit hotter."

Finally, when it was almost white-hot, I said, "I think it is ready. Do you really want to go through with this?"

She gulped, speechless, but nodded vigorously.

I blindfolded her and then washed her thigh with some very hot water. When she felt the touch of the washcloth, she arched and hissed through her teeth, but I said, "I have to make sure it is completely clean; we don't want any infection."

With that, she lay back, but every muscle in her body was standing out in sharp relief.

Then I took the branding iron and held it close to her thigh so she could feel the intense radiated heat. As the skin below the iron became a brighter and brighter shade of red, I asked, "For the last time, do you want to go through with this?"

Again, she nodded.

With one smooth motion, I put aside the branding iron

and pressed hard on the reddened, heat-sensitized skin with an ice cube I had concealed in my other hand. Her scream was earsplitting; she completely lost control of her bowels and bladder and passed out cold.

When she recovered consciousness, I had draped a white cloth over her body (and cleaned up most of the mess). She was almost incoherent in thanking me for what she called the most intense experience of her life. However, when I released her hands and she lifted the sheet, she was completely dumbfounded. I explained what had happened and pointed out that I had never promised to brand her.

Her reaction was a mixture of relief and resentment. I did notice, however, that for the next few days, she would gingerly touch her thigh with a hand as if to check that, indeed, she was not branded.

CHAPTER 11

Saving the Scene on Film

Head back, mouth open, every muscle standing out in bold relief—few things in this world are more beautiful than a submissive in the middle of a session. It is little wonder that most of us have dabbled in photography to make some of their beauty ours forever. The sad truth is that we often manage to capture little of the reality and none of the fantasy. The pictures come out stiff and unreal or technically flawed and serve only as souvenirs to jog our memories.

What went wrong? Probably several things.

The most common errors are to start with too little preparation and to expect too much. We accept that the keys to a good D&S session are preparation and control. Nothing will break a mood faster than the dominant digging through a set of drawers muttering imprecations while searching for a riding crop or discovering that *this* chain won't reach *that* hook.

If you simply pick up a camera for a grab shot, that is what you will get: a grab shot with little to recommend it. Surprisingly for some, the more expensive the camera, the more likely this will be true. Expensive cameras are considerably more versatile than cheap ones, but they are more demanding and less tolerant of sloppy technique. My old Nikon F has literally thousands of possibilities for wrong settings on the controls.

The key to good photos is planning.

Set aside a session for photography. Arrange the room for it. Decide the activities that will yield the most photogenic results. Choreograph the activities so you know everything that will be happening when you take the picture. Photographers call this process "pre-visualization."

Check what will be in the background. Remember that you are creating a mood and don't want distractions. I remember one shot a friend took showing his wife in full suspension. Truly lovely—except that in the background was a crayon sketch their child had made at school that they had stuck on the bedroom wall. It was so incongruous that, instead of appreciation, the picture produced giggles.

One of my pictures has a shelf that seems to be growing out of the side of the subject's head. The impact of a picture can be spoiled by such a little thing as clutter on a bedside table. Even professionals forget to check the background in the heat of the moment—and we do expect those moments to be heated.

After you have gotten rid of the distractions, consider

what kind of background props you might use to enhance the mood. Whips and chains on the walls are nice, of course, but don't forget the power of symbolism. One of my favorite shots shows one of my submissives, arms spread wide, and chained to rings in opposite walls with horizontal chains. Her back is toward the camera, and she is facing a blank wall on which is hanging a crucifix.

I have a strong prejudice toward faces. My greatest turn-on is watching the expression on my submissive's face. Therefore my camera tends to dwell on that part of the anatomy rather than "where the action is."

Don't overlook lighting; it can add immensely to the impact. It helps a lot to have a good camera with manual controls or at least a manual override. However, good results can be had with automatic cameras if you put a little effort into tricking them. You don't need an expensive set of lights (but it helps). You can get clip-on reflectors at the local discount store and photoflood bulbs at a photographic supply store. Note of warning: make sure the reflectors are solid metal. Photofloods are *hot,* and silver-coated plastic won't stand it. For the same reason, handle them with care.

Silhouettes are dramatic, and thanks to apartment owners insisting on white walls, they are easy to obtain. Simply place the lights so that they shine on the walls instead of on the submissive. If you don't have a white wall, tacking up a white sheet will do. (Does anyone still use white sheets?) Try placing a bare bulb—just an ordinary lamp without the shade—behind the subject. This will create a glow around the darkened body and highlight the hair.

Dramatic, contrasty lighting really sets the mood for bondage. Put your lights at right angles to the camera and outside the camera's field of view. If you are using an automatic camera, put something between the lights and the camera; some of the light sensors on automatics have a wider angle than the camera lens and can be confused by an off-camera "hot spot." You can also get really dramatic lighting effects by using a focused source of light like a slide projector.

Another source of contrasty light is candles. Although they are relatively dim, you can use a tripod and the "bulb" setting on a manual camera to keep the shutter open. This takes experimentation, but it is well worth it. An advantage of bondage is that if you do it right, the subject isn't going to move during the exposure.

To soften the effect of candlelight without overpowering it completely, use an electronic flash and a slow shutter speed. By keeping the shutter open for a relatively long time, you capture the image of the candle flame. The instantaneous blast of light from the flash fills in the shadows. Again, a bit of experimentation is needed, but the effects are well worth it.

Another interesting source of light is a strobe. I don't mean the electronic flash unit that has replaced flashbulbs; I'm talking about the blink, blink, blink flasher that was made popular in the 1960s and is still sold by places like Radio Shack.

The beauty of this kind of dramatic lighting is that the flashes are so short that it is virtually impossible for the individual pictures to be blurred. Unlike candlelight, strobe light is most dramatic when the subject is in violent motion because one exposure can capture a number of images depending on how often the light flashes. Any suggestions how the subject can be stimulated into violent motion?

We all want to be part of the action, but leaving the camera and entering the picture has its own set of problems. Ideally, you can leave the camera in another's hands. This will yield incalculably better pictures as the camera is being controlled by a conscious eye and an aware brain. Unfortunately, this isn't the kind of thing you can ask of the helpful next-door neighbor (unless your neighbor is infinitely more fun than mine). Lacking a third body, most people turn to some sort of remote triggering device—and are deeply disappointed in the results.

It seems too simple: set up the camera, set the camera on a tripod, step into the action, and produce an erotic masterpiece. In reality, using a remote-triggered camera for anything more complex than a simple "Okay, everybody, look at the camera and scream" calls for considerable thought and planning if the result is even to approach acceptable standards. While it is difficult to mix a real D&S session with photography, it is almost impossible to mix a session with remote photography. If you want to use a remote camera, plan a photo session which will include D&S, rather than a D&S session which will include photography.

There are several ways to trigger a camera indirectly: self timers, air releases, and wireless releases. The self-timer is the most common and the most difficult to get good pictures with. You set the timer, actuate it, run around into the action, and wait for the timer to run out. This is a bigger mood wrecker than dead batteries in a vibrator.

There is simply no way to maintain the rhythm of a session while fiddling with a camera, running around, and posing. To make this worse, you can't really know when the timer will run out. This makes shooting anything other than a frozen tableau an exercise in frustration. Take a whipping: out of the five seconds it takes for a stroke, only one or less is of any photographic value. Factor in Murphy's Law, and you might as well be playing poker with a guy named "Doc."

An air release is a squeeze bulb connected by a thin, flexible tube to a plunger on the camera. Squeezing the bulb causes the plunger to trigger the camera. Some electronic cameras have replaced the air-operated plunger with a solenoid fired by a button you can hold in your hand, but the principle is the same. This has the advantage that you know exactly when the camera is going to go off. The disadvantage is that the tube or wire may show up in the picture.

Wireless releases work in a similar fashion, except that radio waves or infrared light replace the wire. One of my favorite cameras has this kind of remote trigger. The Canon Sure Shot Ace comes with a built-in infrared remote release. Unfortunately, it has some drawbacks.

First, and most important, it is an idiot camera. You can't interfere with the automatic focusing or exposure controls. It even decides when to fire the built-in flash. This limits creativity a bit. Second, the remote release does not trigger the camera instantly; there is a delay of two to three seconds. I assume that this is so you can hide the remote before the camera fires; however, it does complicate timing a bit. On the plus side, the delay is a lot easier to adapt to than the 15- to 30-second delay on conventional self-timers.

As important as planning is in a conventional photo session, it is an order of magnitude more important when you are using a remote camera. One of the most common errors is to cut off your own head or lose an arm to a picture border. (We could call this photographic edge-play.)

Use the submissive as a registration point and plan what you are going to do around that point. Don't forget to allow for perspective. If you are going to be in front of the registration point, you will be larger and will be more likely to be cut off. This problem is heightened if you are using a wide-angle lens which amplifies perspective. The easiest thing is to stay in the same plane, the same distance from the camera as the submissive, or to get behind him or her.

I also block out the frame. Before the session, I set up several camera locations and mark where the tripod touches the floor with masking tape. Then, sighting through the camera, I have the submissive mark the floor at the edges of the camera's frame (what it can "see") with strips of tape.

That way, when I have set up the camera at one of the marked locations, I can just look down at the floor to see if I am in the horizontal part of the frame.

Blocking the vertical parts are more difficult; that is why I suggest you remain in the same plane with the submissive; by remembering where his or her head is in reference to the edge of the frame, you can judge how you are fitting. I also use a spare light stand. By putting it where I intend to stand, with the top of the lamp where my head will be, I can adjust the camera so I will be completely in the frame when I take my position replacing the light stand.

Whether we are part of the picture or our camera

dwells on the magnificence of submission, the beauty we create in our submissives can be ours forever. The camera is a natural adjunct to chains, whips, and the erotic stimulation we lavish on those we control.

CHAPTER 12
Making Leather Toys

Naked, but for leather cuffs and collar, the submissive stands before the master. Clad from head to toe in leather, the mistress enters the dungeon. Cool leather against the throat and the touch of a leather glove sliding possessively along the small of the back.

There is something about leather: its texture, its color, even its smell. It calls to us. Unfortunately, that call has a price tag. Leather goods are not cheap, and the very special items we use in the scene are even more expensive than the semi-vanilla coats, dresses, and gloves we admire in the display windows of such paragons of the status quo as Saks and Bergdorf Goodman.

The flip side of this is that *somebody* did make the

whips, cuffs, and collars we admire. There is no magic in leatherwork. A whip need not be made in the dark of the night while obscure odors rise from a nearby bubbling pot and ancient hags chant in a forgotten language. (It might be fun, but you don't have to do it that way.)

For basic leatherwork, only a few basic tools and supplies are needed:

A metal straightedge to allow you to draw straight lines and make straight cuts

Shears with serrated blades—invaluable when cutting light- and medium-weight leather

A Stript-Ease draw gauge with a replaceable razor blade to cut straps of even widths

A mat knife with replaceable blades

A moderately light hammer for setting rivets and other fasteners

A pounce wheel or space marker for indicating evenly spaced marks for hand sewing

An edge beveler which takes a sliver off a thick piece of leather to give a beveled trim along the side. It comes in various sizes, but for beginners, a 4 or 5 will do in most circumstances.

A rotary punch with tubes of various sizes for punching holes in leather. In the more expensive models, the tubes are replaceable.

A cutting board, which should be made out of soft wood

An anvil touse as a backstop for hammering or pounding. It can be made of metal or stone.

A few heavy needles for sewing the pieces of leather together

Leather glue

Waxed thread
Sharpening stone

Perhaps most important is to recognize that you are going to make mistakes at first. True, leather is expensive, but it is better to "waste" some leather practicing than to make the mistakes during a major project. Begin by practicing techniques on scrap leather.

First, let's look at some basic techniques.

There are three basic ways to cut leather: with freehand knives, with shears, and with a draw gauge.

When cutting with a knife, always place the leather flat against a soft wood surface. Press a ruler against the leather and draw the knife along the ruler's edge. There is no need to cut completely through the leather with one stroke. Repeated strokes will cut even the thickest piece.

Don't hesitate to resharpen the knife frequently. There is no such thing as too sharp a knife. Even replaceable blades can be touched up with the sharpening stone.

Shears can be used to cut both light- and medium-thickness leather and are preferred when there a lot of curves to be cut. However, knives work best on long, straight runs.

A draw gauge cuts even strips and is invaluable for collars, cuffs, and whip lashes. After you make a single guide cut, it will make another cut a constant distance from the first. It requires a firm grip and a steady pull, but it produces a fine, even cut. One version of the draw gauge, called the Strip-Ease, is inexpensive and uses replaceable razor blades.

Use an edging tool to put a bevel in the edge of heavy leather you are going to use for a collar or cuff. They come in sizes 1 (smallest) to 5 (largest) and have a U-shaped blade that you push along the edge. To make the bevel smoother, you can sand it with fine sandpaper or emery paper.

There are several ways to attach two pieces of leather together. The two most common are sewing and gluing; often they are used in conjunction with each other.

Hand sewing is quite simple because you aren't expected to shove the needle through leather. Use the pounce wheel and a ruler to make a series of evenly spaced marks on the leather and then poke a hole through with a hammer and punch or with what is called a saddler's awl. With the hole already in place, sewing is a cinch.

Two basic stitches are the running stitch and the backstitch. With the running stitch, you simply go down through one hole and up through the next. The backstitch is made after the running stitch is completed. While the running stitch went down through the first hole, with the backstitch, you come up through that hole. This way, thread is on both sides of the leather.

Often you will want to glue two pieces together before sewing; in fact, for some applications, you can just glue and avoid sewing.

There are adhesives sold specifically for leather. One of my favorites is Tandy Leathercraft Cement; however, there are many others, and most do a very good job.

The basic process is to coat both pieces of leather with the cement, let them dry and then press the pieces together. They will form a permanent bond almost instantly; however, you should tap them with a mallet to ensure that the bond is solid.

Because the bond is instantaneous, if you are connecting two pieces that have to be in perfect alignment, use the slip-sheet method. Prepare the pieces with cement and let them dry; then put a sheet of paper or clear plastic over one piece. Put the other piece on top of the paper or plastic. Make sure that the pieces are in perfect alignment, and then slowly pull the paper or plastic from between them, pressing down on each section as the pieces come in contact.

Rivets can be used for decoration or as another method of fastening two or more pieces of leather together. First, use your rotary punch to make a hole through the leather. Lay the rivet post over the pounding board and place the punched leather over the post. Make sure that the pretty side is up. If you are connecting two pieces of leather, make sure that the bottom one has the pretty side down.

Choose a rivet that is the correct size; this may take a bit of practice. A rivet that is too short will not make a permanent connection; one that is too long will not make a firm connection. About 1/8 inch of the male part of the rivet should be showing above the leather after you have inserted in the hole in the leather. Just put the female end of the rivet onto the prong and strike it sharply with the setting tool. The two will be permanently connected.

Snaps are easy to close and easy to take off. For this reason, they aren't really useful for anything that will be used for restraint; however, they are great for decorative collars and cuffs.

There are four parts to a snap: two go together in one piece and two go together in the other. Each brand is slightly different, so follow the instructions carefully. As with rivets, practice is essential before you attempt to set a snap in a serious project.

Buckles are effective fasteners for items you will use for restraint. Generally, the simplest—a single-bar buckle—is best. The oblong slot for the prong can be cut away with your mat knife, but special oblong punches are also available. You can expect your buckles to be taking a lot of pressure, so it is wise to glue, sew, *and* rivet them in place.

Black leather is traditional for scene activities and, while any color is acceptable, many people like the look of black. This means that your leather will have to be dyed. Fortunately, it is quite easy.

The basic rule is that the leather must be clean and dry before you begin. If the leather has grease or oil on it, you should get some leather-cleaning solution. Do not use saddle soap for cleaning at this point. That is for cleaning *finished* projects.

Dyes are available in both oil- and water-base formula. Since scene gear is often worn close to the skin, and during a scene sweating is not uncommon, I recommend an oil-base dye.

Dye can be applied in several ways. For large areas, use a soft cloth or piece of woolskin you can buy at leathercraft stores. If you use woolskin, soak it in mineral oil to keep it from absorbing too much of the dye. Put the dye in a shallow pan. Pouring it out from the bottle onto the applicator takes too much time and is likely to result in an uneven application. Apply the dye with broad, smooth strokes. Once you start, *do not stop.* Going back once the dye has dried never produces a good result.

For smaller areas, use a dauber. You can make one with a bit of cotton waste or woolskin on a piece of wire. It looks like the dauber in a shoe-polish bottle.

Once the dye is dry, rub the area with a soft cloth to

remove the excess dye. Finally, for a glossy water-resistant finish, use Omega Finish Coat or Fielding Tan-Kote.

Omega Carnauba Creme gives a soft, lustrous finish. However, saddle soap and even Vaseline petroleum jelly will do the job quite well.

Some Leatherwork Projects

Now, let's look at three simple projects you can make: a whip, a blindfold, and a pair of wrist cuffs.

For the whip, you need an 8-inch by 22-inch rectangular piece of leather and a 6-inch-long dowel. (See diagram on p. 258.)

Draw a line 6 inches from one end of the piece of leather. Next, cut a series of strips, 1/2 inch wide, from the other end to this line. This should give you a fringelike affair of about 16 strips, 1/2 inch wide and 16 inches long.

Put the wooden dowel against one side of the uncut part of the leather and roll the leather around it. You now have a workable cat. All you need to do is nail the leather against the dowel, and you are ready to whip.

Of course, you may want to fancy up the whip by dyeing it or putting rivets or studs in the handle. However, for all practical purposes, you are finished.

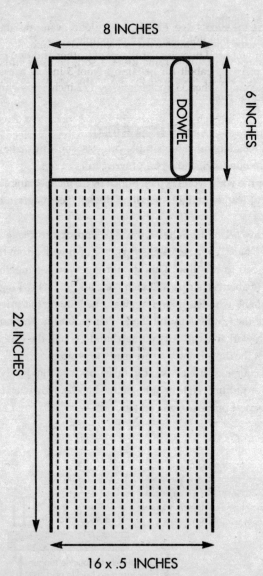

8 INCHES

DOWEL

6 INCHES

22 INCHES

16 x .5 INCHES

Leather Whip

<u>Leather</u> <u>Blindfold</u>

Making the blindfold is a bit more complex.

You will need two circular pieces of leather and two circular pieces of rabbit fur or lamb's wool 3 inches across, one piece of leather 33 inches long by 1/2 inch across, and a metal buckle.

Cut two 3-inch-long pieces off the 33-inch strip. Rivet one of these to the good side of each circular piece of leather. Each strip should have two rivets 1 inch in from the side. This will leave 1 inch between each pair.

Glue the fur circles to the opposite sides of each piece of leather. Attach the buckle with a rivet to the end of the long strip of leather, which should be 27 inches long now. Finally, slide the strap under the leather strips on the circular pieces, and you are finished.

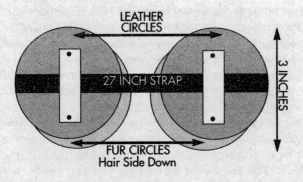

LEATHER CIRCLES

27 INCH STRAP

3 INCHES

FUR CIRCLES
Hair Side Down

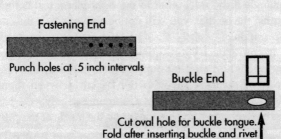

Fastening End

Punch holes at .5 inch intervals

Buckle End

Cut oval hole for buckle tongue.
Fold after inserting buckle and rivet

The most complex project here is a leather cuff. This kind of cuff can be used either on wrists or ankles but cannot be used for suspension.

One cuff requires:

A 10-inch by 2-inch rectangle of heavy leather
A 10-inch by 2-inch rectangle of heavy rabbit fur or lamb's wool
A 16-inch by 3/4-inch strap of leather
A belt-type buckle

Cut an oblong hole in one end of the 16-inch strap to let the tongue of the buckle go through and move. Then glue and rivet the buckle in place. Cut the other end into a V and make holes for the buckle's tongue not more than 1/4 inch apart for at least eight inches.

Put the assembled belt on the leather rectangle. The end of the buckle should be about 1/2 inch from one end. Rivet the belt to the rectangle 4 inches from that end of the rectangle. Put a D-ring over the far end of the belt and slide up until it is against the rivet.

The next step is important. Bend the incomplete cuff around an object until you can fasten the belt as tightly as you ever expect to do it. *Now*, mark the position for the next rivet on both the strap and on the leather rectangle. It should go 7 inches farther along the strap than the first rivet. You can now unbuckle the belt and set the rivet. The belt should be buckling out from the leather rectangle if the rivet is set in the right place. If it is tight against the leather, you will not be able to curve the cuff to put it on.

If you expect your submissive to enjoy struggling, you might add another pair of rivets half-way between the two you have set with the D-ring between them. It isn't necessary, but it holds a bit more securely.

The final step is to glue the fur on the inside of the cuff.

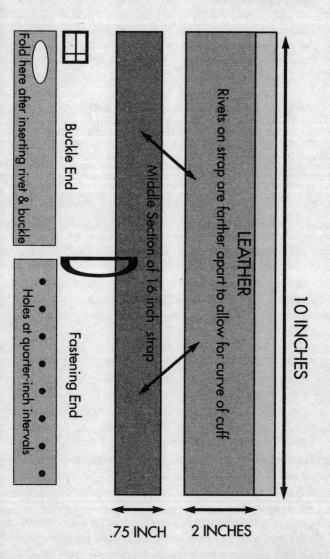

Fold here after inserting rivet & buckle

Buckle End

Holes at quarter-inch intervals

Fastening End

Middle Section of 16 inch strap

Rivets on strap are farther apart to allow for curve of cuff

LEATHER

10 INCHES

.75 INCH

2 INCHES

Leather Cuffs

CHAPTER 13
Your Secret Dungeon

Recently I was invited into a personal dungeon belonging to some members of Black Rose, the Washington, D.C., D&S group. Located in a finished basement, it was a fantasy paradise. The walls and ceiling were painted black and decorated with a profusion of straps, paddles, ropes, and whips; wall-to-wall red carpeting covered the floor, and the place was lighted with a number of aimed, colored, accent lights on the ceiling. The equipment included a suspension frame made of heavy timbers, a leather-covered spanking bench, and a barred jail cell.

Not all of us are lucky enough to have a space that we can set aside for such a room. In fact, this particular dungeon was almost as large as many New York apartments.

However, with a little imagination, we can put together a room suitable for entertaining vanilla friends which can quickly be converted to more energetic activities. The key to this decorating is a term I borrowed from friends in the intelligence community: plausible deniability. This means that every item has a plausible vanilla use, so you can answer any suspicion with an innocent blank stare.

The centerpiece of such a room is a table suitable for bondage. If you look at the coffee tables in a furniture store, you will find that some of them are too delicate for such activities, but others are quite firmly put together. Get one at least four feet long. This length will support any head and torso combination. The legs can be allowed to bend at the knees and hang over. However, my feeling is, the longer the better. There is something delicious about a submissive spread out and available like a buffet.

When you get the table home, put a series of attachment points about 6 to 12 inches *underneath* the overhang of the top. Of course, if you really want to generate curious questions, you can put them along the edge. Screw eyes are acceptable, but I prefer cleats from a marine-supply store. These are used to attach boats to piers and look like squashed Hs resting on their sides. Their advantage is that ropes attached to them can be untied quickly and easily.

If your submissive enjoys a bit of additional stimulation while tied up, get a nonskid chair pad from an office-supply store, and trim it so it fits the top of the table. The little plastic spikes on the bottom of the pad provide an interesting surface for any submissive to lie on. You should provide padding or make a cutout in the pad so the submissive's head and, if appropriate, knees or elbows are protected from the bed-of-nails effect. The pad can be easily stored out of sight when it is not in use.

As I noted in the "Cutting and Piercing" section of the "Fun and Games" chapter, a futon frame, with or without its pad, is the perfect bondage frame. However, most are put together too delicately to restrain an enthusiastic submissive. You need to drill a few pilot holes and reinforce where each slat is connected to its brace. The original screw and a 3-inch reinforcing screw will withstand almost any conceivable stress that a submissive bound in place on the frame could produce. Naturally, this is another place where the reversed office mat can find an application.

By throwing the futon over the frame's raised back, you have a perfect surface for spanking or cropping. Have the submissive stand behind the futon frame and bend forward over the back so his or her hands are touching the seat below. Tie the hands to the crossbars at the front of the seat and the legs to the vertical braces on either end of the frame. This provides a beautiful spread target. If, despite the pad, the submissive is uncomfortable, try doubling up the pad to cut down on the pressure on his or her stomach.

Another piece of Oriental furniture that lends itself to bondage is a Korean papa-san chair. It is shaped like a bowl made of heavy pieces of curved bamboo, with a circular pad that fits inside the bowl. The whole thing rests on something that looks like a giant egg-holder. This chair can be used for bondage in its "normal" configuration, with the submissive either sitting with feet on the floor and hands and knees tied to the rim, or with the submissive's hands tied to the rim while sitting in the lotus position with the knees tied to the rim.

However, if you put the bamboo-frame bowl upside

down on the floor, its real potential for bondage is revealed. Here we have a dome-shaped frame on which a submissive can be tied in a multitude of ways while arched to receive stimulation. Simply as an objet d'art, such a combination of bamboo and flesh is a prize to be cherished.

If you enjoy spanking, a heavily padded love seat (what an appropriate name) or an antique cobbler's bench provides a perfect surface while not exciting any comments at all from vanilla visitors.

If you have exposed beams, you have an ideal place to put a few screw eyes. Paint them black or the same color as the beams, and most people won't notice them. Few of us ever look up unless something catches our eye. Further camouflage can be provided by a hanging plant or two.

For the floor, I've seen some plate-and-ring units that fit right into the floor and, when not in use, lie perfectly flat. Of course, they require that you use a chisel or router to make an appropriately sized hole in the floor but, once in place, they are almost unnoticeable. The people who had them said that they were purchased at a marine-supply store. (Those *are* handy places.)

If you don't want to put in permanent eyebolts, get a pair of heavy carpentry clamps and fasten them to the top of a door. You can then put someone in standing bondage against the door. Exercise stores also sell removable chinning bars that provide an attachment point that should be fairly secure.

While it wouldn't be appropriate for the living room, a freestanding swing set would not be out of place in a playroom or in the cellar and provides a perfect brace for standing bondage or even a bit of suspension. If you don't have children, you can deflect suspicion with a casual comments such as "The last tenants left this, and we haven't gotten around to taking it down" or "Isn't it cute? We got it to try to recapture some of the memories of our youth."

Even more discreet is a simple ladder. After all, everyone needs to change light bulbs or dust for cobwebs. Even an ordinary ladder provides a multitude of attachment points for naughty submissives, and modern technology has made the ladder even better. A neighbor has a Rube Goldberg–type ladder called a MultiMatic™, so jointed that it can be converted into a conventional straight ladder, a stepladder, a scaffolding, or into a number of other forms. Occasionally, I borrow the ladder with an appropriately vague excuse. If only he knew.

In the bedroom, a four-poster or a Shaker-style pencil-post bed fits right in. However, you should make your attachments as close as possible to the frame. A friend literally pulled her pencil-post bed apart when her lover tied the ropes from her legs to the top of the posts. The combination of her orgasm, the strength in her legs, and the leverage provided by the long post was too much for the antique. The bed was repaired; the relationship did not fare as well.

Antique brass beds provide a multitude of attachment points; modern beds, especially water beds or those designed like water beds, are less congenial. However, a series of marine cleats or screw eyes along the base of the bed, under the mattress overhang, increase the utility of these beds from a bondage point of view. If you have a water bed, make sure that the attaching screws have not penetrated the wood to rest against the mattress material.

This kind of oversight could give a whole new meaning to the term "water sports."

Modern beds can be turned into exceptionally versatile bondage surfaces by adding Sport Sheets. These are described in more detail in the "Opening the Toybox" chapter.

Lighting is important in setting the scene. In most cases, this is as simple as unscrewing the white bulbs in a few selected sockets and replacing them with colored lights. However, anyone who has watched late-night movies knows that dungeons often have flickering torches. Unfortunately for the modern dungeonmaster, the old dungeons also had stone walls. Romantic torches are not kind to wallboard walls and ceilings. However, I have found electric lights that flicker just like candle flames. A cluster of these gives an impression of a torch (if you squint really hard).

With a little work and a bit of imagination, you can have it all: kinky dungeon and vanilla home.

CHAPTER 14
Party Manners

Being invited to your first scene party can be a great thrill but, at the same time, it can be a nerve-racking experience. However, if you are reasonably able to deal with people as people, have been housebroken to the point that you won't embarrass yourself and others in a well-run mall, and have a bit of common sense, you shouldn't have any problems.

Of course, rules among groups vary. Some groups, like Threshold on the West Coast, won't even let you attend one of their parties until you have attended an orientation meeting. Most, however, assume that you are sufficiently intelligent to ask if you're uncertain. The problem lies with knowing what to ask about.

Clothing

Most scene people are casual about clothing, but at the same time, an Izod shirt and Eddie Bauer jeans can suck energy from a scene. This doesn't mean you have to invest two months' pay in a leather outfit complete with codpiece. Basic black is always acceptable. Ladies can let their imaginations run wild. I have never seen an outfit too extreme for a scene party.

However—and this is a big however—when the party is held in a private home, the hosts may not want to advertise their orientation to the entire neighborhood. It might be a good idea to slip on something over your outfit or to carry your clothing in a paper bag (more subtle than a suitcase).

Punctuality

In much of the vanilla world, 8:00 P.M. means sometime after 8:30. If you are going to a scene party, arriving at 8:45 may mean facing darkened windows and locked doors. Both for security (imagine a neighbor coming over for a cup of sugar) and to prevent the rhythm of the scenes being broken, many parties lock the doors after the action begins.

Parking

You may be told to park in a particular place. Do it! Many people don't want to advertise the party with cars lining the streets outside their houses.

Tag-along Guests

Even more than at a sit-down dinner for a head of state, unwanted and unknown guests are not wanted at a scene party. It is all right to ask, once, but if the answer is "no," drop it right there.

Anonymity

Expect to cultivate a selective amnesia about people. At the party, they are who they say they are. You might make a hit by saying, "Gee, I recognize you; I loved your last picture," but it is more likely you'll find yourself shunned as a barbarian. After the party, forget who you met until the next party. You may think you are being cute by saying, "Remember me? We met at Irene's party," to a familiar face, but a more likely result is no more invitations. If you see someone, a shy smile indicating vague recognition is about as far as you can go unless he or she responds.

If you really want to meet that little redheaded submissive you played with last night, it is permissible to call the host and give him or her *your* phone number to pass on, if possible. It is the height of bad manners to ask for anyone else's phone number, except from the person in question.

To make this easier, I keep some small printed cards in my toy belt. They have my name, post-office-box address, and telephone number. It is a lot easier to give someone a card like this than to try to make out a phone number scribbled on the back of a matchbook the next day.

Dungeonmasters

At large parties, there are occasionally experienced players—usually dominants, but not always—who are in charge of keeping order and making sure that people play safely. They are usually very polite, but their word is law. If one of them says something like "I don't think it is safe to do that," stop it immediately. The reasonable tone is not an invitation to a debate.

Scene Behavior

Usually, there will be one or more areas set aside for scenes. While you are in these areas, keep the casual chitchat to a minimum. It can be very distracting to both the submissive and the dominant in the midst of a scene to overhear someone discussing the stock market. Take the discussion out into a social area.

Give people room to play. By the same token, if you are playing, keep your play reasonable for the space available. You may be proud of your ability to use a bullwhip, but a 10x12 scene room during a party is no place to demonstrate it.

If you want to ask someone who is in the middle of a scene a question, ask it after the scene is over. Breaking into a scene is always disruptive and can be dangerous. In some scenes, concentration is vital; in all of them, it is part of the pleasure.

If your scene is messy, clean up after yourself or have your submissive do it. A thoughtful dominant who brings a sheet to catch bits of wax or shaving cream is much more likely to be invited back than one who leaves a pile of litter behind.

If you think that someone's scene is dangerous, you can seek out a dungeonmaster or the host and draw it to his or her attention. Again, debate is not an option. Accept the master's opinion. What you cannot do is stop it yourself or criticize it.

If you simply find a scene distasteful, go somewhere else. No one is making you watch. As an extension of this, displays of homophobia (or, for that matter, heterophobia) are in the worst possible taste.

Intoxication

This varies a lot according to the group, but most D&S groups are pretty straitlaced when it comes to drugs and booze. Some forbid it entirely; others expect you to limit yourself to a single beer. Drunkenness is a sure ticket to the door. Remember, under the present laws, if you are caught by the police with drugs, the party giver could have his or her house confiscated. That is not good manners.

Party Manners

Some people feel that if they wear their whip on the left side, it somehow excuses them from conventional manners. Actually, the opposite is true. Manners didn't arise from the lower classes; they were developed by a bunch of very dominant individuals to keep them from cutting each others' throats at the slightest jostle. Saying "please" and "thank you" to the serving submissives doesn't weaken your air of dominance; it enhances it. The same goes for cleaning up after yourself.

Never use or even touch another person's toys without asking. Most people are proud of their collections and enjoy showing them off. If you damage a toy, offer to replace or pay for it. These things can be very expensive. Assume that the first refusal is a courtesy. I would recommend asking three times to show you are serious.

As in the public clubs, submissives are to be looked at but not touched or used in any way unless you are given specific permission. There may be submissives serving the food. Unless you have been told that it is desired, do not attempt to humiliate them in any way.

Safe Words

You may assign or have your submissive choose a safe word. However, some parties have a house safe word. This is usually something common like "red light." This assures that the dungeonmasters can check on the consensuality of the scene and that any "pickup" scenes are fully consensual.

Even more than at public clubs, your behavior at private parties can make or break your reputation. You want to make sure that everything you do enhances the reputation that is your most important scene possession.

Sending a short note thanking your hosts is always appropriate.

Note:

Sydney Biddle Barrows's *Mayflower Manners* has an excellent section on D&S parties beginning on page 124.

CHAPTER 15
First-aid for the Scene

Just because we are playing does not mean that our submissive won't get hurt at one time or another. We are playing, but often we are playing rough. People get hurt riding bicycles, skating, jogging. My local newspaper carried an item about an elderly lady who, excited about winning at bingo, stood up too quickly, fell back over her chair, and broke her collarbone.

This does not mean that we should accept any injuries as part of the game. After everything has returned to normal, it is incumbent upon both of you to sit down and try to prevent whatever happened from happening again. There is nothing contradictory between playing hot and playing safe.

This section is far from a complete first-aid guide. I strongly recommend that you supplement it with a conventional first-aid manual and with Pat Califia's *The Lesbian S/M Safety Manual*. Read them *before* something happens. When someone is bleeding is no time to learn first-aid. It is a sad fact of life: many dominants know more about taking care of their toys than their of submissives. If I were licensing dominants, I would make a basic first-aid course— including CPR—one of the minimum requirements.

Make sure your submissive has read this section. While most injuries *do* happen to submissives, dominants have been known to fall, set themselves on fire during a waxing, or cut themselves with straight razors. I use the word "submissive" throughout for consistency, but don't assume you are somehow bulletproof.

Both of you should also *practice* emergency procedures. When things go wrong, sometimes people panic and take refuge in the familiar. One woman vacuumed her carpet while waiting for the paramedics to arrive when her husband had a heart attack. Make the emergency procedures familiar and commonplace, and you'll be much better off when all hell breaks loose.

Cuts and Bruises

The most common injuries in the scene, as almost everywhere else, are cuts and bruises. Bruises are unsightly, except to those who wear them as badges of pride, but generally they will disappear after a while. You can speed up healing by putting ice packs on them for no more than a half-hour. Hot water will only increase the size and discoloration, and because the skin is not broken, antiseptic or astringent solutions are useless.

You should already have asked if your submissive has a clotting disorder or takes any kind of anticoagulant drug (like Coumadin). That would make him or her bruise much more easily.

The greatest danger from cuts is infection. Clean the area with warm water and a mild soap. Then sterilize it with Betadine (a generic term for this is Povodine/Iodine) or alcohol and have the submissive hold a bit of clean gauze against the cut until the bleeding stops. (Hydrogen peroxide, recommended by some first-aid books, doesn't sterilize as well and, with repeated use, may actually retard healing.) If you think you may have gotten any blood on you, wash carefully with soap and hot water. A Band-Aid can be used to keep the injury clean after the bleeding has stopped.

If, later, the cut gets red and swells, you see red-purple streaks under the skin, or it is sensitive to a light touch, it is probably infected. Go to a doctor. Aside from simply being dangerous, an infection greatly increase the chances that a scar will form.

If the bleeding is severe or if it spurts, apply tight pressure with your hand or an elastic bandage over the site of the bleeding, and call 911. A person can die from a severed artery in seconds. Do not attempt to use a tourniquet unless you have been trained in how to apply one. A poorly applied tourniquet can cause much more damage than you realize.

Unconsciousness

Simply because of the excitement of the scene, because their air supply has been inadvertently cut off or because they have been standing in one place too long, submissives occasionally faint. Some people have the habit of holding their breath during orgasms, which causes them to faint; it is called orgasmic syncope. Diabetics may faint if violent activity causes their blood-sugar level to drop. As I noted in an earlier chapter, you should know your submissive's medical history before you begin to play.

Immediately remove all bondage. If it won't come off fast, cut it off. This is where the EMT scissors or bolt cutters come in handy. The submissive should be on his or her back without anything under the head, with the legs elevated slightly. Smelling salts can be used *carefully* to rouse the submissive. Do not attempt CPR unless the submissive has stopped breathing *and* you know how. CPR is a wonderful technique, but its application is limited to very specific circumstances.

If the submissive remains unconscious for more than a couple of minutes, seek medical help. However, if the submissive recovers and seems all right, you should still keep him or her lying down for at least a half-hour. If he or she is a diabetic, administer some juice with a little sugar in it or regular soda, not sugar-free.

Severe chest pains spreading to the shoulder, neck, or arm and/or a crushing feeling in the chest accompanying a shortness of breath might mean a heart attack. *Call 911 immediately, before you do anything else.*

If it turns out that your submissive was using drugs or alcohol, you have some soul searching to do. First, why didn't you notice before this? Second, do you want to continue to play with a person who would do such a stupid thing? Obviously, many people will disagree with me, but my basic rule is that drugs and the scene do not mix.

Convulsions

The submissive's going into a convulsion can be a more frightening experience. Remove any bondage immediately and place a loop of rope or a piece of soft leather in his or her mouth to protect the tongue. Do not use something hard, like a whip handle, or something vulnerable, like your fingers. The first may cause damage to the teeth; the second will be damaged.

Loosen any clothing around the neck and waist, and place pillows, cushions, or rolled blankets around the body. Unless you have reason to believe that these convulsions are not signs of trauma, call for medical assistance.

Head Injuries

Head injuries can be time bombs. Television and detective fiction have made people casual about blows to the head. Any blow to the head severe enough to cause unconsciousness calls for a trip to the hospital. If the membrane covering the brain inside the skull is bruised, a subdural hematoma can form slowly over a period of hours, eventually causing unconsciousness and, possibly, death.

At the very least, the injured party should be under observation for a full day following the injury and have regular follow-up for a few days after that.

Symptoms of serious injury include returning unconsciousness, nausea and/or vomiting, swelling, severe headache, stumbling or knocking things over, and confusion. One check for the last is to ask three questions, called "orientation times three": "What is your name? Where are you? What is today's date?" Any errors indicate possible serious problems.

"Misplaced" Toys

What do you do when you "lose something inside?" If it is in the vagina and is doesn't have any sharp edges or points, relax. There isn't anyplace for it to go. Like Mary's lamb, it will soon come back. Losing something in the rectum is more of a problem. Do not try to get it out with an enema. You also shouldn't try to reach in and get it. I know one panicked individual who tried to use what looked like salad tongs. Don't do it!

Lubricate the anus and go sit on the toilet. Bring a good book—this one, maybe. Wait, don't force it. After all, your body wants to get rid of it as much as you do. If it doesn't come out in a few hours, or if there is severe pain, go to a doctor—and next time don't use something that can slide all the way in.

Heat-related Injuries

Certain kinds of mummification, bondage, or vigorous scenes in hot weather can lead to heat cramps, heat exhaustion, or heatstroke. Heat cramps are painful muscle spasms caused by excessive sweating and the loss of salt. This can be treated simply by consuming food or liquid containing salt. While none of the injuries in this chapter are limited to submissives, heat-related conditions are a particular threat to dominants who do scenes in hot weather. We tend to pay so much attention to the submissive that we tend to neglect our own needs.

Heat exhaustion is indicated by nausea, faintness, dizziness, excessive sweating, and weakness. The individual's skin is pale and clammy, and he or she has a weak pulse and may show signs of shock. The affected person should lie flat with the head down and take *small sips* of cool, slightly salty liquids every few minutes. Never offer food or drink to anyone unless he or she can speak and hold up his or her head.

Heatstroke is potentially lethal. Initial symptoms begin like those of heat exhaustion, but soon the individual develops a fever of more than 104 degrees and may experience convulsions or become unconscious. Cool him or her immediately. Packing in ice or snow is not too extreme, but a more common treatment is wet towels or sheets and a fan. Call 911. While waiting, check his or her temperature often to make sure that you don't overdo the cooling. You want to reduce the temperature, not chill the victim.

Burns

Burns sometimes occur during waxings when a beeswax candle is used, or if you are too busy watching where the wax is falling that you don't notice where the flame is going. Electricity can also cause burns.

Reddened skin is the sign of a first-degree burn. Immerse the area in *cold* water or cool with an ice pack and apply a used tea bag that has been allowed to cool. Aloe vera gel will moderate the pain. Commercial burn ointments are made for this kind of burn. *Do not use petroleum jelly or butter.* If blisters form, it is a second-degree burn. Again, the initial treatment is cold water. Then cover the blister with a sterile gauze pad. If the blisters fill with a clear fluid, leave them alone; do not open them. If the fluid is cloudy, they may be infected; this calls for a trip to the doctor.

Third-degree burns are very serious. The injury may at first resemble a second-degree burn but progresses quickly to a charred or whitish color, and the surface may be warm and dry. Interestingly enough, it may not be painful at first. This is not because the injury is not serious; it is because the pain nerves have been damaged.

This kind of injury is beyond first aid. If you are not trained and equipped to handle this kind of burn, get the submissive to a doctor. *Do not use cold water or burn ointment.* You can, however, cover the burn with a sterile dressing.

Bone and Muscle Injuries

Occasionally, something goes wrong and a submissive takes a severe fall or crashes against something. In most cases, these "accidents" were caused by simple carelessness. To be precise, your carelessness. A common cause of falls is a littered playroom, one with wires or ropes scattered about, or one with an ultra-shag carpet that acts as a trap for high heels.

In any case, if there is serious damage, such as broken bones or torn ligaments, you need immediate medical assistance. If you suspect a break, immobilize the limb by tying a rolled-up magazine or ruler to it with a bandage or scarf and get the person to a doctor.

If the muscle is only strained, the treatment is exactly the opposite as with bruises. Apply warmth: I tend to lean toward fluffy towels soaked in hot water. That should get the blood flowing again. Wrap it with an Ace bandage and elevate it on a stool or a few pillows.

If a muscle has a minor tear, you will see a large bruise; apply an ice pack. Over-the-counter painkillers will help. If the pain continues, go to a doctor.

Dungeon First-aid Kit

A good dungeon first-aid kit includes many of the same items as a good home first-aid kit—with two additions. If you do handcuff or chain bondage, it should contain a pair of bolt cutters and an extra set of keys.

At a minimum, I recommend:

4x4 sterile dressings
Ace bandages
Adhesive tape
Aloe vera gel
Anesthetic spray
Antibiotic ointment
Band-Aids and/or rubbing alcohol
Burn ointment
EMT scissors
Ice pack
K-Y Jelly
Sling bandage (triangular)
Smelling salts
Splint
Sterile cotton
Sterile bandage roll
Tweezers

A Final Note

I have written several times "go to a doctor" or "call 911." In the middle of a scene, you—and probably your submissive—are going to be reluctant to climb out of the closet this way. Don't worry—they have seen it before. One of my friends, a lovely dominant and a New York City EMT, was confronted by a man who admitted sticking a gerbil "up there" into his wife, where it had "passed to its reward" and was now stuck. Without looking up from her notepad, my friend asked, "Vagina or anus?" They have seen it before! You probably won't even make the top 100.

Second, but more important, is your responsibility to another individual. You have accepted responsibility for another. To allow him or her to be put in danger simply because you are embarrassed is irresponsible. You have a duty to seek medical aid.

To minimize embarrassment, if there is time, change into vanilla clothing. Medical people do tend to give a bit more respect to those who look "normal." If there isn't, grab something out of the closet. If the ER is anything like most, you will have long enough to *make* a complete outfit from fabric before they get around to you. You can easily change clothes in the restroom. Another thing to bring along is a notepad. Keep track of those who have talked with you. You may want to hand out condemnation or compliments later. In any case, the sight of someone politely taking notes *does* tend to make people behave.

You don't have to tell the complete story of the scene. If, for example, your submissive fell from a suspension frame and broke her leg, a simple "she fell" should be sufficient. Male dominants are especially at risk in this area. In today's political-medical environment, if there is a suspicion of "abuse," the less on the chart, the better. However, you should never withhold information that could be necessary to the treatment.

APPENDIX A
Where to Find What

Because so many of us are relatively isolated. I have put together a list of mail-order suppliers and other useful addresses.

Bookstores

Eve's Garden, 119 West 57th Street, Suite 420, New York, NY 10019. (800) 848-3837

Come Again, 353 East 53rd Street, New York, NY 10022. (212) 308-9394

Prometheus Books, 59 John Glenn Drive, Buffalo, NY 14228-9827. (800) 421-0351

Sexuality Library, 938 Howard Street, San Francisco, CA 94103. (415) 974-8990

QSM, PO Box 8822342, San Francisco, CA 94188. (414) 550-7776

Computer Bulletin Boards

2/3 Board	217-877-1138
Adult Action BBS	514-483-5164
Afternoon Delight BBS	407-957-0231
Backdoor	415-756-6238
Boothill	213-962-7436
Bound for Pleasure BBS	617-374-9255
Connecticut Adult Connections	203-889-0735
Denver Exchange	303-623-4965
Der Baron's Schloss	206-324-2121
Fantasy Realization I	617-784-8251
Fantasy Realization II	617-397-8844
Final Frontier	312-334-8638
Forum BBS	215-722-1482
Fountains of Pleasure	313-348-7854
Harbor Bytes	410-235-6753
Hedonism BBS	310-631-7697
Images At Twilight	519-649-2672
Inferno	609-886-6818
Laura's Lair	417-683-5534
Lifestyles	516-698-5390
LuvCat's Lair	215-467-7407
Mirrored Dragon's Dream	402-734-2073
Montreal's Electronic Dungeon	514-522-FUNN
MoonDog BBS	718-692-2498
Multicom 4	716-463-4070
North Keep	503-289-4872
Pizazz TBBS	816-HOT-6900
Pleasure Dome	804-490-LUST
Plumber's Helper	601-832-5132
Rapture BBS	707-573-9438/0927

Scheherazade BBS	206-650-1469
SM Board	818-508-6796
Stephanie's Playhouse	619-569-TSTV
Swingers Connection	215-727-8406
The Cat House BBS	904-778-4236
The Covenant BBS	717-394-2819
The Digital Obsession BBS	215-678-4214
The English Palace	908-739-1755
The Exchange	704-342-2333
The Exchange	713-521-2191
The Farmer's Daughter	414-728-4058
The Great Escape	310-676-3534
The Love Connection	317-236-6740
The Pig Pen	613-723-3143
The Wee Cabin	619-552-0449
Throbnet	314-327-LUST
TITAN	904-476-1270

D&S Supplies:

While all of these companies provide products that are useful in the scene, some do not look upon us with favor. The notation "be discreet" simply means not to mention D&S in your order.

Constance Enterprises, PO Box 43079, Upper Montclair, NJ 07043. (Scene clothing, books and movies and cross-dressing supplies)

Diversified Services, PO Box 35737, Brighton, MA 02135. No phone (Scene supplies and things to coax lovers and hint about D&S interests)

Eastern Currents, 3040 Childer Lane, Santa Cruz, CA 95062. (800) 946-9264 (Acupuncture needles and supplies)

Gauntlet, 8720 Santa Monica Boulevard, Los Angeles, CA 94101. (415) 431-3133 (Piercing and piercing supplies)

Gravity Plus, PO Box 2182, La Jolla, CA 92038. (800) 383-8056 (Gravity boots and inversion tables)

Heartwood Whips of Passion, 412 North Coast Highway, #210, Laguna Beach, CA 92651. (714) 376-9558 (Stock and custom-made whips)

Hedonic Engineering, 2215-R Market Street #107, San Francisco, CA 94114. (Whips and leather goods—will do custom designs)

Humane Restraint, PO Box 16, Madison, WI 53701-0016. (608) 849-6313 (Provides restraint equipment to law enforcement and hospitals. The catalog is chock-full of goodies—be discreet.)

Lucifer's Armory, 874 Broadway, Suite 801, New York, NY 10003. No phone (Vampire Gloves and Sports Sheets—mail order only)

Raelyn Gallina, PO Box 20034, Oakland, CA 94620. (510) 655-2855 (Piercing jewelry, body piercing, branding)

SAM Co., Box 514, 9728 Third Avenue, Brooklyn, NY 11209. No phone (Custom leather work)

Sandmutopian Supply Co., PO Box 11314, San Francisco, CA 94101–1314. (General scene supplies)

Sweater Bumpers, PO Box 1854, Los Lunas, NM 87031. (505) 865-1488 (Nonpierced nipple rings/feminine beauty rings) There is a $5 charge for a sizing chart that must be used before placing an order.

The Noose, 261 West 19th Street, New York, NY 10011. (General scene supplies)

The Utopian Network, PO Box 1146, New York, NY 10156. (Whips and leather goods—will do custom designs)

Vernon's Specialities, 386G Moody Street, Waltham, MA 02154. (617) 894-1744 (Scene and TV clothing)

Versatile Fashions, PO Box 1051, Tustin, CA 92681. (714) 776-1510 (Scene and TV clothing)

Miscellaneous Sources

Earth Guild, 33 Haywood Street, Asheville, NC 28801. (800) 327-8448 (Dye for nylon rope and scene equipment)

Tandy Leather Company, 1400 Everman Parkway, Fort Worth, TX 76140. (Leather and leather-working supplies —be discreet)

Organizations

As these are all not-for-profit organizations, common courtesy would dictate enclosing a self addressed, stamped envelope with any request for information.

Arizona Power Exchange, 5821 North 67th Avenue #103-276, Glendale, AZ 85301. (602) 491-1009, ext. 2739

Black Rose, PO Box 11161, Arlington, VA 22210-1161. (301) 369-7667

Chicagoland Discussion Group, Box 250009, Chicago, IL 60625. (312) 281-1098

Eulenspiegel Society, PO Box 2783, Grand Central Station, New York, NY 10163. (212) 388-7022

Lone Star PEP, PO Box 810715, Dallas, TX 75381. (214) 601-1320

NLA: Columbus, PO Box 16235, Columbus, OH 43216. No phone

NLA: National HQ, 584 Castro Street, Suite 444, San Francisco, CA 94114-2500.

NLA: New England, PO Box N-1111, New Bedford, MA 02746. No phone

NLA: Portland, PO Box 5161, Portland, OR 97208.
(503) 727-3148/(503) 727-3148
Orgasm, PO Box 5702, Portland, OR 97208. (503) 688-0669

PEP Albuquerque, 1113 Delamar NW, Albuquerque, NM 87107. No phone

PEP: Nashville, PO Box 174, St. Bethlehem, TN 37155.
(617) 648-1937

Society of Janus, PO Box 6794, San Francisco, CA 94101.
(415) 848-0452

Threshold, 2554 Lincoln Boulevard #381, Marina del Rey,
CA 90291. (310) 452-0616

United Leatherfolk of Connecticut, PO Box 281172, East
Hartford, CT 06128–1172. No phone

Pansexual Advertising Magazines That Have Some Good 'Serious' Articles

Kinky People, Places, and Things, PO Box 99770, Seattle,
WA 98199. No phone

S&M News, Carter Stevens Studios, Inc., PO Box 727,
Pocono Summit, PA 18346.

Stand Corrected, c/o Shadow Lane, PO Box 1910, Studio
City, CA 91614-0910. No phone

Wild Side, PO Box 101178, Nashville, TN 37210. No phone

Safe-sex Supplies and Toys

Eve's Garden, 119 West 57th Street, Suite 420, New York,
NY 10019.

Good Vibrations, 938 Howard Street, San Francisco, CA
94103. (415) 974-8990

"Serious" Scene Publications

Do not neglect the gay and lesbian publications. They are an excellent source of ideas. After all, a male or female submissive is a male or female submissive regardless of the sex of the dominant.

Bad Attitude (lesbian), PO Box 390110, Cambridge, MA 02139.

Drummer (gay) PO Box 410390, San Francisco, CA 94141-0390. (415) 252-1195

Dungeonmaster (pansexual), PO Box 410390, San Francisco, CA 94141-0390. (415) 252-1195

On Our Backs (lesbian), PO Box 421916, San Francisco, CA 94142. (415) 861-4723

The S&M News, Carter Stevens Presents, PO Box 551, Pocono Summit, PA 18346. (717) 839-2512

The Sandmutopian Guardian (pansexual), PO Box 11314, San Francisco, CA 94101-0390. (415) 252-1195

Journal of Sexual Liberty, PO Box 422385, San Francisco, CA 94142-2385. No phone

Videotapes

Bon-Vue Enterprises, PO Box 92889, Long Beach, CA 90809-2889. (310) 631-1600

Cal Star, 641 West Avenue J, Suite 413, Lancaster, CA 93534. (805) 265-9827

Calbrat Enterprises, PO Box 637, Capitola, CA 95010. No phone

Cameo Classics, PO Box 857, Williamsville, NY 14231. No phone)

Carter Stevens Presents, PO Box 727, Pocono Summit, PA 18346. (717)839-2512

HOM, PO Box 7302, Van Nuys, CA 91409-9987. (818) 780-5898

Kurt Stevens, Suite 187, 12B The Ellipse, Mount Laurel NJ 08054. (609) 786-3737

Nu-West, PO Box 1239, San Marcos, CA 92069. No phone

Redboard Video, PO Box 2069, San Francisco, CA 94126. No phone

Shadow Lane, PO Box 1910, Studio City, CA 91614-0910. (818) 985-9151

Sudden Impact Productions, 226 East 54th Street, Suite 301, New York, NY 10022. (212) 753-2544

T.V.I., 847A 2nd Avenue, Suite 319, New York, NY 10017. No phone

Rock-hard Reading

Nonfiction Books

Encyclopedia of Unusual Sex Practices, Brenda Love. (Barricade Books, Fort Lee, NJ, 1992). From Abduction to Weight Training, this is a comprehensive look at D&S — as well as other sexual practices. Aside from its other values, you can mystify your friends by casually referring to acrophilia or furtling.

The Black Book, Bill Brent. (PO Box 31155, San Francisco, CA 94131-0155, 1993). This is a yearly "catalog" of all kinds of kinky companies. Bill doesn't charge for his listings so there is wide range of outfits you wouldn't hear of otherwise. I'd put this near the top of my must-buy list.

The Breathless Orgasm: A Lovemap Biography of Asphyxiophilia, Gordon Money, Gordon Wainright, David Higsburger. (Prometheus, Buffalo, NY) This is a treatise on a subject so delicate that I will not touch it in *The Loving Dominant*, but rather than leave those who might have an interest in this subject out, I'm including this citation.

Coming to Power: Writings and Graphics on Lesbian S/M, edited by Samois. Samois (named for Anne-Marie's estate in *The Story of O*) is a group of lesbians interested in D&S. This is a collection of essays and prose writings. It is an amazingly honest look at this complex subject, including the therapeutic effects of D&S and how to be feminist and a D&S player at the same time. For those unfamiliar with feminist politics, that section alone is an eye-opener.

Erotic Power: An Exploration of Dominance and Submission, Gini Graham Scott, Ph.D. This is a sociological treatise and in-depth exploration of the physical as well as the psychological dynamics of D&S. The author functioned both as an observer of and as a participant in the scene. The primary limitation is that it gives short shrift to male doms.

Masochism: A Jungian View, Lyn Cowan. (Spring Publications, Dallas.) This book presents an interesting theory of masochism. However, I'm a bit uncomfortable with the relatively unfriendly treatment accorded to the active partner. Dr. Cowan seems unwilling to differentiate between sadists who seek unwilling victims and dominants who cooperate in fulfilling mutual needs.

The Sexually Dominant Woman: A Workbook for Nervous Beginners, Lady Green. (3739 Balboa Avenue #195, San Francisco, CA, 1993). Although relatively short at 60 pages, this comb-bound book is just what it says it is—a handbook for a woman learning to exercise her dominant side. I suspect that a number of these volumes are sold to men who present them hopefully to their lady loves.

Learning the Ropes, Race Bannon. (Daedalus Publishing Company, Los Angeles, 1992). This book is a good overview of the scene. If I knew someone to whom I wanted to give a quick view of the positive side of D&S, this would be one of the books I would recommend.

The Leatherman's Handbook II, Larry Townsend. (Carlyle Communications, New York, 1989). This is often billed as the definitive D&S handbook. It doesn't quite live up to that billing, because it is completely gay oriented. However, it does cover quite a bit of ground—perhaps more than you wanted to cover. The first-person accounts can be exciting to some readers; however, others find them an obstacle to overcome on the way to the information.

Lesbian S/M Safety Manual, edited by Pat Califia. (Alyson Publications, Boston, 1988). This book is a *must* for anyone, straight or gay, who plays in D&S. It is a comprehensive guide to safe playing. It covers both physical and psychological threats, as well as some of the finest safe sex advice I have ever encountered.

Mayflower Manners, Sydney Biddle Barrows and Ellis Weiner. (Doubleday, New York, 1990). Although the section on D&S in this book is relatively short (pages 120 to 126), it is excellent, and the remainder of the book is packed with information missing from other etiquette books.

Pleasure and Danger: Exploring Female Sexuality, Carol Vance, ed. (Routledge, Boston, 1984). The Scholar and Feminist Conference at Barnard in 1982 was almost ripped apart when politically correct feminists tried to suppress feminists who wanted the freedom to enjoy power exchange. This is a collection of papers and talks from this watershed of the woman's movement.

SM 101, Jay Wiseman. (PO Box 1261, Berkeley, CA). This is an excellent extensive treatment of D&S technique and philosophy. I may disagree with Jay on a few points, but I can't fault his thoroughness. The biggest problem is that it is self-published and has a very limited circulation.

S&M: Studies in Sadomasochism, Thomas Weinberg and G.W. Kamel, eds. (Prometheus Books, Buffalo, NY 1983). This is a collection of essays on the nature, origin, and development of what they call sadomasochism. Some are decent; some have points of interest; a number are so far off the mark as to be laughable.

Sadomasochism in Everyday Life, Lynn S. Chancer. (Rutgers University Press, New Brunswick, 1992). This book has a good background on sadomasochistic theory; its primary weakness is that it was plainly a thesis or dissertation, and the hoops the author had to jump through to please members of the committee are painfully obvious. It just goes to prove the truism that all graduate students are masochistic.

A Taste for Pain: On Masochism and Female Sexuality, Maria Marcus. (St. Martins Press, New York, 1981). The author, a self-admitted masochist, explores the existing literature on sadomasochism from a very personal, insightful point of view.

Whips and Kisses: Parting the Leather Curtain, Mistress Jacqueline. (Prometheus Books, Buffalo, NY). This is a book, written by a professional dominatrix with the assistance of a pair of ghostwriters. Much of it is trite, but there are a few interesting insights.

Fiction Books

I've given you all a pretty heavy list of serious D&S reading. Now let's look at some of the fun titles. While all of these are erotic, none are poorly written or simpleminded.

The Claiming of Sleeping Beauty, Beauty's Punishment, and *Beauty's Release*, A.N. Roquelaure. (E.P. Dutton, New York, 1984). One of the worst-kept secrets in modern literature is that Roquelaure (the French word for "cloak") is really Anne Rice of *The Vampire Trilogy* fame. These are—and deserve to be—classics. Sensual with rich imagery. The characters have real depth and mature from book to book.

Dangerous Lessons, Anonymous. (Masquerade Books, New York, 1994). One of what I call the "classic-fluff series." This one is a collection of short stories set across a broad span of time and space. Priests from the Inquisition rub pages with lecherous nobles from prerevolutionary Russia.

Doc and Fluff, Pat Califia. (Alyson Publications, Boston, 1990). Would you believe a lesbian D&S postapocalypse science-fiction biker novel? This is it. You will *never* look at your motorcycle battery the same way again. Califia is a founding fath...er, mother of Samois and one of the best sex writers around.

The First Stroke, Cappy Kotz. (Lace Publications, Seattle, 1988). This is hot and hardboiled lesbian D&S. These are strong women with knives who know how to use them and buffed submissives who glory in their submission. Koltz has a tight style like the best of the old detective writers, but with a sensuality that makes the words smoke on the page.

Macho Sluts, Pat Califia. (Alyson Publications, Boston, 1988). These stories revolve around the exchange of power and the dynamics of lesbian D&S relationships. They also manage to break about every taboo most people can think of and are replete with graphic detail.

The Raging Peace, Dreams of Vengeance, Thrown of Council, Artemis Oakgrove. (Alyson Publications, Boston).Would you believe a lesbian D&S romance novel? How about three of them?

Sacred Passions, Anonymous. (Masquerade Books. New York, 1991). More of the classic-fluff series. This one is about a cross-dresser who tries to hide in a convent and finds that the discipline there is not just for the soul.

Satanic Adventures, Anonymous. Another in the classic-fluff series. This one is about a naïve young woman who meets a man who is not naïve about anything.

The Story of O, Pauline Réage. More than one dreamer has had his or her fantasies made more real by this classic. It is the tale of the psychological journey of a submissive through her submission to several men.

Venus in Furs, Leopold von Sacher-Masoch. (Rhinoceros Books, New York, 1993). What *The Story of O* did for female submissives, *Venus in Furs* does for males. This Victorian novel by the man whose name gave us "masochism" details in sensual and psychological terms the mistress/slave relationship.

APPENDIX C
Scrubbing Up Afterward

Cleaning up after a scene can present some interesting problems that are often not completely covered in *Good Housekeeping* books. While you may delegate the actual cleanup to your submissive, it is, after all, your property, and you will probably want to supervise, with or without a riding crop.

Cooled wax from your submissive's skin can easily be vacuumed up if this is done before it is ground into a carpet or into the cracks in a wood floor. Hot wax that falls on fabric is more difficult to remove. However, if you put a soft, absorbent cloth over the cooled wax and then heat the cloth with an iron, the wax will melt and be absorbed into the cloth. I have had particularly good luck with using this technique on a black velvet-covered chair I occasionally use for waxing.

Leather hoods, straps, and clothing can be cleaned with saddle soap. Smooth the soap on and then rub it until foam appears. Wipe off the foam, and you are finished. This not only cleans the leather, but it replaces the natural oils and helps it remain soft and supple for many years. Every six months or so, leather articles should be treated with neat's-foot oil. Use several light coats and finish by polishing with a soft cloth. Do not use too much; you want to oil it, not drown it. If leather has to be stored, simply hang it up. Do not seal it in plastic; it needs air.

Because leather whips come in such intimate—and forceful—contact with the submissive's skin, there is a chance that they could pick up a bit of blood. For this reason, first wipe them with a rag soaked in hot, soapy water; then, with an alcohol-dampened rag and, finally, with a rag soaked in hot, clean water. After they have been allowed to dry, they should be lubricated to prevent them from becoming stiff.

I use a thin layer of butter—yes, butter—to soften whip tails. It is a natural lubricant that contains little to irritate or inflame sensitive or broken skin. I just stroke it on and rub the surface dry. Some other dominants use mink oil for the softening agent. Saddle soap can also be used, but because it contains chemicals that could cause an allergic reaction, I tend to avoid it.

Toys like dildos, douche nozzles, needles, and knives, should be washed in hot, soapy water and allowed to soak for half an hour in rubbing alcohol or a mixture of one part household bleach and nine parts water. I strongly recommend that you not use the same toy on different submissives. Dildos can be made easier to clean by covering them before use with a condom.

Vibrators should be wiped with a rag soaked in hot, soapy water and another with alcohol. However, because of the construction of most vibrators, they cannot be soaked. Instead, they should be covered with a condom before use. For those too large to cover with a condom (although you will be surprised how much one stretches), use a surgical glove. Some vibrators like the Hitachi Magic Wand and the Oster Stick Massager have attachments that can be soaked in alcohol or water-bleach mixture.

Condoms, dental dams, finger cots, and latex gloves should be sealed in a plastic bag with a bit of alcohol and disposed of in the trash. Ideally, they should be treated like biohazard materials and incinerated in a sanitary manner, but sometimes the principal way to make sure that the wrong thing is done is to make the right thing too complex to do. Let's just keep it simple; dispose of them in a sealed container full of alcohol fumes.

Rope and nylon strapping can be washed in an ordinary washing machine. However, first put them into a bag to minimize knotting and to prevent them from becoming tangled in the agitator. A mesh bag like those used to wash delicate fabrics is ideal. However, a pillowcase will do.

APPENDIX D
Who in the Heck Are We?

Prodigy D&S Users

In 1992 I participated in two surveys of D&S groups. Because each was of a rather small group, neither gives a true indication of the scene. However, each provides a valuable look at groups not normally surveyed.

The first was an impromptu survey by one of the users of *other* users of the D&S section of the Frank Discussion bulletin board on the Prodigy computer system. A series of questions were posed, and readers were urged either to post their answers on public board or to send them by electronic mail to a specific user code.

There were 87 tabulated responses.

1. Sex:
   58 Males
   29 Females

2. Age:
   Under 21= 5
   Under 25= 5
   Under 30= 10
   Under 35= 17
   Under 45= 34
   Under 55= 15
   Over 55= none

3. Residence:
   38 from large towns
   19 medium towns
   26 small towns
   2   said "burbs"

4. Scene orientation:
   15 doms
   49 subs
   17 switchables
   6 don't know

5. Marital status:
   52 Married
   9   Divorced
   34 Single
   1 said Gay (Three people said they were gay. Only one
   regarded it as significant in discussing marital status.)

6. Age at which D&S interest discovered:
   Preteen= 17
   Teenager= 35
   Adult= 21
   Unknown= 6

7. How interest discovered:
   Dreams= 3
   Fantasies= 26
   Reading= 26
   Computer BBS= 4
   Discussion w/significant other= 1
   Introduced by friend(s)= 18
   Childhood games= 7
   Not Sure= 8

8. Does your significant other know?
   Yes= 46
   No= 13
   NA= 23
   No Answer= 1

8a. Does your significant other approve?
   Yes= 30
   No= 11
   NA= 33
   No Answer= 2

9. Are you actively participating in D&S?
   Yes= 48
   No= 39

10. Favorite activities within D&S: (see footnote)
   Discipline= 27
   Humiliation= 17
   Pleasing= 19
   CBT= 1
   Bondage= 33
   Cross-dressing= 9
   Baby games= 2, Ice= 1
   Fantasy rape= 1
   All= 4
   Tickling= 2

Sensory deprivation= 7
Teasing= 7
Water sports/enemas= 4
Anal= 1
NA= 22

11. Activities you want to try:
    Discipline= 9
    Humiliation = 7
    All= 17
    Maid service= 1
    Bondage= 12
    Cross-dressing= 1
    Public scenes= 3
    Teasing= 3
    Water sports= 3
    Fantasy rape= 1
    Sensory deprivation= 2
    Pleasing= 9
    More= 18
    Unsure= 8
    NA= 12

12. Are you full-time/life-style D&S?
    Yes= 1
    No= 86

13. Do you want to be life-style?
    Yes= 23
    No= 41
    Unsure= 23

14. If dom, how many subs do you have?
    None= 8
    One= 6
    More= 6
    NA= 63

15. If sub, how many doms do you serve?
    None= 27
    One= 21
    More= 5
    NA= 28

16. Have you ever been to a professional?
    Yes= 17
    No= 70

17. Have you been to a public D&S club?
    Yes= 18
    No= 69

18. Is specific attire important?
    Yes= 50
    No= 23
    Unsure= 8

19. How many other people know your D&S interest outside BBSs?
    No one= 12
    One= 23
    Two= 10
    More= 36
    Unsure= 1

20. Is D&S better as fantasy or reality?
    Reality= 34
    Fantasy= 15
    Sometimes either= 21
    Unsure= 11

21. Highest education level:
    No HS= 1
    HS= 3
    Some college= 24

College degree= 25
Some graduate school= 8
Advanced degree= 22

Eulenspiegel Survey

The second survey consisted of a four-page professionally designed and printed survey sent to members of the Eulenspiegel Society, one of the oldest continuously active D&S groups in the world. I'm not going to include all the questions, but here is a selection.

There were 130 tabulated responses

Sex:
    Male= 104
    Female= 18
    Transsexual= 3

Scene orientation:
    Dominant= 37
    Submissive= 36
    Switchable= 49

Age:
    18-29= 10
    30-39= 38
    40-49= 45
    50-59= 27
    60+= 5

Education:
    High school= 10
    Some college= 22
    College graduate= 20
    Some postgraduate= 21
    Advanced degree= 39

Respondents were given an opportunity to rate topics based on how interested they were in them. The following is a list arranged from most popular to least popular:

- Fantasy
- Bondage
- Safety
- Spanking
- The psychology of S&M
- Toys
- Discussing limits
- Relations in S&M
- How to find a partner
- Scene etiquette
- Lingerie
- Ritual
- Strapping
- Flogging
- Leather
- Exhibitionism
- Fashion
- Humiliation
- Caning
- History of S&M
- Voyeurism
- Dungeon construction
- Hot wax
- Piercing
- Electricity
- Rubber
- Tattooing
- Sex magic
- Golden showers

Female cross-dressing
Transsexuality
Cutting
Male cross-dressing

Toys used in scenes:

45.4%= crop
44.6%= collar
43.8%= dildo
43.8%= ropes
43.1%= blindfold
43.1%= whip
42.3%= nipple clamps
39.2%= leather cuffs
35.4%= battery vibrator
33.8%= clothespins
32.3%= buttplug
30.8%= chains
30.8%= handcuffs
30.0%= wax candles
26.9%= AC vibrator
26.2%= gag
25.4%= cockring
24.6%= scene clothing
16.9%= harnesses
10.0%= stock
10.0%= hood
7.7%= electric devices

About the fantasy aspect of D&S:

Only 7.7% said they thought it would always be a fantasy.

But 22.3% said that up to that time it had been a fantasy.

Scene locations were:
  76.9%= in a bedroom
  47.7%= at clubs
  36.9%= at parties
  24.6%= in a dungeon
  20.0%= in public

Acceptable scene partners were:
  62.3%= spouse
  44.6%= a few close friends
  23.1%= hot-looking strangers
  17.7%= anyone
  8.5%= friends

Respondents met scene partners:
  50.0%= at Eulenspiegel
  43.8%= at D&S clubs
  29.2%= by placing newspaper and newsletter advertisements
  29.2%= by answering newspaper and newsletter advertisements
  18.5%= by placing magazine advertisements
  14.6%= by answering magazine advertisements
  5.4%= through computer bulletin boards
  3.8%= through telephone chat lines

Scenes involved:
  69.2%= equipment
  65.4%= sex toys
  49.2%= costumes
  38.5%= theatrical-type props

Contracts

Here are the contracts entered into by two different dominant/submissive couples. The styles are quite different, but the basic features remain constant.

Master Morgan's and Leah's Contract

1. Leah agrees to place control of her body, thoughts, and behaviors in the hands of Master Morgan while they are in direct contact. She will follow all commands that fit within the limits of this contract completely, faithfully, and with immediate speed. She will answer all questions honestly and completely. She agrees to receive punishment if she fails to comply with the above.

2. Master Morgan accepts the responsibility for leading Leah in the exploration of her sexuality. Morgan agrees to protect Leah's sense of internal self-worth while removing ego barriers that have prohibited her from exploring these areas on her own. Morgan agrees to a long-term goal that Leah will become comfortable in the knowledge of her sexual desires, as expanded by this training. She shall achieve her "graduation" when she is able to control her own sexuality because her restructured sexual ego and sense of self-esteem are in harmony.

3. The choice of behaviors, sexual partners, physical devices, and punishments is determined by Master Morgan, with the following exceptions:

a. Leah may stop any activity at any time by the clear use of her safe word;

b. Leah and Morgan may leave this agreement temporarily and return to the outside world at any time simply by requesting it;

c. While the level of acceptable force will be learned by mutual exploration and may change with time, nothing will be done to cause physical injury to Leah. Nor will she be exposed to risks of pregnancy, arrest, nor disease.

d. Verbal humiliation will be used only as it affects Leah's preconceived notions about sexual morality. It will never be used to describe her general worth as a human being nor her nonsexual behaviors, except her unwillingness to follow orders.

4. This contract expires immediately upon clear notice by either party that the contract is terminated.

Sir Spencer's and M's Contract

That the two of us have become united as closely as we have in our lives, I now unite and align myself with you in the signing of this agreement and state as carefully my own additional commitment to the strength and assurance of our relationship. We thus compose and provide this document as our original "Agreement of Submission" as a statement of our devotion to our continued relationship and to provide the sense of solidity that we both so very much want.

Of my own free will, as of (date), I, (M's name here), hereby submit to you as my master, and grant you full ownership and use of my body and mind from now until (date about six months later). I further understand and agree to the conditions of the sharing of my body, mind, heart, and soul which I desire to give over to you, and submission as you have detailed herein.

I will strive diligently to acquaint my personal self, my habits, and my attitudes with those that are in that are in keeping with your particular interests and desires for me as your submissive. I will thus always seek to discover new ways of pleasing you and will be observant that I always do those things that you have already indicated that you enjoy. I will gracefully accept any criticism you may choose to inform me of.

For example, when deciding modes of dress, rather than dictating what they should be in this document, to maintain a more flexible position, I am allowed by you here to assist in the planning and negotiation of what forms and fashions of apparel are to be worn by me.

As another example, I will gladly honor at your desire and request, to undertake the public display and to exhibit the exact condition of the state of my submission through the symbols we have chosen and will choose in the future.

I will not conceal or hold private from you, any aspects of this component of my life and existence. I will advise you immediately and without hesitation of all events and occurrences in this and related aspects of my life. Especially, of anything which may affect our special relationship and the condition and status of my ownership and submission.

Thus to this end, I will always look toward and seek your kind assistance. I will be firm in my assurance with conviction and understanding, that you do hold with love and concern, my best and highest interests. I will try to please you and thus achieve any rewards you may so kindly deign to give me., I will obey you at all times and will wholeheartedly seek your pleasure and well-being above all other considerations.

Accordingly, I know that you sincerely have my own safety and hopes at heart and will thus ensure that my obedience is complete and I thus may safely entrust myself to your exacting care and attention with no fears or apprehensions on my part.

I am aware that this agreement is not to be considered as being synonymous with a slave contract. In the main intent and context of our agreement, I will obey you at all times during the period of this agreement.

Again, in keeping with the context and intent of this document, I thus give over to you the direction of my own privileges to my own pleasure, comfort, or gratification insofar as you desire or permit them. Or in this aspect I will, at all times, first ask you for your kind permission, before I may be allowed to enjoy my own pleasure in some particular manner or way. This would be any type of activity at all beyond routine sexual "selfpleasure," which use and frequency you have allowed me to negotiate with you.

In keeping with the intent of this agreement, I will answer any question posed by you immediately and without hesitation, fully and truthfully. As a counterpoint to this, and as you have expressly wished, I will understand that you want me to feel free to express, also without hesitation, any question, interest, desire or need, in keeping with the nature and condition of my submission and my desire for your pleasure, knowing that you do insist upon this questioning. However, I am first to ask permission in any case that I may desire to do something or to ask you a question.

In regard to the conditions of my ownership I agree to the following: I freely offer to you, in this aspect, the full and sole possession of my self; and that with the addition of the special clauses detailed herein, the condition of my ownership shall be fully determined by you.

As to exclusivity: As we have discussed and agreed; in addition to the condition of ownership, you have hereby allowed me to share time and activity in submitting to J. W. as my Mentor, just as you are my Master. For this additional consideration, I am very grateful to you and to J. W., as I know it will please both you and him, to allow for this arrangement.

In regard to the giving of myself to any other Masters, Mistresses, or any Dominants of any design, I hereby renounce any rights or privileges to do so; unless by special arrangement discussed with you directly, on an exception basis, and which may also include a three-way discussion between you, myself, and Mentor J. W.

Also in connection with the conditions of my submission and ownership, I will also be responsible to maintain myself in condition pleasing to you. I will heed your wishes as regards to during which portions of my day-to-day existence you wish me to be fully aware of the condition of my ownership and submission, and during what times of day and night these requirements are to be in force.

I also understand that you will determine the time and occurrences of our encounters, but that also during times in between our personal encounters, in order to please you, I may be also required to engage in my own remote training at your direction.

I understand that I need to maintain my own personal diary of events and emotions that I have had and felt since the very moment that I began to embark on this unique life adventure. Therefore I know that it is my responsibility to dutifully maintain my diary, and from time to time read to you from it, upon your request.

I understand that my failure to comply in any way with the intent, or with the clauses and conditions of this contract will constitute sufficient cause for me to face possible punishment of your sole determination.

Accordingly, I have humbly and at your instigation asked for the single "safe" word of "Prodigy," should I need to plead for a cessation of some treatment. You have assured me here and now that we may discuss and agree to any future change or addition to the safety signal.

You have further assured me herein that you may give audience to my pleas in regards to some particular method or treatment that you may desire to place me under. I am assured and trusting that you will always consider the current state of my limitations in making any determination and imposition of any treatments I am to receive or endure. I am fully aware with my entire conscious being that your treatments of me, my body, flesh, mind, and spirit will be imposed always with your care and love.

Beyond these requests and considerations, I graciously allow and submit myself to receive any nature of treatment that you so desire to give me.

At my request, I gratefully understand that a minimum of one weekend a month will be set aside for my personal attention and further training.

Due to the unique nature of our relationship, the duration of the agreement (contract) of this relationship has been determined as stated at the top of this document. At a time approaching the termination of this agreement, you have assured me that you and I will discuss its renewal.

Also at that time any planning for modifications or updating of the terms and clauses of the agreement may be discussed. At that time, I understand, as you have told me, that we may discuss some sort of award based on my successful and pleasing completion of the terms of this agreement. The nature of this award may take the form of some type of emblem or insignia, or even some adornment, be it of a temporary or permanent nature, to mark the end of this first period of my grateful submission. Future emblematic awards may be further granted at the ends of each subsequent passing period of renewal as representative of the continuation and deepening of our relationship.

Master_____ date_____
Submissive_____ date_____

The following was added at a later date, as negotiated:

I, (Spencer's name here), vow to keep myself only unto you, in these things which we share and enjoy with each other, and participate with no others, except those which we have already discussed with other. This would include the clause in our main agreement document for Mentor, and now in this addendum for myself, to participate on occasion with K. T. and A. I. I will hereby also vow that I will not engage in, nor seek to engage in any new activities with any parties, unless you and I have thoroughly and completely assessed and discussed the particulars of the situation with each other, and are both in complete agreement and anticipation of such outside activity.

Excluding the exceptions already stated, we will not engage in any of these pursuits without the presence of the other. As our two rings which we will always wear have become symbols of our relationship.

Master_____ date_____

Submissive_____ date_____

APPENDIX F
What Color Is Your Handkerchief?

Almost everyone who has come in contact with the scene has heard about "the handkerchief code"; even the title of this section was taken from a well-respected, although out-of-publication, book by the lesbian D&S group, Samois. However, to most people, the signals remain a mystery. There is a good reason for this: there is no consistent, nationwide, mutually agreed upon set of signals. Each city and group has some local or personal variation from a ambiguous and nebulous norm. Handkerchief codes are most common in gay and lesbian circles, but some hetero groups have adopted them.

The closest thing to a norm is a vague agreement that right-side display indicates submissive and left dominant, but in the real world, a handkerchief in the left pocket or a set of keys on the left side of the pants may simply indicate a left-handed person.

Some of the more common colors are:

Black = Heavy into the scene
Gray = Bondage
Red = Fistfucker
Dark blue = Anal sex
Light blue = Oral sex
Purple = Into piercing
Green = Wants money or is willing to pay
Brown = Shit scenes (scat)
Yellow = Piss scenes (golden showers)
Pink = Breast fondler
Orange = Anything goes
White = Wants or is novice
White lace = Victorian scenes (lesbian or cross-dressing)
Maroon = Likes menstruating women or is menstruating (lesbian)

Unfortunately, to make things even more complex, headbangers and other fringe groups have adopted wearing handkerchiefs in their belts or carrying them in their pockets, recognizing only that they indicate some sort of socially forbidden behavior.

Once, at an Eulenspiegel meeting, Lenny, the owner of the Vault and a large, imposing gentleman who clearly has had more than a passing acquaintance with leather and motorcycles, gleefully told about approaching two youngsters who were defiantly sporting brightly colored handkerchiefs in their pockets. As he told it, he walked up to them, looked pointedly at their handkerchiefs while they tried to decide whether to run or to stand their ground and said, "So, you want to get your asses fucked and drink some piss." That persuaded them. They ran.

Spencer's Questionnaire

The following is a questionnaire that a colleague, Master Spencer, developed for delving into the fantasies of submissives.

A. Preliminary Idea/Format: Do you like something that is highly planned, or spontaneous, unplanned, and unstructured? Or perhaps something with elements of both?

Do you like the planning and negotiating to be oral or written or a little bit of both? Do you prefer knowing what will happen:
—Completely
—Mostly

—Somewhat
—Very little
—Not at all

B. Roles and Fantasies (Those that you like to be doing as the Bottom):

a. A role which is set in the present, the here and now, and you are "yourself," and "getting it" just as you are. For example, just because you "like to" or to "atone" for certain emotions present or past.

b. A role which is set in the present, and you are being "yourself," but some "fantasy" becomes more involved in these roles. For example, you are "in role" as a type of person who has certain faults and failings for which you need to atone, be corrected, or punished. In these types of roles you may either "remember" and describe the things you need correction for, or may maintain an "imaginary" or real "Logbook" or "Diary." Common imaginary or real failings are such things as:

—Assignments and things not carried out.
—"Faults" of timeliness: late to work, for appointments, or not calling when coming home late.
—Making a clutter, failing to clean the kitchen or the windows, failing to vacuum or dust or do other assigned tasks.
—Causing loss and breakage, auto fender benders, personal possessions of yourself or your Top, housewares, small collectibles, large or valuable collectibles and possessions.
—Behaving in a naughty, way like being argumentative, pouty, bored, and moody, in a foul, nasty, mood or aloof, sassy, sarcastic, and teasing, "flirtatious," other scandalous or exhibitionistic behavior.

—Money things. Spending too much on big items, or too much on small items, forgetting items you were told to buy.

—Appearance, not dressed to please deliberately, accidentally, or dressed entirely inappropriately for the occasion.

c. Fantasy roles where you may be "being" someone other than yourself, either in present day circumstances, or in times and places past.

These types of fantasy roles can be sort of grouped into several different types of circumstances. In a sense, these tend gradually to increase the level of the (Bottom) player's role.

(1) Fantasy roles in which the "victim"/Bottom/submissive is involuntarily "captured" and/or kidnapped and either "dealt with" randomly without any reason, or as a symbol of some oppressed cause:

—In the present time: by terrorists, mercenary soldiers, as "Westernized" women in Islamic states, Western women by Islamic courts, by bikers, a liberal woman by a community of reactionary "survivalists," (UK) "skinheads" vs. the wealthy class, a socialite kidnapped for ransom.

—Set in the past: a "heretic" by the Inquisition, the noble classes of old France and Russia, the village girl captured by de Sade, the Indian girl by cowboys or Western pioneers.

(2) In a very servile, subservient, even "slavelike" situation, often "punished" for very little provocation, these settings seem to be mostly in the "past":

—The heroine of the Science Fantasy/Sword and Sorcerer/Sword and Sandal epic stories: Norman, S. Greene, Gene Wolf's *Shadow of the Torturer*

—A slavegirl in the secret seraglio in the Topkapi Palace of Suleiman the Magnificent in Istanbul

—Girl on a plantation ruled by a tyrannical owner/overseer
—Girl in an English women's reformatory of about the 1880s
—A young hooker being "disciplined" by her pimp

(3) In a community where breaches of "standards" are dealt with most harshly by ritualistically inflicted corporal punishments:
—In colonial American jails for theft
—The frontier "schoolmarm" by locals
—On the English country estate by the lordly masterly owner, the girl in the employ for offenses of "manor" or "manner"
—Lady in her late teens or early twenties who is still receiving punishment from a stern "parental/guardian" figure.

(4) In circumstances "sort of" semiforced into accepting corporal punishment when some wrong has occurred or been committed:
—A modern British (or even American) woman being disciplined by her partner for something, and who both happen to have lurid D&S life-style passions
—Woman working in a bookstore, for being too inquisitive into subjects of sexual deviation
—A store employee, where some error or pilferage is suspected
—A member of a conservative/ Bible-oriented secret community who punish the women for sinful thoughts or behavior.

(5) An accepted submissive who is actively involved in the "life-style":
—Assigned to go out to a "dangerous" S/M bar, and pick up dominant. She is to be the "feature exhibition" at a display/ exhibition at a B&D party, or a B&D club.

—An actress/model in B&D flicks being done, postfilming, by a dominant who is getting "carried away"
—A lady in a B&D parlor/salon in the United States, Amsterdam, or Bangkok, or simply rented out to a dominant.

(6) Roles you like or prefer your Top to appear in/as:
—Alternating between punishing, soothing, praising, comforting
—Straightforward no-nonsense, silent, impassive, punisher
—Any kind of "humiliation" dominance, or degradation
—Mostly just himself/(or herself), with a touch of some of the above in it.

C. Play and Treatments:
—Are there any particular types of treatments you like?
—What are your "turn-ons"?
—Any particular parts of yourself you like or prefer being "treated"?
—Are there any particular types of treatments you don't like; won't do or try, or can't handle?
—What are your "turn-offs"?
—Any parts of yourself you do not like or want to be "treated"?

Anything you haven't tried yet, but might want to or would like to consider? Or do you like to have things suggested and talk about them with your Top, to get some ideas about what you might like to try as things develop?

What particular safety or code words or signals do you like or have?

One idea for determining a particular discipline to be appropriate for certain circumstances, is the "punishments jar" or "punishments box." Or even better, three of these "punishments jars." One each for light punishments, medium punishments, and heavy punishments. Then each type of failure, problem, or offense in the "Logbook" is accorded its own appropriate "level" of punishment to "choose" from that particular "punishments jar". Then one merely fills up the jar with little bits of paper upon which are written various punishments of the level indicated on the jar. If, for example the Bottom has recorded certain things in her "Logbook" which indicate that a punishment from the "medium" level jar is to be dealt, she gets to reach in that jar and pick one out at random, not knowing what it will be until, of course, she opens it up and reads it (aloud of course).

D. Scene, Setup, Costume, Dress:
—What sorts of costumes do you like to "dress up" in? Or do you like to tailor the costume to the developing scene?
—What sorts of costumes do you like your Top to "dress up" in? Or, likewise, do you like him/her also to tailor the fashion to the scene?

Do you like any music, or do you prefer silence, or should the scene fantasy be considered?

Do you like to view appropriate B&D videos preparatory to or during and in context with the scene, or while "relaxing"?

Do you like any refreshments to be available?

APPENDIX H
A Highly Idiosyncratic Glossary

B&D—Bondage and Discipline. A subgroup within D&S which is largely involved in making the submissive physically helpless and applying stimuli which outside of a scene would be painful. *See* Bondage, Discipline.

Blood sports—A group of techniques in which the submissive's skin is broken and blood is allowed to escape. Since the advent of AIDS and the spread of hepatitis, interest in blood sports has declined, and those who practice it have developed techniques to protect themselves. The most common blood sport is cutting. *See* Cutting.

Bondage—A group of techniques for rendering a submissive physically helpless. These include rope ties, handcuffs and manacles, wrapping, and mummification. *See* B&D; Decorative binding; Immobilization, Mummification.

Bottom—A submissive.

CBT—Cock-and-ball torture.

Cutting—A technique in which cuts are carefully made in the submissive's skin to produce an aesthetically pleasing pattern and stimulation to the submissive. The cuts are sometimes made into permanent markings by placing sterile foreign substances in them before they heal. *See* Blood sports.

Decorative binding—Using rope or cord to compress or tie a portion of the body where struggle will not cause it to tighten or cut into the submissive. *See* Immobilization.

Discipline—The application of stimuli which, outside of a scene, would be considered painful. Common discipline techniques are whipping, spanking, and strapping. *See* B&D.

Dominant—An individual who accepts the submissive's power and uses it for his or her mutual pleasure. *See* Sadist.

Edge play—These are particularly dangerous D&S that are looked upon with some trepidation. Because there is no formal "ruling body" in D&S, what is called edge play is up to the individual. Therefore, something that to one person might be considered edge play might not be edge play to another.

Edge player—A person who takes part in edge play. Example: "The guy is a real edge player; he's into heavy blood sports and asphyxia."

Go word—A signal by the submissive that everything is all right and you can continue with or increase the present level of stimulation. *See* Slow word; Stop word.

Golden showers—A humiliation technique in which the dominant urinates on the submissive. Consumption of the urine may be part of this scene.

Immobilization—Using rope or other bondage tools to render a submissive relatively helpless despite his or her struggles. *See* Decorative binding.

Masochism—The ability to derive pleasure from pain. Derives from the writings of Leopold von Sacher-Masoch. *See* S&M.

Panic snap—A linking device used with cable and chain that allows two lengths to be disconnected even when there is tension in the system. A safety device.

S&M—Sadism and Masochism—A term often used to describe the D&S scene; however, it is falling into disrepute because it is both inaccurate (Dominants are not sadists) and overly limited (all submissives are not masochists). *See* Masochism; Sadism.

Sadist—An individual who enjoys causing pain in a non-consensual manner, or regardless of the presence of absence or consent. Derives from the writings of the Marquis de Sade. *See* S&M.

Safe word—A word or phrase which permits the submissive to withdraw consent and terminate the scene at any point without endangering the illusion that the dominant is in complete control. *See* Go word; Slow word.

Scat—A slang term for scatophilia, taking pleasure in playing with and sometimes eating feces. While this is occasionally used as a means of humiliation, it presents a relatively severe health risk, not limited to AIDS and hepatitis.

Slow word—A signal by the submissive that things are getting too intense and you should change or decrease the stimulation. *See* Go word; Safe word.

SAM—Smart-Assed Masochist. A pseudo submissive who attempts to control everything the dominant does. A term of contempt. Example: "She's cute and willing, but she's a real SAM; you will spend most of your time trying to keep her from telling you which whip to use and how to swing it." *See* "Topping from the bottom."

Scene (A)—An individual session of whatever duration where the participants are in their D&S roles. Example: "It was a tremendously hot scene last night when Master Jim waxed Lisa at the Vault."

Scene (The)—The gamut of D&S activities and people considered as a whole. Example: "The scene contains some of the nicest people I have ever met."

Slave—Often used interchangeably with "submissive." However, generally reflecting a more intense level of submission or nonsexual or sexual-plus submission. For example, a slave might be someone who remains in a 24-hour-per-day submission and cooks, cleans, and otherwise takes care of a dominant's house. *See* Submissive.

Strapple—An elongated paddle with a bit more flex so that it is something intermediate between a strap and a paddle.

Submissive—An individual who gives up power in a D&S relationship for the mutual pleasure of those involved.

Suspension—A set of techniques for hanging a submissive, using ropes, webbing, or chain so that no part of the body touches the floor. This is a highly specialized technique, and great care must be used to prevent damage.

Switch (Switchable)—A person who enjoys both the dominant and submissive roles. A switch may be dominant with one person and submissive with another or may be dominant or submissive with the same person at different times.

Top—A dominant.

Topping from the bottom—A submissive's dictating the precise action in a scene. A term of contempt. Example: "She's cute and willing, but she's always topping from the bottom; you will spend most of your time trying to keep her from telling you which whip to use and how to swing it." *See* SAM

TT—Tit torture. The term applies to both males and females.

Vanilla—Not in the scene. A term used to describe ordinary, conventional life both sexual and otherwise. While it can be used in a pejorative sense, it is more often used to distinguish between scene and nonscene activities and people. Example: "I have to be careful in my vanilla life that people don't find out that I'm a dominant."

MASQUERADE BOOKS

ERICA BRONTE

LUST, INC.
$6.50/467-4

Explore the extremes of passion that lurk beneath even the most businesslike exteriors. Join the sexy escapades of a group of professionals whose idea of office decorum is like nothing you've ever encountered!

ATAULLAH MARDAAN

KAMA HOURI/DEVA DASI
$7.95/512-3

"Mardaan excels in crowding her pages with the sights and smells of India, and her erotic descriptions are convincingly realistic."
—Michael Perkins,
The Secret Record: Modern Erotic Literature

Kama Houri details the life of a sheltered Western woman who finds herself living within the confines of a harem—where she discovers herself thrilled with the extent of her servitude. *Deva Dasi* is a tale dedicated to the sacred women of India who devoted their lives to the fulfillment of the senses.

VISCOUNT LADYWOOD

GYNECOCRACY
$9.95/511-5

Julian is sent to a very special private school, where he discovers that his program of study has been devised by the deliciously stern Mademoiselle de Chambonnard. In no time, Julian is learning the many ways of pleasure and pain—under the firm hand of this beautifully demanding headmistress.

N. T. MORLEY

THE CONTRACT
$6.95/575-1

Meet Carlton and Sarah, two true connoisseurs of discipline. Sarah is experiencing some difficulty in training her current submissive. This unusual situation prompts Carlton to propose an unusual wager: if Carlton is unsuccessful in bringing Tina to a full appreciation of Sarah's domination, Carlton himself will become Sarah's devoted slave....

THE LIMOUSINE
$6.95/555-7

Brenda was enthralled with her roommate Kristi's illicit sex life: a never ending parade of men who satisfied Kristi's desire to be dominated. Brenda decides to embark on a trip into submission, beginning in the long, white limousine where Kristi first met the Master.

THE CASTLE
$6.95/530-1

Tess Roberts is held captive by a crew of disciplinarians intent on making all her dreams come true—even those she'd never admitted to herself. While anyone can arrange for a stay at the Castle, Tess proves herself one of the most gifted applicants yet....

THE PARLOR
$6.50/496-8

The mysterious John and Sarah ask Kathryn to be their slave—an idea that turns her on so much that she can't refuse! Little by little, Kathryn not only learns to serve, but comes to know the inner secrets of her keepers.

J. A. GUERRA, ED.

COME QUICKLY:
For Couples on the Go
$6.50/461-5

The increasing pace of daily life is no reason to forgo a little carnal pleasure whenever the mood strikes. Here are over sixty of the hottest fantasies around—all designed especially for modern couples on a hectic schedule.

VANESSA DURIÈS

THE TIES THAT BIND
$6.50/510-7

This true story will keep you gasping with its vivid depictions of sensual abandon. At the hand of Masters Georges, Patrick, Pierre and others, this submissive seductress experiences pleasures she never knew existed.... One of modern erotica's best-selling accounts of real-life dominance and submission.

M. S. VALENTINE

THE GOVERNESS
$6.95/562-X

Lovely Miss Hunnicut eagerly embarks upon a career as a governess, hoping to escape the memories of her broken engagement. Little does she know that Crawleigh Manor is far from the upstanding household it appears. Mr. Crawleigh, in particular, devotes himself to Miss Hunnicut's thorough defiling.

ELYSIAN DAYS AND NIGHTS
$6.95/536-0

From around the world, neglected young wives arrive at the Elysium Spa intent on receiving a little heavy-duty pampering. Luckily for them, the spa's proprietor is a true devotee of the female form—and has dedicated himself to the pure pleasure of every woman who steps foot across their threshold....

MASQUERADE BOOKS

THE CAPTIVITY OF CELIA
$6.50/453-4
Celia's lover, Colin, is considered the prime suspect in a murder, forcing him to seek refuge with his cousin, Sir Jason Hardwicke. In exchange for Colin's safety, Jason demands Celia's unquestioning submission....

AMANDA WARE
BINDING CONTRACT
$6.50/491-7
Louise was responsible for bringing many clients into Claremont's salon—so he was more than willing to have her miss a little work in order to pleasure one of his most important customers. But Eleanor Cavendish had her mind set on something more rigorous than a simple wash and set—dooming Louise to a life of sexual slavery!

BOUND TO THE PAST
$6.50/452-6
Doing research in an old Tudor mansion, Anne finds herself aroused by James, a descendant of the property's owners. Together they uncover the perverse desires of the mansion's long-dead master—desires that bind Anne inexorably to the past—not to mention the bedpost!

SACHI MIZUNO
SHINJUKU NIGHTS
$6.50/493-3
A tour through the lives and libidos of the seductive East. Using Tokyo's infamous red light district as his backdrop, Sachi Mizuno weaves an intricate web of sensual desire, wherein many characters are ensnared and enraptured by the demands of their carnal natures.

PASSION IN TOKYO
$6.50/454-2
Tokyo—one of Asia's most historic and seductive cities. Come behind the closed doors of its citizens, and witness the many pleasures that await. Lusty men and women from every stratum of society free themselves of all inhibitions.

MARTINE GLOWINSKI
POINT OF VIEW
$6.50/433-X
The story of one woman's extraordinary erotic awakening. With the assistance of her new, unexpectedly kinky lover, she discovers and explores her exhibitionist tendencies—until there is virtually nothing she won't do before the horny audiences her man arranges. Soon she is infamous for her unabashed sexual performances!

RICHARD McGOWAN
A HARLOT OF VENUS
$6.50/425-9
A highly fanciful, epic tale of lust on Mars! Cavortia—the most famous and sought-after courtesan in the cosmopolitan city of Venus—finds love and much more during her adventures with some cosmic characters. A sexy, sci-fi fairytale.

M. ORLANDO
THE SLEEPING PALACE
$6.95/582-4
Another thrilling volume of erotic reveries from the author of *The Architecture of Desire*. *Maison Bizarre* is the scene of unspeakable erotic cruelty; the *Lust Akademie* holds captive only the most luscious students of the sensual arts; *Baden-Eros* is the luxurious retreat of one's nastiest dreams.

CHET ROTHWELL
KISS ME, KATHERINE
$5.95/410-0
Beautiful Katherine can hardly believe her luck. Not only is she married to the charming Nelson, she's free to live out all her erotic fantasies with other men. Katherine's desires are more than any one man can handle—and plenty of men wait to fulfill her extraordinary needs!

MARCO VASSI
THE STONED APOCALYPSE
$5.95/401-1/Mass market
"Marco Vassi is our champion sexual energist."　—VLS

During his lifetime, Marco Vassi's reputation as a champion of sexual experimentation was worldwide. *The Stoned Apocalypse* is Vassi's autobiography; chronicling a cross-country trip on America's erotic byways, it offers a rare an stimulating glimpse of a generation's sexual imagination.

THE SALINE SOLUTION
$6.95/568-9/Mass market
"I've always read Marco's work with interest and I have the highest opinion not only of his talent but his intellectual boldness."
　　　　　　　　　　　—Norman Mailer

During the Sexual Revolution, Vassi established himself as an explorer of an uncharted sexual landscape. He also distinguished himself as a novelist. Through the story of one couple's brief affair and the events that lead them to desperately reassess their lives, Vassi examines the dangers of intimacy in an age of extraordinary freedom.

MASQUERADE BOOKS

ROBIN WILDE

TABITHA'S TEASE
$6.95/597-2
When poor Robin arrives at The Valentine Academy, he finds himself subject to the torturous teasing of Tabitha—the Academy's most notoriously domineering co-ed. But Tabitha is pledge-mistress of a secret sorority dedicated to enslaving young men. Robin finds himself the utterly helpless (and wildly excited) captive of Tabitha & Company's weird desires! A marathon of ticklish torture!

TABITHA'S TICKLE
$6.50/468-2
Tabitha's back! The story of this vicious vixen didn't end with *Tabitha's Tease*. Once again, men fall under the spell of scrumptious co-eds and find themselves enslaved to demands and desires they never dreamed existed. Think it's a man's world? Guess again. With Tabitha around, no man gets what he wants until she's completely satisfied....

ERICA BRONTE

PIRATE'S SLAVE
$5.95/376-7
Lovely young Erica is stranded in a country where lust knows no bounds. Desperate to escape, she finds herself trading her firm, luscious body to any and all men willing and able to help her. Her adventure has its ups and downs, ins and outs—all to the pleasure of the increasingly lusty Erica!

CHARLES G. WOOD

HELLFIRE
$5.95/358-9
A vicious murderer is running amok in New York's sexual underground—and Nick O'Shay, a virile detective with the NYPD, plunges deep into the case. He soon becomes embroiled in the Big Apples notorious nightworld of dungeons and sex clubs, hunting a madman seeking to purge America with fire and blood sacrifices.

CHARISSE VAN DER LYN

SEX ON THE NET
$5.95/399-6
Electrifying erotica from one of the Internet's hottest authors. Encounters of all kinds—straight, lesbian, dominant/submissive and all sorts of extreme passions—are explored in thrilling detail.

STANLEY CARTEN

NAUGHTY MESSAGE
$5.95/333-3
Wesley Arthur discovers a lascivious message on his answering machine. Aroused beyond his wildest dreams by the acts described, he becomes obsessed with tracking down the woman behind the seductive voice. His search takes him through strip clubs, sex parlors and no-tell motels—before finally leading him to his randy reward....

AKBAR DEL PIOMBO

THE FETISH CROWD
$6.95/556-5
An infamous trilogy presented in one special volume guaranteed to appeal to the modern sophisticate. Separately, *Paula the Piquôse*, the infamous *Duke Cosimo*, and *The Double-Bellied Companion* are rightly considered masterpieces.

A CRUMBLING FAÇADE
$4.95/3043-1
The return of that incorrigible rogue, Henry Pike, who continues his pursuit of sex, fair or otherwise, in the homes of the most debauched aristocrats. Ultimately, every woman succumbs to Pike's charms—and submits to his whims!

CAROLE REMY

FANTASY IMPROMPTU
$6.50/513-1
Kidnapped to a remote island retreat, Chantal finds herself catering to every sexual whim of the mysterious Bran. Bran is determined to bring Chantal to a full embracing of her sensual nature, even while revealing himself to be something far more than human....

BEAUTY OF THE BEAST
$5.95/332-5
A shocking tell-all, written from the point-of-view of a prize-winning reporter. All the secrets of an uninhibited life are revealed.

ANONYMOUS

DANIELLE: DIARY OF A SLAVE GIRL
$6.95/591-3
At the age of 19, Danielle Appleton vanishes. The frantic efforts of her family notwithstanding, she is never seen by them again. After her disappearance, Danielle finds herself doomed to a life of sexual slavery, obliged to become the ultimate instrument of pleasure to the man—or men—who own her and dictate her every move and desire.

BUY ANY 4 BOOKS & CHOOSE 1 ADDITIONAL BOOK, OF EQUAL OR LESSER VALUE, AS YOUR FREE GIFT

MASQUERADE BOOKS

LYN DAVENPORT
THE GUARDIAN II
$6.50/505-0
The tale of submissive Felicia Brookes continues. No sooner has Felicia come to love Rodney than she discovers that she has been sold—and must now accustom herself to the guardianship of the debauched Duke of Smithton. Surely Rodney will rescue her from the domination of this depraved stranger. *Won't he?*

GWYNETH JAMES
DREAM CRUISE
$4.95/3045-8
Angelia has it all—exciting career and breathtaking beauty. But she longs to kick up her high heels and have some fun, so she takes an island vacation and vows to leave her inhibitions behind. From the moment her plane takes off, she finds herself in one steamy encounter after another—and wishes her horny holiday would never end!

LIZBETH DUSSEAU
MEMBER OF THE CLUB
$6.95/608-1
A restless woman yearns to realize her most secret, licentious desires. There is a club that exists for the fulfillment of such fantasies—a club devoted to the pleasures of the flesh, and the gratification of every hunger. When its members call she is compelled to answer—and serve each in an endless quest for satisfaction.... The ultimate sex club.
SPANISH HOLIDAY
$4.95/185-3
Lauren didn't mean to fall in love with the enigmatic Sam, but a once-in-a-lifetime European vacation gives her all the evidence she needs that this hot, insatiable man might be the one for her....Soon, both lovers are eagerly exploring the furthest reaches of their desires.

ANTHONY BOBARZYNSKI
STASI SLUT
$4.95/3050-4
Adina lives in East Germany, where she can only dream about the sexual freedoms of the West. But then she meets a group of ruthless and corrupt STASI agents. They use her body for their own gratification, while she opts to use her sensual talents in a bid for total freedom!

JOCELYN JOYCE
PRIVATE LIVES
$4.95/309-0
The dirty habits of the illustrious make for a sizzling tale of French erotic life. A widow has a craving for a young busboy; he's sleeping with a rich businessman's wife; her husband is minding his sex business elsewhere!
SABINE
$4.95/3046-6
There is no one who can refuse her once she casts her spell; no lover can do anything less than give up his whole life for her. Great men and empires fall at her feet; but she is haughty, distracted, impervious. It is the eve of WW II, and Sabine must find a new lover equal to her talents and her tastes.
THE JAZZ AGE
$4.95/48-3
An attorney becomes suspicious of his mistress while his wife has an interlude with a lesbian lover. A romp of erotic realism from the heyday of the flapper and the speakeasy—when rules existed to be broken!

SARA H. FRENCH
MASTER OF TIMBERLAND
$6.95/595-6
A tale of sexual slavery at the ultimate paradise resort—where sizzling submissives serve their masters without question. One of our bestselling titles, this trek to Timberland has ignited passions the world over—and stands poised to become one of modern erotica's legendary tales.

MARY LOVE
ANGELA
$6.95/545-X
Angela's game is "look but don't touch," and she drives everyone mad with desire, dancing for their pleasure but never allowing a single caress. Soon her sensual spell is cast, and she's the only one who can break it!
MASTERING MARY SUE
$5.95/351-1
Mary Sue is a rich nymphomaniac whose husband is determined to declare her mentally incompetent and gain control of her fortune. He brings her to a castle where, to Mary Sue's delight, she is unleashed for a veritable sex-fest!

MASQUERADE BOOKS

MASQUERADE BOOKS

CAPTIVE MAIDENS
$5.95/440-2

Three young women find themselves powerless against the debauched landowners of 1824 England. They are banished to a sex colony, where they are subjected to unspeakable perversions.

THE PRISONER
$5.95/330-9

Judge Black has built a secret room below a penitentiary, where he sentences his female prisoners to hours of exhibition and torment while his friends watch. Judge Black's brand of rough justice keeps his captives on the brink of utter pleasure!

TEARS OF THE INQUISITION
$4.95/146-2

A staggering account of pleasure and punishment, set during a viciously immoral age. "There was a tickling inside her as her nervous system reminded her she was ready for sex. But before her was...the Inquisitor!"

DOUBLE NOVEL
$6.95/86-6

The Metamorphosis of Lisette Joyaux tells the story of a young woman initiated into an incredible world world of lesbian lusts. *The Story of Monique* reveals the twisted sexual rituals that beckon the ripe and willing Monique.

SLAVE ISLAND
$5.95/441-0

A leisure cruise is waylaid by Lord Henry Philbrock, a sadistic genius. The ship's passengers are kidnapped and spirited to his island prison, where the women are trained to accommodate the most bizarre sexual cravings of the rich and perverted. A perennially bestselling title.

....

ALIZARIN LAKE

CLARA
$6.95/548-4

The mysterious death of a beautiful woman leads her old boyfriend on a harrowing journey of discovery. His search uncovers a woman on a quest for deeper and more unusual sensations, each more shocking than the one before!

SEX ON DOCTOR'S ORDERS
$5.95/402-X

Beth, a nubile young nurse, uses her considerable skills to further medical science by offering insatiable assistance in the gathering of important specimens. Soon she's involved everyone in her horny work.

THE EROTIC ADVENTURES OF HARRY TEMPLE
$4.95/127-6

Harry Temple's memoirs chronicle his incredibly amorous adventures—from his initiation at the hands of insatiable sirens, through his stay at a house of hot repute, to his encounters with a chastity-belted nympho, and much more!

....

JOHN NORMAN

TARNSMAN OF GOR
$6.95/486-0

This controversial series returns! Tarl Cabot is transported to Gor. He must quickly accustom himself to the ways of this world, including the caste system which exalts some as Priest-Kings or Warriors, and debases others as slaves. The beginning of the mammoth epic which made Norman a household name among fans of both science fiction and dominance/submission.

OUTLAW OF GOR
$6.95/487-9

Tarl Cabot returns to Gor. Upon arriving, he discovers that his name, his city and the names of those he loves have become unspeakable. Once a respected Tarnsman, Cabot has become an outlaw, and must discover his new purpose on this strange planet, where even simple answers have their price....

PRIEST-KINGS OF GOR
$6.95/488-7

Tarl Cabot searches for his lovely wife Talena. Does she live, or was she destroyed by the all-powerful Priest-Kings? Cabot is determined to find out—though no one who has approached the mountain stronghold of the Priest-Kings has ever returned alive....

NOMADS OF GOR
$6.95/527-1

Cabot finds his way across Gor, pledged to serve the Priest-Kings in their quest for survival. Unfortunately for Cabot, his mission leads him to the savage Wagon People—nomads who may very well kill before surrendering any secrets....

ASSASSIN OF GOR
$6.95/538-7

The chronicles of Counter-Earth continue with this examination of Gorean society. Here is the brutal caste system of Gor: from the Assassin Kuurus, on a mission of bloody vengeance, to Pleasure Slaves, trained in the ways of personal ecstasy.

MASQUERADE BOOKS

RAIDERS OF GOR
$6.95/558-1

Tarl Cabot descends into the depths of Port Kar—the most degenerate port city of the Counter-Earth. There Cabot learns the ways of Kar, whose residents are renowned for the grip in which they hold their voluptuous slaves....

SYDNEY ST. JAMES
RIVE GAUCHE
$5.95/317-1

The Latin Quarter, Paris, circa 1920. Expatriate bohemians couple with abandon—before eventually abandoning their ambitions amidst the intoxicating temptations waiting to be indulged in every bedroom.

DON WINSLOW
SLAVE GIRLS OF ROME
$6.95/577-8

Never were women so relentlessly used as were ancient Rome's voluptuous slaves! With no choice but to serve their lustful masters, these captive beauties learn to perform their duties with the passion and purpose of Venus herself.

THE FALL OF THE ICE QUEEN
$6.50/520-4

Rahn the Conqueror chose a true beauty as his Consort. But the regal disregard with which she treated Rahn was not to be endured. It was decided that she would submit to his will—and as so many had learned, Rahn's depraved expectations have made his court infamous.

PRIVATE PLEASURES
$6.50/504-2

Frantic voyeurs and licentious exhibitionists are here displayed in all their wanton glory—laid bare by the perverse and probing eye of Don Winslow.

THE INSATIABLE MISTRESS OF ROSEDALE
$6.50/494-1

Edward and Lady Penelope reside in Rosedale manor. While Edward is a connoisseur of sexual perversion, it is Lady Penelope whose mastery of complete sensual pleasure makes their home infamous. Indulging one another's bizarre whims is a way of life for this wicked couple....

SECRETS OF CHEATEM MANOR
$6.50/434-8

Edward returns to oversee his late father's estate, only to find it being run by the majestic Lady Amanda. Edward can hardly believe his luck—Lady Amanda is assisted by her two beautiful daughters, Catherine and Prudence. What the randy young man soon comes to realize is the love of discipline that all three beauties share.

KATERINA IN CHARGE
$5.95/409-7

When invited to a country retreat by a mysterious couple, two randy young ladies can hardly resist! Soon after they arrive, the imperious Katerina makes her desires known—and demands that they be fulfilled...

THE MANY PLEASURES OF IRONWOOD
$5.95/310-4

Seven lovely young women are employed by The Ironwood Sportsmen's Club, where their natural talents in the sensual arts are put to creative use. Winslow explores the ins and outs of this small and exclusive club—where members live out each of their fantasies with one (or all!) of these seven carefully selected sexual playthings.

CLAIRE'S GIRLS
$5.95/442-9

You knew when she walked by that she was something special. She was one of Claire's girls, a woman carefully dressed and groomed to fill a role, to capture a look, to fit an image crafted by the sophisticated proprietress of an exclusive escort agency.

MARCUS VAN HELLER
KIDNAP
$4.95/90-4

P.I. Harding is called in to investigate a kidnapping case involving the rich and powerful. Along the way he has the pleasure of "interrogating" an exotic dancer and a beautiful English reporter, as he finds himself enmeshed in the sleazy international underworld.

ALEXANDER TROCCHI
YOUNG ADAM
$4.95/63-7

Two British barge operators discover a girl drowned in the river Clyde. Her lover, a plumber, is arrested for her murder. But he is innocent. Joe, the barge assistant, knows that. As the plumber is tried and sentenced to hang, this knowledge lends poignancy to Joe's romances with the women along the river whom he will love then... well, read on.

N. WHALLEN
THE EDUCATION OF SITA MANSOOR
$6.95/567-0

On the eve of her wedding, Sita Mansoor is left without a bridegroom. Sita travels to America, where she hopes to become educated in the ways of a permissive society. She could never have imagined the wide variety of tutors—both male and female—who would be waiting to take on so beautiful a pupil.

MASQUERADE BOOKS

TAU'TEVU
$6.50/426-7
Statuesque and beautiful Vivian learns to subject herself to the hand of a domineering man. He systematically helps her prove her own strength, and brings to life in her an unimagined sensual fire.

ISADORA ALMAN
ASK ISADORA
$4.95/61-0
Six years' worth of Isadora's syndicated columns on sex and relationships. Alman's been called a "hip Dr. Ruth," and a "sexy Dear Abby," based upon the wit of her advice. Today's world is more perplexing than ever— and Alman is just the expert to help untangle the most personal of knots.

THE CLASSIC COLLECTION
THE ENGLISH GOVERNESS
$5.95/373-2
When Lord Lovell's son was expelled from his prep school for masturbation, his father hired a very proper governess to tutor the boy— giving her strict instructions not to spare the rod to break him of his bad habits. Luckily, Harriet Marwood was addicted to domination.

PROTESTS, PLEASURES, RAPTURES
$5.95/400-3
Invited for an allegedly quiet weekend at a country vicarage, a young woman is stunned to find herself surrounded by shocking acts of sexual sadism. Soon she begins to explore her own capacities for delicious sexual cruelty.

THE YELLOW ROOM
$5.95/378-3
The "yellow room" holds the secrets of lust, lechery, and the lash. There, bare-bottomed, spread-eagled, and open to the world, demure Alice Darvell soon learns to love her lickings.

SCHOOL DAYS IN PARIS
$5.95/325-2
Few Universities provide the profound and pleasurable lessons one learns in after-hours study— particularly if one is young and available, and lucky enough to have Paris as a playground. Here are all the randy pursuits of young adulthood.

MAN WITH A MAID
$4.95/307-4
The adventures of Jack and Alice have delighted readers for eight decades! A classic of its genre, Man with a Maid tells a tale of desire, revenge, and submission.

MASQUERADE READERS
INTIMATE PLEASURES
$4.95/38-6
Indulge your most private penchants with this specially chosen selection of Masquerade's hottest moments. Try a tempting morsel of The Prodigal Virgin and Eveline, the bizarre public displays of carnality in The Gilded Lily or the relentless and shocking carnality of The Story of Monique.

CLASSIC EROTIC BIOGRAPHIES
JENNIFER AGAIN
$4.95/220-5
The uncensored life of one of modern erotica's most popular heroines. Once again, the insatiable Jennifer seizes the day and extracts every last drop of sensual pleasure! A thrilling peak at the mores of the uninhibited 1970s.

JENNIFER #3
$5.95/292-2
The adventures of erotica's most daring heroine. Jennifer has a photographer's eye for details—particularly of the male variety! One by one, her subjects submit to her demands for pleasure.

PAULINE
$4.95/129-2
From rural America to the royal court of Austria, Pauline follows her ever-growing sexual desires: "I would never see them again. Why shouldn't I give myself to them that they might become more and more inspired to deeds of greater lust!"

RHINOCEROS

LEOPOLD VON SACHER-MASOCH
VENUS IN FURS
$7.95/589-1
The alliance of Severin and Wanda epitomizes Sacher-Masoch's obsession with a cruel goddess and the urges that drive the man held in her thrall. Exclusive to this edition are letters exchanged between Sacher-Masoch and Emilie Mataja—an aspiring writer he sought as the avatar of his desires.

JOHN NORMAN
IMAGINATIVE SEX
$7.95/561-1
The author of the Gor novels outlines his philosophy on relations between the sexes, and presents fifty-three scenarios designed to reintroduce fantasy to the bedroom.

MASQUERADE BOOKS

KATHLEEN K.
SWEET TALKERS
$6.95/516-6

"If you enjoy eavesdropping on explicit conversations about sex... this book is for you."
—*Spectator*

Kathleen K. ran a phone-sex company in the late 80s, and she opens up her diary for a peek at the life of a phone-sex operator. Transcripts of actual conversations are included.
Trade /$12.95/192-6

THOMAS S. ROCHE
DARK MATTER
$6.95/484-4

"*Dark Matter* is sure to please gender outlaws, bodymod junkies, goth vampires, boys who wish they were dykes, and anybody who's not to sure where the fine line should be drawn between pleasure and pain. It's a handful."—Pat Califia

"Here is the erotica of the cumming millennium.... You will be deliciously disturbed, but never disappointed."
—Poppy Z. Brite

NOIROTICA 2: PULP FRICTION
$7.95/584-0
Another volume of criminally seductive stories set in the murky terrain of the erotic and noir genres. Thomas Roche has gathered the darkest jewels from today's edgiest writers to create this provocative collection. A must for all fans of contemporary erotica.

NOIROTICA: An Anthology of Erotic Crime Stories (Ed.)
$6.95/390-2
A collection of darkly sexy tales, taking place at the crossroads of the crime and erotic genres. Here are some of today's finest writers, all of whom explore the arousing terrain where desire runs irrevocably afoul of the law.

DAVID MELTZER
UNDER
$6.95/290-6
The story of a 21st century sex professional living at the bottom of the social heap. After surgeries designed to increase his physical allure, corrupt government forces drive the cyber-gigolo underground, where even more bizarre cultures await....

ORF
$6.95/110-1
Meltzer's celebrated exploration of Eros and modern mythology returns. Orf is the ultimate hero—the idol of thousands, the fevered dream of many more. Every last drop of feeling is squeezed from a modern-day troubadour and his lady love in this psychedelic bacchanal.

LAURA ANTONIOU, ED.
SOME WOMEN
$7.95/573-5
Introduction by Pat Califia
"Makes the reader think about the wide range of SM experiences, beyond the glamour of fiction and fantasy, or the clever-clever prose of the perverati."
—*SKIN TWO*

Over forty essays written by women actively involved in consensual dominance and submission. Professional mistresses, lifestyle leatherdykes, whipmakers, titleholders—women from every conceivable walk of life lay bare their true feelings about issues as explosive as feminism, abuse, pleasure and public image. A bestselling title, Some Women is a valuable resource for anyone interested in sexuality.

NO OTHER TRIBUTE
$7.95/603-0
Tales of women kept in bondage to their lovers by their deepest passions. Love pushes these women beyond acceptable limits, rendering them helpless to deny anything to the men and women they adore. A volume certain to challenge political correctness as few have before.

BY HER SUBDUED
$6.95/281-7
These tales all involve women in control—of their lives and their lovers. So much in control that they can remorselessly break rules to become powerful goddesses of those who sacrifice all to worship at their feet.

AMELIA G, ED.
BACKSTAGE PASSES:
Rock n' Roll Erotica from the Pages of *Blue Blood* Magazine
$6.95/438-0
Amelia G, editor of the goth-sex journal *Blue Blood*, has brought together some of today's most irreverent writers, each of whom has outdone themselves with an edgy, antic tale of modern lust.

ROMY ROSEN
SPUNK
$6.95/492-5
Casey, a lovely model poised upon the verge of super-celebrity, falls for an insatiable young rock singer—not suspecting that his sexual appetite has led him to experiment with a dangerous new aphrodisiac. Soon, Casey becomes addicted to the drug, and her craving plunges her into a strange underworld, and into an alliance with a shadowy young man with secrets of his own....

MASQUERADE BOOKS

MOLLY WEATHERFIELD
CARRIE'S STORY
$6.95/485-2

"I was stunned by how well it was written and how intensely foreign I found its sexual world.... And, since this is a world I don't frequent... I thoroughly enjoyed the National Geo tour."
—*bOING bOING*

"Hilarious and harrowing... just when you think things can't get any wilder, they do."
—*Black Sheets*

Weatherfield's bestselling examination of dominance and submission. "I had been Jonathan's slave for about a year when he told me he wanted to sell me at an auction...." A rare piece of erotica, both thoughtful and hot!

CYBERSEX CONSORTIUM
CYBERSEX: The Perv's Guide to Finding Sex on the Internet
$6.95/471-2

You've heard the objections: cyberspace is soaked with sex, mired in immorality. Okay—so where is it!? Tracking down the good stuff—the real good stuff—can waste an awful lot of expensive time, and frequently leave you high and dry. The Cybersex Consortium presents an easy-to-use guide for those intrepid adults who know what they want.

LAURA ANTONIOU
("Sara Adamson")

"Ms. Adamson's friendly, conversational writing style perfectly couches what to some will be shocking material. Ms. Adamson creates a wonderfully diverse world of lesbian, gay, straight, bi and transgendered characters, all mixing delightfully in the melting pot of sadomasochism and planting the genre more firmly in the culture at large. I for one am cheering her on!"
—*Kate Bornstein*

THE MARKETPLACE
$7.95/602-2

The first title in Antoniou's thrilling Marketplace Trilogy, following the lives an lusts of those who have been deemed worthy to participate in the ultimate BDSM arena.

THE SLAVE
$7.95/601-4

The second volume in the "Marketplace" trilogy. *The Slave* covers the experience of one talented submissive who longs to join the ranks of those who have proven themselves worthy of entry into the Marketplace. But the price, while delicious, is staggeringly high....

THE TRAINER
$6.95/249-3

The Marketplace Trilogy concludes with the story of the trainers, and the desires and paths that led them to become the ultimate figures of authority.

GERI NETTICK WITH BETH ELLIOT
MIRRORS: Portrait of a Lesbian Transsexual
$6.95/435-6

Born a male, Geri Nettick knew something just didn't fit. Even after coming to terms with her own gender dysphoria she still fought to be accepted by the lesbian feminist community to which she felt she belonged. A true story.

TRISTAN TAORMINO & DAVID AARON CLARK, EDS.
RITUAL SEX
$6.95/391-0

The contributors to *Ritual Sex* know that body and soul share more common ground than society feels comfortable acknowledging. From memoirs of ecstatic revelation, to quests to reconcile sex and spirit, *Ritual Sex* provides an unprecedented look at private life.

TAMMY JO ECKHART
AMAZONS: Erotic Explorations of Ancient Myths
$7.95/534-4

The Amazon—the fierce woman warrior—appears in the traditions of many cultures, but never before has the erotic potential of this archetype been explored with such imagination. Powerful pleasures await anyone lucky enough to encounter Eckhart's spitfires.

PUNISHMENT FOR THE CRIME
$6.95/427-5

Stories that explore dominance and submission. From an encounter between two of society's most despised individuals, to the explorations of longtime friends, these tales take you where few others have ever dared....

AMARANTHA KNIGHT, ED.
SEDUCTIVE SPECTRES
$6.95/464-X

Tours through the erotic supernatural via the imaginations of today's best writers. Never have ghostly encounters been so alluring, thanks to otherworldly characters well-acquainted with the pleasures of the flesh.

MASQUERADE BOOKS

SEX MACABRE
$6.95/392-9
Horror tales designed for dark and sexy nights—sure to make your skin crawl, and heart beat faster.

FLESH FANTASTIC
$6.95/352-X
Humans have long toyed with the idea of "playing God": creating life from nothingness, bringing life to the inanimate. Now Amarantha Knight collects stories exploring not only the act of Creation, but the lust that follows.

GARY BOWEN
DIARY OF A VAMPIRE
$6.95/331-7
"Gifted with a darkly sensual vision and a fresh voice, [Bowen] is a writer to watch out for."　　　　—Cecilia Tan

Rafael, a red-blooded male with an insatiable hunger for the same, is the perfect antidote to the effete malcontents haunting bookstores today. The emergence of a bold and brilliant vision, rooted in past and present.

RENÉ MAIZEROY
FLESHLY ATTRACTIONS
$6.95/299-X
Lucien was the son of the wantonly beautiful actress, Marie-Rose Hardanges. When she decides to let a "friend" introduce her son to the pleasures of love, Marie-Rose could not have foretold the excesses that would lead to her own ruin and that of her cherished son.

JEAN STINE
THRILL CITY
$6.95/411-9
Thrill City is the seat of the world's increasing depravity, and this classic novel transports you there with a vivid style you'd be hard pressed to ignore. No writer is better suited to describe the extremes of this modern Babylon.

SEASON OF THE WITCH
$6.95/268-X
"A future in which it is technically possible to transfer the total mind...of a rapist killer into the brain dead but physically living body of his female victim. Remarkable for intense psychological technique. There is eroticism but it is necessary to mark the differences between the sexes and the subtle altering of a man into a woman."　　—*The Science Fiction Critic*

Jean Stine's undisputed masterpiece, and one of the earliest science-fiction novels to explore the complexities and contradictions of gender.

GRANT ANTREWS
LEGACIES
$7.95/605-7
Kathi Lawton discovers that she has inherited the troubling secret of her late mother's scandalous sexuality. In an effort to understand what motivated her mother's desires, Kathi embarks on an exploration of SM that leads her into the arms of Horace Moore, a mysterious man who seems to see into her very soul. As she begins falling for her new master, Kathi finds herself wondering just how far she'll go to prove her love....

ROGUES GALLERY
$6.95/522-0
A stirring evocation of dominant/submissive love. Two doctors meet and slowly fall in love. Once Beth reveals her hidden desires to Jim, the two explore the forbidden acts that will come to define their distinctly exotic affair.

MY DARLING DOMINATRIX
$7.95/566-2
When a man and a woman fall in love, it's supposed to be simple, uncomplicated, easy—unless that woman happens to be a dominatrix. This highly praised and unpretentious love story captures the richness and depth of this very special kind of love without leering or smirking.

SUBMISSIONS
$6.95/207-8
Antrews portrays the very special elements of the dominant/submissive relationship with restraint—this time with the story of a lonely man, a winning lottery ticket, and a demanding dominatrix.

JOHN WARREN
THE TORQUEMADA KILLER
$6.95/367-8
Detective Eva Hernandez gets her first "big case": a string of murders taking place within New York's SM community. Eva assembles the evidence, revealing a picture of a world misunderstood and under attack—and gradually comes to face her own hidden longings.

THE LOVING DOMINANT
$7.95/600-6
Everything you need to know about an infamous sexual variation, and an unspoken type of love. Warren is a longtime player in the dominance/submission scene, and he guides readers through this rarely seen world, and offers clear-eyed advice guaranteed to enlighten the most jaded erotic explorers.

MASQUERADE BOOKS

DAVID AARON CLARK
SISTER RADIANCE
$6.95/215-9
A meditation on love, sex, and death. The vicissitudes of lust and romance are examined against a backdrop of urban decay in this testament to the allure of the forbidden.

THE WET FOREVER
$6.95/117-9
The story of Janus and Madchen—a small-time hood and a beautiful sex worker on the run—examines themes of loyalty, sacrifice, redemption and obsession amidst Manhattan's sex parlors and underground S/M clubs.

MICHAEL PERKINS
EVIL COMPANIONS
$6.95/3067-X
Evil Companions has been hailed as "a frightening classic." A young couple explores the nether reaches of the erotic unconscious in a confrontation with the extremes of passion.

THE SECRET RECORD:
Modern Erotic Literature
$6.95/3039-3
Michael Perkins surveys the field with authority and unique insight. Updated and revised to include the latest trends, tastes, and developments in this misunderstood genre.

AN ANTHOLOGY OF CLASSIC ANONYMOUS EROTIC WRITING
$6.95/140-3
Michael Perkins has collected the best passages from the world's erotic writing. "Anonymous" is one of the most infamous bylines in publishing history—and these excerpts show why!

HELEN HENLEY
ENTER WITH TRUMPETS
$6.95/197-7
Helen Henley was told that women just don't write about sex. So Henley did it alone, flying in the face of "tradition" by writing this touching tale of arousal and devotion in one couple's kinky relationship.

ALICE JOANOU
CANNIBAL FLOWER
$4.95/72-6
"She is waiting in her darkened bedroom, as she has waited throughout history, to seduce the men who are foolish enough to be blinded by her irresistible charms.... She is the goddess of sexuality, and *Cannibal Flower* is her haunting siren song."   —Michael Perkins

BLACK TONGUE
$6.95/258-2
"Joanou has created a series of sumptuous, brooding, dark visions of sexual obsession, and is undoubtedly a name to look out for in the future."
                                   —*Redeemer*

Exploring lust at its most florid and unsparing, *Black Tongue* is redolent of forbidden passions.

TOURNIQUET
$6.95/3060-1
A heady collection of stories and effusions. A complex and riveting series of meditations on desire.

LIESEL KULIG
LOVE IN WARTIME
$6.95/3044-X
Madeleine knew that the handsome SS officer was a dangerous man, but she was just a cabaret singer in Nazi-occupied Paris, trying to survive in a perilous time. When Josef fell in love with her, he discovered that a beautiful woman can sometimes be as dangerous as any warrior.

SAMUEL R. DELANY
THE MAD MAN
$8.99/408-9/Mass market
"Delany develops an insightful dichotomy between [his protagonist]'s two worlds: the one of cerebral philosophy and dry academia, the other of heedless, 'impersonal' obsessive sexual extremism. When these worlds finally collide...the novel achieves a surprisingly satisfying resolution...."
                                   —*Publishers Weekly*

Graduate student John Marr researches the life of Timothy Hasler: a philosopher whose career was cut tragically short over a decade earlier. Marr begins to find himself increasingly drawn toward shocking sexual encounters with the homeless men, until it begins to seem that Hasler's death might hold some key to his own life as a gay man in the age of AIDS.

PHILIP JOSÉ FARMER
A FEAST UNKNOWN
$6.95/276-0
"Sprawling, brawling, shocking, suspenseful, hilarious..."
                                   —Theodore Sturgeon
Slowly, Lord Grandrith—armed with the belief that he is the son of Jack the Ripper—tells the story of his remarkable life. His story begins with his discovery of the secret of immortality—and progresses to encompass the furthest extremes of human behavior.

MASQUERADE BOOKS

FLESH
$6.95/303-1

Stagg explored the galaxies for 800 years, and could only hope that he would be welcomed home by an adoring public. Upon his return, the hero Stagg is made the centerpiece of an incredible public ritual—one that will take him to the heights of ecstasy, and drag him toward the depths of hell.

DANIEL VIAN
ILLUSIONS
$6.95/3074-1

Two tales of danger and desire in Berlin on the eve of WWII. From private homes to lurid cafés, passion is exposed in stark contrast to the brutal violence of the time, as desperate people explore their darkest sexual desires.

PERSUASIONS
$4.95/183-7

"The stockings are drawn tight by the suspender belt, tight enough to be stretched to the limit just above the middle part of her thighs, tight enough so that her calves glow through the sheer silk..." A double novel, including the classics *Adagio* and *Gabriela and the General*, this volume traces lust around the globe.

ANDREI CODRESCU
THE REPENTANCE OF LORRAINE
$6.95/329-5

"One of our most prodigiously talented and magical writers."
—*NYT Book Review*

An aspiring writer, a professor's wife, a secretary, gold anklets, Maoists, Roman harlots—and more—swirl through this spicy tale of a harried quest for a mythic artifact. Written when the author was a young man.

TUPPY OWENS
SENSATIONS
$6.95/3081-4

Tuppy Owens takes a rare peek behind the scenes of *Sensations*—the first big-budget sex flick. Originally commissioned to appear in book form after the release of the film in 1975, *Sensations* is finally released. A .

SOPHIE GALLEYMORE BIRD
MANEATER
$6.95/103-9

Through a bizarre act of creation, a man attains the "perfect" lover—by all appearances a beautiful, sensuous woman, but in reality something far darker. Once brought to life she will accept no mate, seeking instead the prey that will sate her hunger.

BADBOY

DAVID MAY
MADRUGADA
$6.95/574-3

Set in San Francisco's gay leather community, *Madrugada* follows the lives of a group of friends—and their many acquaintances—as they tangle with the thorny issues of love and lust. Uncompromising, mysterious, and arousing, David May weaves a complex web of relationships in this unique story cycle. Guaranteed to leave a lasting impression on any reader.

PETER HEISTER
ISLANDS OF DESIRE
$6.95/480-1

Red-blooded lust on the wine-dark seas of classical Greece. Anacraeon yearns to leave his small, isolated island and find adventure in one of the overseas kingdoms. Accompanied by some randy friends, Anacraeon makes his dream come true—and discovers pleasures he never dreamed of!

KITTY TSUI WRITING AS "ERIC NORTON"
SPARKS FLY
$6.95/551-4

The highest highs—and most wretched depths—of life as Eric Norton, a beautiful wanton living San Francisco's high life. *Sparks Fly* traces Norton's rise, fall, and resurrection, vividly marking the way with the personal affairs that give life meaning.

BARRY ALEXANDER
ALL THE RIGHT PLACES
$6.95/482-8

Stories filled with hot studs in lust and love. From modern masters and slaves to medieval royals and their subjects, Alexander explores the mating rituals men have engaged in for centuries—all in the name of their insatiable desire...

MICHAEL FORD, ED.
BUTCHBOYS:
Stories For Men Who Need It Bad
$6.50/523-9

A big volume of tales dedicated to the rough-and-tumble type who can make a man weak at the knees. Some of today's best erotic writers explore the many possible variations on the age-old fantasy of the thoroughly dominating man.

MASQUERADE BOOKS

WILLIAM J. MANN, ED.
GRAVE PASSIONS:
Gay Tales of the Supernatural
$6.50/405-4

A collection of the most chilling tales of passion currently being penned by today's most provocative gay writers. Unnatural transformations, otherworldly encounters, and deathless desires make for a collection sure to keep readers up late at night.

J. A. GUERRA, ED.
COME QUICKLY:
For Boys on the Go
$6.50/413-1

Here are over sixty of the hottest fantasies around—all designed to get you going in less time than it takes to dial 976. Julian Anthony Guerra, the editor behind the popular *Men at Work* and *Badboy Fantasies*, has put together this volume especially for you—a busy man on a modern schedule, who still appreciates a little old-fashioned action.

JOHN PRESTON
HUSTLING: A Gentleman's Guide to the Fine Art of Homosexual Prostitution
$6.50/517-4

"Fun and highly literary. What more could you expect form such an accomplished activist, author and editor?"—*Drummer*

John Preston solicited the advice and opinions of "working boys" from across the country in his effort to produce the ultimate guide to the hustler's world. *Hustling* covers every practical aspect of the business, from clientele and payment to "specialties," and drawbacks.
Trade $12.95/137-3

MR. BENSON
$4.95/3041-5

Jamie is an aimless young man lucky enough to encounter Mr. Benson. He is soon learns to accept this man as his master. Jamie's incredible adventures never fail to excite—especially when the going gets rough!

TALES FROM THE DARK LORD
$5.95/323-6

Twelve stunning works from the man *Lambda Book Report* called "the Dark Lord of gay erotica." The relentless ritual of lust and surrender is explored in all its manifestations in this heart-stopping triumph of authority and vision.

TALES FROM THE DARK LORD II
$4.95/176-4

THE ARENA
$4.95/3083-0

Preston's take on the ultimate sex club. Men go there to abolish all limits. Only the author of *Mr. Benson* could have imagined so perfect an institution for the satisfaction of male desire.

THE HEIR•THE KING
$4.95/3048-2

The Heir, written in the lyric voice of the ancient myths, tells the story of a world where slaves and masters create a new sexual society. *The King* tells the story of a soldier who discovers his monarch's most secret desires.

THE MISSION OF ALEX KANE
SWEET DREAMS
$4.95/3062-8

It's the triumphant return of gay action hero Alex Kane! In *Sweet Dreams*, Alex travels to Boston where he takes on a street gang that stalks gay teenagers.

GOLDEN YEARS
$4.95/3069-5

When evil threatens the plans of a group of older gay men, Kane's got the muscle to take it head on. Along the way, he wins the support—and very specialized attentions—of a cowboy plucked right out of the Old West.

DEADLY LIES
$4.95/3076-8

Politics is a dirty business and the dirt becomes deadly when a smear campaign targets gay men. Who better to clean things up than Alex Kane!

STOLEN MOMENTS
$4.95/3098-9

Houston's evolving gay community is victimized by a malicious newspaper editor who is more than willing to sacrifice gays on the altar of circulation. He never counted on Alex Kane, fearless defender of gay dreams and desires.

SECRET DANGER
$4.95/111-X

Alex Kane and the faithful Danny are called to a small European country, where a group of gay tourists is being held hostage by terrorists.

LETHAL SILENCE
$4.95/125-X

Chicago becomes the scene of the right-wing's most noxious plan—facilitated by unholy political alliances. Alex and Danny head to the Windy City to battle the mercenaries who would squash gay men underfoot.

MASQUERADE BOOKS

MATT TOWNSEND
SOLIDLY BUILT
$6.50/416-X
The tale of the relationship between Jeff, a young photographer, and Mark, the butch electrician hired to wire Jeff's new home. For Jeff, it's love at first sight; Mark, however, has more than a few hang-ups.

JAY SHAFFER
SHOOTERS
$5.95/284-1
No mere catalog of random acts, *Shooters* tells the stories of a variety of stunning men and the ways they connect in sexual and non-sexual ways. Shaffer always gets his man.

ANIMAL HANDLERS
$4.95/264-7
In Shaffer's world, every man finally succumbs to the animal urges deep inside. And if there's any creature that promises a wild time, it's a beast who's been caged for far too long.

FULL SERVICE
$4.95/150-0
No-nonsense guys bear down hard on each other as they work their way toward release in this finely detailed assortment of fantasies.

D. V. SADERO
IN THE ALLEY
$4.95/144-6
Hardworking men bring their special skills and impressive tools to the most satisfying job of all: capturing and breaking the male animal.

SCOTT O'HARA
DO-IT-YOURSELF PISTON POLISHING
$6.50/489-5
Longtime sex-pro Scott O'Hara draws upon his acute powers of seduction to lure you into a world of hard, horny men long overdue for a tune-up.

SUTTER POWELL
EXECUTIVE PRIVILEGES
$6.50/383-X
No matter how serious or sexy a predicament his characters find themselves in, Powell conveys the sheer exuberance of their encounters with a warm humor rarely seen in contemporary gay erotica.

GARY BOWEN
WESTERN TRAILS
$6.50/477-1
Some of gay literature's brightest stars tell the sexy truth about the many ways a rugged stud found to satisfy himself—and his buddy—in the Very Wild West.

MAN HUNGRY
$5.95/374-0
A riveting collection of stories from one of gay erotica's new stars. Dipping into a variety of genres, Bowen crafts tales of lust unlike anything being published today.

KYLE STONE
THE HIDDEN SLAVE
$6.95/580-8
"This perceptive and finely-crafted work is a joy to discover. Kyle Stone's fiction belongs on the shelf of every serious fan of gay literature."
—Pat Califia

"Once again, Kyle Stone proves that imagination, ingenuity, and sheer intellectual bravado go a long way in making porn hot. This book turns us on and makes us think. Who could ask for anything more?"
—Michael Bronski

HOT BAUDS 2
$6.50/479-8
Stone conducted another heated search through the world's randiest gay bulletin boards, resulting in one of the most scalding follow-ups ever published.

HOT BAUDS
$5.95/285-X
Stone combed cyberspace for the hottest fantasies of the world's horniest hackers. Sexy, shameless, and eminently user-friendly.

FIRE & ICE
$5.95/297-3
A collection of stories from the author of the adventures of PB 500. Stone's characters always promise one thing: enough hot action to burn away your desire for anyone else....

FANTASY BOARD
$4.95/212-4
Explore the future—through the intertwined lives of a collection of randy computer hackers. On the Lambda Gate BBS, every horny male is in search of virtual satisfaction!

THE CITADEL
$4.95/198-5
The sequel to *PB 500*. Micah faces new challenges after entering the Citadel. Only his master knows what awaits—and whether Micah will again distinguish himself as the perfect instrument of pleasure....

THE INITIATION OF PB 500
$4.95/141-1
He is a stranger on their planet, unschooled in their language, and ignorant of their customs. But Micah—now known only by his number—will soon be trained in every detail of erotic service. When his training is complete, he must prove himself worthy of the master who has chosen him....

MASQUERADE BOOKS

RITUALS
$4.95/168-3
Via a computer bulletin board, a young man finds himself drawn into sexual rites that transform him into the willing slave of a mysterious stranger. His former life is thrown off, and he learns to live for his Master's touch....

ROBERT BAHR
SEX SHOW
$4.95/225-6
Luscious dancing boys. Brazen, explicit acts. Take a seat, and get very comfortable, because the curtain's going up on a very special show no discriminating appetite can afford to miss.

JASON FURY
THE ROPE ABOVE, THE BED BELOW
$4.95/269-8
A vicious murderer is preying upon New York's go-go boys. In order to solve this mystery and save lives, each studly suspect must lay bare his soul—and more!

ERIC'S BODY
$4.95/151-9
Follow the irresistible Jason through sexual adventures unlike any you have ever read—touching on the raunchy, the romantic, and a number of highly sensitive areas in between....

LARS EIGHNER
WANK: THE TAPES
$6.95/588-3
Lars Eighner gets back to basics with this look at every guy's favorite pastime. Horny studs bare it all and work up a healthy sweat during these provocative discussions about masturbation.

WHISPERED IN THE DARK
$5.95/286-8
A volume demonstrating Eighner's unique combination of strengths: poetic descriptive power, an unfailing ear for dialogue, and a finely tuned feeling for the nuances of male passion. An extraordinary collection of this influential writer's work.

AMERICAN PRELUDE
$4.95/170-5
Eighner is widely recognized as one of our best, most exciting gay writers. He is also one of gay erotica's true masters, producing wonderfully written tales of all-American lust, peopled with red-blooded, oversexed studs.

DAVID LAURENTS, ED.
SOUTHERN COMFORT
$6.50/466-6
Editor David Laurents now unleashes a collection of tales focusing on the American South—stories reflecting not only Southern literary tradition, but the many sexy contributions the region has made to the iconography of the American Male.

WANDERLUST:
Homoerotic Tales of Travel
$5.95/395-3
A volume dedicated to the special pleasures of faraway places—and the horny men who lie in wait for intrepid tourists. Celebrate the freedom of the open road, and the allure of men who stray from the beaten path....

THE BADBOY BOOK
OF EROTIC POETRY
$5.95/382-1
Erotic poetry has long been the problem child of the literary world—highly creative and provocative, but somehow too frank to be "art." *The Badboy Book of Erotic Poetry* restores eros to its place of honor in gay writing.

AARON TRAVIS
BIG SHOTS
$5.95/448-8
Two fierce tales in one electrifying volume. In *Beirut*, Travis tells the story of ultimate military power and erotic subjugation; *Kip,* Travis' hypersexed and sinister take on *film noir,* appears in unexpurgated form for the first time.

EXPOSED
$4.95/126-8
A unique glimpse of the horny gay male in his natural environment! Cops, college jocks, ancient Romans—even Sherlock Holmes and his loyal Watson—cruise these pages, fresh from the pen of one of our hottest authors.

BEAST OF BURDEN
$4.95/105-5
Innocents surrender to the brutal sexual mastery of their superiors, as taboos are shattered and replaced with the unwritten rules of masculine conquest. Intense and extreme.

MASQUERADE BOOKS

IN THE BLOOD
$5.95/283-3
Early tales from this master of the genre. Includes "In the Blood"—a heart-pounding descent into sexual vampirism.

THE FLESH FABLES
$4.95/243-4
One of Travis' best collections. Includes "Blue Light," as well as other masterpieces that established him as the erotic writer to watch.

BOB VICKERY

SKIN DEEP
$4.95/265-5
So many varied beauties no one will go away unsatisfied. No tantalizing morsel of manflesh is overlooked—or left unexplored!

JR

FRENCH QUARTER NIGHTS
$5.95/337-6
Sensual snapshots of the many places where men get down and dirty—from the steamy French Quarter to the steam room at the old Everard baths.

TOM BACCHUS

RAHM
$5.95/315-5
Tom Bacchus brings to life an extraordinary assortment of characters, from the Father of Us All to the cowpoke next door, the early gay literati to rude, queercore mosh rats.

BONE
$4.95/177-2
Queer musings from the pen of one of today's hottest young talents. Tom Bacchus maps out the tricking ground of a new generation.

KEY LINCOLN

SUBMISSION HOLDS
$4.95/266-3
From tough to tender, the men between these covers stop at nothing to get what they want. These sweat-soaked tales show just how bad boys can really get.

CALDWELL/EIGHNER

QSFX2
$5.95/278-7
Other-worldly yarns from two master story-tellers—Clay Caldwell and Lars Eighner. Both eroticists take a trip to the furthest reaches of the sexual imagination, sending back ten scalding sci-fi stories of male desire.

CLAY CALDWELL

ASK OL' BUDDY
$5.95/346-5
Set in the underground SM world—where men initiate one another into the secrets of the rawest sexual realm of all. And when each stud's initiation is complete, he takes part in the training of another hungry soul....

STUD SHORTS
$5.95/320-1
"If anything, Caldwell's charm is more powerful, his nostalgia more poignant, the horniness he captures more sweetly, achingly acute than ever."
—Aaron Travis

A new collection of this legend's latest sex-fiction. Caldwell tells all about cops, cadets, truckers, farmboys (and many more) in these dirty jewels.

TAILPIPE TRUCKER
$5.95/296-5
Trucker porn! Caldwell tells the truth about Trag and Curly—two men hot for the feeling of sweaty manflesh. Together, they pick up—and turn out—a couple of thrill-seeking punks.

SERVICE, STUD
$5.95/336-8
Another look at the gay future. The setting is the Los Angeles of a distant future. Here the all-male populace is divided between the served and the servants—guaranteeing the erotic satisfaction of all involved.

QUEERS LIKE US
$4.95/262-0
For years the name Clay Caldwell has been synonymous with the hottest, most finely crafted gay tales available. *Queers Like Us* is one of his best: the story of a randy mailman's trek through a landscape of available studs.

ALL-STUD
$4.95/104-7
This classic, sex-soaked tale takes place under the watchful eye of Number Ten: an omniscient figure who has decreed unabashed promiscuity as the law of his all-male land.

CLAY CALDWELL & AARON TRAVIS

TAG TEAM STUDS
$6.50/465-8
Wrestling will never seem the same, once you've made your way through this assortment of sweaty studs. But you'd better be wary—should one catch you off guard, you just might spend the night pinned to the mat....

MASQUERADE BOOKS

LARRY TOWNSEND

LEATHER AD: M
$5.95/380-5
John's curious about what goes on between the leatherclad men he's fantasized about. He takes out a personal ad, and starts a journey of discovery that will leave no part of his life unchanged.

LEATHER AD: S
$5.95/407-0
The tale continues—this time told from a Top's perspective. A simple ad generates many responses, and one man puts these studs through their paces....

BEWARE THE GOD WHO SMILES
$5.95/321-X
Two lusty young Americans are transported to ancient Egypt—where they are embroiled in warfare and taken as slaves by barbarians. The two finally discover that the key to escape lies within their own rampant libidos.

2069 TRILOGY
(This one-volume collection only $6.95)244-2
The early science-fiction trilogy in one volume! Here is the tight plotting and shameless all-male sex action that established Townsend as one of erotica's masters.

MIND MASTER
$4.95/209-4
Who better to explore the territory of erotic dominance than an author who helped define the genre—and knows that ultimate mastery always transcends the physical.

THE LONG LEATHER CORD
$4.95/201-9
Chuck's stepfather never lacks money or male visitors with whom he enacts intense sexual rituals. As Chuck comes to terms with his own desires, he begins to unravel the mystery behind his stepfather's secret life.

THE SCORPIUS EQUATION
$4.95/119-5
The story of a man caught between the demands of two galactic empires. Our randy hero must match wits—and more—with the incredible forces that rule his world.

MAN SWORD
$4.95/188-8
The *trés gai* tale of France's King Henri III, who encounters enough sexual schemers and politicos to alter one's picture of history forever!

THE FAUSTUS CONTRACT
$4.95/167-5
Two cocky young hustlers get more than they bargained for in this story of lust and its discontents.

CHAINS
$4.95/158-6
Picking up street punks has always been risky, but here it sets off a string of events that must be read to be believed. Townsend at his grittiest.

KISS OF LEATHER
$4.95/161-X
A look at the acts and attitudes of an earlier generation of gay leathermen, *Kiss of Leather* is full to bursting with gritty, raw action. Sensual pain and pleasure mix in this classic tale.

RUN, LITTLE LEATHER BOY
$4.95/143-8
A chronic underachiever, Wayne seems to be going nowhere fast. He finds himself drawn to the masculine intensity of a dark and mysterious sexual underground, where he soon finds many goals worth pursuing....

RUN NO MORE
$4.95/152-7
The sequel to *Run, Little Leather Boy*. This volume follows the further adventures of Townsend's leatherclad narrator as he travels every sexual byway available to the S/M male.

THE SEXUAL ADVENTURES OF SHERLOCK HOLMES
$4.95/3097-0
A scandalously sexy take on this legendary sleuth. Via the unexpurgated diary of Holmes' horny sidekick Watson, "A Study in Scarlet" is transformed to expose the Diogenes Club as an S/M arena, and clues only the redoubtable—and horny—Sherlock Holmes could piece together.

THE GAY ADVENTURES OF CAPTAIN GOOSE
$4.95/169-1
Jerome Gander is sentenced to serve aboard a ship manned by the most hardened, unrepentant criminals. In no time, Gander becomes well-versed in the ways of horny men at sea—and becomes one of the most notorious rakehells Merrie Olde England had ever seen.

MASQUERADE BOOKS

DONALD VINING
CABIN FEVER AND OTHER STORIES
$5.95/338-4
"Demonstrates the wisdom experience combined with insight and optimism can create." —*Bay Area Reporter*

Eighteen blistering stories in celebration of the most intimate of male bonding, reaffirming both love and lust in modern gay life.

DEREK ADAMS
MILES DIAMOND AND THE CASE OF THE CRETAN APOLLO
$6.95/381-3
Hired by a wealthy man to track a cheating lover, Miles finds himself involved in ways he could never have imagined! When the jealous Callahan threatens not only Diamond but his innocent an studly assistant, Miles counters with a little undercover work—involving as many horny informants as he can get his hands on!
PRISONER OF DESIRE
$6.50/439-9
Red-blooded, sweat-soaked excursions through the modern gay libido.
THE MARK OF THE WOLF
$5.95/361-3
The past comes back to haunt one well-off stud, whose desires lead him into the arms of many men—and the midst of a mystery.
MY DOUBLE LIFE
$5.95/314-7
Every man leads a double life, dividing his hours between the mundanities of the day and the pursuits of the night. Derek Adams shines a little light on the wicked things men do when no one's looking.
HEAT WAVE
$4.95/159-4
Derek Adams sexy short stories are guaranteed to jump start any libido—and *Heatwave* contains his very best.
MILES DIAMOND AND THE DEMON OF DEATH
$4.95/251-5
Miles always find himself in the stickiest situations—with any stud he meets! This adventure promises another carnal carnival.
THE ADVENTURES OF MILES DIAMOND
$4.95/118-7
The debut of this popular gay gumshoe. "The Case of the Missing Twin" is packed with randy studs. Miles sets about uncovering all as he tracks down the delectable Daniel Travis.

KELVIN BELIELE
IF THE SHOE FITS
$4.95/223-X
An essential volume of tales exploring a world where randy boys can't help but do what comes naturally—as often as possible! Sweaty male bodies grapple in pleasure.

JAMES MEDLEY
THE REVOLUTIONARY & OTHER STORIES
$6.50/417-8
Billy, the son of the station chief of the American Embassy in Guatemala, is kidnapped and held for ransom. Frightened at first, Billy gradually develops an unimaginably close relationship with Juan, the revolutionary assigned to guard him.
HUCK AND BILLY
$4.95/245-0
Young lust knows no bounds—and is often the hottest of one's life! Huck and Billy explore the desires that course through their bodies, determined to plumb the depths of passion.

FLEDERMAUS
FLEDERFICTION: STORIES OF MEN AND TORTURE
$5.95/355-4
Fifteen blistering paeans to men and their suffering. Unafraid of exploring the furthest reaches of pain and pleasure, Fledermaus unleashes his most thrilling tales in this special volume.

VICTOR TERRY
MASTERS
$6.50/418-6
Terry's butchest tales. A powerhouse volume of boot-wearing, whip-wielding, bone-crunching bruisers who've got what it takes to make a grown man grovel.
SM/SD
$6.50/406-2
Set around a South Dakota town called Prairie, these tales offer evidence that the real rough stuff can still be found where men take what they want despite all rules.
WHIPs
$4.95/254-X
Cruising for a hot man? You'd better be, because one way or another, these WHiPs—officers of the Wyoming Highway Patrol—are gonna pull you over for a little impromptu interrogation....

MASQUERADE BOOKS

MAX EXANDER
DEEDS OF THE NIGHT:
Tales of Eros and Passion
$5.95/348-1
MAXimum porn! Exander's a writer who's seen it all—and is more than happy to describe every glorious inch of it in pulsating detail. A whirlwind tour of the hypermasculine libido.

LEATHERSEX
$4.95/210-8
Hard-hitting tales from merciless Max. This time he focuses on the leather clad lust that draws together only the most willing and talented of tops and bottoms—for an all-out orgy of limitless surrender and control....

MANSEX
$4.95/160-8
"Mark was the classic leatherman: a huge, dark stud in chaps, with a big black moustache, hairy chest and enormous muscles. Exactly the kind of men Todd liked—strong, hunky, masculine, ready to take control...."

TOM CAFFREY
TALES FROM THE MEN'S ROOM
$5.95/364-3
Male lust at its most elemental and arousing. The Men's Room is less a place than a state of mind—one that every man finds himself in, day after day....

HITTING HOME
$4.95/222-1
Titillating and compelling, the stories in Hitting Home make a strong case for there being only one thing on a man's mind.

"BIG" BILL JACKSON
EIGHTH WONDER
$4.95/200-0
"Big" Bill Jackson's always the randiest guy in town—no matter what town he's in. From the bright lights and back rooms of New York to the open fields and sweaty bods of a small Southern town, "Big" Bill always manages to cause a scene!

TORSTEN BARRING
GUY TRAYNOR
$6.50/414-3
Some call Guy Traynor a theatrical genius; others say he was a madman. All anyone knows for certain is that his productions were the result of blood, sweat and outrageous erotic torture!

PRISONERS OF TORQUEMADA
$5.95/252-3
Another volume sure to push you over the edge. How cruel is the "therapy" practiced at Casa Torquemada? Barring is just the writer to evoke such steamy sexual malevolence.

SHADOWMAN
$4.95/178-0
From spoiled aristocrats to randy youths sowing wild oats at the local picture show, Barring's imagination works overtime in these steamy vignettes of homolust.

PETER THORNWELL
$4.95/149-7
Follow the exploits of Peter Thornwell and his outrageously horny cohorts as he goes from misspent youth to scandalous stardom, all thanks to an insatiable libido and love for the lash.

THE SWITCH
$4.95/3061-X
Sometimes a man needs a good whipping, and The Switch certainly makes a case! Packed with hot studs and unrelenting passions, these stories established Barring as a writer to be watched.

BERT McKENZIE
FRINGE BENEFITS
$5.95/354-6
From the pen of a widely published short story writer comes a volume of highly immodest tales. Not afraid of getting down and dirty, McKenzie produces some of today's most visceral sextales.

CHRISTOPHER MORGAN
STEAM GAUGE
$6.50/473-9
This volume abounds in manly men doing what they do best—to, with, or for any hot stud who crosses their paths.

THE SPORTSMEN
$5.95/385-6
A collection of super-hot stories dedicated to the all-American athlete. These writers know just the type of guys that make up every red-blooded male's starting line-up....

MUSCLE BOUND
$4.95/3028-8
In the NYC bodybuilding scene, Tommy joins forces with sexy Will Rodriguez in a battle of wits and biceps at the hottest gym in town, where the weak are bound and crushed by iron-pumping gods.

BUY ANY 4 BOOKS & CHOOSE 1 ADDITIONAL BOOK, OF EQUAL OR LESSER VALUE, AS YOUR FREE GIFT

MASQUERADE BOOKS

SONNY FORD
REUNION IN FLORENCE
$4.95/3070-9
Follow Adrian and Tristan an a sexual odyssey that takes in all ports known to ancient man. From lustful Turks to insatiable Mamluks, these two spread pleasure throughout the classical world! A thrilling tour through the ancient world.

ROGER HARMAN
FIRST PERSON
$4.95/179-9
Each story takes the form of a confessional—told by men who've got plenty to confess! From the "first time ever" to firsts of different kinds....

J. A. GUERRA, ED.
SLOW BURN
$4.95/3042-3
Welcome to the Body Shoppe! Torsos get lean and hard, pecs widen, and stomachs ripple in these sexy stories of the power and perils of physical perfection.

DAVE KINNICK
SORRY I ASKED
$4.95/3090-1
Unexpurgated interviews with gay porn's rank and file. Get personal with the men behind (and under) the "stars," and discover the hot truth about the porn business.

SEAN MARTIN
SCRAPBOOK
$4.95/224-8
From the creator of *Doc and Raider* comes this hot collection of life's horniest moments—all involving studs sure to set your pulse racing!

CARO SOLES & STAN TAL, EDS.
BIZARRE DREAMS
$4.95/187-5
An anthology of voices dedicated to exploring the dark side of human fantasy. Here are the most talented practitioners of "dark fantasy," the most forbidden sexual realm of all.

MICHAEL LOWENTHAL, ED.
THE BADBOY EROTIC LIBRARY
Volume 1
$4.95/190-X
Excerpts from *A Secret Life, Imre, Sins of the Cities of the Plain, Teleny* and others demonstrate the gift for portraying sex between men that led to many of these titles being banned.

THE BADBOY EROTIC LIBRARY
Volume 2
$4.95/211-6
This time, selections are taken from *Mike and Me, Muscle Bound, Men at Work, Badboy Fantasies,* and *Slowburn.*

ERIC BOYD
MIKE AND ME
$5.95/419-4
Mike joined the gym squad to bulk up on muscle. Little did he know he'd be turning on every sexy muscle jock in Minnesota! Hard bodies collide in a series of horny workouts.
MIKE AND THE MARINES
$6.50/497-6
Mike takes on America's most elite corps of studs! Join in on the never-ending sexual escapades of this singularly lustful platoon!

ANONYMOUS
A SECRET LIFE
$4.95/3017-2
Meet Master Charles: eighteen and quite innocent, until his arrival at the Sir Percival's Academy, where the lessons are supplemented with a crash course in pure sexual heat!
SINS OF THE CITIES OF THE PLAIN
$5.95/322-8
indulge yourself in the scorching memoirs of young man-about-town Jack Saul. Jack's sinful escapades grow wilder with every chapter!
IMRE
$4.95/3019-9
An extraordinary lost classic of obsession, gay erotic desire, and romance in a small European town on the eve of WWI.
TELENY
$4.95/3020-2
Often attributed to Oscar Wilde. A young man dedicates himself to a succession of forbidden pleasures.
THE SCARLET PANSY
$4.95/189-6
Randall Etrange travels the world in search of true love. Along the way, his journey becomes a sexual odyssey of truly epic proportions.

PAT CALIFIA, ED.
THE SEXPERT
$4.95/3034-2
From penis size to toy care, bar behavior to AIDS awareness, The Sexpert responds to real concerns with uncanny wisdom and a razor wit.

MASQUERADE BOOKS

HARD CANDY

ELISE D'HAENE
LICKING OUR WOUNDS
$7.95/605-7

"A fresh, engagingly sarcastic and determinedly bawdy voice. D'Haene is blessed with a savvy, iconoclastic view of the world that is mordant but never mean." —Publisher's Weekly

Licking Our Wounds, Elise D'Haene's acclaimed debut novel, is the story of Maria, a young woman coming to terms with the complexities of life in the age of AIDS. Abandoned by her lover and faced with the deaths of her friends, Maria struggles along with the help of Peter, HIV-positive and deeply conflicted about the changes in his own life, and Christie, a lover who is full of her own ideas about truth and the meaning of life.

CHEA VILLANUEVA
BULLETPROOF BUTCHES
$7.95/560-3

"...Gutsy, hungry, and outrageous, but with a tender core... Villanueva is a writer to watch out for: she will teach us something." —Joan Nestle

One of lesbian literature's most uncompromising voices. Never afraid to address the harsh realities of working-class lesbian life, Chea Villanueva charts territory frequently overlooked in the age of "lesbian chic."

KEVIN KILLIAN
ARCTIC SUMMER
$6.95/514-X

An examination of the emptiness lying beneath the rich exterior of America in the 50s. With the story of Liam Reilly—a young gay man of considerable means and numerous secrets—Killian exposes the contradictions of the American Dream.

MICHAEL ROWE
WRITING BELOW THE BELT:
Conversations with Erotic Authors
$7.95/540-9

"An in-depth and enlightening tour of society's love/hate relationship with sex, morality, and censorship." —James White Review

Michael Rowe interviewed the best and brightest erotic writers and presents the collected wisdom in Writing Below the Belt. Includes interviews with such cult sensations as John Preston, Larry Townsend, Pat Califia, and others.

PAUL T. ROGERS
SAUL'S BOOK
$7.95/462-3
Winner of the Editors' Book Award

"A first novel of considerable power... Sinbad the Sailor, thanks to the sympathetic imagination of Paul T. Rogers, speaks to us all." —New York Times Book Review

The story of a Times Square hustler, Sinbad the Sailor, and Saul, a brilliant, self-destructive, alcoholic, dominating character who may be the only love Sinbad will ever know. A classic tale of desire, obsession and the terrible wages of love.

STAN LEVENTHAL
BARBIE IN BONDAGE
$6.95/415-1
Widely regarded as one of the most clear-eyed interpreters of big city gay male life, Leventhal here provides a series of explorations of love and desire between men.

SKYDIVING ON
CHRISTOPHER STREET
$6.95/287-6
"Positively addictive." —Dennis Cooper

Aside from a hateful job, a hateful apartment, a hateful world and an increasingly hateful lover, life seems, well, all right for the protagonist of Stan Leventhal's latest novel. An insightful tale of contemporary urban gay life.

BRAD GOOCH
THE GOLDEN AGE OF PROMISCUITY
$7.95/550-6
"The next best thing to taking a time-machine trip to grovel in the glorious '70s gutter." —San Francisco Chronicle

"A solid, unblinking, unsentimental look at a vanished era. Gooch tells us everything we ever wanted to know about the dark and decadent gay subculture in Manhattan before AIDS altered the landscape." —Kirkus Reviews

PATRICK MOORE
IOWA
$6.95/423-2
"Full of terrific characters etched in acid-sharp prose, soaked through with just enough ambivalence to make it thoroughly romantic." —Felice Picano

The raw tale of one gay man's journey into adulthood, and the roads that bring him home again.

BUY ANY 4 BOOKS & CHOOSE 1 ADDITIONAL BOOK, OF EQUAL OR LESSER VALUE, AS YOUR FREE GIFT

MASQUERADE BOOKS

RACHEL PEREZ
ODD WOMEN
$6.50/526-3
These women are sexy, smart, tough—some even say odd. But who cares! An assortment of Sapphic sirens proves once and for all that comely ladies come best in pairs.

RED JORDAN AROBATEAU
STREET FIGHTER
$6.95/583-2
Another blast of truth from one of today's most notorious plain-speakers. An unsentimental look at the life of a street butch—Woody, the consummate outsider, living on the fringes of San Francisco.

SATAN'S BEST
$6.95/539-5
An epic tale of life with the Outlaws—the ultimate lesbian biker gang. Angel, a lonely butch, joins the Outlaws, and finds herself loving a new breed of woman and facing a new brand of danger on the open road....

ROUGH TRADE
$6.50/470-4
Famous for her unflinching portrayal of lower-class dyke life and love, Arobateau outdoes herself with these tales of butch/femme affairs and unrelenting passions.

BOYS NIGHT OUT
$6.50/463-1
Incendiary short fiction from this lesbian literary sensation. As always, Arobateau takes a good hard look at the lives of everyday women, noting well the struggles and triumphs each experiences.

RANDY TUROFF
LUST NEVER SLEEPS
$6.50/475-5
Highly erotic, powerfully real fiction. Turoff depicts a circle of modern women connected through the bonds of love, friendship, ambition, and lust with accuracy and compassion.

ALISON TYLER
COME QUICKLY:
For Girls on the Go
$6.95/428-3
Here are over sixty of the hottest fantasies around. A volume designed especially for you—a modern girl on a modern schedule, who still appreciates a little old-fashioned action.

VENUS ONLINE
$6.50/521-2
Lovely Alexa spends her days in a boring bank job, saving her energies for the night. That's when Alexa goes online, living out virtual adventures that become more real with each session. Soon Alexa—aka Venus—finds her real and online lives colliding deliciously.

DARK ROOM:
An Online Adventure
$6.50/455-0
Dani, a successful photographer, can't bring herself to face the death of her lover, Kate. Determined to keep the memory of her lover alive, Dani goes online under Kate's screen alias—and begins to uncover the truth behind Kate's shocking death....

BLUE SKY SIDEWAYS
& OTHER STORIES
$6.50/394-5
A variety of women, and their many breathtaking experiences with lovers, friends—and even the occasional sexy stranger.

DIAL "L" FOR LOVELESS
$5.95/386-4
Katrina Loveless—a sexy private eye talented enough to give Sam Spade a run for his money. In her first case, Katrina investigates a murder implicating a host of lovely, lusty ladies.

THE VIRGIN
$5.95/379-1
Seeking the fulfillment of her deepest sexual desires, Veronica answers a personal ad in the "Women Seeking Women" category—and discovers a whole sensual world she had only dreamed existed! Soon she is deflowered with a passion no man could ever show....

K. T. BUTLER
TOOLS OF THE TRADE
$5.95/420-8
A sparkling mix of lesbian erotica and humor. An encounter with ice cream, cappuccino and chocolate cake; an affair with a complete stranger; a pair of faulty handcuffs; and love on a drafting table.

LOVECHILD
GAG
$5.95/369-4
One of the bravest young writers you'll ever encounter. These poems take on hypocrisy with uncommon energy, and announce Lovechild as a writer of unforgettable rage.

MASQUERADE BOOKS

ELIZABETH OLIVER
THE SM MURDER: Murder at Roman Hill
$5.95/353-8
Intrepid lesbian P.I.s Leslie Patrick and Robin Penny take on a really hot case: the murder of the notorious Felicia Roman. The circumstances of the crime lead them through the leatherdyke underground, where motives—and desires—run deep.

SUSAN ANDERS
CITY OF WOMEN
$5.95/375-9
Stories dedicated to women and the passions that draw them together. Designed strictly for the sensual pleasure of women, these tales are set to ignite flames of passion in any reader.
PINK CHAMPAGNE
$5.95/282-5
Tasty, torrid tales of butch/femme couplings. Tough as nails or soft as silk, these women seek out their antitheses, intent on working out the details of their own personal theory of difference.

LAURA ANTONIOU, ED.
LEATHERWOMEN
$6.95/598-0
"...a great new collection of fiction by and about SM dykes."
—SKIN TWO

A groundbreaking anthology. These fantasies, from the pens of new or emerging authors, break every rule imposed on women's fantasies. The hottest stories from some of today's newest writers make this an unforgettable exploration of the female libido. A bestselling title.
LEATHERWOMEN II
$4.95/229-9
Another groundbreaking volume of writing from women on the edge, sure to ignite libidinal flames in any reader. Leave taboos behind, because these Leatherwomen know no limits....

AARONA GRIFFIN
LEDA AND THE HOUSE OF SPIRITS
$6.95/585-9
Two steamy novellas in one volume. Ten years into her relationship with Chrys, Leda decides to take a one-night vacation—at a local lesbian sex club. She soon finds herself reveling in sensual abandon. In the second story, lovely Lydia thinks she has her grand new home all to herself—until strange dreams begin to suggest that this House of Spirits harbors other souls, determined to do some serious partying.

PASSAGE & OTHER STORIES
$6.95/599-9
"A tale of a woman who is brave enough to follow her desire, even if it leads her into the arms of dangerous women."
—Pat Califia
An SM romance. Lovely Nina leads a "safe" life—until she finds herself infatuated with a woman she spots at a local café. One night, Nina follows her, only to find herself enmeshed in an endless maze leading not only to her object of passion, but to a mysterious world of pain and pleasure where women test the edges of sexuality and power.

VALENTINA CILESCU
MY LADY'S PLEASURE: Mistress with a Maid, Volume 1
$5.95/412-7
Claudia Dungarrow, a lovely, powerful professor, attempts to seduce Elizabeth Stanbridge, setting off a chain of events that eventually ruins her career. Claudia vows revenge—and makes her foes pay deliciously....
DARK VENUS: Mistress with a Maid, Volume 2
$6.50/481-X
Claudia Dungarrow's quest for ultimate erotic dominance continues in this scalding second volume! How many maidens will fall prey to her insatiable appetite?
BODY AND SOUL: Mistress with a Maid, Volume 3
$6.50/515-8
Dr. Claudia Dungarrow returns for yet another tour of depravity, subjugating every maiden in sight to her sexual whims. But she has yet to hold Elizabeth in submission. Will she ever?
THE ROSEBUD SUTRA
$4.95/242-6
"Women are hardly ever known in their true light, though they may love others, or become indifferent towards them, may give them delight, or may extract from them all the wealth that they possess."
MISTRESS MINE
$6.50/502-6
Sophia Cranleigh sits in prison, accused of authoring the "obscene" Mistress Mine. What she has done, however, is merely chronicle the events of her life. For Sophia has led no ordinary life, but has slaved and suffered—deliciously—under the hand of Mistress Malin.
THE HAVEN
$4.95/165-9
J craves domination, and her perverse appetites lead her to the Haven: the isolated sanctuary Ros and Annie call home. Soon J forces her way into their world, bringing unspeakable lust into their staid lives.

MASQUERADE BOOKS

LINDSAY WELSH

SEXUAL FANTASIES
$6.95/586-7

A volume of today's hottest lesbian erotica, selected by no less an authority than Lindsay Welsh, bestselling author of *Bad Habits* and *A Circle of Friends*. A dozen sexy stories, ranging from sweet to spicy, *Sexual Fantasies* offers a look at the many desires and depravities indulged in by modern women.

SECOND SIGHT
$6.50/507-7

The debut of lesbian superhero Dana Steel! During an attack by a gang of homophobic youths, Dana is thrown onto subway tracks. Miraculously, she survives, and finds herself the world's first lesbian superhero.

NASTY PERSUASIONS
$6.50/436-4

A hot peek into the behind-the-scenes operations of Rough Trade—one of the world's most famous lesbian clubs. Join Slash, Ramone, Cherry and many others as they bring one another to the height of ecstasy.

MILITARY SECRETS
$5.95/397-X

Colonel Candice Sproule heads a specialized boot camp. Assisted by three dominatrix sergeants, Colonel Sproule takes on the submissives sent to her by secret military contacts. Then along comes Jesse—whose pleasure in being served matches the Colonel's own.

ROMANTIC ENCOUNTERS
$5.95/359-7

Julie, the most powerful editor of romance novels in the industry, spends her days igniting women's passions through books—and her nights fulfilling those needs with a variety of lovers.

THE BEST OF LINDSAY WELSH
$5.95/368-6

Lindsay Welsh was one of Rosebud's early bestsellers, and remains one of our most popular writers. This sampler is set to introduce some of the hottest lesbian erotica to a wider audience.

NECESSARY EVIL
$5.95/277-9

When her Mistress proves too by-the-book, one lovely submissive takes the ultimate chance—creating a Mistress who'll fulfill her heart's desire. Little did she know how difficult it would be—and, in the end, rewarding....

A VICTORIAN ROMANCE
$5.95/365-1

A young Englishwoman realizes her dream—a trip abroad! Soon, blossoming Elaine comes to discover her own sexual talents, as a hot-blooded Parisian named Madelaine takes her Sapphic education in hand.

A CIRCLE OF FRIENDS
$6.50/524-7

The story of a remarkable group of women. The women pair off to explore all the possibilities of lesbian passion, until finally it seems that there is nothing—and no one—they have not dabbled in.

ANNABELLE BARKER

MOROCCO
$6.50/541-7

A young woman stands to inherit a fortune—if she can only withstand the ministrations of her guardian until her twentieth birthday. Lila makes a bid for freedom, only to find that liberty has its own delicious price....

A.L. REINE

DISTANT LOVE & OTHER STORIES
$4.95/3056-3

In the title story, Leah Michaels and her lover, Ranelle, have had four years of blissful, smoldering passion together. When Ranelle is out of town, Leah records an audio "Valentine:" a cassette filled with erotic reminiscences....

A RICHARD KASAK BOOK

LARRY TOWNSEND
THE LEATHERMAN'S HANDBOOK
$12.95/559-X

With introductions by John Preston, Jack Fritscher and Victor Terry

"The real thing, the book that started thousands of bikes roaring to the leather bars and sent thousands of young men off with a road map for adventure in this new world."

—John Preston

A special twenty-fifth anniversary edition of this seminal guide to the gay leather underground, with additional material addressing the realities of radical sex in the 90s. A leathersex volume of extraordinary historical value, the *Handbook* remains relevant to today's reader.

MASQUERADE BOOKS

ASK LARRY
$12.95/289-2

Starting just before the onslaught of AIDS, Townsend wrote the "Leather Notebook" column for *Drummer* magazine. Now, readers can avail themselves of Townsend's collected wisdom, as well as the author's contemporary commentary—a careful consideration of the way life has changed in the AIDS era.

PAT CALIFIA
DIESEL FUEL: Passionate Poetry
$12.95/535-2

"Dead-on direct, these poems burn, pierce, penetrate, soak, and sting.... Califia leaves no sexual stone unturned, clearing new ground for us all." —Gerry Gomez Pearlberg

Pat Califia reveals herself to be a poet of power and frankness, in this first collection of verse. One of this year's must-read explorations of underground culture.

SENSUOUS MAGIC
$12.95/610-X

"*Sensuous Magic* is clear, succinct and engaging even for the reader for whom S/M isn't the sexual behavior of choice.... When she is writing about the dynamics of sex and the technical aspects of it, Califia is the Dr. Ruth of the alternative sexuality set...." —*Lambda Book Report*

"Captures the power of what it means to enter forbidden terrain, and to do so safely with someone else, and to explore the healing potential, spiritual aspects and the depth of S/M." —*Bay Area Reporter*

"Don't take a dangerous trip into the unknown—buy this book and know where you're going!" —*SKIN TWO*

SIMON LEVAY
ALBRICK'S GOLD
$20.95/518-2/Hardcover

"Well-plotted and imaginative... [Levay's] premise and execution are original and engaging." —*Publishers Weekly*

From the man behind the controversial "gay brain" studies comes a tale of medical experimentation run amok. Is Dr. Guy Albrick performing unethical experiments in an attempt at "correcting" homosexuality? Doctor Roger Cavendish is determined to find out, before Albrick's guinea pigs are let loose among an unsuspecting gay community... A thriller based on today's cutting-edge science.

SHAR REDNOUR, ED.
VIRGIN TERRITORY 2
$12.95/506-9

Focusing on the many "firsts" of a woman's erotic life, *VT2* provides one of the sole outlets for serious discussion of the myriad possibilities available to and chosen by many lesbians.

VIRGIN TERRITORY
$12.95/457-7

An anthology of writing by women about their first-time erotic experiences with other women. A groundbreaking examination of contemporary lesbian desire.

MICHAEL BRONSKI, ED.
TAKING LIBERTIES: Gay Men's Essays on Politics, Culture and Sex
$12.95/456-9

Lambda Literary Award Winner

"Offers undeniable proof of a heady, sophisticated, diverse new culture of gay intellectual debate. I cannot recommend it too highly." —Christopher Bram

Some of the gay community's foremost essayists—from radical left to neo-conservative—weigh in on such slippery topics as outing, identity, pornography, pedophilia, and much more.

FLASHPOINT: Gay Male Sexual Writing
$12.95/424-0

Over twenty of the genre's best writers are included in this thrilling and enlightening look at contemporary gay porn. Accompanied by Bronski's insightful analysis, each story illustrates the many approaches to sexuality used by today's gay writers.

HEATHER FINDLAY, ED.
A MOVEMENT OF EROS: 25 Years of Lesbian Erotica
$12.95/421-6

A roster of stellar talents, each represented by their best work. Tracing the course of the genre from its pre-Stonewall roots to its current renaissance, Findlay examines each piece, placing it within the context of lesbian community and politics.

MICHAEL FORD, ED.
ONCE UPON A TIME: Erotic Fairy Tales for Women
$12.95/449-6

How relevant to contemporary lesbians are traditional fairy tales? Some of the biggest names in lesbian literature retell their favorites, adding their own sexy—and surprising—twists.

HAPPILY EVER AFTER: Erotic Fairy Tales for Men
$12.95/450-X

Adapting some of childhood's beloved tales for the adult gay reader, the contributors to *Happily Ever After* dig up the erotic subtext of these hitherto "innocent" diversions.

MASQUERADE BOOKS

CHARLES HENRI FORD & PARKER TYLER
THE YOUNG AND EVIL
$12.95/431-3

"*The Young and Evil* creates [its] generation as *This Side of Paradise* by Fitzgerald created his generation."—Gertrude Stein

Originally published in 1933, *The Young and Evil* was a sensation due to its portrayal of young gay artists living in Greenwich Village. From drag balls to bohemian flats, these characters followed love wherever it led them.

BARRY HOFFMAN, ED.
THE BEST OF GAUNTLET
$12.95/202-7

Gauntlet has always published the widest possible range of opinions. The most provocative articles have been gathered by editor-in-chief Barry Hoffman, to make *The Best of Gauntlet* a riveting exploration of American society's limits.

AMARANTHA KNIGHT, ED.
LOVE BITES
$12.95/234-5

A volume of tales dedicated to legend's sexiest demon—the Vampire. Not only the finest collection of erotic horror available—but a virtual who's who of promising new talent.

MICHAEL ROWE
WRITING BELOW THE BELT:
Conversations with Erotic Authors
$19.95/363-5

"An in-depth and enlightening tour of society's love/hate relationship with sex, morality, and censorship."
　　　　　　　　　　　　　　　—James White Review

Rowe speaks frankly with cult favorites such as Pat Califia, crossover success stories like John Preston, and up-and-comers Michael Lowenthal and Will Leber.

MICHAEL LASSELL
THE HARD WAY
$12.95/231-0

"Lassell is a master of the necessary word. In an age of tepid and whining verse, his bawdy and bittersweet songs are like a plunge in cold champagne."　　　　—Paul Monette

The first collection of renowned gay writer Michael Lassell's poetry, fiction and essays. As much a chronicle of post-Stonewall gay life as a compendium of a remarkable writer's work.

WILLIAM CARNEY
THE REAL THING
$10.95/280-9

"Carney gives us a good look at the mores and lifestyle of the first generation of gay leathermen.　　—Pat Califia

With a new introduction by Michael Bronski. *The Real Thing* returns from exile more than twenty-five years after its initial release, detailing the attitudes and practices of an earlier generation of leathermen.

RANDY TUROFF, ED.
LESBIAN WORDS: State of the Art
$10.95/340-6

"This is a terrific book that should be on every thinking lesbian's bookshelf."　　　　　—Nisa Donnelly

The best of lesbian nonfiction looking at not only the current fashionability the media has brought to the lesbian "image," but considerations of the lesbian past via historical inquiry and personal recollections.

ASSOTTO SAINT
SPELLS OF A VOODOO DOLL
$12.95/393-7
Lambda Literary Award Nominee.
"Angelic and brazen."　　　　　—Jewelle Gomez

A spellbinding collection of the poetry, lyrics, essays and performance texts by one of the most important voices in the renaissance of black gay writing.

EURYDICE
F/32
$10.95/350-3

"It's wonderful to see a woman...celebrating her body and her sexuality by creating a fabulous and funny tale."
　　　　　　　　　　　　　　　—Kathy Acker

A funny, disturbing quest for unity, *f/32* tells the story of Ela and her vagina—the latter of whom embarks on one of the most hilarious road trips in recent fiction.

ROBERT PATRICK
TEMPLE SLAVE
$12.95/191-8

"One of the best ways to learn what it was like to be fabulous, gay, theatrical and loved in a time at once more and less dangerous to gay life than our own."　　—Genre

The story of Greenwich Village and the beginnings of gay theater.

MASQUERADE BOOKS

FELICE PICANO
DRYLAND'S END
$12.95/279-5

Dryland's End takes place in a fabulous techno-empire ruled by intelligent, powerful women. While the Matriarchy has ruled for over two thousand years and altered human society, it is now unraveling. Military rivalries, religious fanaticism and economic competition threaten to destroy the mighty empire.

SAMUEL R. DELANY
THE MOTION OF LIGHT IN WATER
$12.95/133-0

"A very moving, intensely fascinating literary biography from an extraordinary writer....The artist as a young man and a memorable picture of an age." —William Gibson

Samuel R. Delany's autobiography covers the early years of one of science fiction's most important voices. A self-portrait of one of today's most challenging writers.

THE MAD MAN
$23.95/193-4/Hardcover

"What Delany has done here is take the ideas of the Marquis de Sade one step further, by filtering extreme and obsessive sexual behavior through the sieve of post-modern experience...." —Lambda Book Report

"Delany develops an insightful dichotomy between [his protagonist]'s two worlds: the one of cerebral philosophy and dry academia, the other of heedless, 'impersonal' obsessive sexual extremism. When these worlds finally collide ... the novel achieves a surprisingly satisfying resolution...." —Publishers Weekly

For his thesis, graduate student John Marr researches the life and work of the brilliant Timothy Hasler: a philosopher whose career was cut tragically short over a decade earlier. Marr notices parallels between his life and that of his subject—and begins to believe that Hasler's death might hold some key to his own life as a gay man in the age of AIDS.

LUCY TAYLOR
UNNATURAL ACTS
$12.95/181-0

"A topnotch collection..." —Science Fiction Chronicle

A disturbing vision of erotic horror. Unrelenting angels and hungry gods play with souls and bodies in Taylor's murky cosmos: where heaven and hell are merely differences of perspective; where redemption and damnation lie behind the same shocking acts.

TIM WOODWARD, ED.
THE BEST OF SKIN TWO
$12.95/130-6

Skin Two specializes in provocative essays by the finest writers working in the "radical sex" scene. Collected here are the articles that established the magazine's reputation. Including interviews with cult figures Tim Burton, Clive Barker and Jean Paul Gaultier.

LAURA ANTONIOU, ED.
LOOKING FOR MR. PRESTON
$23.95/288-4/Hardcover

Interviews, essays and personal reminiscences of John Preston—a man whose career spanned the gay publishing industry. Ten percent of the proceeds from this book will go to the AIDS Project of Southern Maine, for which Preston served as President of the Board.

CARO SOLES, ED.
MELTDOWN!
An Anthology of Erotic Science Fiction and Dark Fantasy for Gay Men
$12.95/203-5

Meltdown! contains the very best examples of the increasingly popular sub-genre of erotic sci-fi/dark fantasy: stories meant to send a shiver down the spine and start a fire down below.

GUILLERMO BOSCH
RAIN
$12.95/232-9

In a quest to sate his hunger for some knowledge of the world, one man is taken through a series of extraordinary encounters that change the course of civilization around him.

RUSS KICK
OUTPOSTS:
A Catalog of Rare and Disturbing Alternative Information
$18.95/0202-8

A tour through the work of political extremists, conspiracy theorists, sexual explorers, and others whose work has been deemed "too far-out" for consideration by the mainstream.

CECILIA TAN, ED.
SM VISIONS:
The Best of Circlet Press
$10.95/339-2

"Fabulous books! There's nothing else like them." —Susie Bright

Circlet Press, publisher of erotic science fiction and fantasy genre, is now represented by the best of its very best—a most thrilling and eye-opening rides through the erotic imagination.

MASQUERADE BOOKS

DAVID MELTZER
THE AGENCY TRILOGY
$12.95/216-7

"...'The Agency' is clearly Meltzer's paradigm of society; a mindless machine of which we are all 'agents,' including those whom the machine supposedly serves...." —Norman Spinrad

A vision of an America consumed and dehumanized by a lust for power.

MICHAEL PERKINS
THE GOOD PARTS: An Uncensored Guide to Literary Sexuality
$12.95/186-1

A survey of sex as seen/written about in the pages of over 100 major fiction and nonfiction volumes from the past twenty years.

COMING UP: The World's Best Erotic Writing
$12.95/370-8

Michael Perkins has scoured the field of erotic writing to produce an anthology sure to challenge the limits of the most seasoned reader.

MICHAEL LOWENTHAL, ED.
THE BEST OF THE BADBOYS
$12.95/233-7

The best Badboy writers are collected here, in this testament to the artistry that has catapulted them to bestselling status.

LARS EIGHNER
ELEMENTS OF AROUSAL
$12.95/230-2

A guideline for success with one of publishing's best kept secrets: the novice-friendly field of gay erotic writing. Eighner details his craft, providing the reader with sure advice.

JOHN PRESTON
MY LIFE AS A PORNOGRAPHER AND OTHER INDECENT ACTS
$12.95/135-7

"...essential and enlightening... My Life as a Pornographer] is a bridge from the sexually liberated 1970s to the more cautious 1990s, and Preston has walked much of that way as a standard-bearer to the cause for equal rights...." —Library Journal

A collection of author and social critic John Preston's essays, focusing on his work as an erotic writer, and proponent of gay rights.

MARCO VASSI
THE EROTIC COMEDIES
$12.95/136-5

"The comparison to [Henry] Miller is high praise indeed.... But reading Vassi's work, the analogy holds—for he shares with Miller an unabashed joy in sensuality, and a questing after experience that is the root of all great literature, erotic or otherwise...." —David L. Ulin, The Los Angeles Reader

Scathing and humorous, these stories reflect Vassi's belief in the power and primacy of Eros in American life.

THE STONED APOCALYPSE
$12.95/132-2

Vassi's autobiography, financed by the other erotic writing that made him a cult sensation.

A DRIVING PASSION
$12.95/134-9

Famous for the lectures he gave regarding sexuality, A Driving Passion collects these lectures, and distills the philosophy that made him a sensation.

THE SALINE SOLUTION
$12.95/180-2

The story of one couple's affair and the events that lead them to reassess their lives.

CHEA VILLANUEVA
JESSIE'S SONG
$9.95/235-3

"It conjures up the strobe-light confusion and excitement of urban dyke life.... Read about these dykes and you'll love them." —Rebecca Ripley

Touching, arousing portraits of working class butch/femme relations. An underground hit.

STAN TAL, ED.
BIZARRE SEX AND OTHER CRIMES OF PASSION
$12.95/213-2

Over twenty stories of erotic shock, guaranteed to titillate and terrify. This incredible volume includes such masters of erotic horror as Lucy Taylor and Nancy Kilpatrick.

ORDERING IS EASY

MC/VISA orders can be placed by calling our toll-free number
PHONE 800-375-2356/FAX 212-986-7355
HOURS M-F 9am—12am EDT Sat & Sun 12pm—8pm EDT
E-MAIL masqbks@aol.com
or mail this coupon to:
MASQUERADE DIRECT
DEPT. BMRH98 801 2ND AVE., NY, NY 10017

BUY ANY FOUR BOOKS AND CHOOSE ONE ADDITIONAL BOOK, OF EQUAL OR LESSER VALUE, AS YOUR FREE GIFT

QTY.	TITLE	NO.	PRICE
			FREE

DEPT. BMRH98 (please have this code available when placing your order)

We never sell, give or trade any customer's name.

SUBTOTAL	
POSTAGE AND HANDLING	
TOTAL	

In the U.S., please add $1.50 for the first book and 75¢ for each additional book; in Canada, add $2.00 for the first book and $1.25 for each additional book. Foreign countries: add $4.00 for the first book and $2.00 for each additional book. No C.O.D. orders. Please make all checks payable to Masquerade/Direct. Payable in U.S. currency only. NY state residents add 8.25% sales tax. Please allow 4–6 weeks for delivery. Payable in U.S. currency only.

NAME_____

ADDRESS_____

CITY_____ STATE _____ ZIP_____

TEL( )_____

E-MAIL_____

PAYMENT: ☐ CHECK ☐ MONEY ORDER ☐ VISA ☐ MC

CARD NO._____ EXP. DATE _____